TETHERED

CHRIS C BERKNESS

PROLOGUE

On July 12, 2017, an iceberg the size of Delaware breaks away from Antarctica's fourth largest ice shelf, Larsen C, and drifts through the Weddell Sea. It is the largest iceberg to ever break from the Antarctic Peninsula. The crack exposes a dormant ecosystem, hidden from the waking world for over 120,000 years.

One week later, NASA's Aqua satellite identifies an object embedded deep in the fissure. The Department of Defense extracts this object from the ice shelf and transports it to the United States Amundsen-Scott South Research station in Antarctica, where scientists from the Centers for Disease Control and other organizations work to determine exactly what they have on their hands... and what the object's exposure means for mankind.

Five and a half years later, in January 2023, the capsule begins to release airborne morphons that infect victims with a deadly virus. The virus liquefies a human host's internal organs within two weeks. Infected animals display rabid-like symptoms and attack with impunity. They grow light sensitive and adopt nocturnal habits, but they do not die from the virus. The human population, however, is ravaged, leaving only two hundred and fifty million souls alive. Survivors are forced to endure freezing temperatures, where the virus remains dormant.

Fresler Barsness and his girlfriend, Sharon Clary, are two of those survivors. In their small Northern Minnesota cabin, they're currently safe from the deadly virus. But it is February, and Fresler knows that the temperatures will soon rise. They will need to travel further north, to Canada, in order to stay within the safety of the freezing zone.

While fishing in a nearby river, Fresler meets a family of three. John, a detective for the Louisville Metro Police Department and an ex-Army Ranger, is leading his wife, Jackie, and daughter, Jennifer, toward a settlement in Northern Canada. While hiking through the snow, Jackie sprains her ankle. Fresler invites the Williams family to stay with him and Sharon in their small cabin while she recovers.

In the dead of night, Fresler, Sharon, and the Williams family hear a scream outside the cabin. An infected coyote has just attacked a young man, Sean. Fresler rushes outside to help and is bitten for his trouble. Sean and Fresler spend the next two weeks isolated from the group in a small shed about one hundred yards from the cabin.

Sean's traveling companions—his teenaged sister, Tina, and their cousin, Larry—are invited by Sharon to lodge at the cabin while Fresler and Sean remain in quarantine.

At the CDC headquarters in Atlanta, Georgia, Director William Frieden informs his staff that the Department of Defense has shared new intelligence about the capsule. It was made from materials not found on Earth. Additionally, a message was left inside stating that only three individuals on the planet are immune from the virus. Those individuals' blood can be used to create a vaccine and cure. William broadcasts a message asking anyone who is immune to contact the CDC.

After nearly two weeks in isolation, Fresler is almost fully recovered from his coyote bite. Unfortunately, Sean's infection has only worsened. Fearing that Sean's wound will turn septic, John and Sharon travel to nearby abandoned cabins to search for antibiotics.

The medicine they bring back cannot help Sean, who dies from the deadly virus. It is then that Fresler realizes he is immune. Thanks to the CDC's broadcast announcement, he also knows that the government hopes to create a vaccine from his blood.

John and Larry convince the group that they must travel together to Littlefork, a town not far from Fresler's cabin, where they will attempt to contact the CDC. Without an operational SUV, they will have to make the treacherous journey on foot and pray they can avoid the rabid animals. Fresler's immunity must be reported.

While approaching a vacant cabin along the way, the sun sets too soon. In the midst of a mad sprint for the door, Larry saves Fresler from a stalking mountain lion but gives his life in return, leaving Tina entirely without family.

In Littlefork, the survivors cannot find a communication device. They decide they must drive to the CDC headquarters in Atlanta, Georgia. With the help of a local resident, the group finds three SUVs.

Along the drive, they stop at an abandoned mall, where they find a little boy named Benjamin. His parents were killed two weeks earlier by two individuals attempting to steal their family's car. The group takes Benjamin under their wing.

Upon reaching Atlanta, the group stops at a Walmart to stock up on supplies and find a respirator mask for Sharon. In the store, they encounter a fanatical group called the Soldiers of Destiny, whose members believe that the pandemic is God's will. When they discover that Fresler is immune and that his blood will be used to make a vaccine, they attempt to capture the group.

After one of the SoD members takes off Jennifer's respirator mask, exposing her to the virus, John takes action. He kills one of the attackers and knocks the other unconscious so the group can escape.

Desperate to escape the night, the group enters a house in Atlanta that is occupied by a man named Charles. He invites them to stay overnight.

Unfortunately, it becomes clear that Jennifer has contracted the virus. A desperate and grieving John decides to try something that makes no logical sense to save his baby girl.

Using one of diabetic Charles's syringes, John draws Fresler's blood and injects it into Jennifer. Within hours, she is cured of the disease. Fresler's blood, unaltered, is a cure! This worries Tina. This shouldn't be possible. Fresler is clearly not like other humans.

The next morning, the group's way to the CDC headquarters is blockaded by the Soldiers of Destiny. After being pursued down an abandoned road, John takes out two SoD members. He takes their ham radio so he can listen to their communications.

Charles guides the group closer to their destination on foot. When it is clear they can't make it to the CDC by nightfall, they decide to spend the night in an abandoned home that is only a couple miles from the CDC. Before they reach the front door, they hear a car coming down the street and hide. It is a Soldier of Destiny on patrol. He spots them and calls for reinforcements. Listening to their plans on the ham radio, John decides to lead them away from the house in order to keep the group safe. He takes an SUV and drives away from his friends and family.

The SoDs follow John's car around the nearby neighborhood. Eventually, he gets trapped. As he watches the SoDs close in on his SUV, the sun starts to rise. He knows that his family will be safe and that Fresler will make it to the CDC, where they can create a vaccine and cure.

When the group arrives at the CDC headquarters, they meet William, who divulges the truth of the virus' origins, discovered back in 2017. The U.S. government knew of the virus but did not share this information with the rest of the world or with its own citizens.

William has Fresler's blood tested and discovers that it has unique properties. Hoping to learn more, he has Fresler's parents flown to the U.S. from Norway.

As the group settles in at the CDC, soldiers find a body in a nearby neighborhood matching John's description. William asks Jackie to identify the body.

Jackie and Jennifer are devastated to find out that John was killed by the Soldiers of Destiny. They hold a service for him. Fresler, Sharon, and the others will never forget John's sacrifice.

Fresler's parents arrive from Norway. A blood test reveals that Fresler's mother, Gladys, is his genetic parent, but his father, Lars, is not. Fresler doesn't believe that his mother had an affair. He asks Gladys if anything unusual happened during her pregnancy.

Gladys tells Fresler about an incident at a cave in

Akureyri, Iceland, just before she conceived. While at the cave, she passed out at the entrance—and she wasn't the only one. Two other women also lost consciousness. All three became pregnant around the same time.

Gladys knew both women. One of them, Glendoris Jakobson, had a son named Erik. The other, Jalaine Bjorkman, had a daughter, Karena. The three families got together in Minnesota to celebrate the children's 10th birthdays. On that trip, Gladys took a picture of Fresler, Erik, and Karena because they looked like triplets.

This is the connection William and his assistant director, Rodney McDade, have been looking for. The European CDC, based in Sweden, has just announced its own vaccine. It was developed by a Nobel Prize–winning scientist, Karena Wilson—whose maiden name is Bjorkman. They guess that she is one of the three immune individuals.

Fresler takes the hypothesis a step further: what if he, Erik Jakobson, and Karena Wilson are biological siblings? And what if the three of them are somehow connected to the people who created this pandemic that has devastated the planet?

To learn more, he must visit the mysterious cave in Akureyri, Iceland.

* * *

Book 2: Akureyri Gateway

It's 2017. Erik Jakobson is an associate professor with the University of Minnesota, presenting his work in neural pathways under the Human Connectome Project (HCP) at a neuroscience conference.

Shortly thereafter, Erik interviews one Timothy Claiborne, a volunteer subject for the HCP. Timothy was referred by Erik's brother-in-law, Stephan Johansson, an oncologist. Erik and Stephan are very close, having been college roommates at the University of Minnesota. Stephan even introduced Erik to his bride, Kristin, who is Stephan's sister. Erik and Kristin now have a daughter, Eria.

In his interview with Timothy, Erik discovers that the man was miraculously cured of both multiple sclerosis and cancer last year. Timothy visited a cave in Akureyri, Iceland, and within a few months was cured. Timothy tells Erik that the boulders surrounding the cave's entrance were levitating. He passed out not long after he walked through the entrance. Timothy further reveals that he discovered the cave via a website that claims that the location is a portal to the afterlife.

The next day, Erik leaves with his family to vacation in St. John. Erik and Kristin are celebrating their anniversary, as well as their daughter's seventh birthday. A tragic car crash cuts the trip and both Kristin and Eria's lives short.

Upon returning to the U.S., Erik sees a familiar woman in black at the airport. He remembers her from the darkest day of his teen life. Erik's mother took her life not long after his father passed away from cancer, and this mysterious woman appeared in his backyard after his mother's funeral service. At that time, she delivered a message: "Do not travel toward the light. Go in the opposite direction."

Erik's childhood friend, Fresler Barsness, attended the funeral service. He found Erik talking to himself in the backyard. He told Erik that there was no one with him, which led Erik to believe he was imagining the woman in black. He assumed he was suffering a psychotic breakdown. Seeing this woman again leaves Erik wondering, "Am I losing my mind, again?"

Stephan helps Erik prepare for Kristin and Eria's funeral

service. Kristin's parents, Hanna and Olafur, cannot attend, because Hanna has cancer and cannot travel.

After the service, Stephan looks at Erik's laptop and discovers a website that talks about the afterlife. Stephan's accidental snooping upsets Erik, so Stephan apologizes and leaves. But as soon as he arrives home, Stephan studies the website, and what he finds makes him rush back to save an unconscious Erik, who has attempted to take his own life.

When Erik awakens in the hospital, an irate Stephan asks Erik to travel with him to Iceland to see Hanna and Olafur. There, they can hold a second service for Kristin and Eria. Erik agrees to the trip on the condition that they visit the mysterious cave in Akureyri.

After a pleasant visit with Hanna and Olafur, Stephan, a trained pilot, flies Erik to the other side of the island. There they meet a man named Uriel. Unbeknownst to Erik, Uriel's father took Erik, Fresler, and Karena's mothers to the cave in 1984.

When they arrive after a strenuous journey, there are no levitating boulders. Erik is disappointed.

That night, while Stephan and Uriel slumber in tents by the cave, Erik sees the northern lights. Then the cave's entrance starts to glow, and the boulders levitate. Erik doesn't wake Stephan but instead rushes through the glowing light.

The next thing Erik sees is Stephan kneeling next to him. Erik is devastated. He was hoping to enter a portal to the afterlife—to see Kristin and Eria again—but instead he merely fainted. The trio hikes back to Akureyri and Erik and Stephan fly back to Reykjavik, then Erik embarks back to the U.S. with his will to live gone. But all is not as it seems.

When Erik arrives at his house in Minnesota, the windows are open and the front door is unlocked. He enters the house cautiously, expecting an intruder. He is shocked to find Kristin in the kitchen making dinner.

His daughter, Eria, runs into the kitchen and hugs him. His dead parents then arrive, and an impossible birthday party, months in advance, is soon in full swing, making Erik wonder if he's lost his mind or has in fact entered the afterlife. But the scene dissolves as Erik falls unconscious.

When he wakes, Erik find an unknown bald man sitting at the end of his hospital bed.

The man introduces himself as Reshal and says that everything that happened since Erik entered the portal was a vivid dream. Reshal then takes Erik to a viewing room, where he sees a spectacular view of the Oort cloud. He is millions of light years from Earth!

Erik traveled through a portal to a space station. The Akureyri cave is one of several portals on Earth. The people on the space station have been observing Earth for thousands of years. Humans that enter the portal are put into a deep state of unconsciousness, evaluated, and then returned to Earth with no missing time.

Reshal tells Erik that his people are also human, but from a planet called Sjel. Their history goes back millions of years. What's more, Earth and Sjel are not the only planets that are inhabited by humans. For instance, the planet Rajik, which the Sjelians once monitored, was destroyed twenty thousand years ago.

The Sjelians have recently discovered another planet in a different galaxy that is also inhabited by humans. It is called Phaelin. An exploration vessel will soon depart from the space station to travel to Phaelin.

Reshal introduces Erik to the leader of the space station, Theran. Theran assigns his daughter, Aleria, as Erik's counselor, tasked with helping him acclimate to the space station. Erik is the first human from Earth to travel through the portal and stay aboard. Reshal tells Erik that he will be allowed to stay because of his unique background in neuroscience and experience mapping neural pathways, which may be useful to the Sjelians.

This is not the whole truth. The real reason Erik was asked to stay aboard the Sjelian space station is that Reshal is Erik, Fresler, and Karena's biological father.

In 1984, Akril, the lead Sjelian scientist studying Earth's atmosphere, concluded that the planet's arctic permafrost would melt by the year 2053. If Earth's humans continued on their present course, by the year 2025 this future would be irreversible due to 1.8 billion tons of carbon released from melted arctic permafrost. Earth, Akril said, would be uninhabitable by the year 2132.

As a result of her findings, the General Council sent two capsules to Earth, each containing deadly morphons. These morphons would infect the human host with a virus. Since the morphons were dormant in freezing temperatures, only a few million Earth inhabitants could potentially survive. With most of the humans no longer living, the planet would survive.

Reshal pleaded with the General Council to provide the people of Earth with a vaccine, but they decided against it. So, Reshal took matters into his own hands. He altered the morphons so that Sjelian blood could be used to create a vaccine and cure. He then impregnated three women from Earth, so that there would be Sjelian DNA on Earth. He left a message in the probe that was sent to Antarctica.

The second capsule was sent to Greenland, but it would be years before that capsule would reach the surface. By then, a vaccine would be developed.

In 2017, Theran realizes that Reshal manipulated Earth

communications—the websites Timothy and Erik visited—
and cured Timothy to ensure that the two would connect
and Erik would travel through the portal.

Theran is furious with his friend. Altering communications on Earth breaks a fundamental tenet of Sjelian law.
Theran knows it is only a matter of time before someone on
the space station figures out what Reshal did. When that
happens, they will both be punished.

Erik is spending all of his time with his gorgeous counselor, Aleria, and begins feeling guilty about his attraction to
another woman so soon after his wife's death.

Aleria, meanwhile, wonders why the Sjelians have
broken protocol and allowed Erik to stay aboard. Erik's
research into neural pathways is interesting, but Sjelian
science and technology far surpass Earth's capabilities.
There must be something more to Erik's presence.

When Erik learns the Sjelian language in a few weeks—
a feat that should be impossible for an Earth human's brain
—Aleria decides to confide in her friend Lina. She tells Lina
she wants to test Erik's DNA. Lina tells Aleria that she would
need permission before doing so, but Aleria does it in secret
anyway.

Thirty days after Erik entered the Akureyri gateway, the
Sjelian crew departs for the newly discovered planet,
Phaelin. En route to Phaelin, Aleria and Lina discover the
truth: Erik's mother was impregnated by a Sjelian. Erik's
Sjelian DNA explains not only his aptitude for the language,
but another unusual ability as well. Erik has telepathic
perception, or the ability to receive messages telepathically.
The mysterious, phantom-like woman in black was a mani-
festation of this telepathic perception.

Erik and Aleria confront Theran and Reshal about Erik's
DNA test. Reshal confesses to his unconventional paternity

and explains he committed these acts to provide the people of Earth with a better chance for survival. Erik is furious to find out the truth—both about his parentage and the Sjelian General Council's choice of genocide.

Feeling betrayed, Erik demands to return to Earth immediately to avert the looming catastrophe with his blood sample. It is currently 2017, and the Sjelians suspect that the morphons will not be released from the first capsule until 2023. But Theran tells Erik that they cannot return to Earth. They are not yet done with their mission.

On the long journey to Phaelin, Erik learns that Aleria had a life partner who died when traveling through a collapsed wormhole. She also has a son and granddaughter. She is forty-five years old, but Sjelians' slowed aging makes her look like she is in her twenties. As the months pass, Erik falls in love with Aleria. Still, guilt gnaws at him as he grapples with grief.

When they reach Phaelin in June 2020, the Sjelians send probes to study its atmosphere and monitor electronic communications. They discover that the planet will soon be uninhabitable. As they are completing their initial scans, they are shocked when a vessel approaches undetected. The cloaking device this vessel has is beyond Sjelian technology and seems to contradict the Sjelian intelligence that suggested Phaelinians' evolution was on par with Earth humans.

The Phaelinians invite the Sjelians to visit the planet's surface. Theran agrees. He, Erik, Aleria, and Kralo, the Sjelians' lead pilot and engineer, travel to the surface in a shuttle and are introduced to Skithaell, the Phaelinian leader.

Skithaell tells Theran that an advanced race of humans, from the planet Nekses, landed on their planet years ago, hoping to relocate before their own planet's imminent destruction. While on Phaelin, the Neksesians destroyed Phaelin's oceans—the planet's only source of oxygen. It is because of the Neksesians that Phaelin is dying.

The Neksesians left Phaelin in search of another planet, but not before the Phaelinians confiscated a Neksesian vessel. They have learned how to operate the vessel, but they cannot access its portal drive. Without the portal drive, they have no way of traveling beyond their solar system. The Phaelinians need to obtain this technology in order to get their people off their dying planet.

Skithaell asks Theran to provide the Phaelinians with the technology to travel beyond their solar system. In return, they will give the Sjelians the Neksesian cloaking technology. Sensing trouble, Theran tells Skithaell that he needs permission from the Sjelian General Council to agree to this exchange of technology—knowing full well they'll never take such a deal.

When Skithaell finds out that Kralo is the Sjelians' lead engineer, he tells Theran that Kralo will have to stay on the surface of Phaelin as their guest while Theran, Erik, and Aleria return to the Sjelian vessel to communicate with the General Council. An enraged Theran has no choice but to comply, but Erik, who has befriended Kralo, won't leave the engineer alone on Phaelin. He lies to Skithaell, telling him that he has knowledge of portal travel, and Skithaell takes him prisoner as well, while Aleria and Theran return to the vessel.

Later that night, a Phaelinian named Alesta breaks into Erik and Kralo's holding cell. She says she wants to help them escape. She also reveals that the Neksesians did not destroy Phaelin's oceans. Phaelin is responsible for its own fate. The innocent Neksesians have been detained because of their advanced technology. The Neksesian leader and their lead engineer are prisoners here on the surface of Phaelin, while their fellow Nekesians are prisoners on their orbiting vessel.

Alesta leads Erik and Kralo to the captive Neksesians, Gott and Telfas. Telfas has an advanced form of telepathic perception. He can read any human's thoughts and also send messages to those with telepathic perception —like Erik.

Erik asks Telfas how long it would take the Neksesian vessel, with its advanced portal technology, to travel to Earth. Telfas tells Erik that unlike the Sjelian vessel, which will take years, the Neksesian vessel will take less than four weeks. If Erik can secure the Neksesian vessel, he can return to Earth in time to use his blood to synthesize a vaccine long before the pandemic arrives.

Telfas gives Erik one more piece of information: activating the Neksesian portal drive requires a key, which is the medallion he wears around his neck, as well as an eye scan. The self-destruct is accessed the same way.

Alesta tells Erik, Kralo, Gott, and Telfas that they can escape using a shuttle docked at the top of the building. Erik will need to trigger an alarm to alert the guards and cause a diversion, allowing his allies to reach the shuttle bay.

Instead of following the plan, Erik goes to Skithaell. Erik tells Skithaell about the Neksesian medallion key and the required retinal scans from Gott and Telfas.

When the others are captured and brought before Skithaell, Kralo is crushed to learn that his friend has betrayed them. Alesta, too, was working for Skithaell all along, feigning aid to discover how to access the portal drive.

When Skithaell asks why Erik would betray his friends,

Erik explains about the virus capsules sent to kill his people. He can use the Neksesian vessel to return to his planet... with the Phaelinians' help.

Gott, Telfas, and Kralo are taken to the Neksesian vessel to access the portal drive. On board the ship, Erik convinces Skithaell to send Kralo, Gott, and the other captured Neksesians to the Sjelian vessel. Once their shuttle reaches the Sjelian vessel, the Phaelinians will destroy it.

Kralo cannot understand how Erik could do such a thing. Destroying the Sjelian vessel means killing Aleria, whom Kralo believed Erik loved.

Erik tells Kralo that he no longer has any allegiance to the Sjelians, after what they did to Earth.

Erik and Telfas access the portal drive on the Neksesian vessel. Once the shuttle carrying Kralo, Gott, and the other Neksesians reaches the Sjelian vessel, Skithaell and the other Phaelinians enter the viewing room to watch the destruction.

In the control room, Erik and Telfas overpower their one remaining guard, lock the viewing room, and accesses the vessel's self-destruct mechanism. With Skithaell, Alesta, and the other Phaelinians locked in the viewing room, Erik and Telfas run toward the escape pods with only minutes to get clear of the impending explosion.

Erik is shot by a guard who had remained behind. Telfas drags him onto the pod, and together they escape in time.

With the Neksesian vessel destroyed, Erik and Telfas reach the Sjelian vessel. Erik is rushed to the medical bay, where he receives treatment for his wound.

While Erik recuperates, Telfas explains to the others that he always knew that Alesta was a foe, thanks to his telepathy. Sensing Erik's telepathic perception, Telfas mentally communicated a plan to save them all. It involved

Erik gaining the Phaelinians' trust—and it was executed perfectly.

However, Erik and Telfas were fortunate that Skithaell and the others wanted to view the destruction of the Sjelian vessel. If the Phaelinians hadn't walked into the viewing room, allowing Telfas to lock them in, Erik and Telfas would have died in the self-destruct blast. Erik was willing to sacrifice his life to save Aleria.

Aleria professes her love for Erik upon his waking in the med bay. Now, as the Sjelian vessel returns to the space station, they have a new worry: can they make it back to Earth in time to save Erik's people from the deadly morphons?

* * *

Book 3: Biogenic Convergence

It's January 26th, 2023. Karena Bjorkman Wilson is in Paris with her husband, Ludvig, and her mother, Jalaine, for the 2023 L'Oréal-UNESCO International Awards for Women in Science, where Karena is the keynote speaker.

At the luxurious Hotel Le Meurice before the ceremony, Ludvig is glued to the television set. The news is filled with stories about an outbreak of a new infectious disease in Argentina.

At a reception after the ceremony, Karena is introduced to Walter and Anna Krause. Walter is a general in the German army and his daughter, Anna, is one of the evening's five award recipients. Anna is awestruck by Karena's celebrity status. Karena was the 2020 Nobel Prize winner in Physics for her breakthrough discovery in fusion.

The group also talks to another 2023 L'Oréal-UNESCO award recipient, Maria Pena from Argentina. Maria isn't feeling well but brushes off her symptoms as the common cold.

After the reception, Karena, Ludvig, and Jalaine ride back to their hotel with the general and his daughter. They learn that the general is flying to Hamburg in the morning on a private jet.

In their hotel room, they turn on the news to discover that the new virus is spreading at a rapid pace. It has already infected over fifty million people and has spread as far as Colombia. Karena calls her friend Janice Ammon, the director of the European Centers for Disease Control. Janice tells Karena that this new disease could prove deadly. Karena immediately changes her family's flight so they will return home to Sweden early in the morning.

The next morning, they learn that the virus has spread to Morocco. Over two hundred million are now infected. Karena is notified that their flight is canceled. In fact, all flights out of Paris are canceled. They decide to ask Walter Krause for help, with the use of his private jet. He agrees to take them to Hamburg.

In Hamburg, Walter uses his connections to get Karena, Jalaine, and Ludvig on a train to Copenhagen, Denmark. By this point, the virus has reached the U.S. and there is officially an outbreak in Paris. Even worse, Jalaine is developing a fever.

As soon as their train reaches Denmark, they attempt to book another train to Malmo, Sweden. The day's trains to Malmo are sold out, so Karena buys tickets for the morning.

The next morning, Jalaine has a high fever. Karena heads to a local pharmacy to get some ibuprofen. At the pharmacy, the clerk informs her that the first person infected with the virus died last night. A few hours later, there are over seven hundred thousand confirmed deaths.

The Danish Home Guard is imposing a curfew, and the Danish government has declared a state of emergency.

The clerk at the pharmacy asks Karena for ID to purchase the ibuprofen. Not wanting to put her mother at risk, Karena lies to him. She returns to the hotel and tells Ludvig and Jalaine that they can no longer travel to Malmo. The borders are closed.

Reading the latest news reports, Ludvig discovers that there are over two hundred million infected in the U.S.

Ludvig now has a fever. Worried about her mother and husband, Karena calls her friend Janice. Janice tells Karena that if they can get to Malmo, she will arrange transportation for them to complete their journey home to Solna, Sweden. But with both Jalaine and Ludvig ill, Karena decides they can't travel. She has no choice but to stay in the hotel and hope no one finds out they are sick.

Karena has not yet shown any symptoms.

Two weeks pass. Jalaine and Ludvig deteriorate. When Jalaine realizes her days are numbered, she tells Karena a troubling secret: she and Karena's father had not had marital relations for over a year before discovering she was pregnant with Karena. Her father assumed that she was the product of an affair, but Jalaine insists that she was never with another man. Karena doesn't know what to think.

Jalaine shows Karena the picture of her with Fresler Barsness and Erik Jakobson when they were ten. They look like triplets. Karena's father believed that picture was the key to understanding his wife's pregnancy.

Jalaine passes away. A day later, Ludvig also succumbs to the deadly virus. Heartbroken, Karena travels to Malmo alone, where she is able to rendezvous with Janice's people to complete her journey to Solna.

Karena is now certain she is immune from the virus.

What's more, her blood may be the key to developing a vaccine.

On the Sjelian space vessel, Erik is desperate to return to Earth. En route to the space station, Erik finds out that the morphons have started infecting the people of Earth. At this point, only two hundred and fifty million are still alive. He is crushed that he didn't make it back in time, but he is hopeful that he can save those who remain.

Erik thinks back to 2020, when he learned the Neksesians traveled to Phaelin in search of a relocation planet to escape an impending destructive anomaly. The Neksesians' studies of this rift in space revealed that though it is not a black hole, anything that passes through it is consumed. As of March 2023, Nekses will be obliterated within months.

In that 2020 meeting shortly after the escape from Phaelin, Erik also learned the Sjelians sent the morphons to Earth not only to save the planet from destruction, but also to provide the Sjelians with a site for relocation, should the anomaly eventually reach Sjel. The General Council decided to preserve Earth as a new home for Sjelians.

The second capsule the Sjelians sent to Earth, buried in Greenland, contains a much deadlier morphon. Unlike the morphons in the first capsule in Antarctica, these morphons will not be dormant in freezing temperatures—and there is no vaccine or cure. Erik, Karena, and Fresler's blood will be of no use if this second capsule opens.

In 2023, Erik has a conversation with Aleria, Theran, and Kralo to devise a plan to disable the second capsule. Because the capsule's transmitters were altered, Erik will have to disable it remotely. To do so, he must be within five thousand feet of the capsule. This means he must return to Earth.

Erik will travel through the Akureyri portal and make his way to Reykjavik, where he will see Stephan, Hanna, and Olafur. Erik hopes that Stephan will fly him to Greenland, where he can disable the second capsule.

Meanwhile, in Sweden, Karena has developed a vaccine with her blood.

Janice has been in communication with William Frieden at the U.S. Centers for Disease Control in Atlanta. They share their knowledge of immunity to the virus, and the Americans reveal their plan to travel to Solna—by way of Akureyri, Iceland.

Fresler, Sharon, William, and CDC assistant director Rodney McDade fly into Reykjavik, Iceland. There they hope to find someone to take them to the cave in Akureyri where Fresler, Erik, and Karena's mothers passed out and later became pregnant.

At the Reykjavik airport, they encounter Erik's brother-in-law, Stephan. He transports supplies and doses of the European vaccine to other parts of the island in his small plane, which can land almost anywhere thanks to its skis.

William explains to Stephan that they need to visit a cave in Akureyri. Stephan immediately recognizes it as the cave where Erik disappeared almost six years ago. Interest piqued, Stephan agrees to fly the Americans to the cave.

At the cave's entrance, Stephan tells the group about Timothy Claiborne, who was cured of multiple sclerosis and cancer. When Stephan mentions referring Timothy to the Human Connectome Project study, Fresler puts the pieces together. Though Fresler and Stephan have never met, they are linked by one missing man: Erik Jakobson.

On the Sjelian space station, Erik says goodbye to Aleria, Theran, Reshal, and Kralo. He enters the portal to the

Akureyri cave, where he will begin his journey to Greenland.

Erik wakes in the snow at the cave's entrance. He can hear a plane in the distance, but he doesn't know that it's Stephan's plane—or that Fresler is aboard.

Fresler senses Erik's presence as the plane flies overhead, but he thinks it must be a mistake. There was no one at the cave.

Erik hikes from the cave's entrance to the town of Akureyri. There, he visits Uriel, his guide from almost six years ago. Uriel lets Erik borrow his car so he can drive to Reykjavik.

At Hanna and Olafur's house, Erik is shocked to learn that Hanna's cancer has metastasized and that she doesn't have long to live. But he is overjoyed to see Stephan again. Stephan, who believed Erik dead, breaks down.

Erik tells his in-laws about his adventures with the Sjelians. They find the story hard to believe until Erik gives Hanna a macrophage that he took from the Sjelians' lead physician, Mandal. Hanna begins to recover from her cancer immediately.

Stephan tells Erik that he met Fresler and that Fresler believes they are related. Fresler and the others are on their way to Solna, Sweden. Erik asks Stephan to fly him to Sweden so he can see Karena and Fresler.

But the clock is ticking: Erik has only seventy-two hours to disable the capsule in Greenland and return to the Akureyri portal. At the end of that window, the Sjelian space vessel will depart for Nekses to study the anomaly. Aleria has already committed to joining the mission to Nekses, and Erik wants to be on that vessel with the woman he loves.

William, Rodney, Sharon, and Fresler arrive at the ECDC headquarters, where they meet Janice and Karena.

Fresler and Karena are excited to reunite. They only wish Erik could be there with them.

A DNA test confirms that Karena and Fresler are half-siblings. Satisfied that this question has been resolved and eager to continue work on an American vaccine, William and Rodney return to Atlanta. Shortly thereafter, Erik arrives, and the three siblings are reunited.

Erik relays tales about his time in space with the Sjelians and informs them of the second capsule, which he must disable within forty-three hours. Fresler, Sharon, and Karena agree to go with Erik and Stephan to Greenland. Next, Erik explains the anomaly and its threat to the planet Nekses. He wants Fresler, Sharon, Stephan, and Karena to join him on the exploration vessel leaving for Nekses.

The next morning, the group starts their journey to Greenland. They stop over in Reykjavik to switch planes. Sharon decides to stay behind due to a sprained ankle.

In Greenland, Stephan lands his plane within half a mile of the site where the capsule is embedded in a crack in the ice shelf. The remote device Erik wears around his neck will deactivate the capsule if it is within five thousand feet.

Stephan stays with the plane while Erik, Karena, and Fresler hike to the capsule. When they reach the site, they discover that the capsule has slid out of range inside the chasm. They will need to lower someone down into the chasm for the signal to reach. Karena volunteers since she is the lightest.

After successfully disabling the capsule, the siblings encounter an infected polar bear on their hike back to the plane. They barely escape the vicious beast, losing valuable minutes.

On the plane, Erik does the math and realizes that he cannot make it back to the Akureyri portal in time. The

Sjelian space vessel will depart without him. He may not see Aleria for years.

They pick up Sharon in Reykjavik. Then, Stephan, Fresler, Sharon, and Karena convince Erik to go to the cave, even though it is too late. They all agree to cross the portal, if it is open. But when they arrive, the portal is closed. Erik is crushed.

Then, the boulders around the entrance begin to levitate. Excited, everyone follows Erik into the unknown.

After passing through the portal, they are all put into a deep state of unconsciousness. Erik is the first to wake. He is overjoyed to see Aleria. The Sjelians waited for him to return to the portal before departing for Nekses.

He is eager to introduce everyone to Fresler, Karena, Stephan, and Sharon, but Aleria tells Erik only three other Earth-humans are on the station. Stephan decided to stay behind on Earth.

Erik also learns that Reshal, his biological father, will soon be a grandfather—which means that either Aleria, Sharon, or Karena is pregnant.

* * *

Book 4: Diastassi Connection

On March 1st, 1951, Sarah Wade is born. Her parents, Kaitlyn and Nathan, are overjoyed, but Sarah is no ordinary child.

Nathan does not know it, but Kaitlyn is not from the planet Earth. She was born on the planet Diastassi and escaped with her father when she was thirteen years old. Kaitlyn and her father, Prostatis, each possess special gifts: they can cause pain telepathically and sense others' emotions. Only ten percent of Diastassians have these abilities, and the Diastassian government fears these gifted people will overthrow and dominate the rest of the population. Their inhumane countermeasures include isolation and eugenics, and it is from these that Kaitlyn fled.

Prostatis's father-in-law, who worked for the Diastassian government, provided them with a shuttle and coordinates to an interdimensional portal that would take them to Earth, where they could live in peace and safety.

When the Diastassians created this portal, they also created a rift that is threatening the universe.

Sarah has inherited her mother's abilities. In fact, Sarah's gifts are much more advanced than Kaitlyn's. Kaitlyn tries to help Sarah manage her abilities so that she can acclimate to life on Earth. If she's unsuccessful, Sarah's gifts will lead the Diastassians to their quiet Missouri town and threaten the life they've built.

The Diastassian government has sent trackers to Earth in search of Kaitlyn and Prostatis. These trackers carry devices that help them detect telepathic signals like those that emanate from Kaitlyn, Sarah, and Prostatis when they use their abilities.

For this reason, Prostatis no longer lives with his daughter. Nathan does not even know he exists. Prostatis does, however, check in on his daughter and granddaughter from time to time. As a child, Sarah sees a mysterious white-haired man watching her in a park. When she looks again, he's gone.

Sarah is home-schooled until high school, when she begs to join her peers. On her first day, she is excited to walk into the building with her best friend, Mary Jacobs. In science class, Sarah immediately impresses the teacher, Mr. Fuller, with her advanced knowledge. In English, she is inspired by Mrs. Wright. But at lunch, after being introduced to Mary's friend Kenny, Sarah is accosted by her childhood bully, Mitchell Solheim—the first person upon whom she used her telepathic pain power, back when they were six.

Sarah settles into her new routine, navigating Mitchell's continued abuse along with Kenny's unrequited crush. She excels in her studies, especially in science class, and by her junior year is on track to be valedictorian. Mrs. Wright encourages Sarah to begin thinking about college. Unfortunately, Kaitlyn is against the idea. She worries that her daughter's abilities will be exposed if she is given too much freedom.

That winter, Sarah has a terrible nightmare. Afterward, she runs to her parents' room and wakes them. She knows, somehow, that there's a tornado coming. Initially, Nathan doesn't believe his daughter, but Kaitlyn convinces him to join them in the tornado shelter. The storm passes right overhead, and when they emerge, their house has been destroyed. The Wades move in with Mary's family while they rebuild.

Sarah later learns that her beloved English teacher, Mrs. Wright, was killed by the tornado. She decides that she will follow her dreams and go to college to honor Mrs. Wright, no matter how much her mother disapproves.

After seeing the movie "2001: A Space Odyssey," Sarah decides to build her own computer for her senior science fair project. She is overjoyed when Mr. Fuller he reveals that their school will be loaned a state-of-the-art computer for her to study. Despite instructions to only look at the expensive machine, Sarah decides the only way to learn how it works is to take it apart. Unfortunately, she is interrupted by her teacher before she can put everything back where it goes. As punishment, Mr. Fuller bans her from the science lab.

With Kenny's help, Sarah breaks back into the school after hours and rebuilds the computer. The night is a triumph... until Kenny tries to kiss Sarah. She pulls away, humiliating him.

Mr. Fuller is astonished to discover the computer rebuilt and working perfectly. He says not even the scientists who designed the machine could have disassembled and reassembled it so quickly. He is in awe of Sarah's intellect.

While walking home one night, Sarah witnesses school bully Mitchell being hit by his abusive father, Craig. Without thinking, Sarah uses her ability to psychically hurt Craig, to save Mitchell from further harm.

When Sarah gets home, her mother is waiting for her. Kaitlyn felt Sarah unleash her ability. She says Sarah must never do it again—not even for a just cause. Sarah is frustrated because her mother still won't tell her exactly why she must hide her gift.

The next day at school, Sarah notices Mitchell's distress. She offers an olive branch, which he begrudgingly takes it, and a new friendship begins.

On prom night, Mitchell is Sarah's date—much to Kenny's dismay. At the dance, Sarah and Mitchell kiss, and Sarah doesn't feel any sparks. Feelings hurt, Mitchell lashes out at her and runs from the gym. Sarah leaves as well and is comforted by Mary.

As the friends walk the halls together, they pass the cafeteria, where the science fair exhibits are set up. They see that Sarah's computer has been smashed. It looks like Mitchell is to blame.

Outside in the parking lot, Mitchell and Kenny are fighting. Sarah uses her ability to render Mitchell unconscious.

Mr. Fuller takes Mitchell to the hospital. That's when Kenny confesses he's the one who smashed Sarah's computer—jealous that Sarah kissed Mitchell. Sarah goes to the hospital to check on Mitchell and to apologize for blaming him.

Back at home, Kaitlyn knows Sarah has used her ability again. She finally explains to her daughter what is at stake. Each time Sarah unleashes her gifts, the Diastassian trackers draw closer.

After graduation, Mr. Fuller tells Sarah about a new opportunity: if she can get to San Francisco, a prominent computer engineer will take a look at Sarah's microprocessor, which survived the smashing of her science fair project. If she impresses Mr. Fuller's colleague, Sarah may have a chance at securing a prestigious internship.

Knowing she won't have her parents' approval, Sarah decides to make the long bus trip alone. Mitchell and Mary each promise to join her.

At the bus's first stop, Sarah sees something that makes her blood run cold: the mysterious white-haired man from her childhood. He's gone before she can confront him, but she sees him again outside her hotel when they stop for the night.

The next day, in Cheyenne, Wyoming, things get even stranger. Sarah, Mitchell, and Mary see an odd blue light coming from an alley. When they check it out, they find two men lying unconscious on the ground. They call the police, give a statement, and return to their bus.

When they finally make it to San Francisco, they have time to enjoy the city before Sarah's big meeting the following day. After taking in a free concert in the park, they come across a teen being attacked by two men. Sarah uses her ability to take down the muggers. Grateful, the teen,

Spenser, invites Sarah and her friends to stay at his house overnight. Spenser's father is having a party, and among the luminaries in attendance is none other than John Lennon.

At the computer conference, Sarah's microprocessor impresses several engineers. Sarah is passed along to Ted Hoff at Intel. She earns an interview the next day, which leads to an offer for a salaried job that includes college tuition. But as she and Mary leave Intel's headquarters, they are accosted by two men. They are rescued by the white-haired man, who rushes them both into his car and drives away.

At a nearby diner, the white-haired man—Sarah's grandfather, Prostatis—explains about the Diastassian trackers. Mary is astonished to learn that her childhood friend has telepathic abilities. Mary decides to fly home, wishing Sarah luck.

Sarah and Prostatis drive to Missouri to pick up Kaitlyn and Nathan. At their hotel in Wyoming, they are attacked by more trackers. Sarah demonstrates her superior gift by taking down the men through a wall. Prostatis is astonished. Most Diastassians must see the people on whom they're inflicting telepathic pain.

At home, Kaitlyn confesses all her secrets to Nathan. Then, a pair of trackers breaks into their house and subdues them. The men perform a blood transfusion on Kaitlyn, embedding a tracking device in her bloodstream.

Sarah and Prostatis arrive and rescue Kaitlyn and Nathan. Prostatis takes the group to his hidden shuttle. But not everyone will be able to flee the planet. Because of the blood transfusion, the trackers can now find Kaitlyn wherever she goes. If she is with Sarah, Sarah will never be truly safe.

Using the shuttle's systems, Prostatis locates a Sjelian

vessel. The Diastassians have been observing the Sjelians and know they are a peaceful race. Prostatis and Kaitlyn decide to send Sarah on a direct path to intercept the Sjelian vessel. They hope she will be safe hiding among the Sjelians.

Sarah doesn't want to go alone, but she knows that she has no choice.

Prostatis programs the shuttle and tells Sarah to give the Sjelians a new name—one that does not sound like it is from Earth. She can never tell them who she really is or where she is really from.

The Sjelian vessel discovers Sarah's shuttle, and she is brought on board. When the Sjelians ask Sarah her name, she tells them that it is Kayna—a combination of her parents' names, Kaitlyn and Nathan.

She meets a nice young engineer named Theran. Theran and Kayna fall in love and have a daughter named... Aleria.

* * *

Book 5: Transcendent Anomaly

Picking up immediately after the events of Biogenic Convergence in 2023, Transcendent Anomaly begins as Erik wakes aboard the Sjelian space station after traveling through the Akureyri portal along with his half-brother, Fresler, his half-sister, Karena, and Fresler's girlfriend, Sharon.

Erik and Aleria visit Karena first and inform her that she is pregnant. She conceived a child with her husband, Ludvig, several weeks before he died in the pandemic. Karena is shocked. The news is bittersweet.

They visit Fresler next. Upon waking, Fresler reveals to

Erik, Aleria, and Karena that he has an ability. He can sense
the presence of his siblings, wherever they are. He knew the
moment Erik arrived in Akureyri. He believes the ability
was triggered by the rage he felt after discovering that the
Soldiers of Destiny had killed his friend John Williams.

Sharon is the last to wake, but once she's with the group,
Erik is excited to show everyone the space station where he
spent the past several years.

When they are finally alone together, Aleria tells Erik
about a confrontation she had with Akril, the Sjelian
director of planetary evaluation, while he was on Earth.
Akril told Aleria that she informed the General Council of
their plan to disable the second capsule.

At this revelation, Aleria felt extreme rage. The rage triggered a new ability. Aleria caused Akril to feel severe neurological pain. Akril screamed and passed out, leaving Aleria
feeling ashamed and confused.

Erik reassures Aleria. She did not intentionally hurt
Akril, and Akril did not suffer any permanent damage. Also,
Akril has done more to harm Earth than anyone else on the
space station, so Erik finds it hard to feel sympathy for her.

The next day, the four Earth humans board the Sjelian
space vessel. It departs for the planet Nekses, where the
Sjelians hope to study the anomaly. It will take them six
months to reach the planet.

En route to Nekses, Aleria decides to have her blood
tested. She is curious to learn the source of her new ability.
She discovers that she has Sjelian and Earth DNA, as well as
something unknown. She realizes that the unknown DNA—
and the unique new ability—must have come from her
mother, Kayna, who disappeared when Aleria was sixteen.

Erik has a conversation with Telfas about Aleria's ability
to sense Kristin's presence, which she says is the reason they

cannot become romantically involved. Telfas tells Erik that there are people on Nekses that have the same ability. They can sense the afterlife. In fact, there are some that can bridge the two planes of existence, allowing communication with those who have passed. Telfas's mother has that ability.

Erik asks Telfas if his mother could help him communicate with Kristin and Eria. He wants to have closure, as he believes this is the only way he can eventually have a relationship with Aleria. Aleria first sensed Kristin's presence years ago, and she insists Kristin is still keeping them apart.

Telfas tells Erik that if his mother is still on Nekses, he will arrange a meeting. When Erik relays this to Aleria, she is hopeful their relationship can truly begin soon.

The Earth humans adjust to life on the Sjelian vessel. Erik returns to the brain scan research he did on previous space journeys. Physicist Karena joins the anomaly research team, working alongside Sjelians and Neksesians to understand the strange rift. Fresler studies the Sjelian language and begins to write a book about his adventures. Sharon struggles to fit in, as she is the only one without any Sjelian DNA.

Months pass. When the Sjelian vessel exits the final portal, they are seven days from the planet Nekses. Then, they will finally see the anomaly.

On October 7th, 2023, the vessel is within range of the anomaly.

The colorful, swirling mass looms over the planet Nekses. To the Sjelian crew's chagrin, the anomaly is within four days of devouring the planet. Even worse, its rate of expansion keeps changing, so it is impossible to determine exactly when Nekses will be consumed.

The planet's radiation levels are too high for the Sjelian vessel to land on its surface. In fact, Theran will not allow anyone other than Telfas and Kesh, a Neksesian researcher Karena has befriended, to take a shuttle to the surface. Most Neksesians have already abandoned their planet, and Telfas needs to find out where they went. He plans to visit his mother's house, where he can access the main terminal and download the relocation coordinates. Kesh will take readings that should help them learn more about the anomaly.

Erik is devastated to learn that Theran will not allow him to travel to the surface of Nekses with Telfas. He had so desperately wanted to communicate with Kristin and Eria. It takes Aleria's intervention to convince Theran to let Erik accompany Telfas in Kesh's place.

During his goodbyes to Karena and Aleria before boarding the shuttle, Erik promises to return before Karena gives birth, which could happen any day.

According to Kralo, they now have only five hours before the planet is destroyed.

On the surface of Nekses, the increased radiation forces Telfas and Erik to exchange their Sjelian shuttle for a Neksesian model, causing a delay.

They arrive at Telfas's mother's house, where Telfas is able to retrieve the coordinates he's seeking. Meanwhile Telfas's mother helps Erik communicate with Kristin and Eria.

Erik learns that his wife and daughter are not suffering. They tell Erik that it is time for them to leave. Erik's over-whelming joy and gratitude for the opportunity to say goodbye is cut short by Telfas' shouts.

The anomaly is approaching the surface at a faster rate than anticipated. They must leave immediately. To Telfas' dismay, his mother chooses to stay behind.

In the shuttle, attempting to escape the fast-approaching

anomaly, Erik talks to Aleria over comms and tells her that they can now be together. Kristin and Eria have moved on.

Aleria's excitement turns to devastation when she sees Erik's shuttle swallowed by the anomaly. She blames herself for talking Theran into allowing Erik to go to the surface. Because of her, Erik is gone.

At the very moment that Erik's shuttle is overtaken by the anomaly, Karena gives birth to her son, Winnett. Fresler and Sharon are at Karena's side. When Erik disappears, Fresler experiences a sense of overwhelming loss.

Theran, Gott, and Kralo map out the coordinates that Telfas retrieved from the surface of Nekses and transmitted before the shuttle was consumed. The Neksesians have relocated to a quadrant of the universe that the Sjelians have never explored.

On October 18th, the Sjelian vessel arrives at the mysterious planet, which they learn is called Tria. The planet is incredibly lush and beautiful. They land their vessel on the surface and soon find the Neksesian village.

They are welcomed by a human named Utivos, who is a Borjan. Borjans are far more advanced than Sjelians, Neksesians, and other human races. Utivos explains that Tria is an outpost planet that the Borjans use to monitor other human planets, like Earth, Sjel, Phaelin, and Nekses. When the anomaly approached Nekses, the Borjans decided to offer the Neksesians refuge on Tria.

Aleria asks Utivos about the anomaly. She is holding out hope that Erik is still alive and can be saved. Utivos tells Aleria that to get more information about the anomaly, they need to visit the people who created it. The Borjans have been monitoring this other planet, Diastassi, for millions of years, and will guide the Sjelians there.

Utivos introduces Theran and Aleria to Maskin, who

will be the Borjans' representative on this new mission. Aleria, Theran, Reshal, Kralo, and Mandal leave with Maskin. Gott stays behind to be with his fellow Neksesians. Fresler, Sharon, Karena, and baby Winnett also stay behind.

The Sjelian vessel departs Tria the same day. The situation on board is tense. Aleria is suspicious of Maskin because she cannot sense any emotions from him, making him the first human she has ever encountered without emotions. Additionally, Aleria wonders about Utivos' motivation in sending Maskin along and directing them to Diastassi in the first place. If the Borjans have been monitoring this planet, and if they are truly as advanced as they say, surely they know enough to help locate Erik. Why couldn't Utivos just answer Aleria's questions?

Meanwhile, back on Tria, Karena has a sudden and inexplicable desire to visit the outpost headquarters to talk to the Borjans. Like Aleria, she believes they are withholding information. Fresler and Sharon try to talk her out of it, but she cannot be dissuaded. Karena later learns that this compulsion is a special ability tied to her Sjelian DNA, like those of Fresler and Erik. Hers is powerful intuition.

Fresler and Sharon watch baby Winnett while Karena breaks into the Borjan headquarters. There, she meets a woman named Sibula. Sibula was expecting Karena and is eager to talk.

She informs Karena that there were once nine planets inhabited by humans, each with a different subspecies of human DNA. The Borjans have been observing these planets for millions of years. They are most concerned with five individual humans—five hybrids, or humans with two or more subspecies of human DNA.

Kayna, born Sarah Wade, was the first hybrid. Her mother was Diastassian and her father was from Earth.

When Kayna had Aleria, Aleria became the first human with three subspecies: Earth, Diastassian, and Sjelian. Thus, Aleria's abilities are much more advanced. In her, human evolution fast-forwarded millions of years.

The other three monitored hybrids are Fresler, Erik, and Karena, who each have a Sjelian father and an Earth mother. Unmonitored hybrids include Aleria's son, Emeran, and granddaughter, Kayna, and now Karena's own son, Winnett.

Sibula tells Karena about her own ability to see the future. She had a vision of Erik's future long ago, when he was a young man. He was trapped in the anomaly. When Erik developed his ability to receive telepathic signals at eighteen, she sent him a vision to warn him... while Erik was attending his mother's funeral. Sibula is the woman in black.

In the vision, Sibula told Erik to travel away from the light. That is the only way he can escape the anomaly.

Karena asks Sibula if the Borjans seeded the nine planets, but before the older woman can answer, they are interrupted by a furious Utivos. Karena flees.

Under Maskin's guidance, the Sjelians reach Diastassi. In orbit around the planet, Aleria senses someone that she hasn't seen since she was sixteen years old: her mother. To her amazement, Kayna is on the surface of Diastassi.

A few moments later, the Sjelian vessel is flanked by two Diastassian warships. Their ambassador, Lenix, talks to Theran. She orders them to leave their solar system, but Theran insists on asking her for information about the anomaly. She tells Theran that they are not aware of an anomaly, though she admits that the Diastassians created an interdimensional portal.

Aleria tells Lenix that she can sense that her mother,

Kayna, is on the surface of the planet. Lenix immediately invites Aleria, Theran, and Maskin to board their lead vessel.

In order for the Sjelians and Maskin to visit Diastassi's surface, they need to be inoculated. Theran doesn't like this, but Lenix insists. They have no choice if they want to see Kayna, so they agree.

Lenix takes Theran, Aleria, and Maskin to the isolated village where Kayna lives with other gifted Diastassians, apart from the general population. During a very emotional reunion with Kayna, Theran, and Aleria are introduced to her mother, Kaitlyn, and her father, Nathan. She goes on to explain her absence, detailing the climactic events of Book 4.

Kayna next introduces Aleria and Theran to her grandfather, Prostatis, and her great grandfather, Navik—the person who helped Prostatis and Kaitlyn escape Diastassi all those years ago. He lives with them now, demoted from his leadership position when the government discovered his actions.

Navik is nearing death, but he is still cognizant enough to answer questions about the anomaly. He tells the Sjelians that it is a multidimensional rift created as a byproduct of the portal. It was nothing more than an accident.

Maskin wants to know how to destroy the anomaly. Navik responds that it would take five million tons of dark matter subjected to two billion pounds of pressure to create a vacuum effect that would result in the rift collapsing upon itself. If the rift collapses, the portal will close.

Maskin reveals that Utivos gave him a two-fold mission: to learn how to destroy the rift and to bring Kayna back to Tria. She is key to their survival.

Aleria does not want to destroy the anomaly before

rescuing Erik. She asks if they can enter the rift to save him. Navik responds that the rift is multidimensional, so it would be impossible to locate him. In addition, there is no way to communicate with their shuttle.

There is nothing inside the anomaly. It is a completely empty void. The only thing visible is a light at the entrance. Navik worries that Erik and Telfas will instinctively travel toward the light. If they do, they will be crushed by two billion pounds of pressure.

Aleria asks, if they cannot travel inside the rift to locate Erik and they cannot communicate with him, how can they warn him not to travel toward the light? Navik doesn't have an answer.

Meanwhile, Maskin has come up with a plan. A Neksesian vessel can carry dark matter. If the vessel entered the anomaly and traveled back toward the entrance, the pressure at the entrance would collapse the rift.

Maskin tells the group that they need to return to Tria to prepare a Neksesian vessel with dark matter. Aleria argues that they need to save Erik before the anomaly is destroyed. She asks Navik where the exit to the portal is, just in case Erik figures out that they need to travel in the opposite direction of the light. Navik discloses that the exit is in the same dimension as Diastassi, but he doesn't have the exact location. To complicate matters, it has become clear that the Diastassians have no intention of letting gifted beings like Aleria or Kayna leave their planet. Ever.

As the group strategizes how to escape Diastassi with Kayna, Aleria offers to use her newfound ability to inflict pain. Navik asks Aleria if Lenix injected her with anything. He reveals that her "inoculation" was nothing more than an inhibitor designed to prevent her from using her ability. However, Maskin believes the inhibitor will have no effect on Aleria, since she is much more powerful than anyone the Diastassians have encountered.

To leave the planet, they need to disable the Diastassian defense system. Maskin needs access to their command terminal, which will mean getting a retinal scan from Lenix.

Theran notifies Lenix that the group is ready to return to their vessel. Lenix arrives and transports Aleria, Theran, Maskin, and Kayna to the capital.

When they arrive at the capital, Lenix takes the group to a laboratory, where she will have her medical team perform the sterilization procedure on Aleria. As the group suspected, Lenix has no intention of letting them leave.

Aleria uses her ability to put all of the guards and Lenix into a deep state of unconsciousness. Maskin carries Lenix's limp body to the control center, not far from the laboratory. Once inside, Maskin uses Lenix's retinal scan to access the Diastassian defense system and disable their entire fleet.

To reach the shuttle that will return them to their own vessel, they must pass by hundreds of guards. Maskin tells Aleria that she has the ability to incapacitate thousands of humans in the space of a breath. Aleria does so.

En route to the shuttle, they are confronted by a lone guard. Before Aleria can take him down, he shoots his weapon and hits Maskin in the stomach. Upon examining Maskin's wounds, they learn that he is a machine. He reroutes his programming so he can still function. He pilots the shuttle back to the Sjelian vessel.

The Sjelian vessel returns to Tria, where Maskin prepares a Neksesian vessel with dark matter. He tells Aleria and Theran that it will take him five days to reach the anomaly. The life support in Erik's shuttle will end not long after that, so they need to locate him and return to this dimension before the anomaly is destroyed. Once the anomaly is destroyed, the portal will collapse.

Maskin also tells Utivos and the Sjelians that it is only a matter of time before the Diastassians regain control of their defense system and send a fleet to look for Kayna and Aleria. The Diastassians see them as a threat to their survival, even though they are no longer on the surface of Diastassi. When Aleria asks how the Diastassians can possibly find them, Kayna explains that like her mother, Kaitlyn, she now has a tracking device in her blood.

Relying on her enhanced intuition, Karena convinces the group that Fresler will be able to use his ability to locate Erik if he successfully escaped the anomaly. She believes Erik will escape, thanks to the message Sibula sent him when he was eighteen: "Do not travel toward the light. Go in the opposite direction."

The Neksesian vessel, piloted by Maskin, and the Sjelian vessel depart Tria at the same time. The Sjelians pass through the interdimensional portal to search for Erik on the Diastassian side. Five days pass before Utivos communicates to the Sjelian vessel that Maskin has reached the anomaly and that the Diastassian fleet is approaching fast. Fresler still hasn't sensed Erik's presence.

When it is clear the life support on Erik and Telfas's shuttle has expired, and there is no hope of finding them alive, Theran orders Kralo to return to Tria. The Diastassian fleet will arrive soon, and if the Sjelians don't cross the portal before Maskin destroys the anomaly, they will be trapped in this dimension.

Aleria insists that they cannot return to Tria without Erik. Theran sympathizes with his daughter, but tells her that Erik didn't survive. His concern now lies solely with the

safety of his crew. With Kayna on board, there is no question
that the Diastassian fleet will locate their vessel.

Kayna, meanwhile, regrets coming along. She wonders
how she could possibly be the key to their survival. If the
Diastassians can track them because of her, she is the key to
their capture.

Kralo obeys Theran's order to return to Tria. Overcome
with emotion, Aleria uses her ability to incapacitate her
father, Kralo, and Reshal. She is certain Erik is still alive, and
she won't leave him behind.

While the Sjelians are unconscious, Fresler suddenly
senses Erik's presence. Kralo, Theran, and Reshal awaken,
and, with Fresler's help, they locate Erik and Telfas's shuttle.

Aleria is the first to greet Erik, but amid the joy, she
comes to realize Erik doesn't look like he's been gone for
twenty-four days. When asked how they survived without
life support, Telfas and Erik are confused. They tell the
group that they were only inside the anomaly for three days,
not twenty-four. The anomaly has gravitational time
dilation.

There is no more time for happy reunions. Maskin is
already inside the anomaly. Using his newfound knowledge
of the time dilation, Telfas calculates that Maskin will
destroy the anomaly in thirty-four hours. The Sjelian vessel
has thirty-four hours to reach the interdimensional portal. If
they fail, they will be stuck in this dimension, at the mercy
of the Diastassian fleet.

Unfortunately, the Diastassians are on a direct path to
the Sjelian vessel and will intercept them well before they
can enter the portal. The Diastassian ships are too fast, and
thanks to Kayna's tracking device, there is nowhere to hide.

Twenty-six hours later, the Diastassian fleet catches up
to a shuttle. Kayna's tracking device is inside. Lenix believes

that the Sjelians sacrificed Kayna to aid their escape. Little do they know the shuttle is empty... except for a bag of Kayna's blood.

A few hours later, the Sjelian vessel arrives at the entrance to the portal. With the blood transfusion ruse a complete success, the Diastassian fleet is millions of lightyears away. Not long after the Sjelian vessel crosses the portal, Maskin successfully destroys the rift. The interdimensional portal collapses, leaving no possible way for the Diastassian fleet to cross dimensions.

When they return to Tria, the group has much to celebrate. The successful rescue of Erik from the anomaly. The rescue of Kayna from Diastassi. The destruction of the threatening anomaly.

Best of all, Erik and Aleria can finally be together.

* * *

Book 6: Fatal Resonance

It's July 2nd, 2016. David Schwarz is bringing his family for a long overdue visit to his small Wisconsin hometown. The last thing he expects is to arrive at his childhood farmhouse to find his parents and their entire herd of cattle dead. Even though his old friend, Kevin Schumer, is the lead deputy, David—a police detective in Detroit—wants to solve the case himself. David insinuates himself into the investigation, despite being too emotionally invested to remain objective.

The Schwarzes move in with the Schumers while the investigation begins at the farm and funeral arrangements for Margaret and Stan Schwarz are made. David's wife, Debbie, is friendly with Kevin's wife, Ellie. Thirteen-year-old Maddie Schwarz is the same age as Joey Schumer, and six-year-old Grace Schwarz is close in age to Bethany Schumer. Joey has leukemia, and his illness has cast a shadow over the family. He and Maddie have not seen each other for five years—since before he was diagnosed.

While the local police are looking into natural and pathological causes for Stan and Margaret Schwarzes' deaths, David becomes convinced a neighbor, Gordon Muller, is to blame. Gordon recently wanted to buy the Schwarz farm, but Stan declined to sell. Also, Gordon's son, Bradley, was suspected of poisoning animals as a youth. David is sure his parents were poisoned, despite a lack of evidence.

In Atlanta, epidemiologist Thomas Murphy at the Centers for Disease Control is made aware of a developing situation at a Wisconsin dairy farm. The local coroner cannot establish a clear cause of death for either the cattle or the Schwarzes. Thomas may need to take over the investigation to determine if this is a new, dangerous pathogen.

David and Debbie return to the farmhouse so David can look for clues. After sharing an emotional moment of remembrance in the garden Margaret planted for David's sister, Lizzy, who died of cancer as a teen, they discover something ominous. All of the birds and mice in the barn are dead. This makes it more likely that the deaths are a matter of public health, not murder.

But David is stubborn. Sticking to his hunch, he breaks into Gordon Muller's lawyer's office. He finds a geological survey of his parents' property and the Mullers'. The survey reveals that a valuable mineral deposit straddles the border between the two lots. This explains why Gordon offered to buy the struggling Schwarz farm.

On a trip to town to meet with the funeral director, David learns from Kevin that his parents' official cause of death was a heart attack. But the coroner says that it's as though their blood literally boiled. In order to fully understand what happened, she is calling in reinforcements from the CDC.

While the adults run errands, Maddie and Joey are left to hang out downtown. They have not been getting along. Prickly Maddie wants nothing to do with sickly, dorky Joey, even though they were childhood friends. But when Joey is attacked by two bullies from school, Maddie can't stand by. Trained in in Krav Maga, she uses her skills to take the bullies down. Afterward, she divulges to Joey that her quick temper and fighting prowess got her ostracized at school in Detroit. She and Joey bond over feeling like outcasts.

To placate David, Kevin agrees to send one more patrol out to the Schwarz farm to look for a smoking gun to tie the Mullers to the deaths. The two deputies do their canvass... and discover something strange. But before they can call it in, they're dead.

The investigation kicks into high gear. Thomas Murphy arrives with a team from the CDC. The town is put under quarantine to contain the possible contagion. With the Schwarz property cordoned off, it's not long before the investigators locate something that they can't explain.

During the quarantine, Maddie and Joey grow closer. Maddie teaches Joey to fight, while Joey teaches Maddie to swim. One morning, they wake up early to hike to a place Joey used to go with his other friends, before his leukemia diagnosis. The cliff is on the border of the Schwarz and Muller properties. From the top, they can see the hazmat-suited researchers swarming around a strange tower. They decide to go down to investigate. In the caves below the cliff, Joey collapses.

When the adults discover that the teens are gone, David

and Kevin rush out to search for them. Kevin remembers Joey mentioning the cliff, so they go there. From the top, they also see the mysterious tower.

Joey recovers, and he and Maddie make it to the base of the tower. When Joey touches it, the tower gives off a rumbling vibration that makes him feel tingly. They are about to return to the caves when they see Kevin approaching with Thomas in a government van. Joey and Maddie know they're caught. Before they all leave, Thomas warns Kevin to watch the teens for unexplained symptoms that might result from their proximity to the tower.

That night, Kevin gets a call that everyone on the farm—the CDC research team, the personnel from the Wisconsin Bureau of Communicable Diseases—is dead. Only one man, Terrance Wilkins, survived the slaughter. Thomas was saved by going into town to speak to the sheriff.

At this point, the government thinks the tower may be a weapon of mass destruction. Catherine Harris is sent to Wisconsin from Washington, D.C., to head up a task force comprised of personnel from the FBI, Department of Defense, Homeland Security, and other agencies. Thomas gives his report to Catherine when she arrives, and together they realize there has been a pattern to the deaths: they occur five days apart, between 5:00-5:15 p.m.

The government scientists soon determine that the tower is made of materials not found on Earth. Based on that information, the FBI director decides to investigate a connection to a mysterious incident from 1969 in Cheyenne, Wyoming. Agents are sent to San Francisco to speak with Mitchell Solheim and Mary Jacobs Miller, the two living witnesses to the Cheyenne incident.

The agents also interview Sarah Wade Solheim, Mitchell's daughter. Sarah was named after Mitchell's friend Sarah Wade, who disappeared in 1969. Sarah Solheim is a professor at Stockholm University and teaches part-time at U.C. Berkeley in the summer months. She has expertise with the type of signals the tower is producing. Sarah also believes in the existence of extraterrestrial life.

The FBI director invites Sarah to join the investigation on the Schwarz farm. He shows her a rectangular device that was recovered from the unconscious men in the alley in Cheyenne in 1969. The device is made from elements that do not exist on Earth, just like the tower in Wisconsin.

Sarah arrives at the Schwarz property and meets with Catherine Harris. The two discuss infrasound—soundwaves on the lowest end of the frequency spectrum that cannot be heard by humans. They wonder whether the tower is producing blasts of high-decibel infrasound every five days, which would account for the deaths.

Joey has an appointment with his oncologist to see whether his cancer treatments are working. To everyone's astonishment, his levels are close to normal. This drastic improvement means he's almost in remission. The adults credit the chemotherapy, but Joey knows the truth: touching that mysterious tower healed him. He is determined to return to the tower.

At the farm, Sarah is frustrated by her continued lack of progress in understanding either the tower or the device from Cheyenne. She goes to find Catherine at the tower, and the small device found in Cheyenne suddenly powers on in her pocket. The women postulate that the tower's signal vibrates at the same frequency as blood.

Joey and Maddie sneak out to return to the tower. They make it there without problems, but in the cave on the way back, they are attacked by a mountain lion. They manage to

seal themselves into a small room within the cave network...
but they are now trapped.

Knowing that Joey wanted to visit the tower again, Kevin
and David go to the farm to find the teens. Unaware of the
cave system, their lengthy search ticks down the clock,
approaching the upcoming deadly blast from the tower at
5:12 that evening. If they aren't out of the blast radius by
then, they could all die.

Finally, David and Kevin discover and enter the cave.
Kevin kills the mountain lion, and they rescue the teens. But
it's too late to escape the blast radius. Using deductive
reasoning, based on Joey's reactions to the tower's frequen-
cies, Maddie realizes that the room they were hiding in will
protect them; it's covered in a chalky graphene residue that
absorbs the soundwaves. They take cover and survive
the blast.

Afterward, Sarah and Catherine reflect on what they've
learned about the strange tower. They know it's sending a
signal...but where? And to whom?

A month later, Joey is officially in remission. His cancer
is cured.

PART I

RETURN TO EARTH

CHAPTER 1

Aboard the Sjelian vessel, en route to the Earth space station - December 8th, 2023

Erik sinks into Karena's couch, mesmerized by the sway of the Sjelian mesh rocking chair as she lulls baby Winnett—just shy of two months old—to sleep.

He grins, remembering his parents' tales of him as a child, obsessed with their wooden rocking chair. "You would spend hours there," his mom would say with a smile.

Winnett seems to share Erik's old love. "He is so peaceful," Erik murmurs.

Karena nods and strokes her son's soft brown hair. "He rarely ever cries," she says, tracing a finger along his cheek and around his ear. "Apparently, I cried all the time... I was colicky." She smirks. "I know how crazy this will sound, but I actually wish he would cry more."

Erik chuckles, now recalling his first months as a parent, awake at all hours with a fussy Eria. "You're right... that does sound crazy. Be thankful."

"Trust me... every single day, *I am thankful*." She plants a gentle kiss on Winnett's forehead.

"Are you excited to be returning to Earth?" Erik asks.

Karena lays Winnett in the wooden crib retrieved from Theran's storage room. The Sjelians had offered to make her a safer, Sjelian crib, but she'd declined. She wanted something from Earth. Or at least, something that looked like it was from Earth.

She shrugs. "I have mixed feelings. I'm excited to see Janice, and I need to get some personal things I left behind, but... Sweden just reminds me of Ludvig and my mom."

Erik nods. That's how he'd felt about Minnesota, all those years ago. "Is Kesh going with you?"

Karena's sharp, delicate features brighten in a flash. "Yes. I can't wait to show him where I grew up."

Erik tilts his head. "Aren't you worried?"

"About what?"

"I know how this will sound, but... he is going to stick out like a sore thumb."

Her hazel eyes cut sideways at him. "Are you referring to his skin tone?"

"It doesn't exactly look like a sunburn," says Erik with a wince.

"I'm not worried," she claims, though she starts fidgeting with her white-blond locks. "The only person that will see him up close is Janice. She'll understand. She won't judge him... like *you're doing*."

Erik puts his hands out. "I'm not judging. I'm just worried someone will think he has a contagious disease. The world is still recovering from a deadly pandemic, you know."

Karena shakes her head. "I know. I'm just giving you a hard time."

"And I only bring it up because I care. I want you to be safe."

Karena acknowledges that with a nod. "Are you and Aleria excited to visit Iceland?"

"Yeah. I can't wait to see Stephan."

"How do you think he will react when he sees you with Aleria?"

Erik shrugs. "Hopefully, he'll be happy for me... but I'm sure it will be awkward at first."

"I'm sure he'll be happy to see that you've moved on."

Erik releases a trapped breath in a whoosh. "Yeah, I hope so."

"Maybe you can find out why he didn't enter the portal with us."

"Oh, I intend to," Erik says with gusto. "And I'm going to convince him to come with us to the space station this time. He's got to at least see the Oort cloud."

"You and that Oort cloud." Karena smiles fondly, turning her focus back to Winnett as his baby blues flutter shut.

* * *

Kayna smiles as she taps a key on John Lennon's piano, sending an alto note ringing through the storage unit. She turns into Theran's chest and squeezes him tight. "I remember when you got this for me. It was our seven-year anniversary. I think Aleria was *three.*"

Theran rests his chin on his life partner's graying, chocolatey hair. "I remember... Now it makes sense why you were so connected to these things."

"I am so sorry I kept the truth from you." She rubs his forearm. "I was worried they would find us."

Theran snorts. "As it turns out, they did find you."

Kayna shakes her head, a wash of sorrow tightening her throat. "I was so devastated..." She lifts Theran's hand and intertwines their fingers. "I am grateful you found me." The knot of their hands is a sight she never thought she'd see again, and the beauty of it, the capture of a moment she longed for every day for years, brings tears to her eyes.

"I never stopped looking." He kisses her cheek.

Kayna spies an antiquated floppy disk computer sitting on the desk beside them and thinks back to 1969 and the trip to San Francisco. She walks over and puts her hand on the computer. "I hope Mary and Mitchell survived the pandemic... I would love to see them again."

Theran nods. "Hopefully, Reshal can locate them. It all depends."

"On what?"

"Cell phone usage. Not long after the outbreak, we lost our ability to track communications on Earth. All we can do is determine their location at the point when everything shut down."

Kayna wets her lips. "Hopefully they weren't in San Francisco at the time...."

Theran nods his bald pate in his stoic way, lids heavy.

She moves to the clothes rack and trails her fingertips along the fabrics. "Let's get you something to wear for our trip to Earth. You'll need to blend in."

Theran looks down at his white gown. "What's wrong with this?"

She clucks her tongue. "No, you can't wear that." She tugs on his sleeve and chuckles. "You'll look like a sixties cult leader."

Theran narrows his eyes at the rack for a moment and then snatches a pair of bell-bottom slacks and a purple silk shirt with a rare giddy grin.

Kayna giggles. "I know you love disco, but you need something more contemporary." She pulls a pair of tan khakis and a blue and white button-down from the rack. "This is more like it." She holds the shirt up to his face. "It matches your eyes."

"Why does that matter?"

Kayna shakes her head. "You're hopeless."

* * *

The Setustofa room's waterfalls create a white noise that encapsulates Sharon and Fresler in a private bubble. Sharon ponders Fresler as he swirls his Slak in his glass, waiting for him to act on the breadcrumb trail she's been laying all morning.

"You don't seem excited about our trip," says Fresler. There it is, but he still isn't really getting it.

"I am! I'm just..."

"What?" Fresler prompts.

She shrugs. "I know you want to move to Minnesota permanently—"

"I didn't say that," interrupts Fresler.

"It's what you're thinking... right?"

He studies the blue liquid in his cup. "I have thought about it. It would be nice to move to Minnesota with my parents."

She exhales sharply. "Don't get me wrong, Fresler. I love them, but I want a place of our own... a place where we can raise a family."

Fresler pulls Sharon close, kissing the top of her golden hair. "I agree... but we can do that in Minnesota... build a home next to the cabin."

Sharon looks up at him through narrowed eyes. "Where are we going to stay while it's being built?"

"We would stay in the cabin," says Fresler, as if it's obvious.

"With your parents?"

"Yes."

Sharon shakes her head. "You expect all four of us to live in that tiny cabin while we build a home for you and me?"

Fresler's jaw tightens. "Wow, I never knew you felt that way about my parents."

"Don't do that." Sharon glares, pointing at his nose.

"Do what?"

Sharon props her hands on her hips. "Put words in my mouth. Or snap at me." Fresler has been tightly wound lately. Sharon is struggling to get used to this shorter-fused version of her once carefree, perpetually mellow partner, and she's not sure she wants to. She adopts a softer tone and continues, "You know I love your parents. That has nothing to do with how I'm feeling." She pauses for a moment, watching the whitecapped water tumble into the fountain designed like a jungle river. "It's just that, I think I... want to stay on Tria."

Fresler blanches. "But Earth is where our family and friends are."

"You have friends and family on Tria."

"Family?"

Sharon throws up her hands. "Erik and Karena."

"You only spent a couple of weeks on Tria. Now you're ready to live there forever?"

"Maybe. I feel like I'm making a difference there, helping the Neksesians rebuild."

"You can help Earth rebuild," Fresler argues.

"Can I? It's not like I can go back to work for the Sierra

Club."

Fresler bites the inside of his lower lip, turning his head away. "We can talk about this later."

* * *

Erik sighs contentedly as he pulls Aleria's back into his chest, one arm wrapped around her shoulders, nestled together in a love seat in the Setustofa room.

Aleria turns her face so her cheek presses against his. "This is nice."

Erik nods.

"After everything we've been through these last few years..."

Erik chuckles. "You mean escaping the anomaly?"

"Yes... and don't forget Phaelin."

Erik wrinkles his nose, flashes of hairy foes chasing him down corridors and a burning pain in his shoulder replaying in his mind. "I haven't."

Aleria pats his leg. "Hopefully we won't have any more adventures like that."

"Hopefully."

"I am excited to meet Stephan," says Aleria.

"You'll love him... and he'll love you." He flinches, hearing the hesitation in his own voice. He's being silly... right?

Aleria shifts beside him. "We'll see."

"What's that supposed to mean?"

"I know you're anxious, Erik. I can sense it. You're worried it will be difficult for Kristin's family to see the two of us together."

Erik bites down on his tongue to trap the boyish denials that flood to the front of his mouth. "Maybe," he says gruffly, knowing full well she wants and deserves the truth.

She cuts her eyes up at him. "Are you going to tell them?"

"Yes... of course. I'll be so proud to introduce you as my life partner. I can't wait until tomorrow."

Aleria brightens, leaning into his chest again. "I am excited too..." She kisses his cheek and then springs up, reaching out for Erik's hand to help him off the soft cushion. He follows her to the water's edge, where a six-foot-tall lavender plant stretches a frond toward them, as if waving. Its twin sways toward it, tipping half its large, pinkish bulbs like a gentleman tipping his hat. "This is where we will hold the ceremony," says Aleria.

"Why here?"

"It is a Sjelian tradition to hold the Life Partner cere-mony by the Lysander plant. It is a symbol of a life- long commitment to love."

"Why is that?"

"These plants grow in pairs. When the flowers bloom, they face each other in perfect symmetry. If one plant were to die, the other would not survive. They need each other."

"Really? We have nothing like that on Earth."

Aleria nods. "They are unique."

"When do they bloom?"

"One month each year... and only for a few hours each day." Aleria kisses Erik's cheek. "They will be in full bloom tomorrow during the ceremony."

Erik reaches out to trail his fingers over the enormous plant's extended, leafy hand. "Incredible."

She gestures to the plants. "We'll each pull a petal from a flower and lay them on top of each other." She studies the purple stems, each leaning toward their mate. "Something truly amazing happens when they touch."

"What?"

"You'll see tomorrow."

"You're going to make me wait to find out?" he says, tickling her side.

Aleria laughs and swats him away. "Absolutely."

Erik draws her in and murmurs, "I can't wait," against her mouth.

* * *

Karena rubs noses with Winnett before relinquishing him

into Sharon's waiting arms. "Thanks for watching him. We won't be long."

Sharon taps Winnett's nose with her index finger. "You take as long as you want."

Karena kisses Winnett on the forehead and waves goodbye with one hand, reaching back with the other to take Kesh's. He nods his bald, pink head to Sharon and then escorts Karena into the hall, arm in arm.

"I so look forward to our time together, Karena," he murmurs when they are alone in the stark white corridor.

"Me too." She rests her head against his shoulder. "Are you looking forward to visiting Earth?"

"Yes, but..." His smile goes sheepish, eyes ducking toward the floor and its trail of recessed lights.

"But?"

"The people of Earth do not believe that there is intelligent life outside of their solar system, correct?"

Karena giggles at his choice of phrasing. "A few do. Most don't."

"Then what will they think... when they see me? You can't tell them I am from another planet. What will they think of my..." He looks at his exposed arm, the color of strawberry taffy. "... skin pigmentation?"

"Don't worry. The person we'll be visiting, my friend Janice—she already knows."

Kesh's eyes pop. "About me?"

"No... about intelligent life outside of Earth. She knows about the Sjelians."

"Ah." Kesh nods. "Does she also know about the... multiple human subspecies?"

"No," Karena admits. "I had no idea about the nine inhabited planets when I last saw her."

Kesh hangs his head. "Now, two of those planets have

been consumed by the anomaly. First Opik, and then Nekses."

Karena gently turns him into her hug, her fingers tracing his high cheekbone. "I am so sorry."

"Thanks. At least we have a place we can call home, on Tria."

Karena drops her hand from his face into his palm, and they start walking again, fingers interlocked. "It's strange," she says. "The Borjans provided your people safe refuge from the anomaly, but not the humans on Opik. Why is that?"

"I think it is because the Opikians were still in the beginning stages of human evolution."

"That doesn't mean they didn't deserve a chance to live," Karena says in a low voice.

Kesh nods. "True."

"Did you ever meet an Opikian?"

"No. That planet was destroyed by the anomaly before I joined the team. My first mission was the one to Phaelin. That was also my first contact with another human subspecies."

"And now you've met Sjelians, Earthlings, and Diastassians."

"The universe is indeed vaster than I'd imagined."

Karena pauses mid-step. "That's something I've been wondering about, actually."

He gives her a curious look.

"How did the Neksesians learn about Opik and Phaelin in the first place? The odds of finding another planet inhabited by humans... when they are millions of light years apart... are *insurmountable*."

"I honestly don't know," Kesh says. "The only thing I do know is that we sent out millions of probes in search of intelligent life and found those two planets."

Karena scrunches her eyes. "It doesn't make any sense."

"Well, what about the Sjelians?"

"What about them?"

"They also identified other human-occupied planets that were millions of light years apart from each other: Earth, Phaelin, and Rajik."

"Rajik," says Karena, voice sinking with dismay. "Erik told me about Rajik."

"The Sjelians identified Rajik over twenty thousand years ago," Kesh says. "They monitored it, like they are currently doing with Earth... up until the point that the humans perished."

Karena doesn't like to think about Rajik, the planet that the Sjelians chose *not* to help. Then again, their idea of "help" on Earth was eradicating most of the population— including her beloved Ludvig. She rubs at an ache in her temple.

"Kralo told me that the Sjelians used probes to locate Earth, Phaelin, and Rajik," Kesh goes on. "Millions of probes, just as we did on Nekses."

Karena scoffs. "I don't care if they sent trillions of probes out into the universe... there is no *possible way* they could locate three planets that happen to be inhabited by humans. The Sjelians are hiding something... and so are your people."

"Hiding what?"

"I don't know, exactly." Karena feels the tug of her ability —her intuition. "A random probe didn't find those planets. Something or someone helped them."

"Maybe you're right. The Borjans claim to have known about the nine planets for millions of years."

Karena makes a skeptical hum in the back of her throat. "I don't think it was them."

"Then who?"

"I... have no idea." Karena purses her lips. "But I have a feeling it's extremely important that we find out."

CHAPTER 2

December 9th, 2023

Erik's white silk ceremonial robes are loose and soft, yet he has an overwhelming urge to tug at the collar. His heart is pounding with happiness, but the rapid beat and the few nervous jitters lingering in his muscles are making it hard to draw in a satisfying breath. Half of Aleria's long hair is twisted up into a braided knot, with the other strands curling down her back. The Lysander plants give off a heady, almost musky scent that he didn't notice yesterday. He looks around at the small audience gathered in the Setustofa room. Theran, Kayna, and Reshal stand behind Aleria. Karena, with baby Winnett nestled into the crook of her arm, Sharon, and Fresler are Erik's half of the ceremonial party, standing behind him with cheesy grins. Kralo, his life partner Mandal, and Aleria's friend Lina gather around in a semicircle, their faces as giddy as stoic Sjelians can be.

Aleria takes Erik's hand, pulling his gaze back to her face, and some of his nerves dissipate, drawn out by her touch. "We start the ceremony by describing the moment..."

A tear trembles on her lower lashes, but she holds it captive. "The first moment you knew you were in love." She smiles that special, soft smile reserved only for him—vulnerable in the intensity of its love. "I'll go first. This will sound strange... but for me, it was when I found you at my workstation after you had taken my PAD without my knowledge. I knew then that I loved you."

Erik nearly laughs in shock. "That moment almost drove us apart," he says, incredulous.

"I felt such pain, such betrayal," Aleria explains. "If I hadn't loved you then, I would have simply been mad at you."

Understanding ignites a warmth that spreads through his veins and stills his jittery limbs.

"But the birthday present I received from you," she continues, "was what told me you were someone I could commit to as a life partner. When you arranged, with Kralo's help—" She smiles at Kralo. "—for me to see my son and granddaughter, I knew how deep my love was for you. It has been proven over and over, never more clearly than when I thought I had lost you in that anomaly."

Erik lets his free hand trail down the side of her face, following the line of one of her loose curls, then places it atop their already intertwined fingers. "For me," he begins, "it was at the celebration after we exited the second portal on the way to Phaelin. Dancing with you to that song... 'The First Time Ever I Saw Your Face.'" A shiver of delight races along his spine at the memory of her white dress, her head on his chest as he turned her in smooth, careful circles on the dance floor. It still makes him tremble. "Holding you in my arms for the first time. The love I felt for you in that moment... is just..." He shakes his head. "I can't explain it. Every day... my love for you grows." A crack in his timbre forces him to slow down and breathe. "When I was trapped in that anomaly, the only thing I could think about was seeing your beautiful face one more time. And of course, you were the first person that I saw when I exited that shuttle. I love you."

Aleria's smile is strong enough to leave him dazed. "I love you, too."

Sharon sniffles behind Erik. Behind Aleria, Kayna leans into Theran, and Erik hears her whisper, "Remember our vows, love?" Theran presses his cheek against her hair as he nods.

Aleria drops Erik's hands and turns to their family and friends. "Now we will each take a petal from the Lysander flower to symbolize our commitment to a life partnership." She leads Erik to the beautiful flowers that are now in full bloom, pink stamens rising proudly out of a lush base of mauve teardrop petals the size of Erik's hand. Golden speckles dot their surface like a dusting of glitter. Aleria pulls a petal off the leftmost plant, and Erik follows her lead with a petal from its mate.

Aleria gently coaxes him to face her again and holds her petal aloft between them. "This Lysander petal symbolizes my commitment as life partner to you, Erik, my one true love," Aleria says, her pupils dilating as she holds his gaze. She leans closer to whisper, "Your turn."

"Do I just say what you said?"

Aleria smiles. "Yes."

Erik holds up his petal. "This Lysander petal symbolizes my commitment to you, Aleria, as my life partner. My one true love."

"We now press the petals together." Aleria brings hers most of the way to meet his.

As the golden speckles touch, they fuse, and Erik gasps

in surprise. The rounded petals' edges fold into one another, forming a seal that leaves them indistinguishable from each other—a single entity.

Aleria holds up the melded petal and says, "Like this petal, we are now one." She flushes as she leans in with a grin.

For this part, at least, Erik knows what he's doing. He meets her halfway in a kiss that leaves the back of his neck hot. Cheering fills his ears, and he pulls away to find even baby Winnett grinning at him.

He looks at Aleria. "Is it over?"

She nods. "We are now life partners."

He lifts her off her feet and twirls her in an embrace. "Let's celebrate!"

"To the Slak!" says Fresler, earning a chorus of laughter.

Erik and Aleria lead the way to the dispenser.

Close behind them, Sharon says to Fresler, "That was so beautiful, don't you think?"

Fresler nods.

"I know we decided years ago that marriage is just a legal ritual that we don't believe in, but I loved that ceremony," says Sharon, and Fresler can feel the gravity of her words. He slows his pace to give her his full attention. "I would like us to be life partners," she says. "To make that commitment in front of the people that we love most."

"Let's do it," says Fresler, pulling her into a hug and brushing his lips against her ear as he adds, "I love you, Sharon."

"I love you, too." She pauses, grimacing a little. "But we still need to discuss our plans for when we return to Earth. I don't like the way we ended that conversation yesterday."

Fresler stiffens. "I agree, but not now. Let's celebrate with Erik and Aleria."

* * *

December 10th, 2023

Reshal greets Theran and Kayna with a serene half-smile, hands folded atop his desk, as they enter his office hand in hand. Kayna is short of breath with anticipation as Theran scoots in her chair. The evaluation center office is rather cramped compared to Theran's commander's quarters, but since Reshal is presenting his own research, his office made more sense.

Reshal accesses his computer by placing his hand on the pad built into his desk. Images of Mary Jacobs Miller and Mitchell Solheim appear on the holographic screen, hovering perfectly in Kayna's line of vision. It's like sitting face to face with her old friends.

Kayna stifles a sob with her hand. The driver's license photos depict a man and a woman clearly in their seventies. Even with the wrinkles and thinning gray hairlines, Kayna relishes the familiar angles and curves of their faces. She can almost hear Mary complaining good-naturedly about Kayna's far slower aging process. *"You've barely aged a day over thirty-five, and here I am, an old lady! Of course, I still look better than Mitchell here, the old windbag."*

"I can't believe it," Kayna whispers. She reads the driver's license addresses. "They both ended up living in San Francisco?"

Reshal nods. "Yes, not far from each other."

"Amazing." Kayna gazes wistfully at the screen as memories of strolling San Francisco's streets with her two friends play in her head. "Did they marry?"

"Not each other, but yes. Mitchell married Linda Colburn, now deceased, from La Crescenta, California.

They had one child, a daughter they named Sarah Wade Solheim."

Kayna gasps.

Theran squeezes her hand tight. "What is it?"

"That was my name... on Earth. Sarah Olivia Wade."

Theran blinks. "Your name was Sarah?"

"Yes," she says through tears. "Mitchell named his daughter after me."

"Wow... you clearly had an impact on his life."

Kayna wipes her face clean and asks Reshal, "What did Mitchell do for a living?"

Reshal swipes to change the page on his holographic screen. "He owned four restaurants. Two in San Francisco, one in San Jose, and the other in Salt Lake City."

Kayna's surprised giggle sounds more like a hiccup. "Salt Lake City? I wonder if that has anything to do with our trip to San Francisco."

"Why would it?" asks Reshal.

"Salt Lake City was one of our stops. We visited the Mormon library to research the origin of the name Diastassi."

"You knew about the planet Diastassi?" asks Theran.

"Not at the time. My mother always told me that Diastassi was her maiden name."

"Ah. I'd like to hear the whole story of your trip sometime."

"You name the time and place," says Kayna with a smile before turning back to the computer. "What about their daughter, Sarah? What does she do for a living?"

Reshal types in a few words, and a photo of a red-haired woman in her early forties appears. "She is a professor at Stockholm University. She teaches physics."

Kayna's brows rise. "Wow... impressive."

"She received her PhD from U.C. Berkeley," Reshal continues, "where she teaches during the summer months."

"And Mary?" Kayna says eagerly. "Tell me about her life."

Reshal accesses Mary's file. "Mary Jacobs moved to San Francisco in 1970 and attended the UCSF School of Medicine. She became a cardiologist at Saint Francis Memorial in San Francisco."

"She said she wanted to be a nurse." Kayna shakes her head, a smile budding. "And she became a cardiologist." She kisses a finger and taps it lightly against the hologram, on Mary's cheek, making the image flicker. "Did she marry and have children?"

"Yes, she married Lawrence Miller. They had two boys, Jared and Evan." Reshal puts their pictures on the holographic screen.

"Mary did it," Kayna breathes, chest swelling with love. "She moved back to San Francisco and became a medical doctor. Got married and had two boys. I am so proud of her." She squeezes Theran's hand. "What about her husband?"

"He was also a medical doctor," says Reshal.

"Are her two boys doctors?" asks Kayna.

"No, neither went into the medical profession. Evan works with Mitchell, running his Salt Lake City restaurant, and Jared is an engineer."

"It sounds like they've all had... wonderful lives." Kayna's smile wavers, and she straightens her spine as if bracing for impact. "Did they survive the pandemic?"

Reshal's eyes move slower across his desk screen. "According to the last data transfer before the satellites became non-operational... Mitchell was in San Francisco when the morphons reached the United States." He looks up at Kayna. "The temperature in San Francisco was well above freezing. It is unlikely that he survived. I'm sorry."

Kayna's spine cannot withstand the blow, and she folds herself over the desk, gasping for air.

Theran rubs her back and exchanges a look of helpless sorrow with Reshal.

Kayna gathers herself and rises with a sniffle. "And Mary?"

Reshal draws a deep breath. "I'm sorry, Kayna, but it seems that Mary was also in San Francisco when the morphons reached the U.S."

"What about her family?"

"Mary's husband, Lawrence, and her son Jared were in San Francisco... but Evan was in Salt Lake City."

Kayna fixes her gaze on the picture of the more delicately featured brother. His deep, friendly eyes are framed by circular, silver glasses. "Evan may have survived. The temperatures should have been below freezing. He could have lived long enough to receive the vaccine."

Theran pats her hand. "It's possible."

Kayna looks back over at Reshal. "And Sarah, Mitchell's daughter... What about her?"

"She was in Zurich, Switzerland, at the time of the outbreak, attending an academic conference."

Kayna smiles through her tears, imagining Switzerland's snow-topped mountains and ski chalets. "She probably survived."

Reshal brightens a fraction. "Yes. It's very likely that she did."

"We have to find her!" Kayna turns to Theran and takes both his hands, pleading with her eyes. "Evan, too!"

"We can try," he says without hesitation.

"I have Sarah's last known address," says Reshal. "She

was staying in an apartment in town, within walking distance of the university."

"Thanks, Reshal."

He nods.

Theran lifts his life partner's hands to his lips. "I'll let the others know we'll be making some additional stops while we're on Earth."

"Thank you," Kayna murmurs, staring at the image of the red-haired woman in Reshal's file. She can see Mitchell in Sarah's features, just as she can see Mary in Evan and Jared's. "Switzerland first, and then Salt Lake City." If her friends' children are still alive, she will find them.

* * *

Sjelian space station — December 12th, 2023

Theran waits by the vessel's main doors as the space station arm pulls them onto the dock. The doors open with a whoosh, and Lathal is waiting with a ring of assistants. He looks just as he did ten months ago, when Theran and his crew departed the space station en route to Nekses. In truth, Lathal appears exactly as he did six years ago, when he took Theran's place as Space Station Leader. After an expedition full of such... eventful happenings—each of which left Theran feeling as though his emotions were caught in a warp speed jump, bouncing from one to the next far faster than his mind could keep up—a bit of familiarity is an immense comfort.

Lathal greets him with a wide smile that brightens his hazel eyes. "Theran, it is so good to see you."

"It's good to see you too, Lathal."

The assistants trail behind at a respectful distance as Lathal gestures for Theran to walk beside him through the station's labyrinthian corridors. "You and your crew are heroes," he says, some uncharacteristic pep slipping into his voice. "You destroyed the anomaly."

"Anyone would have done the same."

Lathal chuckles. "That's not true. You made the decision to travel to another dimension without approval from the General Council. You ignored their directive." Lathal grows somber, two creases between his brows. "I wouldn't have done so, and the universe would still be in jeopardy. You defied orders... and saved us all."

Theran holds up a hand. "I would love to take credit, but most of it goes to Aleria. Without her, we would still be on Diastassi and the anomaly would still be wreaking havoc."

"You haven't changed," says Lathal.

Theran shifts uncomfortably under Lathal's admiring gaze and changes the subject. "Did the General Council update you with regard to our plans?"

"Yes, they mentioned that you want to access the portal in Iceland, to allow the four Earth humans to return home."

Theran nods and opens his mouth to divulge the latest changes to plan—that in fact nine of them will travel to Earth... and that at least a few of the Earth humans intend to return to the space station, and then on to Sjel.

"Unfortunately," Lathal says, before Theran can speak, "the General Council has ordered me to close all portals to Earth."

"What?" Theran exclaims. "That is not what the General Council agreed upon when we communicated."

"They reversed their position. They feel keeping the portals open is now too risky."

Theran struggles to keep his voice calm. "Risky how?"

"Reshal impregnated three women from Earth. The General Council insists this must never happen again."

Theran jerks. "You know about that?"

"Yes, but I am the only one on this station who is aware of what Reshal did."

Theran resists the urge to groan, instead pressing his fingertips together in a meditative pose in front of his chest. "Tell me, are the planet's satellites operational?"

"Not yet, but they should be soon."

"I appreciate the update."

Lathal's commiserating gaze turns slightly suspicious. "What are you planning, Theran?"

Theran gives his friend a sidelong glance. "It is probably best that I don't tell you."

Lathal cracks a smile. "I understand."

* * *

Aleria can sense the bad news in Theran's urgent message to her and Erik's PADs, asking them to meet. She urges Erik off the bed and tosses his turtleneck at him. Picking up on her tension, he stays fairly quiet as they dress and make their way toward the conference room, until their paths cross with Kayna, Kesh, Reshal, Fresler, Sharon, and Karena, who's wearing Winnett in a wrap around her chest.

"Anyone have a clue what's going on?" Erik asks, wiggling a finger to tickle Winnett behind the ear.

After a few grunts and head shakes, Fresler says, "Well, I guess we're about to find out."

Theran is waiting at the head of the table. Aleria can sense his unease, but the determined set to his mouth eases her own worry. When everyone is seated except for Karena, who remains standing to bounce Winnett as he dozes off, Theran clears his throat.

"Lathal has informed me that the Council has closed all portals on Earth."

"Why?" asks Reshal.

Theran's mouth twitches to the left, a clear sign to Aleria that he's uncomfortable sharing the true answer. All he says is, "To eliminate risk."

Reshal's forehead wrinkles. "That doesn't make any sense."

"Regardless, the portals are closed."

Aleria notes all four Earth humans' immediate alarm and says, "What are we going to do?"

"We need to visit Earth," Erik chimes in, no doubt thinking of Stephan.

Theran meets each pair of eyes in turn before speaking, as is his way. Aleria has always thought the habit's intention is to make each individual feel important in a time of stress or need, and the gesture always makes her pay closer attention to whatever words should follow.

"The portal was never a viable option." Theran looks to Winnett, now droopy-eyed and drooling against Karena's chest. "We will have an infant with us. The temperature at the portal in Iceland will be at or below freezing. The journey from the portal to Reykjavik would be too dangerous for our group. Not to mention we wouldn't have transportation to our destinations in Sweden, Switzerland, and the U.S." He shakes his head. "We have always needed another plan."

Aleria catches on first. "You're planning to take a shuttle, aren't you?"

Theran's smile shows in his eyes rather than his mouth. "Yes. We will take this vessel's shuttle to the surface. We will first land near the CDC headquarters in Atlanta, where Fresler and Sharon will depart. We will then travel to

Iceland." He looks over at Aleria and Erik. "Sweden will be our next destination, for Karena and Kesh. Finally, Kayna and I will land in Switzerland."

"Did you get approval from the General Council to take the shuttle?" asks Reshal through an ornery grin.

Theran scoffs. "I'm not asking for permission."

Reshal leans back and folds his hands over his chest with a satisfied nod.

"Won't the shuttle be discovered once it reaches Earth's atmosphere?" asks Kayna.

"We will travel under cover of darkness. Lathal informed me that the planet's satellites are still inoperable. That means they will have no way of tracking our shuttle."

Fresler leans forward to meet Theran's eye around Sharon's thick head of hair. "It is still dangerous to be out at night."

"Are you referring to the infected animals?" asks Theran.

"Yes."

"They are no longer infected."

Sharon jumps in, her head obscuring Fresler's view once more. "Were they cured? How?"

"No. The morphons expired five months ago," says Theran.

"What do you mean... *they expired*?" says Karena, bouncing Winnett faster.

Reshal answers for Theran. "All morphons are coded to terminate at a certain date. The morphons that were sent to Earth terminated five months ago. Thus, the remaining animals are no longer infected."

"Humans too?" Karena asks.

Theran nods.

Beside Aleria, Erik's eyes go wide. "Wow."

Karena nods sharply. "When do we leave?"

"We will meet at the shuttle bay in two hours," Theran says. He stands to dismiss them all.

Erik pops out of his seat. "I need to say goodbye to Kralo. I'll see you at the shuttle bay in two hours." He kisses Aleria softly before heading out.

Aleria's smile fades as Kayna stands beside her. She grabs her mom's arm and says, "Why are you and Dad traveling to Switzerland? I thought you would come to Reykjavik with us, to meet Erik's in-laws."

"I would love to," Kayna says earnestly, "but I'm hoping to find the daughter of a friend of mine. He and I went to high school together."

Aleria brightens at the excitement in her mother's voice. "It's so odd. Knowing that you lived a life on Earth, and I don't really know much about it."

"I am sorry I had to keep that part of my life secret."

Aleria simply inclines her head in true Sjelian fashion. "Tell me about your friend."

"His name was Mitchell Solheim. He and my other best friend, Mary Jacobs Miller, took a pretty amazing bus trip with me back in 1969."

"And he... died?" Aleria asks, sensing her mother's surge of grief. "They both did?"

Kayna exhales sharply, blowing a strand of hair off Aleria's face. "It appears as though neither survived the pandemic. But two of their children may have. Sarah Solheim was in Zurich, Switzerland, at the time of the outbreak. Evan Miller was in Salt Lake City, Utah. I would like to meet them both."

Aleria smiles, hoping against hope her mother's sweet enthusiasm isn't replaced by disappointment. Kayna deserves this, to touch the first life she was forced to leave, just as she has been able to finally reconnect with the second life, the Sjelian life... Aleria's life... that the Diastassians took from her.

"Good luck," Aleria says.

"Thanks," says Kayna, a little sheepishly.

"Can you tell me more about them?" Aleria asks.

"Well... before we were friends, Mitchell was the first person I used my ability on. I hurt him—twice. I had good reason to do so... at least, I thought I did." Kayna frowns. "What's wrong, Aleria?"

Aleria startles. She's not used to someone reading *her* emotions. She kept her face neutral, she's sure, but Kayna sensed the shift. Time to come clean, she supposes.

"How did you deal with the pain of using your ability to hurt others?"

Kayna nods, understanding. "I could tell that had been troubling you."

Aleria scoffs, thinking "troubling" isn't a strong enough word.

"You may be my daughter, but you have Sjelian blood running through your veins. That is why you are so conflicted. I never struggled emotionally with using my ability. But I'm not Sjelian. I was not raised to view conflict as something to avoid... as something I should have evolved beyond." Kayna touches her daughter's arm. "Your Sjelian side is at war with your Earth and Diastassian sides. It's a lot to process. Please know that you can always talk to me. I will never judge you."

"Thanks." Aleria nods, but her mother's answer has only brought up more questions.

Above all else: which side of herself is right?

* * *

Erik enters the pristine command center to find it almost
peaceful—filled with a comfortable silence permeated by
occasional soft beeps. Kralo is the only person inside,
leaning in his secure seat in front of the controls, his holographic screen hovering an inch over the tiny lens that
projects it from inside the control deck. He turns with a soft
smile and gestures his bald head toward the enormous main
screen taking up the entire front of the room. Jupiter's
orange and cream hues are far more vibrant than any
picture Erik ever saw in a textbook or on an Earth computer.
The stripes swirl in mesmerizing patterns, but there is
something untamed and dangerous in the way they move.

"I wanted to say goodbye," Erik says, peeling his eyes
from the screen.

Kralo stands, alarm flickering across his features. "Goodbye? But... I will see you again, won't I? You're not planning
to stay on Earth?"

"I'll just be gone a few days," Erik reassures his friend.
"Aleria and I will be traveling to Sjel after our visit to Earth.
She wants to see her son and granddaughter."

Kralo looks relieved. "That makes sense."

"What about you, Kralo?"

Kralo shrugs. "What about me?"

"What are your plans after we return to Sjel?"

"Mandal and I are going to spend some time on Sjel, but
we both like serving on this vessel. If there is another
mission, we will want to be a part of it."

Erik smirks. "No plans for *offspring*, as Reshal likes to
call them?"

Kralo chuckles. "We have talked about it and agree that
we would like to have one *offspring*."

"That's great news," says Erik through a genuine grin.

"What about you and Aleria?"

The image of his lost daughter, Eria, flashes through Erik's mind's eye. "I don't know."

"Well... I hope your trip to Earth is pleasant."

"Me too. I am hoping to convince my friend Stephan to join us this time."

"I would like to meet him."

"Yes, I have a feeling the two of you would be great friends. You're a lot alike."

Kralo inclines his head. "I hope you're successful in convincing him."

"Thanks, Kralo. See you in a couple of days."

* * *

At the appointed time, Erik joins the others in the shuttle bay. Once he reaches the slate flooring, he follows the trail of blue lights in it to the door of the designated shuttle, where his friends wait in a disorganized clump.

When Theran opens the door, they all board in a rush, looking over their shoulders for any curious eyes who might wonder why a shuttle is preparing for launch without authorization. With the door shut securely behind them, Theran hands out communication devices that attach to their wrists. They look like digital wristwatches, except the entirety of the sleek black bands can act like a screen. They will allow the party to communicate with each other and act as a tracking device.

Theran returns to the front to address the group. "If you need help for any reason while we are on the surface of Earth, please contact me. I will be with the shuttle at all times."

They wave, nod, and grunt their understanding. Theran takes the controls, and Erik leans over the arm rest of his seat to watch the small screen just above Theran's head. Earth rushes to meet them like an old friend, and Erik is startled by the flood of affection those familiar green blotches stir in his chest.

As they enter Earth's atmosphere with a mild bump, the screen offers a stunning view of a sunset on the horizon. The last time Fresler, Sharon, Karena, and Erik were on Earth was March 30th, 2023, at the portal in Akureyri, Iceland. They'd just successfully deactivated the second capsule of deadly morphons. Erik remembers the panic of that moment, watching his deadline to return to Aleria shrink while the possibility of saving some bit of Earth became a more likely reality. He'd thought that he would never see Aleria again, but now... they are life partners, forever bound. He looks to his right and studies her profile. Her face is more his home than even Earth.

Using the darkness as cover, Theran navigates the shuttle to North America, to Georgia, to Atlanta, and finally to the CDC building. The shuttle's stealth mode quiets the engines and kills the lights. Not a single leaf in the wooded area surrounding the facility is shaken out of place by their arrival. Theran swiftly lands in a clearing in the woods, obscuring them entirely from the main entrance.

Erik is the first to embrace Fresler and Sharon. "We'll see you soon. Probably in two days."

Karena grabs her half-brother in a hug that's more like a chokehold, slinging an arm around his neck and yanking him in, then gives Sharon a much gentler embrace. Aleria moves in for handshakes but is pulled into a group bear hug. Kayna and Theran receive the handshakes Aleria wanted, and baby Winnett is cuddled and kissed.

And then it's time.

Erik watches through the open door as Fresler and

Sharon disembark and head for the nearby checkpoint, visible only as two spotlights shining through the trees. The stairs retract as Sharon and Fresler turn to wave goodbye. The shuttle door closes, blocking out their silhouettes.

"Next stop, Iceland," Erik murmurs as the shuttle lifts off from the ground with a low boom.

CHAPTER 3

CDC Headquarters, Atlanta, Georgia — December 12th, 2023 — 6:00 p.m. local time

As Fresler and Sharon approach the CDC checkpoint, Fresler is brought back to a time when aliens were only a vague possibility and the last thing on his mind. This very checkpoint had marked the end of a quest, the chance for a cure from the unknown plague that had decimated the world, but it wasn't exactly a happy or triumphant entrance. John had been missing, and he would never arrive. They had lost so many loved ones. This time, though, they are on their way to meet friends.

The thought makes Fresler smile... until he and Sharon step through the line of trees and are greeted by the sound of assault weapons cocking.

Fresler throws his hands up. "I'm Fresler Barsness, and this is Sharon Clary. We are here to see William Frieden and Rodney McDade."

"You're Fresler Barsness?" One of the soldiers steps forward, weapon still raised.

"You know these two?" one of the others asks.

"He's the guy who..." The first soldier fades off. "Never mind. We can stand down. They aren't SoDs."

"Why would you think we're SoD?" Fresler mutters under his breath.

After a swift pat-down that no one involved appreciates, Fresler and Sharon are escorted to the main entrance. The separate add-on room where they were once cleansed of the virus is gone. The double front doors look refreshingly ordinary, and only one guard is posted inside. The soldier who recognized Fresler's name waits with them while the guard calls for William.

A few minutes later, William walks downstairs, a little out of breath. "Fresler! Sharon! It's great to see you again." He embraces them like close family come to call over the holidays. That's what this reunion feels like to Fresler, anyway. A homecoming, to family and to friends who might as well be.

"You're not going to believe what's happened to us these last eight months," says Fresler with a smile of his own.

William loosens his tie and bounces on the balls of his feet like a child waiting for the adults to serve cake at a stuffy party. "I can't wait to hear the whole story," he says. "Let's walk to my office. Rodney is waiting for us." He nods at the soldier standing behind Fresler and Sharon. "I'll take it from here."

The man hesitates, but then gives a sharp nod and goes back to his post outside.

They begin walking, and Fresler launches into his tale. But before he can get any further than, "We were on another —" William shushes him.

"Let's wait for Rodney," the CDC director says with a laugh that, to Fresler's ear, sounds a little forced. "Don't want you to have to tell it twice."

No one speaks again until William swings open his office door. Rodney is buried in a lazy chair in the corner, and it takes him a few seconds to get up when Fresler and Sharon greet him with cheery hellos. He shakes their hands so hard that Sharon's ponytail bobs. Rodney then immediately flops back into the chair. Fresler notes the puffy rings under his eyes look less purple. He's sleeping better these days. A good sign.

"Now can I tell the story?" Fresler asks, once they're all seated.

William waves his hand to say, *Go ahead.*

Fresler tells the two men about discovering Tria and befriending the Neksesians. He shares the gripping tale of how Aleria used her ability to get the crew safely off Diastassi. Finally, he tells his slack-jawed audience how they rescued Erik's shuttle from the anomaly, before destroying the universe-threatening rift for good.

Rodney can hardly blink properly, his eyes are so wide. He swivels his head between Sharon and Fresler, looking particularly owl-like. "Wow! It sounds like a science fiction novel."

"As it happens, I'm working on a novel based on our story," says Fresler, looking pleased.

"You mean to tell me," says William, jabbing a finger onto his desk, "that this woman, Aleria, is capable of causing neurological pain... *telepathically?*"

"Yes, she actually caused hundreds of people to fall to their knees in pain!" insists Fresler.

"You saw it?"

"Well... not that time. But I was there when she did it to Theran, Reshal, and Kralo."

William shakes his head. "You realize how this all sounds."

"I do," says Sharon, raising a hand with a smirk.

"If I hadn't seen it with my own eyes, I wouldn't have believed it," says Fresler.

Rodney, who has been tugging on his chin, suddenly fans a hand at Fresler to grab his attention. "You mean it was a robot... a cyborg that actually destroyed the anomaly?"

"Yes."

"Like Data?" asks Rodney.

"Data?" repeats Fresler, confused.

"You know, from Star Trek, on the Enterprise."

Sharon laughs. "Yes, but way more realistic. You would never know he was a machine. He looked human."

"Incredible." Rodney's usually drooping, basset-like face lifts in a giddy smile that makes Fresler believe Rodney could have actually been a child once.

Fresler leans back in his chair and says wistfully, "After all that adventure, I can't wait to see my parents... and our friends."

The mood in the room changes in an instant. William's whole face drops, and Fresler's gut goes with it.

He instinctively reaches for Sharon, sitting in the second spare chair across from William's desk. "What?" he asks, his tired voice cracking.

"There is something that I have to tell you..." William says slowly. "It's about your father."

Sharon squeezes Fresler's hand, but he barely feels it. "What is it?"

"He and Charles are missing."

"*Missing!*" Fresler shoots forward in his chair. "I don't understand... how could they be missing?"

"Charles wanted to visit his home to gather some of his belongings," William says. "Since it is only a few miles from this building... I allowed it."

"And my father?"

"Your father and Charles have become good friends. They went together, along with an armed guard. The Soldiers of Destiny were waiting at Charles's house. They killed the armed guard and kidnapped your father and Charles."

"Oh my God," Sharon squeaks.

Fresler's free hand balls into a fist. "When did this happen?"

"Two weeks ago," says William, cringing.

"Two weeks ago! Why haven't you done something to get them back?!"

William flinches at Fresler's enraged shout. "It's not that simple."

"How is it not that simple?"

"The Soldiers of Destiny have been..." William puffs out a breath. "An ongoing problem."

"They're just hillbillies," Fresler argues, remembering the ones he'd encountered at the Walmart back in March. "What can they do against a squad of trained soldiers?"

"Homemade bombs, for one thing," Rodney says. "They blew up one of our checkpoints in August. Luckily, no one was killed, but two men lost limbs."

"They planted an incendiary device on one of our vaccine transport vehicles as well," William says, shaking his head. "That one was disarmed in time. And they've tried sniping visitors."

"They have snipers?" Fresler runs a hand over his forehead. Perhaps the SODs aren't quite the ragtag militia he thought. "So that's why there's so much more security outside."

"The new general in charge of this facility, Dennis Martell, is committed to protecting those stationed here at all costs," Rodney says.

"And two weeks ago, I failed to do that." William's shoulders sag. "A man died because of me."

"You can't blame yourself for that," says Sharon.

"It was my decision to let Lars and Charles leave the premises with only one guard," William says, "and the general won't let me forget it. I am no longer in command of the military personnel stationed at this facility."

Fresler releases his fist with a long breath and massages the bridge of his nose. "I need to talk to the general. I have to convince him to rescue Charles and my dad."

Rodney shakes his head, his basset hound expression back in place. "We have already made that request. General Martell said that there aren't enough guards assigned to this building for a rescue mission. They are needed here in a defensive position."

"Then the Department of Defense needs to assign more soldiers to this building," Fresler snaps. "Who can we petition about that?"

Rodney and William exchange a look. "There isn't really a... Department of Defense anymore," Rodney says.

"What?" Sharon exclaims.

"There is," William clarifies, "but the president is the only person making decisions about allocation of resources. That includes military postings."

"Well..." Fresler blusters for a moment. "I'll introduce myself to the general anyway. Does he know that it's *my* father who's missing? I'm one of the three immune individuals responsible for the vaccine. That soldier outside... he knew my name. Surely he and some of his squad would be willing to—"

"Unfortunately, that won't help," says Rodney. "Yes, some of the men stationed here know what you did, but they're under strict orders not to talk about it."

"Unbelievable! We saved millions of lives! You would think they would consider us heroes." The words feel sour on Fresler's tongue, but he'll scream them from the rooftops if it means saving his father.

William clears his throat. "The president has decided to credit the CDC for creating the vaccine and cure... without mentioning the immune individuals. He doesn't want the public to know that it was synthesized from... *alien* blood."

Sharon releases Fresler's hand to leap from her seat and throw up her arms. "You've got to be kidding!"

"The public doesn't have to know it's alien blood," says Fresler, fighting to keep his jaw loose, "just that it is human blood—which is true."

William sighs. "If people learn that there is alien blood in the cure and vaccine, the president worries that it will lead to the revelation that the virus was created by aliens."

"I know what he's really worried about," Fresler says as realization dawns. "He is worried the public will find out that our government knew about the virus *years* ago and decided to keep it secret."

"Yes, that's exactly it," says Rodney, voice dripping with cynicism.

Sharon turns her glower back on William. "Fresler and everyone that made that journey to the CDC should be considered heroes. John died making sure that a vaccine and cure would be created... and what?! We're supposed to pretend it never happened?!"

"I agree with you, Sharon," says William, looking weary. "There should be a statue in front of this building in honor of John."

"Those damn SoDs killed him, and now they have my father!" yells Fresler.

"Please, keep your voice down," William says, glancing at the door. "Our relationship with General Martell and his men is... tenuous."

"Sorry," Fresler grumbles.

Sharon's sound of disgust rattles around in her throat. "How are the Soldiers of Destiny even still alive? Were they given the vaccine?"

William shrugs. "I highly doubt they would accept the vaccine. We think they built a facility at their compound capable of protecting them from the virus. And now, of course, the pandemic seems to have died down on its own."

Fresler and Sharon look at each other, not sure whether to share what Theran said about morphons having an expiration date.

"That group has been preparing for the apocalypse for decades," William says into the silence. "As it turns out... they were right."

* * *

Fresler power-walks through the residential corridors of the CDC, resisting the urge to sprint so he won't leave Sharon in his dust. The meeting with William and Rodney has left him jittery and unsettled. His frustration, anxiety, and anger are bees buzzing around inside him. There is only one thing that can ease his mind: a mother's hug.

He pastes on a smile as he raps his knuckles against his mother's door. There's a shuffle, and then the door opens on Gladys's curious face. A hand flies to her mouth, and she bursts into tears.

"Mom!" He wraps her in a hug.

"Fresler! I wasn't sure if I would ever see you again," she says, clinging to his shoulders. She pulls him down to kiss his cheek.

"I missed you, Mom," he says, tickled by her frizzing red hair.

She wipes away her tears and beckons Sharon into her arms with fingers flapping like butterfly wings. "Sharon, it's so good to see you."

"It's good to see you too," Sharon says, going in for her embrace.

Gladys looks at Fresler over Sharon's shoulder. "You

heard what happened to your father?" The pain suddenly dulling her eyes causes a fresh stab of rage-tinged sorrow in Fresler's chest.

"Yes," he says, choking on the word.

"I am worried sick. I don't know what to do." Fresh tears spill toward her smile lines. "I've pleaded with that new general, but he has a heart of stone."

Fresler lets out a growl at the thought of his sweet mother begging General Martell, whom he imagines as a hulking, scowling, lantern-jawed type, to save her husband.

"Let's talk inside," Sharon says softly, checking up and down the hall.

Gladys waves them into her modest living space.

"I'm going to talk to that man," Fresler mutters, the moment the door is shut.

"I told you, he can't be reasoned with," Gladys says.

"I'm not going to ask him to help us," Fresler says. "I'm going to *make him*."

"What do you mean?" his mother asks.

"What if we threaten him with the truth?"

"Threaten a general?" asks Sharon, jerking around in surprise, her ponytail flying over her shoulder.

"Yes, threaten to expose the truth about the capsules and the morphons... about the fact that our government knew a crisis was coming for *years* and didn't warn anyone."

Sharon's brows rise, and Fresler can see the idea's appeal growing in her brain, giving her eyes a new spark. But her mouth remains a firm, unreadable line until she finally says, "Assume for a second that the general calls your bluff. How are you going to make this public? We don't have the internet to spread the word. We don't even know where the survivors are living, to reach them."

Fresler huffs. "Do you have a better idea?"

"Maybe…" One side of Sharon's mouth curls up in a mischievous grin, and she lifts her wrist to display the Sjelian communication device. "I think we should use this. But—" She flips her hand to stop Fresler as he opens his mouth. "Before we start making plans, I think we need to check in with our friends."

* * *

Fresler's stomach is still knotted with worry, but the scents wafting down the hall from the cafeteria coax a greedy rumble from his gut. It's dinnertime, after all. Plus, he hasn't had anything but bland Sjelian food cubes since they left Tria.

He opens the cafeteria door for Sharon, who gasps in delight the moment she steps inside. "Jackie?"

Fresler follows Sharon's gaze to see Jackie eating alone at a table. On his own, he might not have recognized her from this distance. Her hair, which she'd had to crush beneath a hat and a respirator mask on their long journey to the CDC, has grown out into a thick, shiny afro. Each curl is styled and coiled with great care, keeping them bouncy and full.

She turns toward Sharon's voice and drops her fork. "Oh, my God!" she says, jaw dangling.

Fresler and Sharon rush to her table, and she pulls them both into a hug.

"Where have you been these last…" She pauses to do the math. "Eight months? You were heading to Iceland. Did you stay in Europe?"

"Not exactly," Fresler says.

"What does that mean?" Jackie asks.

Sharon smiles. "If we told you… you wouldn't believe us."

Jackie scoffs. "After everything we've been through, I'll believe anything."

"We'll see about that," Sharon says through a giggle.

"Where are the girls... and Benjamin?" asks Fresler.

"They'll be here soon," Jackie says. "Tina is working as a lab technician. Jennifer and Benjamin like to pick her up at the end of her shift. Those three are inseparable."

"Wow, that's great," Sharon says. "What have you been doing?"

"I am actually teaching aerobics and yoga. I have a couple classes that are pretty popular with the scientists here. They need to stretch out after spending all day bending over those microscopes."

"That sounds nice," Sharon says.

Jackie nods, but her face falls as she turns back to Fresler. "You heard the news?" she asks in a lower, more somber voice.

"About Charles and my dad? Yes."

Jackie squeezes Fresler's arm and says, "I am so sorry."

"Thanks."

Jackie grits her teeth. "Those Soldiers of Destiny... first they took my husband, and now your dad and Charles. I wish we could..." She shakes her head. "I won't finish that thought."

"I'll finish it," Fresler spits. "I would like to see them all die for what they did!"

Jackie flinches and then cocks her head. She looks even more surprised than William and Rodney did at Fresler's rarely shown capacity for rage.

"Fresler," Sharon says, putting a hand on his arm. "Not here."

"She's right," Jackie says in an undertone, eyes flicking

toward the corner of the ceiling. "You never know who's listening these days."

Fresler follows her gaze and spies a small, round video camera watching over the tables. It's Fresler's last straw. He spins on his heel. "I'm going to talk to this general. Now."

"Wait," Jackie barks in the stern voice of a chastising teacher, It halting Fresler on the spot. "A lot changed while you were away."

"Obviously," Fresler snorts.

"You need to know what you're dealing with before you approach General Martell." Jackie points to an open chair. "Sit."

After a moment's debate, he does. Sharon sits beside him as Jackie returns to her seat across the table.

"Our government is back in control of the country," Jackie says, pushing her mostly empty plate away. "Except there is no legislative or judicial branch."

"Wait... doesn't that make it a dictatorship?" asks Sharon.

Jackie shushes her. "Yes, I suppose it does," she murmurs, "but I wouldn't say that too loud if I were you. The president reassures us each week, during his radio broadcast, that everything will eventually return to normal and that there will once again be three branches of government, but for the time being it is in our best interest to just have one person making decisions: *him*."

Sharon scrunches her whole face. "Really?"

Fresler taps his fingers nervously on the table. "The military answers to the president?"

"Yes, and the military is running things everywhere now. Each citizen is required to register with the military," says Jackie darkly. "We were all assigned a new identification card... it's basically like a driver's license. It has everything that a driver's license would have, except it also has our assigned job."

Fresler chokes on his own spit. "Assigned job?"

"Yeah, as well as our living zone."

"Living zone?" Fresler says, voice rising.

Jackie shushes him again. "There are two zones that we can choose from. Two communities with housing and power... electricity and running water."

"Where are they?" asks Sharon.

"The largest is in the west, in the state of Washington. The power comes from the Grand Coulee Dam, which I'm told is the largest power grid in the U.S. The other is in New York, and the power source is the Robert Moses Niagara power plant. I guess our government actually runs it with the Canadians. It powers most of the northeast."

"I'm glad they are using hydro power," says Sharon, lightening her voice, though the cheeriness fails to drip into her smile.

"Me too," says Fresler. At least there's one silver lining.

"Apparently, it's easier to maintain," says Jackie.

"But..." Fresler frowns. "Who is operating those power plants? Each one probably requires hundreds of people... many of whom would have been killed by the pandemic."

Jackie shakes her head, mouth twisting in a sour expression that doesn't match her next words. "William told me that all of the people that ran both power plants survived."

"What?!" Fresler looks around, surprised by his own outburst. He lowers his voice before Jackie has to shush him again. "Impossible."

Jackie scoffs. "Not so impossible when our government decides to make it so. As it turns out, this building—" she waves a hand, "—is not the only facility equipped to withstand a pandemic. I guess they built thousands of these... and hand-picked who would live in them."

"You mean our government actually came up with a list of people that they felt deserved to survive the pandemic?" Fresler says, feeling sick to his stomach.

"Yes. Over one million of our military personnel survived. All of the people that worked in the relevant power plants were chosen, as well, along with others who were deemed... essential."

"How did that work exactly? Did they tell them that they would be living in these buildings before the pandemic? How was it kept secret?" Fresler hears his volume rising at the end of each question but can't stop it.

"William said that the people that were picked did not know anything about it until the outbreak started. They only had a few days from the time the first person was infected in Argentina until it spread to the U.S. to get all those people safely inside the buildings. He said there were 14,000 buildings and each could house around two hundred people... so, just under three million were selected to survive."

Sharon leans on the table and presses her forehead into one hand. "Wow, someone had to decide who lived and who died."

Jackie nods. "They based it on age, health, number of close family members, and of course contribution. Scientists, medical professionals, engineers, military... you get the idea."

Sharon nods. "So, a Noah's Ark, so to speak?"

"That's one way to put it," Jackie says.

For a moment, they're all silent. Of all the unbelievable things Fresler's seen and experienced this year, the cold, analytical actions of his government and what they've done

to his country—to his fellow citizens—are the hardest to
swallow. When put up against the existence of other inhabited planets and universe-destroying anomalies, that's really
saying something.

"Have you chosen a living zone yet?" asks Sharon, trying
to bring the conversation back around.

Jackie clears her throat. "Everyone in this building has
been cleared to stay here, if they want."

"Are you going to stay?" asks Fresler.

"I don't know yet." Jackie rubs her forehead. "Jennifer,
Tina, Benjamin, Charles, and I talked about moving to
Washington, but after Charles and your father were
captured, we put our plans on hold."

"You could go back to your farm," Fresler says, thinking
of his own cabin in Minnesota.

Jackie sucks air through her teeth. "We can't go back to
our homes. Our government now owns all property in this
country, and we need approval from them before we can
decide where to live."

"That's insane!" yells Fresler.

"Anyway," Jackie says, eyes finding the camera but
letting this latest shout slide without comment, "there's only
electricity and running water in the living zones and in
government facilities like this one. Also, we'd have no
currency."

"You could live off the land," Fresler says stubbornly.

"We'd still need supplies, and the dollar is worthless
now. Our currency is all electronic. You get credits when you
work in an approved job." Jackie's smile is harsh and sear-
ing, like a knife wound. "Or you can get paid for
procreating."

"What?" Sharon sputters.

"The government wants our population to... expand, so

they are willing to pay us for each child. Otherwise, you have to get a job on the list."

"The list?" Sharon asks.

"Most everyone that was picked to survive already has an essential job. Anyone who survived on their own and chooses to live in one of the two zones has to select from a list of eight career paths." Jackie ticks them off on her fingers. "There's medicine, agriculture, power, waste management, military, science, housing, and education."

Fresler narrows his eyes. "Housing?"

"That category includes handymen, plumbers, electricians, roofers... anything related to keeping people off the streets."

"Right. But... I'm a writer," Fresler says. "Tina's a musician. What are we supposed to do?"

"You won't be allowed to pursue those activities as jobs... not until things are back to normal. That's why Tina is currently working in a lab."

Sharon chews on her lip, hugging herself tight. "I guess I could choose education..." she says. "Or maybe agriculture? I did have that greenhouse at the cabin..."

"I don't think anyone should have to choose from this list," Fresler huffs. "And if there has to be a list, I think they should include entertainment as an essential category. We still need musicians, painters, and writers. What kind of world would this be without... *art?* We need it more than ever."

"I agree," says Jackie in a tired voice that makes Fresler think she's had this same conversation with Tina several times.

"Well, it doesn't matter, since Sharon and I will be living in Minnesota," says Fresler. "We don't need government permission or electronic credits. We'll be fine on our own."

Jackie shakes her head. "You won't be able to get there. Only the military can operate motorized vehicles. They seized all the oil in this country. They're using the strategic petroleum oil reserve. Apparently, there are eight-hundred million barrels of oil in underground tanks in Louisiana and Texas."

Sharon makes a guttural sound of disapproval. "Really? Oil."

"I'll just siphon off gas from an abandoned car... like we did when we traveled here," says Fresler, feeling frenzied.

As much as he enjoyed his time away from Earth, he's held the cabin—his beloved home—close to his heart. He always knew he'd return. Now new roadblocks fly from Jackie's mouth faster than he can think of ways around the last ones. Home is drifting further and further away.

"If you're caught on the road, you will be detained," says Jackie morosely.

Fresler sags in defeat, biting down on his tongue to stop another outburst.

Sharon puts her head in her hands. "This is hard to take in. Is it like this everywhere in the world?"

"Yeah, what about other countries?" asks Fresler, thinking about their friends, on their way to Europe.

"The only viable governments left are in northern Europe and Asia. The other continents were too decimated. Anyone who survived from Africa, Australia, South America, and the southern parts of Europe and Asia has migrated north. The countries there want to organize one worldwide nation—one country. The U.S. refused to join."

"Why?" asks Fresler.

"Why else? They wanted control."

"Of course," says Sharon sarcastically.

"Each country in the alliance was supposed to get a

single vote, with twelve leaders total. So, the U.S. would have had one of those twelve votes for decisions that would affect everyone in the world."

"But?" Sharon asks through gritted teeth.

"But our president felt like we needed to have at least five of the twelve votes. The reason he gave was that we are the only country with a military operating at almost full capacity. He wasn't about to be told how to run this country, since we have the only military force in the world."

Fresler scoffs. "That's because the U.S. had time to prepare... no one else did."

Sharon pops up in her seat like a jack-in-the-box. "Wait! What about Canada?"

"They agreed to join the European nation." Jackie narrows her eyes at Fresler as if she can see exactly where his head is going. "Even if you could make it up to the border, you couldn't cross. It's heavily militarized now."

Fresler sighs. "So, we're trapped."

"We all are. I can't even leave this building." Jackie shrugs. "Supposedly, in Washington, we'd have a little more freedom, even with the assigned jobs... but I don't know."

Fresler struggles to find his voice. He had hoped for some level of normalcy when he returned. He'd thought he'd be able to see the fruits of his and his friends' efforts to deliver a cure taking root in the form of pastoral tranquility and national unity. Now the notion seems incredibly naive.

"I'm still going to talk to the general," he finally says. "But I think... maybe... I need to gather my thoughts first."

Sharon puts her hand on Fresler's forearm. "We can contact Theran. Maybe the Sjelians can help."

"The who?" asks Jackie, frowning at the unfamiliar word.

"The Sjelians. They're the ones we've been..." Sharon looks at Fresler. "We should start from the beginning."

"Yes, you should," says Jackie, "but not until the others get seated." She waves over Fresler and Sharon's shoulders. "Jennifer! Tina! Benjamin! Look who's back!"

Fresler and Sharon turn to see the younger contingent from their epic journey standing in the cafeteria doorway. Tina and Jennifer look the same, albeit more rested and well-fed. Benjamin seems older—his face less rounded, his nose more defined, his limbs longer. All three of them gawk when they see who's at Jackie's table.

"You two go get some food, too," Jackie says.

On cue, Fresler's stomach growls. "Okay." He stands, extending a hand to Sharon. "But I want to make an appointment to meet with General Martell first thing in the morning."

"First thing in the morning," Sharon echoes with a sigh.

That gives them time to strategize. To rehearse what they'll say. And to rest.

CHAPTER 4

Reykjavik, Iceland — December 12th, 2023 — 11:30 p.m. local time

E rik's hair batters his forehead as the shuttle takes off in front of the Johansson house, leaving him and Aleria behind. It hovers in the clouds and vanishes in a blink, with a low boom that could easily be mistaken for rolling thunder.

He takes Aleria's hand as they turn to the house. With a deep breath, he leads the way to the front door. "I can't wait for you to meet them."

Aleria offers a nervous smile. "It's so late. Are you sure they'll be awake?"

"They're night owls. I bet Olafur is having a sandwich before bed."

"A sandwich! At this hour?" Aleria looks mildly scandalized.

"It's always sandwich time in this house," Erik says with feigned solemnity. "So, are you ready... *life partner*?" He nudges her playfully until her grin becomes more genuine.

Erik knocks on the door, and it seems an eternity before he hears footsteps on the other side. His palm grows sweaty in Aleria's grip. The door opens slowly at first, but once Hanna's hazel eye spies Erik, it flies the rest of the way. She reaches over the threshold and drags him into a tight hug, making him laugh as his head is tugged down to her level so she can kiss his cheek. She looks better than he has ever seen her... better than even the first time he laid eyes on her. With her health restored, her blonde hair thick and her face filled out over high cheekbones, she looks so much like Kristin. His heart gives a dull pang when he looks in her eyes—extra green thanks to the emerald nightgown she wears. Kristin's eyes used to shift, too, depending on the time of year and what color she wore. The feeling that sinks into his gut at the thought of her is no longer grief or guilt, just a distant longing. It's the feeling of missing a loved one who has moved away.

"I didn't think we would see you this soon," says Hanna, wiping away a stray tear. "I assumed it would be years, like last time. What a great surprise!" She turns into the home and yells over her shoulder, "Olafur... Erik is here!" She blinks in surprise when she finally notices Aleria, then smiles wide. "Who do we have here?"

Erik moves his hand to the small of Aleria's back and says, "This is my life partner, Aleria."

"Your what?" says Hanna, smile wavering.

"Life partner... basically my wife, but without the marriage certificate."

There is a split-second pause that makes Erik's heart skip, and then Hanna's mouth pops into a happy 'O' and she throws up her hands. "Congratulations!"

Aleria puts out her hand awkwardly to shake.

Hanna bats lightly at it and says, "That won't do. A hug is more appropriate for a... *life partner*."

Aleria walks into Hanna's inviting arms, her cheeks flushing as she smiles.

Olafur wanders into the living room carrying half a sandwich and stops in his tracks. "Erik!" he cries after a harsh swallow. He drops his sandwich on the coffee table, then rushes to embrace Erik, who meets him halfway.

Erik pats Olafur's back. "It's great to see you."

"I missed you, Erik."

Hanna takes Aleria's hand and leads her to Olafur. "Erik brought his life partner, Aleria."

"His what?" says Olafur, brows coming together.

Hanna chuckles. "Apparently a life partner is like a spouse, but without the legality. She's his wife."

Olafur makes a low "oh" sound as he nods, then claps Erik on the shoulder. "Congratulations, son." He opens his arms for Aleria, who accepts the hug with a soft sigh of relief that only Erik catches. "Welcome to the family, Aleria. We think of Erik as our son, so... I guess that makes you our daughter."

Aleria's eyes glisten. "That's so sweet."

"Have you eaten? I can make us something," says Hanna, shifting into mom mode.

Erik grins, feeling warm head to toe. "It's late. I don't want you to go to the trouble."

"No trouble at all. How about I make us some more sandwiches?" she says, eyeing the fourth that Olafur left on the low table. Mustard has leaked from its center onto the wood.

He snatches it up with an apology to his wife in his eyes.

Erik knows better than to argue with Hanna. "Sure," he says. "We'd love a bite to eat."

When Aleria shoots him a bemused look, he shrugs. Earth food is an experience, while Sjelian nutrition cubes are a daily chore finished hastily. Food is one of the two things he deeply misses about his home planet. The other is family.

They walk into the kitchen, where Hanna starts pulling supplies out of the fridge.

Aleria whispers in Erik's ear, "Remember what happened last time you ate here... be careful."

"That won't happen again," says Erik, stomach flipping at the memory of spending hours hugging the toilet on Stephan's plane. He pulls a block of Sjelian food partially out of his pocket for her to see. He won't be overloading his perfectly balanced system with Earth food this time.

After they take seats in the living room around the coffee table, Erik asks, "Where is Stephan?"

"He had a late delivery," says Olafur. "He should be back soon."

"How is he? Still working at the hospital?" asks Erik.

Hanna shakes her head and clucks her tongue. "Yes, and still making delivery runs with that little plane. I worry about him every time he flies in that thing."

Olafur scoffs. "It's perfectly safe, as long as you know what you are doing... and Stephan is an excellent pilot."

Erik studies the grain of the table as he changes the subject. "Did he ever tell you why he decided to stay behind?" he says as nonchalantly as he can manage. "I was surprised when he didn't walk through the portal."

Olafur shrugs. "No, he didn't really say much to us. Just that he wanted to look after your mom to make sure she was fully recovered."

Hanna swats the air. "I am fully recovered. That thing you gave me was a miracle cure."

Aleria's head whips Erik's way. "What thing did Erik give you?"

Erik sinks a little in his chair. He never did tell Aleria that he "borrowed" a vial of macrophage activator from Mandal's office.

"I think you called it a macro... *something*," Olafur says before Erik can signal him.

"Macrophage?" says Aleria sharply, and Erik cringes.

Olafur points at Aleria. "Yes, that's it."

She nods and crosses her arms. Erik can feel the fury radiating off her as she glares sidelong at him.

He looks to Hanna in a silent plea, only to find her already coming to his rescue. She stands behind him and puts her hand on his shoulder.

"I would have died if it hadn't been for what Erik did. I owe him my life," she says, voice fervent as her eyes well with tears.

"He saved her life and mine," says Olafur softly. "Without my Hanna, I wouldn't want to go on living."

Hanna swats at his arm when he reaches for her hand. "Don't say such things. Of course you would continue living."

"Well, I can't wait to see Stephan," Erik says a little too loudly.

"He can't wait to see you," says Hanna.

The sound of the front door opening makes everyone turn.

"And there he is!" says Hanna, sounding as delighted as if she had manifested him herself.

"What are you two still doing awake?" Stephan drops his backpack on the floor. "I told you, you don't have to wait up for me—" He looks up and freezes with his keys halfway to the designated wall hook.

"Hi," Erik says.

"Erik!" Stephan thunders into the living room in his boots.

Erik jumps up from the table, but Stephan nearly knocks him back down with the force of his bear hug. Winded from the impact, Erik slaps Stephan on the back and then holds him tight until Stephan pulls away for a better look. Tears shine in his eyes.

"I didn't think I would see you for..." He shakes his head. "Years."

Erik nods. "We finished our mission much sooner than I thought... and, well... I missed you, Stephan."

"I missed you too." Stephan looks over Erik's shoulder and sees Aleria standing next to Hanna with her lashes lowered and her hands folded in front of her.

Erik steps back and holds out a hand for Aleria. "Sorry... Stephan, this is Aleria."

She steps forward.

Stephan ignores Aleria's outstretched hand and wraps her in a hug only slightly less crushing than the one bestowed on Erik. Aleria smiles wide as he lifts her onto her tiptoes.

"You're the reason for that... *timer* around Erik's neck." Stephan chuckles. "He was so depressed when we ran out of time."

Erik rolls his eyes but can't contain his smile. Stephan has put the whole room at ease. Erik can hardly remember why he was a ball of nerves in the first place.

Aleria reaches for Erik's hand and smiles as she leans her head against his shoulder.

Erik looks up at his brother-in-law. "Aleria and I are life partners."

Stephan looks at his parents, as if unsure how to

respond. Olafur stands up and pats Stephan's shoulder. "It's like they're married, son."

"But without the marriage certificate," Hanna adds, nodding wisely.

Erik's breath catches as Stephan turns back to him, but then the corners of Stephan's mouth perk up, lighting his eyes. "I'm happy for you, Erik. Congratulations."

Erik releases his breath in what he hopes is an inaudible sigh.

"Thanks," Aleria says for them both.

"I wish you could have been there for the ceremony. It was beautiful," says Erik, words gushing from him like a fountain now.

Stephan nods. "I'm sure it was. You'll have to tell me all about it. And the mission. I want to hear how you destroyed that... *anomaly*." He pauses. "I'm assuming it was destroyed?"

"It was," Erik says firmly, "but that may be a story for tomorrow. It's going to take a while."

Stephan looks at his watch and scoffs. "I don't care... I can sleep in tomorrow. I can't wait to hear all the details." He waves them into the living room and plops down on the couch, placing his hands on his knees like an eager child.

"What about you two?" Erik asks Olafur and Hanna.

"Oh, we couldn't possibly sleep now," Hanna says, adopting a pose almost exactly like her son's.

Erik looks over at Aleria and raises his eyebrows. "Okay. Here goes."

* * *

By the time the tale is told, Hanna and Olafur are rubbing

their eyes. Even Aleria, who rarely shows fatigue, is close to dozing off, cheek drifting toward her shoulder.

"Why don't we call it a night?" Erik asks, watching his life partner politely suppress a yawn.

"Yes, let me show Aleria to the guest room," Hanna says.

"Stephan and I will take care of this mess." Erik gathers empty sandwich plates and sweeps crumbs onto them. Aleria stands, kisses the top of his head, and follows Hanna out of the room.

Erik and Stephan finish tidying and return to the kitchen. Side by side over the double sink, they stare out the window.

"That was some story," Stephan says. "I can't believe Aleria has special powers."

"I owe my life to her," Erik says simply.

"She disabled thousands of people at once. *Unbelievable.*" For a moment, Stephan looks like a young boy exiting the theater after an awesome superhero movie.

Erik can't help but chuckle. "Yeah… and she has other abilities as well."

"Like what?"

"She can sense emotions," Erik says. "All emotions—so she knows if you're lying."

"Damn, I'd better be careful then." Stephan smacks the back of his hand against Erik's shoulder. "Glad you told me." He chuckles at his own joke.

Erik smirks. "So, you were planning to lie to her?"

"Maybe. But only when telling stories about the two of us, from college." Stephan shakes his head, eyes twinkling at the memories. Then he sobers. "I can't believe I missed so much by not going with you."

Erik looks over. "I wanted to ask you about that. Why didn't you walk through the portal with us?"

Stephan exhales sharply. "I was planning to."

"What happened?"

"Do you remember... right before you entered the portal, you whispered something to Fresler and Karena?"

"Vaguely. I think I mentioned that they would be amazed by how real the dream would be when they entered the portal."

Stephan shrugs one shoulder and looks down at the dishes drying in the dish rack. "When I saw the three of you together, it hit me. You three are Sjelians. You were entering a Sjelian portal to be with other Sjelians. I'm not Sjelian. My place is here on Earth, with my parents." He looks up with a soft smile. "Plus, I just got my mother back... healthy again."

Erik squeezes Stephan's shoulder, shaking him playfully. "I may have Sjelian blood in my veins, but I am from Earth and you are my family. There is no one in this or any other universe that knows me better than you. No one who has all the history that you do with me. I love you."

Stephan's stance relaxes, tension falling out of his shoulders. "I love you, too."

Now it's Erik's turn to sheepishly avert his gaze. "I was worried about how you would react when you found out about Aleria."

"Why?" asks Stephan with a snort.

"We're life partners now. I thought..." Erik rubs the back of his neck, searching for words. "I thought it would be difficult for you to see me with someone else."

Stephan blinks at Erik, and his smile shrinks a smidge. "I'm not going to lie... it is weird seeing you with someone else. But I am happy for you."

"I know you are," says Erik, reading it in Stephan's face. He opens his mouth twice without any sound, then forces out a sigh before trying again. "There is something else that

I wanted to tell you. It involves Kristin and Eria, but... I don't want you to think I'm crazy."

Stephan offers a lopsided grin. "I would never think that you are crazy, Erik."

"Well, considering my past... you know, the woman in black... I can see how you would."

"What is it?"

Erik does his best to hold Stephan's gaze. "Certain humans have the ability to sense the presence of those that have passed."

Stephan narrows his eyes. "You mean... they can see dead people?"

"Not see. Sense their presence. For the first few years I was with the Sjelians, Aleria could sense Kristin's presence still with me. It was one of the things that kept us apart. And I met someone else, on the planet Nekses... she could sense both Kristin and Eria."

Stephan takes a step back, eyes roving around Erik's face but never landing on it. "Are they with you now?"

"No... but they were. They've moved on. I communicated with them. Said goodbye."

"How is that possible?"

Erik swallows a lump in his throat. "The woman I told you about, on Nekses. She had the ability to bridge the two planes of existence... ours and the afterlife. She was able to connect me with Kristin and Eria so that I could communicate with them."

"You realize how this all sounds?" says Stephan with a nervous chuckle.

"Of course. I sometimes wonder if it was real myself— but deep down, I know it was."

Stephan nods slowly. "I guess I shouldn't be surprised. If you'd told me that an alien macrophage would save my mother's life, I would have told you that you were crazy, but..." He points at the ceiling, where they can hear Hanna's footsteps moving around the master bedroom. "There's the living proof. Nothing should surprise me now." Stephan pauses as a soft, wistful smile creeps onto his face. "What was it like?"

The whole way back to Earth, Erik had practiced how he might explain the experience, reworking the speech in his head as he lay awake at night. Nothing he'd come up with was exactly right. Now, he settles on keeping it simple... as much as such a thing can really be simplified.

"I was put into a deep state of unconsciousness," he begins. "In that state, I connected with them. It seemed so real. The way they smelled and looked was just like before the accident. Eria was wearing that yellow dress, from her first day of school..." Erik's voice catches, but he powers on. "They seemed like themselves, but they were actually so different."

"How?"

"When Eria was alive, she was so vibrant—you remember?"

"Of course," Stephan murmurs.

"This version of her was... stoic. *Emotionless*. Kristin too. She said she loved me, but she may as well have been talking about the weather. It was unsettling." Erik shudders. "They told me they'd felt the depth of my pain after they died. They knew I'd..." He clears his throat rather than mention his suicide attempt out loud. "That's why they were still with me. They were worried about me."

Stephan nods, jaw working as he takes this in.

"I told them that I was worried they were suffering. The accident was so horrific... and I didn't get a chance to say goodbye. But Kristin said that they were fine. That they loved me. And when I said I was ready to move on with my life, she said it was time for them to leave."

Stephan hangs his head, tears dripping into the sink.

Erik lets him mourn, working to quell his own tears.

Stephan regains his composure with a hard sniff, rubbing a hand down his face. "That must have been difficult."

"It was... but it also made me feel at peace."

"What happened after that?"

"They vanished. I came out of my state of unconsciousness. Aleria confirmed that they're no longer with me." Erik gulps. "They must be in a better place, right?"

"I know they are." Stephan looks out the window into the darkness, and then at a painting hanging on the kitchen wall. It's of Hanna and Olafur's home, nestled into the green hills, with a blue sky above. The house looks friendly. Welcoming. In the painting, it's a little bit of paradise.

Staring at the depiction, Erik suddenly can't imagine how anyone would ever want to leave this place.

Before nostalgia makes him lose his nerve, he blurts, "I want you to come back to the space station with us. Please come."

Stephan startles. "Why—"

"I want to show you the Oort cloud and planets from the Sjelian vessel. It's incredible."

Stephan shakes his head. "I'm sure it is."

"Will you consider joining us?"

"I don't know." After a moment of thought, he turns to Erik. "For how long?"

"Not long. I just want you to see the view for yourself."

Olafur appears in the kitchen doorway. "Come on, boys. Time for us all to get some sleep."

They follow him upstairs, but before heading into their separate rooms, Stephan murmurs, "I'll think about it."

CHAPTER 5

Solna, Sweden — December 13th, 2023 — 1:00 a.m. local time

The gust of chilly wind sent swirling through Karena's hair by the departing shuttle makes her teeth chatter. The shuttle makes the spruces vibrate as it rises, hovering over Solna, Sweden, for a blink before disappearing with a soft boom.

Karena leans into Kesh's side as they approach the front door of ECDC Director Janice Ammon's house. She does her best to shield Winnett's sweet face from the winter chill, but it's difficult without a coat to wrap him in. The wooded driveway is dark, quiet, and cold. Perhaps too dark, too quiet —and definitely too cold. Karena suddenly regrets the late hour. Is Janice a sound sleeper? If she wakes, will she even open the door? Winnett shouldn't be outside in this weather for long.

"We should have sent a message to let Janice know we were coming," Karena says, voice vibrating as a shiver wracks her.

"How?" Kesh asks. "Aren't satellite communications

down?"

Karena nods as she lifts a numb hand to ring the door-bell. She hears it echo inside, the chime familiar from her many visits to Janice's home over the years.

Kesh holds her and the baby tighter, rubbing Karena's arms to build heat. After a few minutes go by without an answer, she tries the metal door knocker. Still no answer.

"Should we check the perimeter?" Kesh asks.

"I suppose. I just hope she's not spending the night at her office." Karena had asked Theran to drop them here, hoping to avoid anyone other than Janice seeing Kesh. Janice's home is tucked away in the mountains, with only towering evergreens for company. There are no neighbors close by. It seemed like the best option, to stay away from the ECDC entirely.

Karena leads Kesh around the side of the house. There's a single light on, from what Karena remembers as the bedroom window. She hands baby Winnett to Kesh and bangs on the glass. A loud thump answers, and then the curtain slowly opens. Janice's petite face peeks out, partially obscured by a fat stun gun she holds at the ready. When she sees Karena, her mouth drops open.

"Can we come inside?" Karena shouts, hoping the wind won't carry her words away.

Janice smiles wide and gestures to the front door.

They hurry back around the house, and Janice opens the door, screaming, "Karena!" Her sweatshirt is soft, and her arms are warm as she pulls Karena into a tight hug. "You scared me to death. What are you doing here at this hour?"

"I wanted to see you," says Karena. She drinks her friend in. She's cut her hair shorter, into a stylish bob. The tangles in the back are the only evidence that their visit pulled her out of bed.

Janice looks over at Kesh, and her eyes spark when she spies the baby cuddled in his arms. In the dim porchlight, Kesh's skin doesn't look much different than Winnett's.

"Come on in, you must be freezing." Janice ushers them inside and leans in to tickle Winnett under the chin as she says, "Who do we have here?" When she straightens, she does a double take, noting Kesh's pink skin.

"Janice, this is Kesh. I don't know how to tell you this, but... he is not from Earth. He is from Nekses."

Janice's jaw drops, and she quickly covers it with her hand. "I was going to guess that he wasn't from Earth," she says. Excitement makes her voice breathy, and Karena instantly relaxes, smiling at Kesh. "Nice to meet you, Kesh," says Janice.

He inclines his head in a regal fashion that makes Janice press one hand to her chest in delighted shock.

"Is that..." Janice coos in Winnett's direction.

"This is my baby boy, Winnett," says Karena.

"He is so beautiful," Janice says in an awed whisper, mouth forming that special happy pout reserved for beings so cute it hurts. "*And peaceful*," she goes on. She holds out her hands. "Can I?"

"Of course," says Karena, gently passing Winnett from Kesh to Janice.

"He's amazing," says Janice, tearing up. "Is Ludvig the..." Her eyes flick to Kesh as the words fade out.

Karena smiles. "Yes. Ludvig is the father. I didn't know I was pregnant when I left." She grabs Kesh's hand and says, "Kesh is a good friend of mine. We worked together on the... space station."

"You'll have to tell me everything." Janice gently bounces Winnett as she walks over to a rocking chair in the living room.

Karena looks at her watch, which reads 1:24 a.m. "It's a long story. Maybe I should start it after we get some sleep."

"Maybe you're right," Janice says dreamily, gazing at Winnett as she rocks. "He just stares into my eyes without blinking. How is that possible?"

"That's what everyone says. I don't know."

Janice looks back up at Karena. "Why did you return?"

"Like I said, I wanted to see you... and to show Kesh a bit of Sweden." Karena loops her arm through Kesh's, then asks Janice, "Do you still have my things?"

"Yes, the boxes are in the garage."

"Great. I also wanted to get some of my family photos, to have to show Winnett when he gets older."

"Of course." Janice rises from the chair, once more transfixed by Winnett's gaze. "Let me get you set up in the guest room."

"Thanks." Karena reaches for her son. "I should feed him before we go to sleep."

"Do you need anything to eat?" Janice asks, handing the baby over. "I don't know how far you've traveled..."

Karena is about to say no when her stomach betrays her by rumbling. She blushes, saying, "I'd love something small. Breastfeeding always makes me hungry."

"Kesh?" Janice asks, looking toward him.

"I will have whatever Karena is having," he says courteously.

Five minutes later, Janice returns from the kitchen with open-faced sandwiches. While Karena nurses Winnett, Kesh flips through a Swedish magazine.

"So, one of these magazines is printed every day... for people to read?" he asks Janice.

"That's an old magazine." She grins when she takes a

closer look and realizes he's reading *Cosmo*. "They would print those once a month... until the pandemic."

"Amazing." Kesh ogles the pictures. "This is how the people of Earth dress?" He holds up a page featuring a woman in a bikini. "She is in her undergarments."

Janice and Karena burst into laughter.

"I can see how you would think that," says Janice, "but that is called a bikini. It is worn when you go swimming."

"Do people from Earth often wear undergarments in public?"

Janice shakes her head. "No, that would be inappropriate."

Kesh lays the magazine in his lap and looks between the two women, three creases appearing in his pink forehead. "I don't understand. It's okay to wear undergarments if you are swimming, but if you are not... you cannot wear them?"

Karena chuckles. "There's a lot about this planet that probably doesn't make any sense."

"So, what is your plan for tomorrow?" Janice asks.

"I want to go into Stockholm and show Kesh where I grew up. Can we borrow your car?"

Janice nods. "Of course. I can have one of my assistants pick me up before work. But..." Janice looks meaningfully at Kesh's bright pink skin. "Are you sure going out in public is a good idea?"

Karena hands baby Winnett to Kesh to burp and helps herself to the sandwich Janice made. "I don't plan on walking around the city. We will keep our distance from everyone."

"Hm." Janice nods, but her eyes are still crinkled with concern. "There are fewer people out and about these days... but it's not just Kesh I'm worried about."

Karena chews and swallows. "What do you mean?"

"The Swedish government has proclaimed you a national hero. You're a Swedish-born Nobel Prize–winning physicist, and you created the vaccine and cure that saved millions. They wanted to honor you at the capital. They actually had a statue made in your likeness."

Karena's mouth drops open. "National hero?"

"Yes."

Kesh smiles wide. "That is good news, isn't it?"

Karena shakes her head. "But I didn't create the cure. I *was* the cure. I mean, my blood was... because I am actually part alien."

"Well, the government doesn't know that, and if they did, they wouldn't want to make that public," Janice says matter-of-factly. "Anyway, they tried to contact you shortly after you left with your half-brothers. I had to decide what to tell them... so I said you'd disappeared."

"Why didn't you say I went to Greenland?"

"I thought about that, but they would have wanted to know why. They would have investigated. I didn't want them to know that you were in Greenland to disable another capsule carrying more deadly morphons. I just thought it was easier to say I didn't know."

Karena nods. "I suppose that makes sense." She reaches for Winnett, who is droopy-eyed now that he has a full belly. She begins to rock him as she finishes her sandwich.

"Unfortunately, the government ran an investigation into your disappearance. And they found—"

"What?" Karena asks when Janice breaks off.

Janice looks over at Kesh, then back at Karena. "I don't want to be rude, but can we speak alone?"

Kesh stands. "I can put Winnett to bed, Karena." He pats the baby's back and looks to Janice. "Where should I take him?"

"The third door on the left. I don't have a crib, but—"

"I will figure something out." Kesh smiles kindly at her, and then heads down the hall.

"Let's go to my study," Janice says. She stands, and Karena follows her. After shutting the door, she goes straight to the computer on her desk and logs in. "There is something I need to show you."

Karena hovers over Janice's shoulder as she takes a seat in her plush office chair. "You're making me nervous."

Janice doesn't respond, and her strained expression only compounds Karena's unease. Janice pulls up a file and clicks on it. Scanned copies of documents appear in a row. Janice clicks on one, which depicts a damaged Land Cruiser being pulled out of a lake.

Karena's confusion overtakes her nerves as she recognizes the smashed vehicle. "That's a photo of my car accident in 2005. Why would you have those pictures?"

"What do you remember about this incident?"

Karena shrugs. "Not much... the road was icy, and I lost control of my vehicle. It flew off the embankment. Luckily, I was thrown from the car before it plunged into the lake... otherwise I would have drowned. Not to mention that someone saw the accident and called for help."

"You don't remember anything else?"

"No, why would you ask?" The question comes out as a hoarse whisper. Karena doesn't like the way Janice is looking at her.

"As I told you, when you disappeared, the government ran an investigation into your past. They pulled all of the files from this accident." She gestures to the picture.

"Why? It was just a car crash."

"They were trying to determine why their national hero went missing."

"And...?"

"And... they found something." Janice clicks through the pictures of the scene. "What I am about to show you may come as a shock. These pictures were taken by the CCTV camera across the street."

Janice stops on an image of two people on the shoulder of the highway. Karena leans in for a better look and recognizes herself, lying unconscious with her head in a man's lap.

"What...? I don't remember this at all."

Janice clicks further into the slideshow, moving slowly backward in time. The man onscreen drags Karena through the grass, his arms under her armpits. "This man pulled you out of the car and dragged you to the side of the road... after notifying emergency services."

"No, that's impossible. I was thrown from the vehicle."

"Karena, you can see from this picture that the man is pulling you out of the car. You weren't thrown."

The next image shows the lake, not far from the side of the road. The picture is fuzzy, but it shows a man half-submerged in the water, pulling a woman through the car window as the vehicle sinks nose-first into the lake.

"Who is that?" Karena asks, stomach churning with anticipation and dread.

Janice exhales sharply, then clicks one last time to pull up the first in the series of photographs of the rescue. In this one, the man's face is clear.

Karena gasps and puts her hand over her mouth. "Impossible!"

The man is... Ludvig.

Karena supports herself on Janice's office chair as her knees go weak. Her breath comes in short gasps as she stares at the photo.

"That's impossible," she repeats, shaking her head as if the frantic movement might make the image blur and reform into something else... something that makes sense. "We didn't meet for another two years. Why wouldn't he mention that he'd saved my life?"

Janice scans Karena with sympathetic eyes. "What do you know about Ludvig's family?"

"Not much... only that he was an only child... and the same with his parents. They didn't have siblings."

"You told me once that his parents died before the two of you met. Did he have any friends or family at your wedding?"

"No," says Karena, her mouth dry.

"Didn't you find that odd?" asks Janice.

"I thought it was... sad," Karena says. "But what does that have to do with the fact that Ludvig pulled me from a sinking car—that he saved my life two years before we met! Why wouldn't he tell me?"

"It seems he didn't want anyone to know," Janice says solemnly. "When the police and paramedics arrived, he was long gone. There was no mention of him in the police report."

"That's not like him," Karena says forcefully. But her next words come out timid, as a small voice in her mind whispers unpleasant possibilities. "At least... it's not like the man I thought I knew."

Janice pauses, finger hovering over the mouse, and looks over her shoulder at Karena. "Do you have anything that would have a sample of his DNA?"

"His DNA? Why?"

"When the government verified that it was Ludvig at the scene of your accident, they decided to check into his past. They couldn't find anything."

Karena scrunches her eyes closed. "That doesn't make any sense. He had a driver's license and a birth certificate. He had a passport."

"That is true, but there are no government records for his parents. No ownership of property, no driver's licenses, no birth certificates... *nothing.*"

"What are you saying?" asks Karena, massaging her temples.

"I don't know." Janice shrugs, and then repeats, "Do you have anything that has his DNA?"

Karena freezes, breath catching, and then lets her arms fall limp to her sides. "Yes," she says softly. "Do you still have *all* my clothes from when you sold my house?"

"Yes, everything is in the garage. Why?"

"When Ludvig died, he was spitting up blood. It got all over my blouse," Karena croaks. "It was in my suitcase when I traveled to Solna. I never washed it."

Janice stands up. "Let's check the garage."

Karena drifts after Janice, feeling disembodied. In the garage, the scent of cardboard overpowers everything else. Together, they sift through the boxes, and Karena finds the blood-stained blouse in the third one. Tears make her vision fuzzy as she holds it out to Janice. "Here it is."

"I'll have this analyzed first thing tomorrow. We should also analyze Winnett's blood."

Karena jolts. She hadn't even considered how this news affected her child.

Janice lays her hand on Karena's arm and gives a comforting squeeze. "I know this is hard," she says, "but I'm here for you. Now, you need to rest. We'll learn more in the morning."

With a numb nod, Karena follows her friend back inside.

CHAPTER 6

Zurich, Switzerland — December 13th, 2023 — 7:00 a.m. local time

Kayna wakes with the shift of the light outside the shuttle's windows. It's not yet dawn, but a soft gray world has replaced the pitch-black canvas that greeted them when they arrived a few hours ago. Her neck twinges as she turns toward Theran in the reclined chair beside her. He is already half-awake, shifting in his seat. It seems he, too, had a restless night.

Kayna takes his hand to pull him fully out of sleep. "I'll start getting ready," she says, motioning toward the window. "I can leave at sunrise." A few rooftops are visible through the trees surrounding the secluded area where they parked the shuttle. Sarah Solheim may be beneath one of those roofs. The idea makes Kayna's heart speed up.

Theran kisses Kayna on the cheek. "I'll stay here with the shuttle," he says, knowing without being told that she's itching to get going.

"She might not be there," Kayna says, rising from her

seat on legs full of pins and needles. The thought makes her racing heart beat an uneven rhythm. "She probably isn't. It's been months and months—"

"Don't think like that," Theran says. "We have to start somewhere."

Half an hour later, Kayna exits the shuttle with a full but uneasy stomach, freshly brushed hair, and a light layer of makeup borrowed from Karena. She looks down at the flowy white blouse, flared jeans, and wool pea coat taken from her curated stash of Earth clothes, wondering if they make her look dated. For some reason, she's terrified of making a bad impression on Mitchell's daughter, as if it will reflect badly on her lost, beloved friend.

She walks for several miles, first through the trees and then along streets that are surprisingly well-kept, considering that there was a global pandemic just months ago. There's no litter. Many shops are open, complete with boards advertising the day's wares along with any shortages. A few people are out walking, though all keep their heads down as they go about their business. It's quiet, like perhaps the town is still mourning humanity's great loss.

Sarah Solheim's last known location was an apartment complex near the university, where she was speaking at an academic conference about recent developments in the field of infrasound. Following Theran's scribbled directions, Kayna turns down a side street and finds the address.

After climbing a few flights of stairs, Kayna knocks on the door. Her heart pounds with anticipation, but there's no answer. Her excitement trickles away over the next ten minutes, as she looks up and down the corridor, hoping Sarah will appear at any moment. She knocks a few more times. Nothing. She tries the knob, but it doesn't turn.

Kayna taps her communication device, and Theran's face materializes on the screen. "No answer."

"Is there anyone else around?"

"I'll see if there's a building manager." Kayna scours the outskirts of the building and the entire bottom floor for the manager's office. Nothing is marked as an office. On her second pass, she sees a man exit his apartment. Time to test out the Swiss German she studied aboard the Sjelian space station.

"Excuse me," she says, making him look around as he locks his door. "Do you happen to know where I can find the apartment manager?"

"Sure, he is in apartment 1A."

With a soft sigh, she goes back the way she came. After locating 1A, she knocks on the door. A scruffy, gray-haired man answers. "Yeah?"

"I was hoping you could help me locate my niece," Kayna says in Swiss German. "She was previously renting apartment 8B. I knocked on her door, but there was no answer."

"When was she here?" the man asks.

"January," Kayna says.

"January!" the man exclaims. "Back then, these were short-term rentals. Then the building became a refugee shelter for people fleeing north. She may have been here in January, but she certainly wouldn't be here now. I'm afraid I can't help you."

Kayna's throat tightens as the slow, creeping dread that's been building all morning rises to the surface. "Please. I am worried that something has happened to her."

"And you're probably right to worry. If you haven't heard from her, your niece must have died in the pandemic, God

rest her soul." The man crosses himself and looks
heavenward.

"I don't believe she did. Could you just let me into the
apartment? I could see if she left anything behind—
anything that could help me locate her now."

The building manager stares for a few moments,
working his mouth like he can't spit out his words. At last,
he simply says, "Follow me."

He grabs the large key chain hanging by his head on the
wall and leads Kayna up the stairs to 8B. He looks over the
key chain and finds the correct one.

"I have to be with you the entire time," he says as he
turns it in the lock. "You can't take anything from this apartment. The whole complex is government property now."

Kayna nods as the door swings open. "I understand."

The stench of death overwhelms Kayna's senses before
she sets foot inside the door. The manager chokes and pulls
his shirt over his mouth and nose. Kayna goes cold.

Maybe Sarah didn't make it, after all.

The manager apologizes a few times, but Kayna can't
respond. She follows him through the main living space,
both bedrooms, and finally the hall bathroom, where the
vile smell makes Kayna's eyes water. The manager's curse
bounces off the tile. A frail, dead cat is curled inside the tub.

"When was the last time you were in this apartment?"
asks Kayna, covering her face to try and block the stench.

The old man shrugs. "It's been months," he says through
a cough, eyeing the cat's corpse like it might bite. "I don't
keep tabs on who moves in and out. I just take care of issues
when the residents bring them to my attention." He's shifty
eyed, never meeting her gaze, obviously aware that the
current situation is a dereliction of his managerial duties.
"Was this your niece's cat?"

"I don't know." Kayna hurries back into the bedroom and checks the closet. A red suitcase stands up in the back. She returns to the bathroom and frowns at the cat, a white paw nestled under its black head as though it's sleeping. Kayna inspects the cupboards. Nothing unusual. And not much missing, by the looks of things. Every surface is covered by a fine layer of dust. The apartment hasn't been occupied in some time. If someone's been here since Sarah rented it in January, it was months and months ago.

Kayna wanders into the living room and notices a cell phone sitting on the counter, plugged into the charger. When she turns to check on the manager, she nearly bumps into him, hovering behind her.

"Can you shut the bathroom door?" she asks. "The smell is… *awful*."

As soon as the manager turns to walk back down the hall, Kayna grabs the cell phone and shoves it in her jeans pocket.

"Everything seems to be in order," says the manager as he traipses back from the bathroom. "Except of course the cat. Did you see anything to help you find your niece?"

"Unfortunately not," Kayna says, the cell phone feeling hot and conspicuous against her leg.

The manager shrugs. "Sorry. But as I said, many people have passed through this building in the past eleven months." He walks to the door and swings it open, extending his arm for Kayna to step out first.

"Thanks anyway for your help," Kayna says as the manager locks the door behind them. She hurries down the hallway, eager to check if the phone works. She feels a pang of guilt for stealing, but if this is Sarah's phone… it will be worth it.

"Wait a second," the manager says when she's nearly to the stairs.

Kayna swallows hard as he trots toward her. He must know she took the phone. Should she use her ability on him or just run?

He pulls a card out of his pocket. "If you know of anyone looking for a place to stay, call that number on the card. I have some..." he clears his throat, looking uncomfortable, "...empty units."

Kayna takes the card and slides it into the pocket opposite the cell phone. "I will. But... the cell towers aren't operational yet."

"They will be soon," the man says confidently. "Our new government has promised us that."

Kayna makes a mental note of that—*new government*—but simply says, "Thank you." Then she hikes back toward the shuttle.

Once she's safely hidden amongst the trees, she pulls out the phone and presses several buttons, hoping to turn it on. The screen stays black. It occurs to her then that none of the lights were on in the apartment; without a tenant, the electricity must have been turned off. So, despite the charger, the battery is long dead.

As she crests a small hill, she sees Theran waving to her from the grass. Kayna smiles with relief at the sight of him and runs the rest of the way. She puts the cell phone in his waiting hand.

Theran studies it. "A communication device?"

Kayna nods. "A phone."

"Is it Sarah's?"

"I hope so. It's all I found." Kayna pauses. "Well, the phone, a suitcase, and a dead cat."

Theran's eyebrows lift. "Sounds as though Sarah left in a hurry."

"Someone did." Kayna searches Theran's face, finding comfort in its familiar serenity. "Can we access the phone using the shuttle's control system?"

"We can."

"Even if the battery's dead?"

"That won't be a problem." Theran beckons Kayna back into the shuttle. He sits at the controls and places the phone into the terminal slot.

"What if it's password-protected?" asks Kayna as a copy of the phone's screen blinks to life on the main control panel screen. As she thought, a keypad prompts them for a password.

"That won't prevent us from accessing it," says Theran with a calm smile.

Within seconds, the phone is unlocked. The picture on the home screen is of the red-haired woman Reshal showed Kayna a few days ago, her cheek pressed against another young woman's, both of them smiling with cocktails in their hands. "It's her," Kayna breathes, astonished. "It's Sarah. Can you pull up her contact list?"

Theran taps on his screen, and a list of names appears in alphabetical order. There are over a hundred, but only seven are listed under *Favorites*. Kayna recognizes some of the names: Evan, Jared, Mary, and Mitchell, saved as "Dad." She doesn't recognize the others: Gretchen, Leslie, and Malcolm.

"What are the addresses?" Kayna asks. "Are they local?"

Theran clicks on each name, but only one contact has an address in Switzerland: Gretchen. Theran types the address into the shuttle's computer.

"Only a block away from the university," he says,

swiveling in his chair toward Kayna. "Maybe she was a
colleague or a mentor."

Kayna leans in for a closer look at the map. "I think I
passed this street earlier."

"I hope she's still in Zurich," Theran says.

"Me too." Kayna jumps up as Theran scrolls through the
phone's camera roll. The images of Sarah herself show
someone who's full of life. Even her high ponytail—apparently a favorite hairstyle—looks light and happy, like it
would bounce with every step.

I'll find you, Kayna promises, starting her hike back
into town.

Kayna stares at the silver "3A" marking the apartment door
for a long moment. What if this abode is abandoned, too? Is
there more death here? She's not certain she wants to find
out. But the thought of Mitchell finally coaxes her to ring
the doorbell. The sound of movement instantly soothes
her heart.

A slender, blond woman in her mid-thirties opens the
door a fourth of the way. Kayna recognizes her as the
woman from the Sarah's home screen photo.

"Can I help you?" she asks, blinking owlish, hazel eyes.

"I hope so. Are you Gretchen?"

The woman closes the door to a sliver and peeks out
with one narrowed eye. "Who wants to know?"

"I'm trying to locate my niece, Sarah Solheim. I was
hoping you could help."

The woman's skepticism visibly fades. "Are you
Aunt Mary?"

"No, I'm... her other aunt. Kayna."

The suspicion returns, and Gretchen retreats further behind the door. "Sarah never mentioned you."

"Well... it's more of a term of endearment. She was *like* a niece to me. I've been so worried about her."

"Do you have some identification?"

Kayna doesn't have a driver's license or passport, but she pulls out Sarah's phone. "I have this. It's how I found your contact information. How did you know Sarah?"

"We were in the same academic field," the woman says begrudgingly, after a beat. "It's not a particularly large community, and there weren't many women in it when Sarah and I finished our doctorates. We became friends." The woman slips her hand through the crack, and Kayna puts Sarah's phone in it. She powers it on. "Yes, this is her phone."

"And are you Gretchen?"

After a long silence, the woman says, "I am. How did you get this?"

"It was left it in the apartment she was renting."

"In the complex on Rütistrasse?" Gretchen says, sounding surprised. The door opens wider.

"Yes. No one had been in the apartment in months," Kayna says. "There was a dead cat in the bathtub."

Gretchen gasps. "Mimi!"

"Was Mimi Sarah's cat?"

"Not exactly. She was a stray. Sarah took her in when she rented the apartment. She was hoping to tame her and take her home to Sweden after the conference. She kept leaving out bowls of food, closer and closer to the apartment door..." Gretchen sighs. "Poor Mimi."

"Mimi looked to have..." Kayna cringes. There's no delicate way to put this. "Died fairly recently. When was the last time you saw Sarah?"

Gretchen is quiet for a moment. Then she sticks her head out into the hall to look right and left. "Perhaps you should come inside."

Kayna does. Gretchen shuts the door and locks it, and then puts several feet between herself and Kayna before saying, "The last time I saw Sarah was in January. Not long after Argentina." She leans against the wall in her foyer, hugging herself.

"Argentina?"

"You know... when we first learned of the pandemic. I was walking from my class when I saw her in the parking lot on campus with two men."

Kayna's breath catches. "What did the men look like?"

"They were both dressed in dark suits with white earpieces. Like you would see in the movies."

Kayna tilts her head. "What do you mean?"

"You know... like bodyguards or something."

"Do you think they worked for the government?" asks Kayna, her stomach sinking as memories of her teen years and her trip to San Francisco shove their way into the forefront of her brain. What she really means is, what if those men were Diastassian agents? Did they take Sarah away by force, pressing one of their blue-light weapons into her back?

A thought chills her: did merely sharing Kayna's Earth name set Sarah Wade Solheim up for catastrophe?

"It definitely wasn't the Swiss government," Gretchen says, oblivious to Kayna's racing thoughts. "If I had to guess, I'd say... Americans."

"What makes you say that?"

"I ran to try to catch her. I heard them speaking English as they got into a car."

"You haven't seen her since that day?" asks Kayna.

"No. I tried to call, left messages… but then cell service went down. I visited the apartment, but when she didn't answer the door, I figured she had left town. I'd hoped she'd made it home to Sweden before the borders closed."

"Thanks, Gretchen," says Kayna with a heavy sigh. "I appreciate your help."

"Of course. I hope you're able to find Sarah."

The unspoken hovers in the air between them: *at this point, there might not be anyone to find.*

"If you do find her," Gretchen says, filling her voice with forced cheer, "make her return my calls. When the new government gets our cell towers back up, I mean."

"I'll do that. Thank you again."

The two women share a nod, and then Gretchen shows Kayna out the door.

* * *

Kayna hardly remembers her walk back to the shuttle, letting her feet take over as her mind wanders to dark places. The moment she steps inside, Theran asks, "What's wrong?"

She tells him Gretchen's story of two men in dark suits taking Sarah away, all those months ago.

"That was the last time she saw Sarah." She leans her head on Theran's chest, craving the comfort of his arms around her. "It may have been the last time *anyone* saw Sarah."

"Those two men weren't necessarily Diastassian agents."

"True. Gretchen thought they were Americans."

"I wonder if it has anything to do with that project Sarah worked on with the United States government about seven years ago," muses Theran, looping his arms around her waist.

Kayna pulls back her head. "The communication tower she studied?"

"Yes, the one discovered in the state of Wisconsin. It wasn't built by anyone on Earth." Theran pulls up Reshal's file on Sarah Solheim.

"Was the tower Sjelian?" Kayna demands, scrolling and skimming.

"It was not Sjelian. Whoever built it... their technology is more advanced than ours."

"Why do you think that?" asks Kayna.

"Those of us on the space station would have detected a signal before it surfaced. Instead, we learned of its existence on the same day as the humans of Earth did: July 2nd, 2016."

"Sarah studied this tower..." Kayna says, speed reading more about the younger woman's involvement.

"The FBI director recruited her personally."

"Why?"

"I'm not certain. The communications we found were heavily redacted. We think it is related to her knowledge of physics... particularly the electromagnetic spectrum, sound waves, and her theory about gravitons as a form of communication."

"But why would American agents pull Sarah from Zurich the day after a global pandemic begins?" Kayna asks. "How could the two things be connected?"

"I don't know."

"Did you report the discovery of the tower on Earth to the General Council, in 2016?"

"I did. They concluded that it could not have been placed on Earth without us noticing, even with presumably advanced technology. Thus, the tower has been there since before Sjelians began monitoring Earth. It is likely thousands of years old."

"Hm." Kayna still isn't seeing a concrete connection between Sarah Solheim and the pandemic. "Can we ask Reshal to look into whether any U.S. government agents flew to Switzerland around the time the first morphons appeared in Argentina?"

Theran sits down at the control panel, saying, "Right away."

CHAPTER 7

"Remember to keep your cool," Sharon murmurs to Fresler as they follow an armed soldier to General Martell's office for their meeting. "Don't lose your temper."

"Me? Lose my temper? Never!" Fresler says it jokingly, but Sharon doesn't laugh. They stayed up late planning what they would say to convince the general to rescue Lars and Charles, but Fresler can tell Sharon's still on edge. She doesn't trust him to stick to the script. He supposes he can't blame her. She's not used to his new temperament yet. Ever since John's death at the hands of the Soldiers of Destiny, he's stopped rolling over so easily, and he's unafraid to raise his voice. It was a promise he made to himself, that he'd never let another friend go it alone or allow trouble to come for his friends while he stayed silent and docile. Now a friend and his father are in trouble, and it's time to raise hell.

Two armed guards flank the entrance to General

Martell's office. Fresler and Sharon step between them into a small room, most of which is taken up by a large maple desk. Behind that desk sits the general. He stares at his visitors without expression, and then his eyes dart to their escort soldier. The man exits and shuts the door with a sharp *click*.

"Mr. Barsness, Ms. Clary... have a seat." The general gestures to the two chairs opposite his desk.

"Thank you, sir," says Sharon, sitting.

"Yes, thank you for making time for us, General Martell," Fresler says politely, taking his place beside Sharon.

The general adjusts his gold-embossed cap and sits perfectly straight, flashing numerous metals on his broad chest. He's younger than Fresler expected, his hair still a rich brown beneath his cap and only some mild crow's feet afflicting his otherwise smooth face. "What can I do for you?" he asks.

"Well, to get right to the point," Fresler says in what he hopes is a calm, no-nonsense voice, "I am hoping that you can help us locate my father, Lars Barsness, and our friend Charles Radnor."

The general frowns. "I was afraid that was why you asked for this appointment. The answer is no."

Fresler breathes in sharply, and Sharon puts her hand on his knee. "May I ask why you keep refusing?"

"It's a waste of resources," the general says, his tone clipped. "We must think of our soldiers' safety."

"Two lives are at stake," Fresler says through gritted teeth.

"One life has already been lost," the general shoots back. "Director Frieden was careless to let your father and Mr.

Radnor leave the facility. One of my men paid dearly for that carelessness."

"We were hoping that you'd consider a rescue mission as a thank you for Fresler's service to this country," Sharon tries, keeping her tone friendly.

General Martell's eyebrows raise. "Are you a veteran? I wasn't aware."

Fresler barks out a laugh. "No. She means the vaccine."

"Ah. Of course. We are all very grateful to you for the journey you made to get here," the general says.

"Then why won't you let your people talk about my role in creating the vaccine?" Fresler counters, grit entering his tone despite his best efforts.

"The president has decided it's in the country's best interest not to know the true provenance of the vaccine," General Martell says.

"The president is wrong," Fresler says forcefully.

The general's eyes narrow. "Would you like me to pass that message along to him?"

Fresler opens his mouth to retort, but Sharon gets there first with their next tactic.

"The Soldiers of Destiny are a threat," she says. "Letting them get away with kidnapping two civilians from this facility will only embolden them."

"We are handling the SoD threat," the general says.

"You can handle it while rescuing my dad!" Fresler shouts.

General Martell stiffens. "I know we've only just met," he says, rolling back his shoulders and jutting his prominent chin forward like a cobra about to strike. "But I would recommend not raising your voice to me."

"Or what?" Fresler hisses, ignoring Sharon's hand squeezing his knee.

"I will inform the president that you inquired about your father and Mr. Radnor." The general stands. "Is there anything else I can do for you?"

Fresler scoffs, looking over at Sharon in disbelief. "Is there anything else... Are you serious?!"

"I'm sure the president will send his gratitude for your endeavors."

That snaps Fresler's last fraying nerve. "When you talk to the president, ask him how he would feel if I told everyone that he knew about the pandemic years before it struck, and he did nothing!"

Sharon digs her nails into Fresler's leg. "What are you doing?" she hisses under her breath.

The general's face turns crimson. "Are you threatening the president of the United States?"

"You know what? Yes! That's exactly what I'm doing!" Fresler booms.

Sharon tugs on his arm. "Fresler, please—"

She's shoved away by one of the burly soldiers, drawn into the room by the shouts.

"Take him away," the general commands.

"Get your hands off me!" Fresler tries to yank free, but the soldier tightens his grip, ensuring a bruise later. "You can't do this!"

"I assure you," the general says. "I can. You seem to have become a threat to national security."

"Please!" Sharon shrieks, but none of the men even spare her a glance.

Fresler is a burning ball of rage. He is without fear, without anxiety, without rational thought. His blazing fury turns everything else to ash.

Until he looks at Sharon's distraught face. Tears streak down her cheeks as she stumbled into the hall after them, clutching the doorframe for support. Sobbing helplessly, she half runs half falls to his side. "Fresler!" she cries, throwing her arms around his neck.

The raw agony in the way she says his name brings him back to himself. "Call Theran," he whispers quickly into her ear before they're forced apart and he's marched through another guarded set of double doors.

* * *

Zurich, Switzerland — December 13th, 2023 — 2:30 p.m. local time

Kayna and Theran recline the front row of shuttle seats and have a Sjelian cube each for lunch. Kayna lays her head on Theran's shoulder and watches the control panel screen, waiting for the cheery tone and blinking light that will signal Reshal's response to their message.

"I wonder how our daughter is doing..." she muses to take her mind off the waiting. "It must be difficult meeting the family of Erik's late wife."

Theran shrugs, making Kayna's head bob.

Kayna chuckles. "I forget how different Sjelians are."

"What do you mean?"

"People from Earth are so much more emotional. You—"

Kayna is interrupted by the chime of the computer. Theran leans forward and stretches an arm to tap the holographic keypad. Reshal's face appears on the main screen.

"Hello, Theran, Kayna," Reshal says. "I was able to confirm that two FBI agents traveled from Washington, DC, to Zurich, Switzerland on January 20th, 2023. They returned to the United States on the same day."

"Back to Washington, DC?" asks Kayna.

"No. They flew to Atlanta, Georgia."

"Were you able to determine if Sarah Solheim was with them on the return trip?" asks Theran.

"There is a third person listed on the travel manifest, but this person is not identified."

"Thanks, Reshal," says Theran, and ends the transmission. He looks to Kayna. "What do you think?"

"It could be the two men that Gretchen saw. The way she described them... they could have been FBI agents. Sarah would be the unidentified third traveler."

"It seems likely. Our next logical step would be to—"

Theran's wrist communicator interrupts him. When he answers the call, Sharon's torso appears. She wipes tears away from red-rimmed eyes and gulps down a sob. Theran sits straighter, eyes narrowing slightly with concern. "What is it?"

"It's Fresler. He's been taken into custody."

"Why?" Kayna asks.

"He threatened the president," Sharon whispers. "I don't know where they've taken him or what they'll do to him. We need your help."

"Of course. Let me call the others." With a few keystrokes, Theran adds Karena, Kesh, Erik, and Aleria to the discussion.

Erik picks up first. His torso hovers beside Sharon's. "Hi, Theran. Everything okay?"

"We have a situation in Atlanta," Theran says.

"What is it?" Karena's face appears above Erik and Sharon's, forming a pyramid. She looks exhausted, like she had a rough night. Kayna wonders if Winnett kept her up, or if there's something else going on.

Before Kayna can ask, Sharon jumps in. "Fresler's in trouble. He was just arrested for threatening national security. Also, his father and another friend of ours are being held hostage by a local militia group. We have to free Fresler, and then rescue Lars and Charles." She takes in a shuddering breath and finishes, "We need help."

"What kind of help?" Aleria asks, materializing beside Karena's hologram to create a square.

Kayna can't sense her daughter's emotions over the communicator, but she can hear the worry in Aleria's voice. A mother always knows. Aleria doesn't want to be asked to use her ability. Kayna saves her from having to make the decision. "Theran and I will fly to Atlanta."

"You can pick us up on the way," Erik says.

"No," Kayna says, before Theran can agree. "We can handle this. You two enjoy your time with the Johanssons."

"Are you sure?" Aleria asks uncertainly.

"Yes," Kayna says.

"Karena, are you ready to return to Atlanta?" Theran asks.

"No," Karena says after a beat. "There's something I'm... looking into here. I could use a bit more time."

"Then it's settled," Kayna says. "Sharon, we'll talk more en route."

"Mom, if you need my help..." Aleria says.

"We'll be just fine," Kayna assures.

"Stephan is a pilot," Erik says loudly. "He can fly us to Atlanta. We can pick up Karena, Kesh, and Winnett and join you in the U.S."

"We'll let you know when Karena's ready," Kesh says, half his face appearing behind Karena's shoulder.

"Great." Theran nods once. "We'll be in touch." He ends the group call and looks at his life partner. "Are you ready?"

"Yes, back to Atlanta," she says, thinking not only of Fresler, but also of Sarah Solheim. Is it possible that someone there might know what happened to her?

* * *

Stockholm, Sweden — December 13th, 2023 — 2:45 p.m. local time

"Do you want to cut our day short?" Kesh asks from the passenger seat.

Karena relaxes her white-knuckle grip on the steering wheel. "No, of course not," she says. Sharon's call was worrisome, but she trusts Theran and Kayna to resolve the situation. Plus, she has bigger things on her mind today.

Ludvig... her beloved Ludvig... *lied to her.*

The thought haunted her all night. She must find out why, for her sanity.

But to do that, she has to wait for Janice to finish analyzing his blood. Nothing else to do but wait. It's killing her. An excursion with Kesh will be a good distraction.

"Karena?" Kesh says softly.

She's been quiet too long. "Sorry, sorry. I'm fine." Karena turns the key in the ignition. "Should we go to the Royal National City Park next?"

Kesh puts a hand over hers. "I know something's bothering you. I believe even Winnett can tell." He nods toward the back seat, where Winnett stares, solemn-faced, from the car seat Janice borrowed from a neighbor.

"Nothing's wrong." Karena blinks as her eyes fill with tears.

"You don't have to tell me what it is," Kesh says. "I understand that it may be private. But perhaps talking about it would ease your pain..."

"I just wanted to have a nice day," Karena mutters stubbornly. "I wanted to show you where I grew up and introduce you to my closest friend."

"You have done both of those things. We've been to Gamla Stan. You showed me the Royal Palace, the Parliament House, and the cathedral. Stockholm is beautiful, albeit very different than Nekses. And Janice is extremely hospitable."

Karena forces a smile, gathering herself. "She is."

"I would consider the day a success." Kesh pauses, pink skin flushing a shade darker. "Especially as I am spending it with you."

Now it's Karena's turn to flush. To hide it, she looks out her driver's side window.

When Theran's call came through, she'd pulled into an empty parking lot outside a café. The café claims to be open, but no one has entered or exited since they've been here. That's how most of Stockholm appears: quiet and empty. Janice told her this morning that citizens are permitted to be out and about, not only for essential work and to buy necessary items, but also for fresh air, exercise, and socialization. However, many people still choose to stay home whenever possible.

The pandemic has dulled this once-vibrant city. Karena isn't sure whether her current malaise is due to that... or the fact that her husband was lying to her from the first moment they met.

But maybe basking in nature will improve her mood. "The park," Karena says, shifting Janice's car into drive. "It's so big, I'm sure we can find somewhere to get out and walk around."

Kesh pulls down the cap Janice loaned him to shadow his face. "I would like that. I think a stroll would do us good."

Karena peeks at Winnett in the rear-view mirror. As she turns out onto the main road, he catches her eye and a toothless smile breaks through his solemn visage. She thinks perhaps her infant son agrees.

* * *

By 3:45 p.m., the sun is setting as Karena and Kesh complete their stroll and return to the car. The exercise has soothed some of her anxiety, and Winnett is content and cooing against her chest after his nursing breach on a secluded park bench. After a pleasant afternoon of fresh air, sunshine, and peaceful conversation among the beauty of the local flora and fauna, it's time to get back to Janice's house.

Karena wants to be there the instant Janice gets home, wasting no time in finding out what she discovered at the lab.

On the drive, all is still and quiet—until blue-and-white lights flash in the night. Karena's heart sinks as she recognizes the vehicle: military police. She pulls over, turns off the overhead light, and prays the officer won't shine his flashlight too far inside.

The officer walks to her window, and she rolls it down. "Can I help you?"

"This road is off-limits," the officer says. "Government vehicles only."

"Oh! I'm sorry, I didn't realize. I've been... away," Karena finishes awkwardly, hoping the man doesn't press for more information.

Unfortunately, he does. "Away... where? Are you a Swedish citizen?"

"I am."

"Can I see some ID?"

Karena's mind flashes to the cardboard boxes in Janice's

garage. Thanks to the earth-shattering revelations about Ludvig, she'd completely forgotten to unearth her driver's license. "I'm sorry, officer... I don't have anything with me," she says. "This car belongs to my friend, Janice Ammon. She is the Director of the ECDC."

The officer nods as if he recognizes Janice's name, but his face is still suspicious. "What is your name?"

"Karena Wilson."

The officer's eyes widen, and he bends down for a closer look. "*The* Karena Wilson?" he demands. "There's a statue of you in the Nobel Prize Museum, you know."

"So I've heard," Karena says, trying to keep her voice steady. She doesn't want the man to look any closer at her companion.

"You created the vaccine. You saved us."

"I only did what any scientist would do..." Karena fades off as the officer's flashlight beam sneaks past her head and illuminates Kesh in the passenger seat. In the harsh light, Kesh's pink skin appears a deep raspberry tone.

The officer yelps and jumps back, burying his nose and mouth in the crook of his elbow, as if to shield himself from contamination. "What's wrong with him?"

"Nothing. He has a skin condition." Karena looks apologetically at Kesh, who has his eyes on his lap.

"I'm going to have to call this in."

Karena gulps. "I assure you, that isn't necessary—"

The officer holds up his hand to stop her and then turns his back to speak into his radio.

In minutes that feel like hours in confinement, their car is surrounded. "Step out of the vehicle," says a disembodied voice over a megaphone.

"I have a baby in the back!" Karena shouts, her voice cracking with panic.

"Understood," the voice replies a moment later. "Please collect the child, as well as any belongings, exit the vehicle, and prepare to come with us."

* * *

Karena sits inside a plain beige cell, eyes on the analog clock on the wall outside. She watches the second hand go around and around, trying to keep her mind off what they might be doing to Kesh. They separated them as soon as they entered the building.

In her arms, Winnett blinks drowsily. She supposes it's a small comfort that her son so rarely cries.

She jumps when the door at the end of the hall opens, and the officer in charge stomps in, scuffing the floor with his combat boots. "Follow me, please," he says.

Afraid to ask questions she may not like the answer to, Karena follows him silently into his office.

He doesn't shut the door behind him, putting her a little more at ease.

"I am sorry you were detained," he says as he offers her a seat. "You didn't have any identification, so we needed to verify that you are who you say you are. On behalf of the people of Sweden, and the new Eurasian Alliance, it is such an honor to meet you."

Karena nods stiffly. "Thanks. Where is my friend?"

"We have him in isolation."

Karena sucks in a sharp breath. "Why?"

"We are concerned that he has some mutated version of this virus. As a scientist, I'm sure you understand us taking every precaution—"

"Is this because of the color of his skin?"

"Yes."

"He is not infected," Karena says, leaning forward. "I promise you that."

The officer leans back in his chair. "Then... please explain."

Karena purses her lips, thinking a mile a minute. She knows she can't simply tell him the truth. "He has a rare form of psoriasis," she says as confidently as she can manage. "It's a skin condition found in less than one percent of the population."

"I've never heard of anything that would cause the skin to turn such a deep pink color," the man says doubtfully. "It covers his entire body. We checked."

Karena winces at the thought of her kind, dignified friend being subjected to a strip search. "I need to see him," she says.

"We need to keep him in quarantine until we can be certain he is not contagious."

Karena sits tall and keeps her jaw hard while her guts flutter with a swarm of butterflies and her heart gallops like a champion racehorse. "Are you acting on orders from the government?"

"Yes, the Eurasian Alliance is taking public health threats extremely seriously. We have been authorized to bring in anyone whose pathology appears suspicious."

"That seems wise," Karena says in a placating tone, "but my friend is not a threat. Are you familiar with the name Janice Ammon?"

The officer clears his throat, shifting in his seat. "Of course. The Director of the ECDC. You both are national heroes for your work on the vaccine."

"Janice has already tested my friend and confirmed that he does not have the virus—or anything contagious, for that matter. Do you have her number?"

"We have a direct line to the ECDC, yes."

"Call her. She will vouch for us."

After a moment's consideration, the officer dials a number on his land line and presses the speaker button. Karena stokes Winnett's cheek to stave off anxiety as three rings chirp through the office.

"Hello, this is Janice Ammon."

"Janice this is Colonel Karlsson. I have Karena Wilson in my office."

Janice's exhale is sharp, and Karena can read her mind through the phone—*I told you so.*

Karena leans forward hastily. "Hi, Janice. I told the colonel that you have already examined my friend Kesh and have determined that his pink skin was the result of a rare form of psoriasis."

"Yes, Colonel Karlsson," Janice says immediately. "Karena's correct. Kesh does not have a contagious disease."

The colonel eyeballs Karena for a moment before saying, "Thank you for your time."

"You're welcome. See you at home, Karena."

"See you soon."

After hanging up the phone, the colonel pushes an intercom button to order Kesh's release, but Karena doesn't like the way his gaze lingers, like he's reading her body language. She relaxes her muscles and bounces her crossed legs in a lazy fashion, a soft smile playing at her lips. Hopefully, she looks calm, rather than smug. Or guilty.

"He will be brought here, and then you both—you three," the colonel amends, nodding at the sleeping baby, "will be taken back to your vehicle. I am sorry for the inconvenience."

"Thank you," Karena says, thinking but not saying that this was much more than an inconvenience.

The colonel stands, opens the cabinet behind his desk, and pulls out a magazine. He comes around the desk with a sheepish expression, though his posture remains impeccable. "While we wait, would you mind signing this for me?"

With a jolt, Karena looks back into her own eyes on the cover of *Time* magazine. The largest headline declares her the winner of the Nobel Prize in Physics. That day, once one of her most cherished memories, seems a lifetime away. "Of course," she says, scrawling her name below the image of her younger self—a woman who looks so happy.

A woman who had no idea what was coming.

CHAPTER 8

CDC Headquarters, Atlanta, Georgia — December 13th, 2023 — 10:00 a.m. local time

Theran lowers the shuttle into the same cluster of trees behind the CDC, keeping the stealth function in place even as he opens the door for Kayna to exit. They agreed on the hour-long trip from Zurich to Atlanta that Theran would stay with the shuttle, to make sure it wasn't discovered.

Kayna hurries around the building toward the main entrance with a gift from Reshal tucked into her back pocket. The ID card is for a woman, Regina Crawford, who lives in Texas and looks astonishingly like Kayna. Assuming Regina isn't affiliated with the military, the ruse should stand up to scrutiny. Theran informed Sharon of Kayna's fake identity, so she should be waiting... unless something has gone awry.

* * *

"Regina Crawford, you said?" William asks in a low tone. He and Sharon are alone in his office, but the general seems to have ears everywhere.

"Yes."

"And she'll be here soon?"

"Any minute now." *I hope,* Sharon finishes inside her head.

As if on cue, William's phone rings. "Yes?" He puts it on speaker, holding a finger to his mouth in a signal, though Sharon's hardly breathing.

"It's Wilson, at the checkpoint. There's a woman here to see you, sir."

"Name?" William asks crisply.

"Regina Crawford."

"Ah, yes," William says. "We have an appointment. Have her escorted to my office."

"Will do, sir." The guard hangs up.

Sharon and William wait. And wait. And wait.

Almost an hour passes. Sharon is clinging to her last shred of hope when there's a knock at the door.

"Come in," William says.

The door opens, and Kayna steps inside, followed by a soldier.

"Sorry for the delay, sir," the young man says. "General Martell wanted to verify her identity. Her ID card is out of date. It's an old Texas driver's license. She said she lost her current ID card on the way here. We had to run it through the old Texas DMV database."

"And?" William asks.

"She is who she says she is."

"Good. Thanks for your vigilance. We'll see that she gets a new ID, immediately after our meeting." William waves for the soldier to leave.

After a moment, the man complies.

When the door is shut, Sharon leaps up to hug Kayna. "Thank you for coming."

"Of course," says Kayna.

Sharon turns to William. "This is William Frieden, the CDC director."

"Nice to meet you."

"Nice to meet you," William replies, staring thoughtfully at Kayna. "Sharon told me some... very interesting stories about you and your daughter. You have certain abilities?"

"Yes," Kayna says curtly, then turns to Sharon. "Do we know where they're keeping Fresler?"

Sharon looks to William for the answer.

"He is downstairs in a makeshift cell. It was retrofitted before the pandemic. There are two guards posted outside his room. Shift change is every two hours."

"And the next shift change should be...?" Kayna prompts.

William glances at his clock. It's just after 11:00 a.m. "Noon."

"How invested is this General Martell in keeping Fresler detained?" Kayna asks.

William and Sharon exchange a look. "Quite invested," William says. "Fresler made threats toward the president."

Kayna's eyebrows go up. "Bodily harm?"

Sharon makes a face. "Worse. *Knowledge.* Fresler said he'd go public with the information that the U.S. government knew the pandemic was coming and did nothing to warn its citizens."

"We've only recently restored some semblance of order here," William says. "There would be riots."

Sharon glares at him. "People should know they've been lied to and manipulated."

"I agree," William says with a sigh, "but it's not as simple as you and Fresler think. You haven't been here. You weren't in those rooms when we were ordered to—"

"We can hash this out later," Kayna cuts in. "Do you have the keys to Fresler's cell?"

"Yes," William answers. "I can access any room in this building."

Kayna nods. "Good. Where are the exits?"

"There are four," says William. "The one where you entered is the most heavily guarded."

"And which is the least watched?"

"The east exit. During the day, there are as many as fifteen guards, but at night, there are only five."

"What about the perimeter of the building?" asks Kayna.

"There are over one hundred soldiers stationed at various points around the building, but only five at the checkpoint you passed through."

Kayna narrows her eyes, thinking. "So, at night, there are five soldiers inside the building near the east exit, as well as five at the checkpoint? Ten in total, if we take that route?"

"Should be," William says.

Sharon notes the concerned twist of Kayna's mouth. "Can you disable that many?"

"I'm not sure."

"Didn't your daughter, Aleria, disable over a thousand people at once on Diastassi?" William asks.

"Yes," says Kayna, drawing out the word, "but she's not here."

"Then what's your plan?" asks Sharon.

"I don't have my communicator. I was worried that the guards would confiscate it. Where is yours?"

Sharon lifts her wrist, where the device sits like a watch. "Right here. Fresler's is in our room."

"How were you able to get it past the checkpoint?"

"We hid them in a pouch at the bottom of my bag. Earth's metal detectors could never detect this."

"Okay." Kayna nods decisively. "So, we'll wait until nightfall to break Fresler free. I'll update Theran."

"Theran?" asks William.

"My life partner."

Sharon adds, "He is the commander of the space vessel I told you about."

William nods, unable to keep from grinning at Kayna in awe. "Sharon told me everything. Truly amazing. You were rescued from a planet in another universe and helped destroy an anomaly."

Kayna snorts. "I didn't really help."

"Yes, you did," argues Sharon. She tells William, "If it wasn't for Kayna, the Diastassians would have captured us."

Kayna waves off the claim. "They just used my blood because it had a tracking device in it, that's all."

Sharon rolls her eyes but doesn't protest; no use wasting time cracking Kayna's iron-clad humility.

"You grew up on Earth?" William asks Kayna.

"Yes, my mom was a refugee from Diastassi. She met my dad here. I was raised in Potosi, Missouri."

William startles. "Potosi?"

Kayna raises an eyebrow. "You've heard of it?"

"I recently read an FBI briefing that mentioned Potosi."

"Why would an FBI briefing mention Potosi? Nothing ever happens in Potosi," says Kayna with a titter.

"There was an incident many years ago in Cheyenne, Wyoming. The three individuals who filed the police report were from Potosi."

Kayna's eyes widen. "Do you know the names of the individuals?"

"I do, but I'm not allowed to discuss it."

"Was one of them Mitchell Solheim?"

"Yes," says William cautiously.

"What about Mary Jacobs?"

William's mouth drops open. "I can't believe it. Were you the third person? Are you... *Sarah Wade?*"

"Yes."

William shakes his head. "Sarah Wade and her parents disappeared in 1969."

"Yes, we were forced to leave Earth. But... why would the FBI be interested in our police report?"

"It was because of the devices found at the scene. The two unconscious men that you found in the alley had devices on them that were made from materials that don't exist on Earth."

Kayna nods. "They used them to track us."

"Whoa." Sharon holds up her hands, struggling to follow all of this. "Why was the director of the CDC sent an FBI briefing about an incident that happened back in 1969? Did it have something to do with the pandemic?"

"No, this was in reference to a situation in Wisconsin seven years ago."

Sharon gives him a look. "A situation?"

William sighs. "I suppose we're past the point of 'need to know' now. In 2016, our lead epidemiologist, Thomas Murphy, was sent to Wisconsin to investigate whether a cluster of deaths in a small town was due to some new pathogen. But there was no contagion. A communication tower was determined to have caused the deaths."

Kayna is practically vibrating as she asks, "I don't suppose your Thomas Murphy met a woman named Sarah Solheim in Wisconsin?"

William slaps his hands on his desk and leans toward

Kayna like she has her own gravitational pull. "You know Sarah?!"

"Yes... well, not exactly," says Kayna, color blooming on her cheeks as a smile buds on her lips. "But I knew her father."

"Mitchell Solheim," Sharon says, putting the pieces together.

William smiles at Kayna. "As a matter of fact, Sarah Solheim is in this building."

"Oh, my God!" Kayna gushes. "Can I see her?"

* * *

Each dull thud of William's dress shoes on the carpeted hall reverberates in Kayna's head, like hammers striking rock. Her senses are amplified, her nerves shot, her stomach in knots. At the end of this short walk lies Sarah Solheim's office. What if Sarah, Kayna's last link to her dear friend, doesn't like her? Resents her? Fears her, even? It's a childish thing, this burning desire to be liked, but she feels it all the same.

Kayna nearly walks into William's back. They've stopped at a door. William knocks, and a woman says, "Come in."

William opens the door, and Sarah looks up from her desk, her red ponytail sliding off her shoulder. "Hi, William."

"Sarah, I have someone here who would like to meet you."

Kayna steps around William's broad form.

Sarah's lips part. "Oh, my God," she says, shaking her head as if to recover herself. "You look just like someone my dad knew when he was in high school."

William smiles. "I'll leave you two alone."

Kayna walks to the desk and extends her hand. "Hi, Sarah. My name is Kayna... but you'd know me as Sarah Wade."

Sarah doesn't move to shake, and for a moment, Kayna's stomach drops. Then the younger woman says, "You look just like the pictures hanging in our house. How is that possible? You look like you're around my age, in your forties, but your road trip with my dad was, what... fifty years ago?"

"Fifty-three," says Kayna, relaxing as Sarah takes her hand. "I am part Diastassian. We age differently."

"Part *what*?"

"Diastassian. Diastassi is a planet far from Earth. My mother came here when she was thirteen..." Kayna pauses. "It's a long story."

"And I'd like to hear it," Sarah says fervently. "But first, tell me about your special abilities. Dad said you used them on him."

Kayna nods, loosely folding her arms around herself for lack of a better idea what to do with them. "I did. I'm sorry—"

Sarah smirks. "Don't be. He always told me he deserved it." She leans back with a blissful look. "He also said you saved his life."

"I didn't save his life. He saved his own life."

"He believed he would have stayed in Potosi, worked in the mines, and become an alcoholic like his dad, if it wasn't for you."

Kayna takes a seat across from Sarah. "You're... speaking about your father in the past tense. Is he...?"

Sarah's face drops. "I don't know. I hope not."

"If he were alive, where might he be?" Kayna asks delicately.

"I wish I knew."

"What about Mary?"

Sarah brightens. "She should be alive. When I was brought here, before the pandemic hit the U.S., I asked the director of the FBI about Dad and Mary. He assured me that if I cooperated, my family would be saved. It was part of the deal."

"Saved?" says Kayna, so short of breath it comes out a whisper. The hope she thought was snuffed blazes bright.

"Yes. There are thousands of buildings like this one, built to protect us from the pandemic. Certain people were picked to survive the outbreak and live in these buildings. I was one of those people. The director of the FBI promised me that my loved ones would be taken to the facility in San Jose."

"But you said you didn't know where your father was."

"Right. They found Mary, her husband, and Jared," says Sarah with a heavy exhale. "They couldn't find my dad or Evan."

"Have you been in contact with Mary?" asks Kayna, squeezing her hands together too tightly in her lap. "Maybe she knows something."

"We aren't allowed to use the land lines." Sarah's tone sours. "I have to take their word for it that she and her husband and son are safe."

"We can go to San Jose," Kayna says. "And we can try to find your father."

"How? We can't leave this building."

"There is a way. Theran, my life partner, has a shuttle not far from here."

Sarah shakes her head. "They have armed guards at every entrance. They won't let us leave."

Kayna leans forward. "Is this room..." She lowers her voice. "Secure?"

Sarah blinks. "I think so."

"Tonight, Director Frieden is helping me break Fresler Barsness out of detention. Fresler, his girlfriend, Sharon, and I will then meet Theran at the shuttle."

"Fresler Barsness?" Sarah says, sounding astonished. "He's back?"

"He is, and he managed to get himself in trouble with General Martell this morning. I'm here to help him escape." Kayna's next words are barely audible. "Not only Fresler, but his father and their friend, Charles Radnor. They were kidnapped by a local militia."

"The Soldiers of Destiny," Sarah says darkly.

"Yes. The general refuses to send soldiers to recover them."

"I'm not surprised. He wouldn't devote any manpower to tracking down my dad, either. I've asked." Sarah's scowl flips into a hopeful grin. "You really think you'll be able to find him?"

"I am going to try." Kayna smiles at the younger woman. "Do you want to come with us?"

"And find my dad and Mary? Of course!"

"Great. So, as I said, we'll be leaving after sundown, when there should be fewer guards in our way. Here's what we're going to do."

* * *

Solna, Sweden — December 13th, 2023 — 6:15 p.m. local time

Janice gathers her purse and her briefcase, and then exits out the passenger side of her assistant's car. "Thanks for the ride," she says, and waves as the man drives away.

Other than fielding the call to get Karena and Kesh out

of trouble, she spent the entire day analyzing Winnett's blood sample and the bloody blouse. Working alongside trusted colleagues, she separated, copied, tested, and conducted the matching process in just nine hours.

She walks through the door and smiles at Karena. All she can see of Winnett is his little legs, which peek out from beneath the breastfeeding scarf draped across his mother's chest. Kesh sits across the table from them. At the sound of the door, he turns his head slowly, as if pulling himself from a daydream.

"How did it go?" asks Karena.

"I have the results."

Karena peeks beneath the scarf and then lifts Winnett out from under it. She adjusts her clothing and hands the baby to Kesh. "I need to talk with Janice for a minute. Can you watch him?"

"Of course." A huge smile blossoms on Kesh's face as he cradles the child, who gives a toothless grin of his own in return.

Janice and Karena hurry into the office and shut the door.

"What did you find out?" asks Karena as she takes a seat across from Janice's desk.

Janice opens her briefcase, extracts the printed sheet with the DNA results, and hands it to Karena.

She looks it over for a few seconds, shaking her head. She then places the paper on the desk, leans her elbows on it, and covers her face with both hands.

Janice sighs. "Sorry, Karena. I know it's a lot to take in."

Karena starts to cry. "Everything was a lie. All of it," she says, voice muffled by her palms.

"Not all of it. You know that Ludvig truly loved you."

"Do I?" Karena swipes at her wet cheeks. "How can I

know that now?"

"I know it," Janice says firmly. "I saw him with you. I saw the life you built together."

Karena shakes her head, unconvinced. "Not that I need to ask, but did you reference the Sjelian markers in my blood?"

"Yes... Ludvig is not Sjelian." Janice pauses. "But as you can see, he is also not from Earth. All we know is that he is human, like us."

Karena looks up at the ceiling, but her gaze stretches farther, as if reaching out into space to find Ludvig's true home. "Could he be Diastassian?"

"Diastassian? You're referring to the planet in the other dimension?"

"Yes."

Janice sucks in her cheeks, thinking. "I would need a Diastassian's blood sample to compare. But didn't you say there were more planets inhabited by humans?"

"There are nine... well, there *were* nine. Two planets were destroyed by the anomaly. One of those was Kesh's home planet, Nekses." Karena glances at the office door. On the other side, Kesh is caring for her son.

"Right. Ludvig didn't have that pink skin," Janice says. "What do you know about the other planets?"

"I know that the Sjelians were monitoring a different planet until it became uninhabitable twenty thousand years ago. And that Erik visited a planet called Phaelin a few years ago..." Karena throws her hands in the air. "That still leaves us with too many unknowns. How can we ever find out Ludvig's true heritage?"

Janice points to the report. "If you can bring me a sample of Diastassian blood, I could use those markers to see if there is a match."

"Is there enough blood on the blouse to perform another DNA test?" asks Karena.

Janice nods. "More than enough."

"Aleria and Kayna have Diastassian blood," Karena says.

"They're Diastassian?" asks Janice, confused. "I thought they were Sjelian."

"Kayna was born on Earth to a Diastassian mother and an Earth father. She married Theran, a Sjelian. Their daughter, Aleria, has all three DNA strands."

Janice shakes her head. "I still have a hard time wrapping my mind around all of this."

"Me too... and I lived through it." Karena taps the desk, staring into the corner. "What about Winnett's results?"

Janice pulls another sheet of paper from her briefcase and hands it to Karena. "He has the Sjelian and Earth markers from you... and the unknown third marker that matches Ludvig."

Karena's brow furrows. "So Ludvig is clearly Winnett's biological father."

"Was that in doubt?" Janice asks, startled.

Karena clucks her tongue. "I'm not taking anything for granted anymore. Not after learning how I was conceived."

Janice shakes her head to clear it. "What?" she starts to ask, but Karena cuts over her with, "Why would he come to Earth, anyway?"

Janice shrugs. "Maybe it was to save your life."

"People die every day on Earth. Why save *my* life?"

"You're not just anyone."

Karena sighs. "It's all speculation until we figure out what that unknown DNA marker is."

* * *

Reykjavik, Iceland — December 13th, 2023 — 5:45 p.m. local time

"Why didn't you tell me that you took the macrophage for Hanna?" Aleria asks from the guest bathroom at Hanna and Olafur's house.

In the bedroom, Erik sighs. They've had a lovely day touring around the city and spending time together as a family, but part of him has been waiting for this question. He knew she wouldn't forget.

"I broke a tenet," he says. "I didn't want you to be part of that. You once told me that under Sjelian law, if you are aware of an offense, you have to report it. If you don't, you are just as guilty."

Aleria sticks her head out of the bathroom to give him a look. "Seriously?"

Erik tosses up his arms, palms to the ceiling. "I had to do it. I had to save her life."

"Erik." Aleria turns off the sink faucet and comes to sit beside him on the bed. "I understand why you did it. But you need to be honest with me. We can't keep secrets from each other."

"I was scared I would lose you," Erik admits. "I remembered how upset you were after I took your PAD... and I panicked."

"Our relationship is much different than it was then," she says, patting his hand. "I just need you to be honest with me... no secrets."

"Okay," says Erik, nodding like a bobble head. The relief is like a shot of hydrogen in his belly, making him lift off the bed. He feels like he is getting off easy but chalks it up to a perk of the honeymoon phase.

"Did you tell Mandal?" asks Aleria.

"No, but she knew anyways."

"I'm not surprised. She's very meticulous with her supplies."

Erik nods. "She saw there was a vial missing and asked me about it. I told her that I took it to save someone's life—someone very important to me."

"What did she say?" asks Aleria.

"She wasn't happy with me, but she said she couldn't report me. If she did, Kralo would never forgive her."

Aleria chuckles. "She's right. He wouldn't."

Erik's PAD lights up on his wrist. "It's Karena," he says, clicking to answer the call.

"Hi, Erik," Karena says. "Is Aleria there?"

"We both are," Erik says. "Are you all right?"

Karena sighs like she's shouldering the weight of the world. "I'm fine. Winnett's fine. So is Kesh. But…"

Erik braces himself.

"We need you to pick us up. Tonight, if possible."

Erik looks at Aleria. "Tonight?"

"Yes. And then we need to get to Atlanta."

"Why?" Aleria asks.

"Is this your intuition talking?" Erik chimes in.

Karena's disembodied head nods. "How long is the flight from Reykjavik to Stockholm?"

"I'll have to check with Stephan, but… three hours, maybe? Of course, Stephan will have to ready the plane, make us a flight plan, get permission to land at various airports… I don't think we could pick you up before midnight, your time."

"Okay. We'll be ready."

"Are you sure you don't want to wait until tomorrow morning?" Erik asks, as the smell of the dinner Hanna's preparing wafts under the door.

"I don't think we should," Karena says. "I'm sorry for the

short notice." She blinks, and for a moment, she looks utterly wrecked.

Aleria leans in so her face will appear in frame next to Erik's. "Karena... are you all right?"

"Yes. No. It's... a long story. I'll tell you on the plane."

"All right," Erik says cautiously. She still looks like she might burst into tears, and he's not sure how he'll be of any help if she does. "I'll go talk to Stephan and my in-laws. We'll be in touch as soon as we have a departure and arrival time."

"Thanks." Karena signs off before Erik can even reply.

* * *

Erik enters the kitchen, Aleria right behind him. Luckily, Stephan, Olafur, and Hanna are all hanging out together. It will be easier to only have this conversation once.

"That smells amazing," he begins, trying to put his in-laws at ease.

But when Hanna turns around, whatever she sees on his face stops her from thanking him. "You have to go," she guesses, her mouth downturned.

"What?" Olafur exclaims. "I thought we'd get another day, at least."

"Karena called. She needs us to pick her up." Erik turns to his brother-in-law. "Is the plane ready?"

"I can radio ahead and have them fuel up," Stephan says. "And then we'll bring Karena, the baby, and her friend Kesh back here?"

"No, we need to meet the others in Atlanta."

Stephan frowns. "Oh. That's a little more complicated. The Cessna Citation can do Atlantic crossings, but I'll need to map out our refueling stops along the way. Maybe we return here first, since I know the team at the airport. Then we can stop over in Halifax, Nova Scotia..."

"Canada?" Erik says. "Why can't we stop in New York? Wouldn't that be closer?"

"I told you, relations between the U.S. and the Eurasian Alliance are tense." says Stephan, massaging his neck. "I don't want to deal with U.S. officials unless absolutely necessary. If we refuel in Canada, we should be able to make it to Atlanta..." He pulls a piece of paper and pencil out of a junk drawer and starts jotting down notes, muttering to himself.

"But are you sure you have to leave tonight?" Hanna pleads.

"Karena insisted. I'm sorry." Erik hugs her, relishing how warm and solid she feels in his arms. He will never regret what he did to save her. Not for one moment.

"When do you think you'll be back, son?" Olafur asks Stephan.

Stephan looks up from his calculations. "Oh. Well... I'm thinking about going with them to the Sjelian space station."

"For good?" asks Olafur, voice cracking a little.

"No, it'll only be for a few months... right, Erik?"

"Yes, no more than a few months."

"Well, then... I think it's a great idea," says Olafur, his wrinkled face softening with relief.

Hanna nods down at her pot on the stove. Stephan looks to Erik with a question in his eyes, but Erik can only shrug. If Stephan can't gauge his own mother's reaction, how is Erik supposed to?

"So, this is a goodbye dinner," she finally says. Never looking up, she reaches over to add more seasoning.

CHAPTER 9

CDC Headquarters, Atlanta, Georgia — December 13th, 2023 — 7:50 p.m. local time

Sharon exits the CDC cafeteria, tucking the cleaning rag she just swiped off one of the tables into her back pocket. Before closing the door behind her, she looks back. Jackie, Jennifer, Tina, and Benjamin wave at her as though this is just "see you later"... instead of "goodbye."

They don't know what she and Kayna are planning. They don't even know who Kayna—a.k.a. "Regina Crawford"—is. William didn't want her and Sharon to be seen together today, as they're supposed to be total strangers. If their plan to break Fresler out of detention has any chance of succeeding, it has to be a complete surprise. Sharon couldn't even tell Gladys of the dual rescue missions, as much as it broke her heart to leave Fresler's mother in the dark.

With considerable effort, Sharon turns from her friends' smiling faces and heads to William's office. Kayna and Sarah are already there and waiting with the director.

William nods to Sharon and then hands her one of two keys. "This will unlock Fresler's room." He hands Kayna the second. "And this one will unlock the outside door. With shift change at 8:00 p.m., you'll need to reach Fresler by 8:05. Our hope is that it will take longer for the two incapacitated guards in Fresler's cell to be discovered. You'll find five soldiers at the east entrance. I will disable the security cameras in exactly five minutes. They will only be off for three minutes, but that should be plenty of time for you to disable the guards and run for the door."

Kayna nods and looks at Sharon. "I talked with Theran. He is ready for our signal. Do you have both communicators?"

Sharon hands Kayna one of the devices and William the other. She shows him how to use it.

"I will notify you the moment the cameras are disabled." William gestures to the device strapped to his wrist. "Good luck," he says, pulling Sharon into a quick hug.

"Are you ready?" Kayna asks, looking between Sharon and Sarah.

Sharon's stomach flipflops, but she keeps her spine straight for Fresler. "Yes."

Sarah nods. "Goodbye, William. Thank you for everything this year."

The CDC director inclines his head. "You have been a great asset to our research team. You'll be missed. But I hope you locate your father."

Sarah smiles nervously. "Me too."

They exit the office, and William leads the way to the transformer room. The three women wait outside the unmarked black door. There are no security cameras in this hallway to identify them, but Sharon still feels antsy knowing there are two guards watching twenty monitors somewhere in this building.

"They're off." William's voice comes through all their communicators at once, as crisp and clear as if three of him were standing in the hall. "You have three minutes."

"Thanks," says Kayna. Following the route William mapped for her on a sticky note, she leads them to Fresler's holding room.

The women maintain their overly casual pace, and the guards stationed in the hall barely glance at them. Kayna nods to Sharon and Sarah.

Steeling her nerves, Sharon pulls the swiped cleaning rag from her back pocket and holds it behind her back as she approaches the guards. The closer man snaps to attention. "What are you doing here?"

"I would like to see Fresler."

"Sorry, no one can see…"

His words become unintelligible grunts as he drops to his knees at Sharon's feet. He clutches his head and bows forward, as if praying to a feared goddess. Shocked, Sharon hesitates, and the man's first scream cuts into her head like a knife. That spurs her to action. She gets the rag over his mouth to muffle the rest of the outburst. Across from her, Sarah is doing the same to the other guard, using a hand towel. They don't have to struggle long before the men tip forward, unconscious.

Sharon stands too fast and stumbles sideways, light-headed from lack of oxygen. Trying desperately not to hyperventilate, she fumbles the key out of her pocket and opens Fresler's door.

Fresler is lying on the bed, rubbing a hand over his face. "I heard a scream. Is—" His eyes widen at the sight of Sharon. "What are you doing?"

"Breaking you out."

Fresler jumps out of bed, watching Kayna and Sarah drag one of the unconscious guards into the room. He looks at Sarah with a glimmer of confused recognition in his eyes, but he doesn't ask any questions. He quickly helps pull the other man inside.

When the guards have been locked into the holding cell, Kayna says, "We need to go. Now."

Sharon grabs Fresler's hand, and they fly down the hall. As they approach the east exit, Kayna holds up a hand to slow everyone down. She peeks around the corner, looking right and left. After a painful pause, she waves them onward. The exit is in sight.

So are five armed guards.

"Can you disable all of them at once?" Sharon whispers to Kayna.

"I think so."

Not the most promising answer, Sharon thinks, but there is no turning back now.

Kayna mutters into the communicator to alert Theran that they are approaching the door.

He responds, "I'm on my way."

Kayna looks over her shoulder. "Are you ready?"

Everyone nods.

She closes her eyes and clenches her fists. Within seconds, all five guards are grabbing their heads, knees buckling from the tremendous agony forcing wild screams from their lips. The small lobby bounces the cries back and forth in surround sound. It's only a matter of time before more guards arrive. Kayna jumps over a guard's prostrate form and uses William's key to open the glass door. Sharon is the next to sprint. Fresler's long legs quickly overtake her, though, and he pulls her along by the hand. Sarah sticks right behind them.

Their feet hit the pavement outside in a hectic beat, as Kayna whirls around to lock the doors. Sharon scans the front lawn, but no shuttle is waiting. All she can see is a checkpoint less than fifty yards down a concrete drive. As William anticipated, there are five soldiers manning it. One turns to flick a cigarette and notices the fleeing flock of people.

"Stop!" his voice booms on the breeze. He pulls on his uniform to bring his radio closer to his mouth. The other four turn with weapons already rising. Kayna skids to a halt and clenches her fists, eyes scrunched tight. Assault rifles swing loose at the guards' sides as they abandon their triggers to clutch their heads. Over their screams, the low hum of the shuttle makes Sharon gasp with relief. Though its sides look like a shifting mirage, thanks to the stealth function, she can clearly see it bending the trees as it glides over the canopy.

The soldiers go quiet as they fall unconscious, but Sharon spies two Humvees approaching from the north. She can hear vehicles coming from the south as well. The pounding of boots makes her look around to see a swarm of guards inside the building, running toward the exit they just used.

They've got about thirty seconds before they're surrounded.

Sharon's chest burns as she gulps down too much air in her mad dash for safety. The shuttle lands ten yards from the checkpoint, its rear blocking off the Humvees' route. Just when Sharon is sure they're going to make it, the soldiers in the first Humvee open fire on the Sjelian vessel. Sharon ducks instinctively, but Fresler tugs her onward. The shuttle acts as a shield. Bullets bounce off its shimmering sides like rubber balls tossed against a concrete wall.

"It's them we need to worry about!" Fresler shouts over the din, jabbing a thumb over his shoulder.

Sharon looks around to see the guards crashing against the CDC building's doors, shaking the frame as the one in the lead shouts at the others to back up, his cheek smushed against the glass.

The shuttle opens near the nose, releasing a ramp, and Theran's bald head appears, along with a frantically waving arm. Sharon and Fresler reach the ramp first, with Kayna and Sarah right behind.

A round of pops and the crash of shattering glass make Sharon jump. She looks back to see the guards firing on the doors. They bust through in a swarm, break up into a practiced formation, and open fire. Sharon screams as Fresler tosses her inside the shuttle and then leaps in behind her. Sharon falls to her hands and knees, but hops back up in an instant, shouting, "Kayna! Sarah!"

She turns on her heel to see the other two women reach the ramp. Sarah takes the lead and whizzes past Theran, but Kayna's leg buckles halfway up, blood blossoming on her jeans, and her shoulder strikes the metal ramp as she falls. Theran half runs, half slides down the ramp and lifts Kayna to her feet. Fresler waits in the doorway with his arms outstretched and grabs them both by their shirts when they're close enough, yanking them inside. Theran lets Fresler settle Kayna in a seat as he takes the controls and closes the door. The shuttle lifts off the ground, impervious to the hundreds of bullets bouncing off its exterior.

In seconds, the CDC building is a dot in the rear camera projected onscreen. Theran takes the shuttle to a safe place a few miles away.

The moment he lands, he hurries to Kayna's side. She tries to smile at him, but it comes out a grimace as she rolls up her jeans to expose her wounded calf. A fat hole leaks blood on one side, but there is no exit point. Theran examines it with a feather-light touch. "I'll need to remove the bullet."

Sharon sits next to Kayna as Theran fetches the medical supplies, which include a macrophage vial. Unsure what else to do, she takes Kayna's hand and pats it, earning herself a smile.

"They were shooting at us," Sarah murmurs, sinking into a seat across the aisle.

"Just for trying to leave the building," Fresler mutters bitterly.

"Our government is out of control," Sarah says with a melancholy shake of her head.

After Kayna downs the macrophage activator, Theran sets to work removing the bullet. Sarah eyes the thin prongs with a grimace, feeling sick to her stomach, but Kayna doesn't seem to feel much pain. Two creases between her brows are the only indicators that Theran is rooting around in her flesh, and she even introduces Sarah to Theran while he works. Sarah says an awkward hello, gawking with thinly veiled horror at the impromptu surgery. That macrophage must be a hell of a painkiller.

"I'm Fresler Barsness," Fresler says, holding out a hand. "We've met before, haven't we?"

Sarah nods. "Back in March."

"Were you on the vaccine team?"

"No, I'm a physicist, specializing in infrasound and gravitons."

"What were you doing at the CDC?" Sharon asks.

"Mostly the same research I was doing before the

pandemic. Atlanta is…" Sarah fidgets with a modest sterling silver ring on her right hand, avoiding Fresler's eye. "It's where they chose to send me, in January."

It hits Sharon and Fresler simultaneously that Sarah was one of the lucky people the U.S. government hand-picked to save. "Oh," Fresler says.

The bullet is extracted and dropped into a bloody towel. Theran rubs Kayna's shoulder. "Are you still in pain?"

Kayna shakes her head. "No, the macrophage is working. I should be able to walk in a few hours."

He kisses her softly on the cheek in reply, then heads back up the shuttle's aisle to the controls. He logs onto the communications channel. "Reshal was able to locate the Soldiers of Destiny compound."

Sharon startles. "Already?"

"How?" Sarah asks. "Not even our military knows where they're holed up."

Theran rotates his chair and smiles. "Our vessel has thermal infrared sensors. The SoDs are about two miles from our current location." He looks to Kayna. "Should we reach out to Aleria?"

"No, I want her to enjoy her time with Erik's family. I should be fine in a couple of hours," says Kayna. "Besides… I don't want to ask her to use her ability again."

Theran tilts his head. "Are you sure? Reshal was able to identify twenty-six individuals at the compound. We have to assume that they will be heavily armed."

"Yes. I can handle them," Kayna says with more confidence than she truly feels.

Theran stares at her a moment but simply says, "Okay."

"Thank you, Kayna," Fresler says earnestly. "I don't want my dad and Charles in that place any longer than necessary."

"Of course," she says. "While I recover, let's go over the plan."

Theran enters a few commands, summoning a holographic 3D model of the compound from the lens embedded in the panel. He points to the north-east portion and says, "This will be the best place to enter." With a tap on his computer screen, he overlays thermal imaging on the blueprint, and shapes of furniture and people take form in tones of blue and red. "There appears to be five guards at this entrance. There are two individuals in this room." He turns to Fresler and points to the room closest to the entrance, where two red figures sit on what looks to be a futon. "They are the only two who stay in one place, so we believe them to be your father and Charles."

"When are we going in?" Fresler asks.

"Reshal has noticed a decrease in movement between 1 a.m. and 6 a.m., when most of the SoD members are sleeping. We will make our rescue attempt at 3:00 a.m." He looks back at Kayna. "At that hour, there should only be five soldiers for you to disable... assuming we can do this without waking any other soldiers."

"How is that possible? They'll scream when she uses her ability," says Fresler.

"We have to muffle those screams." Theran points to the medical kit beside Kayna, and she pulls out a few small, white towels. "Using those."

"With Kayna doing the disabling, that leaves four of us," Fresler goes on. "One of us will have to take care of two soldiers."

"Yes. We'll figure that out when we see how they're configured at the time of our rescue," Theran says.

"We'll need to be close to them when Kayna uses her ability," counters Fresler. Sharon doesn't like how easily he's poking holes in this plan. It doesn't bode well. But she knows if she proposes they take extra time to work out the kinks, Fresler will protest, and they've had too many arguments lately. She's not sure she should poke this bear. After-all, she's aching to get Lars and Charles back, too.

Theran points to thermal images of the soldiers at the entrance and then glides his finger to the Jeep parked out front. "We can hide behind the Jeep. It is only a few feet away from the soldiers."

"Hopefully it will still be there at 3:00 a.m.," Fresler whispers to Sharon. "I wish Aleria were here. She would just disable the entire camp at once."

Theran stands and appraises the group. "If you feel this is too risky, please tell me now."

Sharon looks to Fresler, wondering if he's got anymore holes to punch, but nobody says anything.

Theran nods. "Okay, let's rest up. We'll set out at 2:30 a.m."

* * *

Halifax, Nova Scotia — December 14th, 2023 — 12:00 a.m. local time

Aleria squeezes Erik's knee as Karena finishes her story about Ludvig and the blood test.

"Maybe it was someone who looked like Ludvig," says Erik, straining to reach around the back of his and Aleria's double seat in the Cessna to take Karena's hand.

"The footage was clear. He was the one who pulled me from the Land Cruiser. Besides, his blood test... he's not from Earth."

"Are you sure?" asks Aleria, concern wrinkling her brow.

"Yes... and he's not Sjelian, either."

There's a *clunk* outside the small plane, and all three of them look toward the door. Stephan is supervising the Canadian team refueling the Cessna. They should be on the last leg of their journey soon. Everyone slept from Stockholm to Reykjavik, and then again during the Atlantic crossing, so even though it's midnight in Halifax, they're wide awake. Only Winnett, in Kesh's arms in the back of the plane, where the white noise from the engine is strongest, is still dozing.

"Did I ever tell you how Ludvig and I met?" asks Karena suddenly.

"I don't think so," Erik says.

"We met on April 21st, 2007, in front of the library at ETH Zurich. It was raining, and he offered to walk me to class under his umbrella. It was so sweet."

"You both attended the same university?" asks Aleria.

"Yes. He was an undergraduate and I was working on my doctoral thesis. We met *two years* after my car accident." Karena lets out a long sigh. "Why would he lie to me?"

"Maybe it was chance," says Erik. "Or maybe he didn't recognize you from the accident."

Karena scoffs. "I think you remember the person whose life you saved, and anyway, he never mentioned having pulled *anyone* from a sinking vehicle, much less... *me*. As for chance..." She sighs again. "If he were from Earth, maybe I could believe it was a coincidence. But he's not from Earth. Why save my life and hide it from me?"

"Maybe," Aleria ventures, "he was sent here to watch over you, but he couldn't risk anyone finding out who he was... or where he was from."

"But why me?" Karena's voice is tortured. "What is so important about me?"

"You did win a Nobel Prize," says Erik. "And your blood did help end a global pandemic."

"Well, he could have watched over me without... If he wanted to keep his identity hidden, he didn't have to..." She presses her fingers to her lips and blinks back tears before trying again. "Why show up at my university? Why bother introducing himself?"

"Maybe he fell in love with you," says Aleria, looking to Erik with compassion in her eyes.

"Before we met? I mean... we'd never talked. What are the chances I'd..." Karena swallows audibly. "I need to find out the truth."

"Is there anything we can do to help?" asks Aleria.

"Actually, there is something. I have a sample of Ludvig's blood."

"How did you get his blood?" asks Erik, startled.

"It was on my blouse... the one I was wearing when he died."

Erik goes quiet, unsure how to respond.

"I want to compare it to yours or your mother's, Aleria," Karena says. "To see if Ludvig was Diastassian."

"Sure, anything you need, Karena," says Aleria, and Erik gives her a thankful peck on the cheek.

"Do you also have samples from the other planets on the space station?" Karena asks.

"We do. We'll be able to rule out Diastassi, Nekses, Phaelin, and Rajik."

"Rajik is the planet Sjelians observed twenty thousand years ago, right?" asks Erik.

"I thought no one on that planet survived," Karena says.

Aleria is quiet for a moment. "No one that we know of," she acknowledges.

Karena hangs her head and lets out a bitter laugh. "I'm

not sure which is worse... Thinking Ludwig's whole race was wiped from the universe twenty thousand years ago, and his death marked their total obliteration, or the idea that we could run every Sjelian test in the book and still know nothing."

* * *

Atlanta, Georgia — December 14th, 2023 — 2:30 a.m. local time

As the shuttle lowers into the backyard of an abandoned home one mile from the compound, no one inside says a word. Kayna can sense the others' anxiety, amplifying her own. The success of the mission rests on her shoulders, but she's never used her ability on this scale before. The uncertainty is gnawing away at her nerves.

She runs through the plan on repeat in her head.

We enter the compound from the north-east entrance. There will be five guards at the entrance; Reshal confirmed. The others are in their quarters. Fresler and Charles are three hundred yards to the right of the entrance, but there are other SoD members slumbering not far from them. We cannot wake the other SoD members.

That last bit is the most important part of the whole plan. Kayna knows disabling twenty-six individuals is well beyond her capabilities. Aleria could do it... but after sensing her daughter's roiling emotions surrounding her ability, Kayna could never ask her to.

As Kayna closes her eyes to run the plan again in more detail, Theran's serene visage, rock steady at the controls, lingers in her mind and helps steady her heart.

When the shuttle's engines power down, Theran checks the time. "It is 2:34 a.m. Time to leave." He stands and hovers his finger over the button that will open the door. "Everyone ready?"

Everyone nods, but nobody rises.

Theran studies their faces and does his best to hold himself like Erik did during their escape from Phaelin. The group needs a confident leader, someone whose bravery is infectious. He wishes Erik were here now, to rally the troops.

Actually, if Theran is honest with himself, he wishes Aleria were with them. With her strength, they could be in and out in two minutes flat, never having to bother with a single SoD radical.

Theran opens the door and leads the rescue mission through overgrown backyards behind dark, abandoned homes. Fresler keeps pace, with Kayna and Sharon right behind and Sarah taking the rear.

A hundred yards from the entrance to the SoD camp, they spy the Jeep. A nearby fire pit lights a covered patio, and the friends make sure to stay well out of its glow as they slink behind a broken-down car in the grass ten yards from the Jeep. The guards by the fire are chatting and guffawing, beers in hand. Two lounge on a couch, while three more sit on fold-out chairs, their fatigue-clad legs stretched toward the warming flames. Each man carries an assault weapon, either hanging from their seat or lying across their laps.

"Let's move behind the Jeep," Theran whispers, glancing over his shoulder at Fresler.

Fresler nods to Theran in solemn silence, but when the Sjelian turns around, he whispers to Sharon, "At least the Jeep is still there."

Everyone but Kayna pulls white towels from their pockets. Fresler has two, and he stares down at them, rubbing his fingers over the thick, scratchy cloth. He wishes that his friend John were with them. Fresler's not sure he can take two SoDs by himself.

Fresler snaps to attention as Theran assigns them each a guard. Fresler will take the two closest to each other, on the couch, for a better chance at reaching both in time.

Kayna takes a deep breath before assuming her attack position, eyes closed and fists clenched. Theran and Fresler rush the guards before they start screaming. Sarah and Sharon are close behind. The three men sitting on fold-out chairs have their backs to the Jeep, but the two on the couch spring up, lifting the barrels of their guns.

Before they can take proper aim, the guns fall as the men's knees hit the patio. Fresler tackles them both, then shoves the towels over their mouths. He looks around to see Sharon sitting on the chest of her guard, both hands pressing her towel over his mouth. Theran and Sarah are already standing up and returning their towels to their pockets, their guards unconscious.

Fresler's two men go limp at almost the same exact moment. Fresler is shocked that the plan actually worked without a hitch. Theran scans the lawn, then points to the right, where Charles and Lars are being held in a small barrack. They quickly make their way to the building.

When they reach the entrance, Fresler hurries to the front and tugs the handle. It doesn't budge. Fresler crouches for a closer examination. It's modified with a deadbolt. "How are we supposed to open it?" he whispers to Theran.

"Check the guards for a key," Theran says. He tucks himself into the shadows by the door, keeping watch, as the others run back to the unconscious men to go through their pockets. Several valuable minutes pass before the group returns, somber-faced and empty-handed.

"Nothing," Fresler mutters, feeling helpless anger rise in his chest.

Theran stares at the door. "We'll have to kick it in."

Fresler clenches his fists and holds in a groan. "They'll hear us. There has to be another way."

"What choice do we have?" Theran narrows his eyes. "Let's make this fast."

Fresler shakes his head. He backs up and rams his shoulder into the door, making a loud boom. The door doesn't budge, but Fresler flies backward and lands hard on his ass. Theran steps in front of the knob and lifts a leg. His shoe strikes just below the deadbolt, and the door swings inward, crashing against the wall hard enough to leave a dent. In the room, illuminated by a small lantern, Charles and Lars jolt up in surprise on the futon. Fresler rushes around Theran to get to his dad, wrapping him in a hug that Sharon soon joins.

"What in the world are you doing here?" asks Lars.

"Rescuing you, Dad."

From outside the door, Theran says, "We need to go now."

Voices carry over the lawn. The SoD members are awake.

Kayna whirls toward the voices, braced to use her ability again... but there are far more than five men on their way.

Fresler grabs Charles's hand and helps him up. Sharon wraps her arm around Charles's midriff in a quick hug and leads him out of the building behind Fresler and Lars. Three men are running toward them from the south side with weapons in hand. Kayna closes her eyes and clenches her fists. All three men fall to their knees, screaming for the whole compound to hear.

Theran leads the sprint back the way they came. On the

patio, the five guards are still unconscious. As they skirt around the Jeep, a man approaches from their right, but Kayna sets to work on him.

Just as he begins to scream, Sharon shouts, "Behind you!"

Fresler turns to see a bearded man hit Kayna in the back of the head with the butt of his rifle. She drops like a rag doll, and Theran rushes to her side. The moment his hand touches hers, the soldier knocks him out, too. Theran and Kayna lie side by side, fingers touching. A trail of blood branches down Theran's bald head. Kayna's hair is darkening with her own blood. Fresler has no time to pounce on the man who attacked them. Assault weapons cock from all sides.

Sarah, Fresler, and Sharon raise their hands in surrender.

* * *

Charles is fuming between Lars and Sarah, bound at the end of the row of prisoners, shaded beneath the compound's front patio. Twenty-six SoD members with assault weapons surround them in a wall of bodies and metal. Charles is sick of these assholes' faces. Sick of their weapons. Sick of their arrogance, their zealotry.

Kayna stirs, her head bobbing and eyes fluttering. She groans, and Charles remembers his own pain when he first came-to in this room weeks ago. Her neck is likely killing her, worse even than that of the throb in her shoulders. She's tied to a chair like him and all their friends, arms twisted behind and tied together at the wrists. A second rope encircles her torso. Her legs are wrapped together with rope secured so tightly she's probably lost proper circulation in her toes. On her left, Theran grunts and meets her eyes, his face darkening as he takes in her state.

Several hours have passed since the failed rescue mission. The sun peeks from behind the tall red oaks, casting a rusty glow that does nothing to warm the cool air. But with everyone now conscious, Charles' two least favorite SoD bastards step front and center.

"I think she's a witch or something," the skinny one with greaseball hair called Skeeter says. He eyes Kayna as he works the massive wad of chew that stays perpetually in his lower lip, making it look like he's got a nasty goiter. He rears back his head and spits tobacco in Kayna's face. Theran grunts, still groggy.

"You're a fool, boy. She ain't no witch," says his giant buddy Chester, wiping a finger over his horseshoe mustache. Chester is so broad, his shaved head looks tiny atop his thick neck. He towers over all the other men, and though he wears a layer of fat over his torso, there's ample muscle beneath. Charles learned that the hard way, on his second day in captivity.

"I saw her with my own eyes, Chester. She made fists and closed her eyes... then Orly and Jasper dropped to their knees."

Orly nods, shifting uneasily and accidentally knocking the barrel of his gun against Chester's. "Skeeter is right. She did something to me. My head really hurt."

Chester flexes the SoD tattoo on his bicep as he crosses his arms and steps toward Kayna and Theran. "Where are you from?"

No one answers.

Chester kicks Theran in the shins. "*You* ain't from around here, that's for damn sure." He holds out Theran's communicator. "This isn't like any gadget I've seen."

"I bet it's Russian," says Orly.

"You a Russian spy?" spits Skeeter, baring yellow teeth.

"I think she's Russian," says Orly, wetting his cracking lips. He fixates on Kayna, drifting forward until he's hovering over her. He cocks his head, and then rips her blouse, popping buttons off into the grass and exposing her white bra.

"Don't you touch her!" Theran screams.

"This one is keen on her, Chester." Skeeter laughs like he has the hiccups.

Skeeter leers over Theran. "What are you... some sort of... *albany?*"

Orly laughs. "It's pronounced albino, dipshit. Albany's the capital of New Jersey."

The other SoD members laugh.

A sigh rumbles from Chester's barrel chest. "You're both dipshits. Albany is the capital of New York. We're getting off track. We need to find out where they're from. This thing..." He holds up the communicator. "... is foreign-made. Where did you get this?" He wiggles the device in Theran's face.

Theran stares back completely expressionless, as if carved from stone by an amateur. Chester pulls a stun gun from his back pocket and zaps Theran on the top of his bald head. His scream is drowned by the SoD bastards' chorus of laughter... and something snaps in Charles's head. The blood rushing to his brain sounds like a forest fire in his ears —the whoosh and crackle of destruction.

"You fucking cowards!" Charles yells. "Why don't you untie me and see what happens to you?"

Beside him, Lars whispers, "What are you doing? Keep quiet."

Chester and Skeeter round on Charles as a hush falls over the crowd of onlookers.

"What did you say to me, old man?" asks Chester through a Cheshire grin.

"I called you a fucking coward!" Charles hisses through his teeth, his cheeks and ears blazing hot.

"That's what I thought you said." Chester zaps Charles in the ear with the stun gun. Charles's teeth clamp together, but still the scream slips through as electricity burns and buzzes through his eardrum. "Untie me, you coward!" he shrieks through the pain.

Chester takes off his shirt, exposing an array of tattoos, all symbols of the Soldiers of Destiny. "Cut him loose. I'm going to teach this old man a lesson."

"Leave him alone!" yells Sharon.

Skeeter hits Sharon in the mouth with the back of his hand. At the sight of blood on her chin, Fresler roars like a caged beast, shaking his chair.

Skeeter doesn't spare Fresler a glance as he moves to cut Charles's bindings with his pocket-knife. Charles tries to leap from his seat, but his numb legs buckle beneath him, and his wild swing misses as he falls forward onto the gritty patio floor. The SoD members howl with laughter.

"Get up, old man," Chester taunts. "I'm going to teach you a lesson... in respect."

Charles hauls himself up, propping his hands on his knees, pretending to pant. When Chester takes a step forward, Charles lowers his head like a billy goat and rams into Chester's stomach, knocking the squishy giant to the ground beneath him. He tries to swing, but Chester blocks his punch and rolls him over, slamming Charles's back against the ground hard enough to steal his breath. Chester swings hard, and Charles's nose explodes with a *pop* that echoes in his head, making his busted ear drum give a mighty throb. Charles doesn't see the next hit coming, but it nearly breaks his jaw. Charles spits out blood as he tries to scramble to his hands and knees.

"Stop this!" yells Fresler.

Skeeter pulls a fat wooden club from a holster on his hip, as a policeman would carry a baton, and cracks it across Fresler's temple. Blood sprays across Sarah's face, and Fresler's head droops to his chest.

"Fresler!" yells Sharon. She glares at Skeeter. "You're an animal."

"That's right, bitch," says Skeeter, grabbing a fistful of her shirt and giving it a hard yank that rips it at the collar.

Chester picks up Charles and sits him on the chair. He hits him hard in the face again, and the world goes black.

Sharon's busted lip quivers as Charles's head goes limp on his neck, knocked unconscious. She tries not to show her terror, not wanting Fresler to act brashly on her behalf, but it's no use. It's all she can do just to keep control of her bladder.

"Anyone else want to call me a coward?" Chester walks up and down the row, daring them to say something. "That's what I thought. Get the acid. I'm going to get answers from this one," he says, jabbing a finger at Theran.

"Do you think the albino will talk?" asks Orly.

Chester shakes his head. "He's not an albino, moron."

"But... his skin is white as a ghost."

Chester's trashcan-lid hand grips Theran's head and tips it backward. "His eyes are blue. He's not albino." He crouches to glare into Kayna's and Theran's eyes. "Where are you from?" Chester zaps Kayna with the stun gun between her breasts, making her scream and whimper as she jerks.

Sharon wants to look away or close her eyes, but she can't. Instead, she bites her tongue hard enough to draw blood to attempt to quell her body's quaking.

"Stop!" yells Theran.

Skeeter comes back with a plastic container labeled muriatic acid.

Chester grabs the container and says, "Take his shoes off."

Skeeter takes off Theran's shoes and exposes his ghostly, perfectly manicured toes.

"I'll give you one more chance. Where are you from?"

Theran's face remains vacant, making Chester grind his teeth.

"Actually, I have a better idea." He points at Kayna's legs and says, "Take her shoes off."

As Skeeter starts to take off Kayna's shoe, Theran's marble features crack, his fear giving his eyes a glossy look. "Stop! I'll tell you what you want to know."

Everyone stares at Theran.

Chester snorts with laughter. "I knew that would work..." He looks around at his fellow SoD members, grinning beneath his mustache, before returning his attention to Theran. "Where are you from?!"

"I am from the planet Sjel," says Theran, and Sharon winces. This isn't going to go over well. He needs to lie! But Sharon has no clue how to signal him, and it's probably too late now.

Chester shakes his head as his fellow SoD members laugh. "You fucking with me? Or do you really believe you're from another planet?"

Theran holds his chin high. "I am from a planet that is over 150 million light years from Earth," he says in a level voice, as if chatting over coffee. "In a different quadrant of the universe."

Chester blinks at Theran. "You are crazy... aren't you?"

"See if he bleeds red, Chester. Maybe he is an alien,"

says Skeeter, panting and hiccup-laughing like a hyena circling a lion's feast.

Chester pulls out his pocket-knife and cuts Theran's foot. With jaw clamped shut, Theran lets out a garbled sound of pain as red blood flows from his foot.

Orly points to Theran's foot. "You're human, just like us."

"I never said I wasn't human," says Theran, breathing heavily as sweat drips into his eyes, "but I am definitely not like you."

Chester scoffs. "Is that supposed to be an insult?" He unscrews the canister of muriatic acid and pours the container over the injured foot.

Sharon's muscles constrict as Theran's high scream of agony rips through her whole body. He passes out from the pain, his head dropping to one shoulder. In the silence that follows, Sharon can't pull her eyes from the skin of his foot, rising in large, pus-and blood-filled bubbles.

Sarah is wheezing and whimpering beside Sharon, just as transfixed by the horrendous damage to Theran's foot. On her other side, Lars sits with head bent in a prayer he mutters under his breath.

Kayna lets out a sound like a furious, wailing spirit and closes her eyes, fists clenched behind her back. Chester's mustache twitches as his face crumples in pain. Another man rushes from the ring and hits Kayna's head from behind with the butt of his gun. As she sags forward, Chester whips a pistol from his utility belt and aims it at her forehead. Sarah and Sharon scream a plea in unison, their words jumbling together...

And then everything stops.

The twenty-six SoD members cry out. They grab their heads and fall to their knees as a unit, like a weird, choreographed dance. The men writhe on the patio cement, in the grass, and on the driveway. They squirm like bugs beneath a magnifying glass on a hot summer day.

They are at the mercy of Aleria's fury.

Aleria stands with fists clenched on the street, seeing red behind her closed lids. She can sense Erik and Karena by her side, shifting uneasily. From behind cars, bushes, and fences, she witnessed her father's mutilation and the violence against her mother as she, Erik, and Karena crept closer, assessing the situation. Her rage is burning her from the inside, so intense it turns all other thought to ash. The only way to rid herself of it is to expel it onto those who caused the pain.

"Aleria," Erik says softly, once the men are all unconscious. "You did it. You can stop."

Her eyes remain shut. Her fists remain clenched.

"Aleria," he tries again.

She doesn't flinch. She barely hears him. Her father's screams and the thud of the gun against her mother's skull are replaying too loudly in her head. She thrusts that pain back on those who inflicted it, stopping only when all twenty-six SoD members stop breathing.

"Aleria!" Erik shakes her.

She slowly opens her eyes. He looks terrified, and for a moment, she cannot figure out why. Are there more enemies? Who's in trouble? Who must she hurt?

But then he hugs her to his chest and says, "Are you okay?"

That is when she realizes *she* is the source of his fear. Tears form in her eyes as feeling rushes back in, replacing the rage. "I... I don't..."

"Shh," Erik says, as she buries her face in his shirt and clasps her shaking hands behind his back. "I've got you."

CHAPTER 10

Erik looks around the shuttle, surveying the damage and the progress. The injured are reclined in their chairs, resting while the macrophage does its work. Stephan is kneeling in the aisle, bandaging Theran's foot. Karena and Kesh are handing out food and water, and Winnett is napping in a shuttle seat that has been converted into a makeshift bassinet.

The only person missing is Aleria. Erik looks out the window and stares down at the top of her head. She sits on a log by herself, gazing out into the woods. Erik wants to comfort her, but he knows he needs to give her some space.

Fresler pats Erik on the shoulder, startling him. Erik looks at the bandage wrapped around his half-brother's head.

"You should sit back—"

"I'm feeling fine now," says Fresler, waving off the concern. "How did you find us?"

"Reshal contacted us and gave us your coordinates," says Erik. "When he didn't hear from you by 4:00 a.m. and saw

that your communicators never left the SoD camp, he
suspected you'd been captured."

"But... how did you get here in time?" Sharon asks from
Fresler's other side. "You didn't have the Sjelian shuttle. If you
left when Reshal contacted you..." She squints like she's trying
to do the math, merging flight times and time zones, and then
winces when the expression tugs at one of the cuts on her face.

"We were actually almost here when Reshal contacted
us," Erik said. "We arrived about half an hour later. Stephan
had to find the nearest open field to land the plane. We
hiked from there."

Fresler looks over his shoulder at Stephan, who waves as
he stuffs gauze and medical wrappings back into his first-aid
kit. "So you left Europe... last night," he says slowly.

"Right. We flew from Reykjavik to Stockholm to pick up
those three." Erik indicates Karena, Kesh, and the baby.
"Then we made our way here, with fuel stops in Reykjavik
and in Nova Scotia."

"But... why?"

"Karena had a feeling." Erik shrugs. "She called us to say
we needed to get here, and so here we are."

Fresler shakes his head. "If you had showed up a minute
later..." He doesn't finish his thought. Instead, he walks over
to his dad and sits beside him. "How are you doing, Dad?"

Lars looks up with glassy eyes. "I'll be fine, son."

Fresler steadies his father's trembling fingers by
enveloping them in his palm. "I love you."

"Oh, Fresler." Lars sighs deeply. "I love you too."

Sharon walks behind Charles and puts her hand on his
shoulder. "How are you holding up, Charles?"

The old man nods. "I'm fine. I only wish I had been
awake to see those... *pricks* die."

Sharon flinches back, eyes wide.

"I said what I said," Charles grumbles.

"Are you still planning to settle back in Minnesota, at the cabin?" Lars asks Fresler.

Fresler looks over to catch Sharon shaking her head. "No," he says, with regret. "Jackie told us about the government seizing all private property in the country."

Lars nods. "It's true."

"Also, that they won't let us travel anywhere without permission," Sharon chimes in.

"Right." Charles scowls.

"And given what happened at the CDC..." Fresler fades off.

"What happened?" asks Charles.

"I sort of..." Fresler clears his throat. "I lost my cool and threatened the president of the United States."

Charles leans around Lars' other side, looking incredulous. "What?"

"I threatened to tell the truth about the virus—that the U.S. government knew about its existence well before it reached Argentina... *and did nothing!*"

"I take it they didn't appreciate your... *candor?*" Charles smirks.

"No, they arrested me. So, I am basically a fugitive now. Which means we cannot live in Minnesota or the two designated settlements," says Fresler.

"What are you two going to do?" Lars asks, knotting his trembling hands together in his lap.

"We're traveling with the Sjelians... to Sjel and then to Tria."

"Your mother will be disappointed," Lars says softly.

Fresler nods slowly. "I know."

Sharon peers around Fresler's head and asks Charles, "Are you all going to Washington?"

"Jackie, Jennifer, Tina, Benjamin, and I are, yes," says Charles. He looks at Fresler. "We are hoping that your mom and dad will join us."

Lars nods. "We would love to. I've already talked it over with Gladys, and she agreed—in the event that Fresler and Sharon didn't stick around."

Fresler pats his dad's shoulder. "I'm glad. I'll feel better knowing you'll be with them."

"We'll take good care of your mom and dad," says Charles.

"Thanks. I know you will."

In the middle row of seats, Kayna whispers to Theran, "I am so sorry." His cheek wipes away some of her tears as she nuzzles against him, kissing along his jaw. "We should have asked Aleria to come along from the beginning. This is all my fault." She rests her head on Theran's shoulder.

Theran strokes her hair and says, "It is not your fault."

Stephan walks to the front near Erik, where he flops into a seat. Erik sits beside him and pats his back. "Thanks for looking everyone over, Stephan. It's good to have a doctor here."

"With that macrophage stuff, anyone can be a doctor."

Erik snorts. "You may be right."

"How is Aleria doing?" Stephan asks.

"I'm going to find out in a minute. I just wanted to give her some space."

"Your girl saved our lives, Erik. You tell her that," says Charles loudly from behind them.

Erik nods. "I will."

Stephan glances over at Sarah, who is sitting alone,

looking out of place and uncertain. "Care to introduce me to the newest member of the gang?"

"I can," Sharon says, walking over. Once the basic introductions and handshakes are exchanged, Stephan sits next to Sarah and starts up a conversation about the macrophage.

Erik leaves them to it and opens the shuttle door. "I'm going to check on Aleria," he announces to whomever might be listening.

He walks down the ramp and looks up at the gray skies. The air is pleasantly cool, but it smells of coming rain. Aleria's back is to him, and she doesn't seem to hear him approach. He coughs to let her know he's coming, but she doesn't turn. He sits beside his life partner and puts his hand on her back. She smiles up at him as she wipes away a tear.

"You okay?"

Aleria nods. "I'll be fine."

"Do you want to talk about...?"

"About what? Killing *twenty-six humans*?!" she snaps, more tears spilling down her cheeks. The question echoes through the trees, quieting the birds.

Worried that he is stepping on a landmine, Erik backtracks, stumbling over his words. "Sorry... I didn't..."

"Are you disappointed in me?" asks Aleria.

Erik shakes his head. "Of course not. I'm proud of you."

She shakes her head, disbelieving. "Proud. No."

"Yes," Erik insists. "You were in an impossible situation, and you saved everyone."

"I didn't have to... you know." She takes a breath. "I lost control."

Erik rests a light hand on her tense back. "Can you move on from this?"

Aleria's shoulders relax, and she takes in a deep breath. "When I used my ability on Diastassi... I felt awful. I hurt a lot of innocent people." She looks up at the darkening clouds. "I used my ability on my own father. I can't tell you how difficult that was for me. I felt so ashamed." She wipes her face with an open hand.

Erik rubs her back, letting her get out what she needs to say without interruption.

"And this time... I didn't just cause pain. I actually killed people."

"It's understandable that you feel bad—"

She shakes her head. "That's the thing. I should feel terrible right now, but I don't. I have no regrets at all. Watching that man pour acid on my father's foot and then... pointing that gun at my mom." She swallows hard, anger flashing in her eyes. "He would have killed her. I could sense his feelings. He was going to pull the trigger. And none of the other SoD members felt conflicted." She looks at Erik. "They wanted her dead."

"I believe you."

"Still, I should feel remorse for my actions. Without that, I'm no better than they are."

"Never think that," Erik says immediately. "You are nothing like those men. *Nothing.*"

Aleria looks over her shoulder instead of answering. "I'm afraid to walk in that shuttle. Everyone must think I'm a... *monster.*"

"Quite the opposite," Erik says. "They're fully aware that you saved their lives, and they are grateful."

"They also know that I didn't need to actually kill those men."

"They're not going to shed any tears... trust me."

Aleria looks sideways at Erik, and he wonders idly if

she's digging through his head for his emotions. He holds her gaze, letting her find the truth: he isn't lying.

Erik puts his hands on her crossed arms. "Charles said he wished he had been conscious when you saved everyone. He wanted me to tell you that." Erik gently coaxes her off the log. "Come on... You'll see."

When they step inside the shuttle, a hush falls over the cabin. Kayna is the first to move, jumping up to hug her daughter. "How are you doing, sweetie?"

Aleria's eyes dart around the seats over Kayna's shoulder. "Fine... I think."

Charles stands and approaches Aleria. "Well, I want to thank you. You are a hero in my book. Thank God for you."

Lars nods, along with Fresler and Sharon. Theran limps over to his daughter and pulls her in for a hug. When her dark hair presses against his chest, she starts to sob. Theran strokes her tresses, making soothing, shushing sounds. "Aleria, you saved our lives," he says when she quiets.

She looks at her dad with bloodshot eyes. "You're not disappointed in me?"

Theran looks down at her slowly, unreadable to everyone but her and Kayna, as usual. "How could I possibly be disappointed in you?"

"I killed those men," she says in a quivering, mousy voice.

Theran smiles softly and says, "*Aleria*... We have been so isolated from violence on Sjel. But we're not on Sjel now, are we? There is violence in this universe, and sometimes we have to respond with violence if we want to survive. I learned that lesson on Phaelin."

Charles pats Aleria on the shoulder and says, "They had it coming... for everything they did to us. You did the right thing, Aleria."

Aleria smiles at everyone's nodding heads. "Thanks."

Theran walks up to the controls and says, "Let's get Charles and Lars back to the CDC and Stephan back to his plane."

"Actually..." Stephan stands and clears his throat. "I thought I'd stay with you all for a while. See the Oort cloud." He winks at Erik.

Fresler laughs out loud. "The more the merrier."

Stephan looks pleased to receive such a warm welcome. "Before I left the plane, I radioed an American contact with its location," he says. "Someone should be able to come pick it up."

"Aren't you worried it will get stolen before they get here?" Sharon asks. "A private plane must be extra valuable in times like these."

"There's no one around this area for miles and miles," Sarah says. "It's just the CDC and the SoDs—and they aren't a problem anymore."

With that settled, everyone takes a seat and buckles in for takeoff. Aleria smiles at Erik and leans her head against his shoulder. She whispers, "You were right."

* * *

The shuttle lands less than half a mile from the CDC building in a different cluster of trees, avoiding the robust guard presence at the closest checkpoint. Charles and Lars stand and start saying their goodbyes.

As he hugs his dad, a new worry rises in Fresler's gut. "What if they punish you?"

"Punish me?" Lars scoffs. "I didn't do anything."

"But I did," Fresler frets. "Right or wrong, I threatened

the president. What if they take it out on you and Mom, or on our friends?"

"We'll request our transfer to the Washington settlement soon," Lars says. "We'll be out of General Martell's hair in no time."

"But what if he—"

"I won't let him, son." Lars claps a hand on Fresler's shoulder and looks into his eyes. "I'll be fine. You go do what you need to do, and don't worry about us."

Fresler wipes away his tears. "I love you, Dad."

"Love you too. When will we see you again?"

"I'm not sure."

Lars squeezes Fresler tight one more time. "Stay safe, Fresler."

"I will, Dad. You, too. Give my love to Mom." Fresler winces as the thorny tendrils of guilt give his heart a squeeze. He never imagined not being able to say a proper goodbye to her.

"Me too," Sharon says, looking equally guilty.

"I will. We love you both."

Fresler disembarks with Charles and Lars and watches them head for the CDC building, waving each time his father looks over his shoulder. He only reenters the shuttle when the trees obscure them entirely.

San Jose, California — December 14th, 2023 — 7:30 a.m. local time

In the twenty minutes that it takes the Sjelian shuttle to fly across the U.S., Karena tells the group what she learned about Ludvig. Everyone is dumbstruck... including Sarah, who barely knows the others well enough to keep up with who's who in the story. Aleria feels the shock seven-fold, rolling off the others in waves until she consciously subdues her ability.

Once the shuttle arrives in San Jose, Theran rises from his seat. "We are about a mile away from the building."

Kayna, Sarah, and Aleria gather their jackets. Aleria taps her communicator, testing it more out of nerves than concern for its function, and then rolls up her pants leg to secure it on her ankle. She plants a quick peck on Erik's lips and moves to follow her mother.

Erik catches her wrist and pulls her in for a hug. He whispers, "Be safe," into her hair.

She nods, patting his cheek, and then exits with Kayna and Sarah. Following a dirt path, the three women settle on Kayna and Aleria's aliases and soon come upon a military checkpoint, where a man's voice booms at them to raise their arms and prepare to be searched. The soldier jogs to them and starts a swift pat-down. Two more come down the path at a leisurely pace, but their hands hover over their holstered weapons. Aleria's heart gallops as the man's large hands travel down her thigh to her calf, nearing her hidden communicator, but he stops short of her ankle.

"Identification cards," the soldier demands, holding out his hand.

"We don't have any identification, unfortunately," says Aleria.

The guard's eyes narrow. "What is your business here?"

"I'm looking for my aunt and uncle," says Sarah. It's not a complete lie since she was raised to call Mary her aunt. "I was told they were brought to this facility."

The lead soldier snaps his fingers, and the other two men return to their post while he appraises the women with thumbs hooked into his pockets. "What are their names... your aunt and uncle?"

"Mary Jacobs Miller and Lawrence Miller."

The guard beckons them forward with a hand. "Follow me. You can wait in the lobby while we confirm your story."

They follow the armed guard through the checkpoint toward the entrance of a long, twenty-story building. Three other guards follow them with assault weapons pointed at their backs. At least twenty more pace the front of the building or lean against its doors. They part to let the group through into an echoey lobby.

Their escort gestures to a row of chairs. "The colonel is on his way."

Aleria sits next to her mother on conjoined white, cushioned chairs. Sarah sits across from them and eyes the armed guards. "This is worse than what we left in Atlanta," she murmurs. "I wonder if it's always like this?"

"Maybe they heard about the escape last night," Kayna says in a low voice.

When one of the men glances their way, all three women smile brightly, as if they don't have a care in the world. "Make small talk," Sarah says through clenched teeth.

Aleria looks at her blankly.

"Tell me about Erik," Sarah prompts. "How did you two meet?"

They chat while the clock above the waiting area ticks away ten minutes. Aleria does her best to avoid Sjelian terms and swap any mention of the "space station" with "the research center," in case the soldiers are eavesdropping.

Finally, an imposing man in a decorated uniform tromps down the steps and approaches their chairs. Sarah cranes her neck to look up at him and thinks that under different circumstances, his clean-shaven face and thick, burnt-umber hair could earn him the title of "tall, dark, and handsome." He'd have to lose the scowl, though.

"My name is Colonel Newman. I am this facility's commanding officer. What are your names?"

Sarah stands. "My name is Sarah Miller. This is Aleria Larsson and Sarah Wade."

He smiles, and Sarah breathes a little easier. "Two Sarahs," he observes. "What brings you here?"

"I'm looking for my aunt and uncle."

"What are their names?"

"Mary Jacobs Miller and Lawrence Miller."

The colonel nods. "Mary and Lawrence are on our medical staff." His head tilts a fraction, his eyes boring into Sarah, and her mouth goes dry. Then, he straightens and offers another small smile. "Follow me."

The three women trail after the colonel as he takes them up the stairs. Three armed guards stick close behind, but thankfully, they are no longer aiming their weapons.

The colonel holds open the first door at the top of the stairs. The second floor looks much like the CDC headquarters, retrofitted to keep the occupants safe from the deadly pandemic. But here the walls are a deep forest green that looks muddy and old.

There is a woman sitting behind a large desk with a computer. The colonel gestures for the women to take a seat in yet another waiting area. Sarah begins to feel like she's in a crappy doctor's office.

"I was told that you don't have any ID," the colonel says. "You'll each need to provide Susan here with your full legal name, address, social security number, and driver's license number."

"I don't have my driver's license number memorized,"

Sarah says apologetically, thinking of the new and old ID cards she left in the shuttle, along with other potentially identifying valuables.

"Do your best. If you are to remain here with us, we'll need to verify your identity and register you with the military. After we call in the request to our main database in D.C., you'll be issued temporary ID cards."

Sarah notes the land-line phone on Susan's desk. "How long will it take to verify our identities?"

"A few hours," the colonel admits. "It's a slow process, without the internet."

"Will I have to wait to see Aunt Mary?" Sarah adds a subtle plea to her voice. "I miss her so much."

After a moment, the colonel nods crisply. "I'll get her. She's just down the hall."

Hearing those words gives Kayna goosebumps.

The colonel leaves with one of the guards. The other two remain behind, standing by the exit.

Susan looks up from her screen. "Who would like to go first?"

Kayna hurries to the desk. "I'll go first."

"Let's start with your complete legal name."

Kayna mines her earliest memories for pieces of her old life to impart to Susan, who seems rather indifferent about the whole affair. Five minutes stretch by, with Kayna pulling names and details out of thin air to form this new version of herself—this new "Sarah Wade." The longer she goes on, the more uncomfortable she feels. This whole building carries an unpleasant weight to it that she can sense but can't define. Until...

"Sarah!" a woman cries.

Kayna whirls to see Mary, her brown hair now gray and

pulled into a braided top knot, staring at Sarah with teary eyes.

"Aunt Mary!" Sarah runs through the waiting area and wraps her arms around Mary. "I was so worried you didn't..." Her words are stifled by a strangled sob.

Kayna's hands are trembling so furiously that she shoves them in her pockets. Mary hasn't noticed her yet, and she doesn't want to disrupt the reunion in progress.

"I'm fine," Mary tells Sarah, "and so are Lawrence and Jared."

"What about Evan?" asks Sarah.

Mary lowers her gaze to the carpet. "They haven't told me anything. I don't know where he is."

As Mary's eyes lift again, she catches sight of Kayna over Sarah's shoulder. She sucks in a harsh gasp. Her arms drop to her side, and her lips part in wonder. Sarah pulls back and follows Mary's gaze. Aleria rises from her seat, caught in the middle of the silent reunion. Mary's hands fly over her mouth. "It's you!"

A tear tickles Kayna's cheek, and she wipes it away hastily, not wanting her vision to blur. "Mary," she says through a tight throat.

Mary's hands shake and tears start to flow down her cheeks. She sobs into her palms.

Unable to wait a moment longer, Kayna sprints to Mary and throws her arms around the seventy-three-year-old woman. "I missed you...so much."

"They haven't seen each other in a really long time," Sarah explains to the colonel, who stands nearby, watching them with mild interest.

The reminder that they have an audience shakes Mary out of her shock. Kayna senses her new alertness, tinged with faint worry. "How?" Mary can't finish her thought.

Kayna looks at the colonel, then back at Mary and says, "I have so much to tell you, but first, I want you to meet my daughter, Aleria."

Aleria smiles as she approaches, no doubt feeling the immense love between the two women.

Mary gasps again and then reaches out for a hug. "Aleria, it's so nice to meet you." She looks back at Kayna and says, "Your daughter is absolutely stunning."

"Yes, she is," says Kayna through a smile.

"Thanks," Aleria says, blushing at Mary.

"You need to meet my son Jared and my husband, Lawrence."

"I would love to."

Mary turns on unsteady ankles to ask the colonel, "Do you mind if I take them to see Lawrence and Jared? They're in the cafeteria downstairs."

"As soon as they've finished with Susan."

After the three women finish rattling off fake names and old or nonexistent addresses to Susan, they follow Mary to the cafeteria. They're banking on the fact that it will take a few hours for the officials to determine that the information they gave is false.

Mary leads the group downstairs, trailed by one guard who keeps a respectful distance, out of earshot. "How are you here?" she murmurs to Kayna, glancing over like she needs reassurance she isn't imagining this. "You look just like you did the day you disappeared." She holds out an arm, showing the loose, silky skin dotted with the marks of age. "I look like an old woman."

Kayna shakes her head. "You look amazing. And I

have aged."

"Not much." Mary rolls her eyes, then drinks Kayna in top to bottom. "Why now?" she asks softly.

"It's a long story..." Kayna whispers. "I'll tell you later."

Mary nods. "Of course."

They hear the cafeteria before they reach it. It's breakfast time, and the place is bustling with life. The door opens for them as they approach, letting a group of women in scrubs exit.

Sarah sees Jared almost immediately and runs through the crowd calling his name.

He looks up, startled, and it takes a moment for recognition to light up his face. "Sarah?!" They collide in a hug, Jared laughing with a wide-eyed look of disbelief. "How did you find us?" he asks, adjusting the glasses their reunion knocked askew.

At the table behind him, Lawrence starts to stand, and Sarah hugs him before he's even fully upright. Over her shoulder, she tells Jared, "I was told that you were brought to this building, but I didn't have any way to get in touch with you."

Mary shuffles up to the table. "They wouldn't tell us anything. I was so worried about you."

"I've been at the CDC headquarters in Atlanta," Sarah says. "The FBI came to get me in Zurich. I told them I wouldn't come with them unless they rescued you all too."

"I had no idea what was going on, when they contacted me," Mary admits. "After the virus was first detected in Argentina, I got a call from the State Department. They told us we had to prepare to be picked up immediately. I barely had time to say yes before they showed up at the house." She tears up. "If only Evan had been home when they came for us."

"Do you know where he is?" asks Sarah.

"We know where he *was*," Lawrence says. "He was in Salt Lake, with Mitchell, at the restaurant."

"Mitchell was in Salt Lake City?" Kayna asks sharply. "His phone was in San Francisco."

"How do you know that?" Mary asks, raising an eyebrow.

"We have ways to… monitor communications," Kayna says. "Never mind that. Are you *certain* Mitchell was in Salt Lake at the time of the outbreak?"

"Yes. Evan sent us a photo of the two of them together right before we were contacted by the State Department," Lawrence says, looking at Kayna with undisguised curiosity.

"Have you heard from either of them?" Sarah asks, though Kayna senses she already knows the answer.

Mary shakes her head sadly.

For a moment, everyone is silent. Then Mary brightens. "Lawrence, Jared… this is Sarah Wade."

"It's Kayna now," Kayna says quietly, "but *they* don't know that." She nods her head toward their guard, who's stationed himself against a wall, watching from afar.

Lawrence's eyes go wide. "I have heard so much about you."

Jared scoffs. "You have no idea."

Mary swats his arm.

"And to think you are the same age as my Mary. Look at you!" Lawrence says, still gawking. "You look like you're in your forties!"

Kayna laughs. "This is my daughter, Aleria."

"Daughter!" Lawrence exclaims. "I would've guessed younger sister!"

Aleria steps forward. "Nice to meet you both," she says to Lawrence and Jared.

The group sits down around the large, circular cafeteria

table, and Sarah pivots the conversation back to the previous topic. "Do you think there's a chance Evan and Dad are still in Salt Lake?"

Lawrence shrugs. "We don't know. They could have fled north, during the initial outbreak. Hopefully, they got the vaccine..."

"Not everyone received it," says Mary, grief in her voice.

"Luckily, the virus is no longer a threat," says Aleria.

"What do you mean?" asks Lawrence.

"The morphons that caused it had a six-month life-span..." Aleria fades off at Mary's sideways look.

"How can you possibly know that?" the older woman asks.

Kayna reaches across the table and grabs her friend's hands. "We have a lot to catch up on."

*　*　*

It takes an hour for Kayna to get the whole story out, starting from the day she disappeared in 1969, and on to the recent adventures on Tria. The constant buzz of conversation in the busy cafeteria makes eavesdropping unlikely, but Kayna still talks as quietly as she can. Mary and her family lean forward, listening in stunned silence.

When Kayna finally finishes and rubs her sore throat, Jared looks at his mother. "You were right all along, Mom. You always said you thought your friend was from another planet."

Sarah nudges Jared's ribs with her elbow. "I told you so."

Jared rolls his eyes.

"I'm assuming you aren't planning to stay here on Earth," Mary says. At Kayna's headshake, she goes on, "What's your plan from here?"

"We still have to find Mitchell and Evan," Kayna says, "so I suppose we'll go to Salt Lake City next. Do you want to come with us?"

"Of course I do." Mary looks around like a bunny hesitant to exit its burrow for fear of a waiting hawk. "Yes, I would do anything to see Evan again."

Lawrence nods. "Count me in."

Sarah looks at Jared. "What about you?"

Jared snorts. "Of course...why would you even ask?"

"How are we supposed to get there?" Mary asks Kayna. "We don't have transportation, and they won't let us leave."

Kayna smiles. "We have a shuttle."

Jared's eyes light up. "Awesome!"

"But...the armed guards...?" asks Lawrence.

Kayna and Aleria share a nod. "That," Kayna says, "won't be a problem."

Just as the group stands, ready to begin their departure, the cafeteria doors burst open. Four armed guards rush in formation to the table, assault weapons aimed at Kayna, Sarah, and Aleria's heads. The colonel strolls over the black scuff marks left by his men's boots, a report clutched in one hand. A hush falls over the bustling cafeteria.

"Everyone but the occupants of this table, leave now," says the colonel, pointing two fingers at Kayna and her friends' table. No one hesitates to obey. The crowd bolts in a tidal wave of scurrying feet.

When the doors shut behind the last person, the colonel slaps his report on the table in front of Sarah. "The names and addresses you gave us... they don't exist in any of our databases. Care to explain?"

Mary stands slowly with palms up and says, "I can vouch for these ladies. This one is my niece."

The colonel shakes his head. "I'm afraid I'll need more

than your word, Dr. Miller."

Lawrence stands too quickly, tipping his chair backward. "I can also vouch for them."

"Me too," says Jared.

The colonel scoffs. "While we were waiting to verify your stories, I received a report from the CDC in Atlanta. Apparently, there was an attack yesterday. Military personnel were injured. Two of the four individuals that perpetrated the attack..." he jabs his index and middle fingers at Sarah and Kayna, "...match the description of these two women."

"Attack?" Mary says, voice rising with outrage. "You can't be serious!"

"You—" the colonel indicates Sarah, "—are Sarah Solheim, a scientist who was stationed at that facility. And you—"he motions at Kayna, "—are Regina Crawford, formerly of Texas." He leans in. "Or was that falsified information as well?"

"I assure you, my name is Sarah Wade," Kayna says calmly.

The colonel snorts derisively.

"When did this attack take place?" Kayna asks, praying her daughter and Sarah will follow her lead.

The colonel lifts a page of the report for a peek. "7:30 p.m. local time."

"Last night?" Kayna asks.

"Yes."

"We couldn't have made it here that quickly," says Sarah, making Kayna breathe easier.

The colonel frowns. "You could have, with the right transportation."

Sarah shakes her head. "Are you saying we have access to military aircraft?"

The colonel blusters a little and then announces, "Until we get this sorted out, you're going to have to be detained."

"Detained!" Mary yells. "No...you can't!"

The colonel turns his head on a stiff neck to stare Mary down. "If you would like to join them, I can arrange it."

Aleria rises, perfectly poised, and smooths the creases of her blouse. "We're done here," she says with a sweet smile.

The colonel nods. "I agree." He snaps for his guards like dogs. "Take them into custody."

Aleria looks around the table, still smiling like a demure politician's wife. "Is everyone ready?"

Before the guards can properly wrap their fingers around Sarah and Kayna's arms, Aleria forms fists. The colonel's head snaps back, and he bloodies his tongue trying not to scream, but in the end, he wails like all his men on his way to the ground for a short snooze.

Jared mutters a curse and Lawrence looks flabbergasted, but Mary turns to Kayna with an eyebrow raised. "She's more powerful than you are?"

"Yes. Much more powerful."

"That was awesome!" crows Jared.

Sarah smacks Jared in the arm. "Really?"

"There is no turning back now," says Lawrence, lifting his gaze to Aleria. "Lead the way. I want to make sure I'm standing next to you the entire time."

Jared chuckles.

Aleria's sugary, close-lipped smile is gone, leaving a stern line in its wake. She turns without a word and leads the exodus from the cafeteria at a steady clip. No one's waiting to arrest them in the hall outside, so she powers on toward the front doors with the others trailing like ducklings.

The main lobby, however, is teeming with at least a

dozen guards. Through the windows, they can see just as many, if not more, at the nearby checkpoint.

Jared whispers to Sarah, "I can't wait to see this." She rolls her eyes at him.

One of the guards takes in Aleria's confident stride, then the gaggle of nervous onlookers behind her, and steps forward with an arm outstretched. "Stop!"

Aleria obliges, then closes her eyes. In seconds, the lobby floor is littered with unconscious guards. They barely have time to whimper on the way down. The men outside, however, let out a few cries of pain that carry over the lawn before falling in a ring around the checkpoint. The three secretaries at the front desk are left standing. They race to the soldiers in the lobby but cower as Aleria walks past them.

Mary takes Kayna's hand and says, "She's incredible."

Jared shakes his head as he says to Sarah, "Twenty soldiers taken down without lifting a finger? I agree with Dad. Let's keep close to her."

CHAPTER 11

Salt Lake City, Utah — December 14th, 2023 — 12:00 p.m. local time

Theran slows the shuttle to hover over the empty parking lot. Salt Lake City, like Atlanta and San Jose, is a ghost town.

It was a quick flight, taken up by introductions and surface level explanations that aren't truly satisfying to anyone.

Sarah can barely focus on the conversations around her. The possibility that she's minutes away from hugging her father, whom she long presumed dead, feels too good to be true.

The shuttle lands with the slightest bump, and Theran opens the door.

Sarah's stomach clenches with anticipation. She has never let the thought that her father was part of the massive death toll left in the pandemic's wake nest in her mind for more than a few minutes at a time. Now, as she descends to the asphalt, she banishes the thought entirely with practiced ease. Her first impression is a good one: the restaurant seems to be cared for. The windows are clean and unbroken. The shrubs out front are neatly pruned. Someone has been here, and recently.

But that *someone* isn't necessarily the people she seeks.

Kayna looks at the large sign above the restaurant and smiles. "Diastassi's," she murmurs.

Mary nudges her and says, "Your mother's maiden name."

Kayna chuckles. "That's what I thought, but it was actually the name of my mom's home planet."

Mary nods. "Incredible."

Sarah, Mary, and Kayna approach first, linking arms to give each other strength. Kayna knocks on the door while Mary presses her forehead to the glass, a hand over her brow to block the glare. It's dark inside, but Kayna knocks again. On her other side, Sarah has her hands cupped around her eyes, squinting into the restaurant's darkest corners.

"Wait, wait!" Mary hoots, waving to Kayna as she starts to step back from the door in defeat. "I see someone coming from the back."

Lawrence goes to Mary's side. "I think it's Evan!"

"I think you're right!" shouts Sarah. Jared squeezes in beside her and lets out a whoop of joy.

Mary starts to tear up, pressing praying hands to her lips.

The figure cocks his head at the window and then bolts to open the door. "Mom! Dad!" Evan pulls them into a group hug and then waves for his brother to join. "Jared! Oh, my God, you're here too!"

"Hey, what about me?" says Sarah.

Jared and Evan create a hole for her to slide into the hug-fest. Kayna rubs Mary's arm. Mary looks up at her friend with tears wetting her cheeks. "My boy…"

Mary introduces Evan to Kayna, Aleria, Erik, Theran, Fresler, Sharon, Karena, Winnett, Kesh, and Stephan.

"How did you get here?" asks Evan.

Jared points to the shuttle in the parking lot.

Evan takes a step back and then tilts his head to get a better view. "What the heck?"

Jared chuckles. "We have a lot to catch up on, bro."

Evan leads the gang inside and turns on the lights. "We have a gasoline generator," he explains. "But we don't want to waste a drop of fuel, so we usually keep the lights off during the daytime."

"We?" Sarah says tremulously, afraid to even ask.

Before Evan can say another word, Mitchell walks backward out of the kitchen, turns, and drops the pan he was holding with a clang.

"Dad!" yells Sarah. Her pulse hammers a happy beat as she races to him, dodging booths and chairs. She jumps into his arms, as if she hasn't aged a day past twelve, and he lifts her off her feet in a bear hug. The missing piece of her heart clicks back into place, and the world is made brighter.

Kayna watches the touching reunion, anticipating the moment when her and Mitchell's eyes will finally meet.

Mitchell smiles as he spies Mary standing next to Jared and Lawrence. He walks toward her, bringing Sarah along by the hand. He embraces Mary, Lawrence, and Jared. "You all made it. I am so thankful. But how in the world did you get here?"

Kayna waits, painfully still, hardly able to breathe.

"I honestly thought..." Mary starts to cry.

"I'm fine, Mary." Mitchell loops her into a one-armed hug... and notices Kayna for the first time. His knees wobble, and Jared braces him with an arm.

Mitchell's mouth is agape. Kayna starts to cry, and the blurred vision only makes him look more like his teenage self, making the red of his hair pop, the thinning patches indistinguishable, the wrinkles smoothing out. He's still a hulking man, broad-chested and stocky.

"Am I... imagining..." he mumbles to Mary.

Mary shakes her head. "No, it's Sarah." She pauses. "She goes by Kayna, now."

"How are you here?" asks Mitchell, choking on a sob.

Kayna cries harder. Mitchell can't seem to move his legs, but Kayna stumbles forward, stopping a foot away, unsure. He looks at her with bloodshot eyes. "Sarah..."

She reaches out, and they fall into each other's arms. He cries into her shoulder.

The whole restaurant goes silent, allowing them their moment. "I missed you, Mitchell," says Kayna.

Mitchell regains his composure, wiping his nose with his apron. "I thought you'd... *died.*"

Kayna shakes her head.

"Why did you leave us?"

"It's a long story."

Mitchell smirks. "I can't wait to hear it." He reaches out for Mary, and the three of them squeeze together for a group hug.

* * *

"Kayna. Does that mean something where you're from?" Mitchell asks after they've caught up a little.

Mary swats Mitchell's arm.

"What?" he says.

"Isn't it obvious?"

"Clearly it's not... otherwise I wouldn't have asked."

Mary rolls her eyes. "It's her mom and dad's names put together."

It takes a second, but Kayna watches the light bulb switch on in Mitchell's head. "Awww, yeah. Kaitlyn and Nathan. I get it. That's nice." He stands, joints popping. "I'm going to make us all some pizza. I'll get some wood for the oven. I have some beer and sodas in the freezer. What do you think?"

Lawrence looks around at the booths. "Your gas generator is able to heat this place?"

"It does all right," Mitchell says gruffly. "We try to dress warmly when the chill sets in."

"You're able to make pizza?" Lawrence asks, a hopeful lilt to his question. "Where are you getting the ingredients?"

Mitchell and Evan exchange a look. "Here, there..." the older man hedges.

Mary squints between the two of them, one brow arced in a "give it up" look.

"There's a sort of... underground community," Evan says. "People who didn't want to move to either of the government settlements. We share resources."

"And you've been living here the whole time?" Sarah asks.

"No," Mitchell says. "When it went above freezing, Evan and I joined a caravan of people trying to get north to Canada. We'd just made it across the border when the vaccines started rolling out."

"After we got vaccinated, the trick was steering clear of our military," Evan jokes, his voice strained.

"They were rounding up survivors," Mitchell says with a shake of his head. "Making people pick a job off some list. Damned if I was going to go along with that."

"You could have become a chef in one of the two settlements," Mary points out.

"I wanted to come back here," Mitchell says, wrapping a knuckle on the table. "Or go to San Francisco, but I heard there was more military activity on the coast than here in Salt Lake. With me and Evan trying to stay under the radar, this seemed like a safer bet."

"This community you're a part of," Sarah says. "They grow food?"

"And forage it. Grocery stores and warehouses still have some non-perishables. And when something shows up that couldn't have come from anywhere other than a military convoy..." Mitchell scratches at the back of his neck sheepishly. "Well, beggars can't be choosers."

"It sounds like it's been a pretty tough year for you,"

Sarah says, softly rubbing her father's arm, thinking about her own private room at the CDC... and its well-stocked cafeteria.

"Never mind that." Mitchell shakes off the memories. "I'm going to fire up the oven."

"Want company?" Kayna asks, and Mitchell waves her after him, saying, "The more the merrier."

Mary and Sarah follow Mitchell into the kitchen, too, hovering around him while he starts up the oven.

Kayna shoves Mitchell's shoulder when he retrieves a box of matches from a drawer. "I love the name you picked for this restaurant."

"Sounds Italian, doesn't it?"

"I guess," says Kayna, lips twitching.

Mitchell shakes his head as he strikes a match and lights the wood-burning oven. "I can't believe it's the name of your home planet."

"I may have Diastassian blood," Kayna says hotly, "but I would never consider that my home."

Mitchell wraps his arm around his Sarah and says, "What do you think of my genius daughter? *Physics professor at the University of Stockholm?*"

Kayna nods. "Very impressive. She's lovely."

Mary snorts. "She got her smarts from her mother."

Mitchell scoffs. "What the fuck?"

Mary punches Mitchell in the arm. "Language."

Mitchell chuckles. "Mary's right, though... Sarah got her smarts from her mother, not me. I wish you could have met Linda. She was amazing."

"I wish I could have met her too," says Kayna.

Mitchell walks into a cold storage room to gather ingredients. He lines everything up on the large twenty-foot counter, then sets to work making the pizza dough.

Kayna leans against the counter and takes in the impressive kitchen. "You really did it, didn't you? You accomplished everything you dreamed."

"All of this is because of you," Mitchell says, rolling a ball of dough in flour. "I owe you everything."

"No, you did it yourself. I always knew you had it in you."

Mary says, "I agree... Mitchell; I knew you would be successful."

"Talk about the successful one, did you know Mary is a surgeon? Fucking incredible... is what that is."

Mary laughs as Lawrence, Evan, and Jared join them in the kitchen.

* * *

Laughter spills from the kitchen into the dining room as Sharon and Fresler slide into the largest, U-shaped corner booth with Stephan, Erik, and Aleria.

"Hearing the story again helped," says Stephan, reclining next to Erik.

Erik chuckles as Karena, Winnett, and Kesh join the party, causing everyone to slide left around the bend. Erik settles at one end of the booth and shifts into a more comfortable position with his arm around Aleria. "Helped with what?"

"It seemed more believable the second time," Stephan says. "You know... it would make a great sci-fi movie."

"I'm already working on the novel," Fresler says.

"Well, when it ends up in Hollywood, I know who will play me," says Erik.

Stephan snorts. "Who did you have in mind?"

"Armie Hammer."

"Huh!" Stephan laughs. "You always did have a man-crush on him."

Sharon nods. "I can see it."

Fresler smiles at Erik. "Well, he would have to play me too, since we look so much alike. He would have to dye his hair red, though."

"Who would play me?" asks Karena.

Erik pauses for a moment and rubs his scruffy chin.

She tilts her head and says, "Be careful..."

Erik snorts. "Either Charlize Theron or Gal Gadot."

Karena aims a finger gun at him. "Great answers."

Theran limps over, favoring his injured foot.

"How is your foot doing?" Stephan asks.

"Fine."

Sharon scoots closer to Fresler and beckons Theran to squeeze into the booth. Karena and Kesh make just enough room for his slender frame.

Conversation splits into various branches, nearest neighbors turning to chat to each other. Fresler and Stephan reminisce about the lives they left behind in Minnesota. Sharon and Karena chat about Winnett's latest milestone: he suddenly wants to "talk" to people he recognizes, cooing and gurgling in response to their words. Aleria and her father discuss Kayna's joy at reuniting with her old friends.

Beside Aleria, Erik can do nothing but smile at this big, messy family he's so lucky to have.

"Oh my God!" yells Sarah, running out of the kitchen and startling the whole booth.

"Jesus, Sarah, you scared me," says Fresler.

"Sorry, it's just that..." She takes a deep breath and comes to stand at the end of the table, gawking at Karena. "It's been killing me...you look so familiar... then it finally hit me. Your last name is Wilson isn't it?"

Karena nods.

"You won the Nobel Peace Prize for physics! Your work in nuclear fusion was truly... *revolutionary.* You're a genius!"

Erik smiles and leans over to whisper to Fresler, "Our sister has an admirer."

Fresler nods. "Looks like it."

* * *

When the pizzas are almost ready, Mitchell pushes two of the square tables flush with the U-booth table to make enough room for everyone to spread out and have elbow room. When the pies come out, steaming in the center of the makeshift banquet table, Mitchell sits like a proud king at the head of the formation and proposes a toast. Fifteen glasses raise.

"I don't know that I've ever been as happy as I am now. Knowing that my daughter survived... and of course Mary, Jared, and Lawrence." Then he stops and looks at Kayna. "And what a miracle, to see my friend again after all these years." Mitchell stands and says, "To family and friends."

Everyone clinks glasses and then tackles the pizza, ripping off slices from every direction.

Kayna takes a bite, and her eyes pop. "This is amazing! You really are an incredible chef."

Everyone nods in agreement, mouths too full to say anything intelligible. The pizza isn't fancy, but the simple ingredients come together into a delicious whole. The tomatoes are tart. The cheese is gooey. The crust has a nice char from the wood-burning oven. Even Theran, who hasn't eaten a bite of Earth food since arriving on the planet's surface two days ago, smacks his lips with appreciation.

When the last slice has been devoured, Mitchell sits

back in his seat and clasps his hands over his stomach. "This is the life," he says. "Now that we're all together, I could stay here forever."

A wrinkle forms between Mary's eyebrows. "I was hoping... you and Evan would come back to San Jose with us. Sarah too," she says. "You're all family to me, and family should stick together in times like these. If you'd prefer, we could all apply to move to the Washington settlement together."

"My parents and several of our friends are hoping to move to Washington soon," Fresler chimes in. "I know you'd all get along."

"My research..." Sarah says slowly. "I was recruited by the government because of my work. From what I understand, the living zones don't have research labs. I don't know if they'll let me live in Washington."

"Well, they can't force you to stay in Atlanta," says Mitchell.

Sarah shakes her head. "Apparently they can. The guards at the CDC building shot at us when we left."

Evan chokes on his drink. "Why did they shoot at you?" he asks, eyes watering while Jared thumps his back unnecessarily hard.

"It's my fault," Fresler admits. "I threatened the president. They put me in a detention cell."

"We broke him out," Sharon says proudly, smiling at Kayna.

"I know they're going to want me back, though," Sarah says, looking like reality is setting in for the first time since leaving the CDC. "After what happened when we were identified in San Jose, I'm certain that if I show my face anywhere, they're going to take me right back to Atlanta."

"Does your work have to do with that government job

you did in Wisconsin a couple of years ago?" Mitchell asks, eyes narrow. "I thought that was resolved."

"It was... and it wasn't. I don't think you knew this, Dad, but they've flown me to Wisconsin a few times a year since then, just to check on things at the site. And with this pandemic... they wanted me to see if I thought the tower had anything to do with it."

Kayna and Theran share a look.

"Wait," says Evan. "Why would a communication tower have anything to do with a global pandemic?"

"This tower was made from elements not from Earth."

"What?" says Jared. "Bullshit."

"She's right," says Theran. "The tower is transmitting signals into space. We've been monitoring it since it first appeared on July 2nd, 2016."

"You monitor us... from a space station..." Evan says faintly.

"Yes," Theran says. "We have been monitoring Earth for about two thousand years. The tower breaching the surface was a notable occurrence for your planet."

"It sends a signal blast every five days," Sarah says. "Like clockwork, since it first appeared."

"Signal blasts... to where?" asks Evan.

Sarah shrugs. "We haven't figured that part out yet." She looks at Theran. "Do *you* know?"

"Unfortunately, we do not. But we are hoping to find out."

"Wow!" Jared braces himself on the table. "This is some serious shit."

Mary smacks Jared's arm.

"July 2nd, 2016..." says Karena, brow scrunched. The date rings a bell, but she can't put her finger on it. She looks into Winnett's eyes, and it hits her. "Oh!"

"What?" asks Erik, startled.

"Sibula told me that July 2nd, 2016, on the Earth calendar, was the date that the anomaly destroyed the planet Opik."

Sarah's head tilts. "Opik?"

"It was one of the nine planets inhabited by human subspecies," says Karena.

"Human subspecies?" says Lawrence, sounding incredulous. "How is that possible, when there is virtually no genetic variation in human DNA?"

"That's exactly what I asked Sibula," says Karena. "She said that beyond Earth, there are significant differences... enough to categorize them as subspecies."

Several people's eyes dart to Kesh, who stares back without comment.

"Who is Sibula?" asks Stephan.

"She's one of the Borjans we met on the planet Tria," says Erik. "She's also..." He gives Stephan a meaningful look. "The woman in black I saw after Mom's funeral."

"What?!" Stephan yelps.

"She has the ability to see the future," Karena says.

Sarah folds her hands on the table. "So, on July 2nd, 2016, an anomaly destroyed a whole planet occupied by humans... *and* a tower surfaced here on Earth and started transmitting signals."

"That can't be a coincidence," says Erik.

"Did you find any evidence that the tower had something to do with the pandemic?" Mitchell asks Sarah. "Maybe whoever put that tower in Wisconsin is responsible for what happened here."

Uncomfortable looks circle the table. Theran's flinch is almost imperceptible flinch, but Aleria goes completely rigid .

"No," Sarah says, unaware of the tension among the Sjelians. "I found nothing to suggest that they're related. But this thing with the anomaly... that's intriguing." She turns to Karena. "Do you have more data on the anomaly?"

Karena nods, nudging Kesh. "We worked together for months, studying it. We'd be happy to show you what we've got."

"And I'll show you my research on the tower," Sarah says eagerly. "It's on the zip drive I was going to access for you earlier."

"Opik was one of the nine planets with human inhabitants," Erik muses. "If the tower on Earth breached the surface because Opik was destroyed, could there be towers on all nine planets?" He looks to Theran. "Do you know if there is a similar tower on Sjel?"

"I'm not aware of one, but that doesn't mean it's not there," says Theran, a twitch of the mouth the only crack in his serene façade. "The General Council isn't exactly forthcoming with information."

"We've been granted an audience with the General Council, thanks to our success destroying the anomaly," says Aleria. "We need to ask them directly."

Karena smiles at Sarah. "What do you think about joining us? You're the only one here that has actually studied the tower."

"I agree," says Theran. "Your input would be valuable."

"I don't know..." Sarah's eyes drift to Mitchell.

"You should go," her father says, patting her hand. "It's your life's ambition, to visit other planets. Besides, I'll feel better knowing that Kayna will be there watching over you."

"I would love nothing more," says Kayna.

"What about you?" asks Sarah. "Do you want to see the universe, Dad?"

Mitchell barks out a laugh. "Me, on a spaceship? I'll take my chances on Earth, thank you very much. Besides, I've got *all* the Millers to take care of now."

Mary rolls her eyes and rests her hand on Mitchell's arm. "You'll always be part of our family."

Mitchell nods. "Then it's settled. You'll go to Sjel with Kayna. I'll stay here with Mary."

Erik shoots Stephan a crooked smirk. "Sounds like we're headed to Sjel. Are you ready to expand your horizons?"

Stephan scoffs. "This goes way beyond expanding one's horizons. But... I think I am ready to travel outside my comfort zone."

Erik's smile overwhelms his face. "Awesome!"

"We'll leave in three hours," Theran announces with a decisive nod.

"In that case, who wants dessert?" Mitchell gets to his feet. "I've got some chocolate chip cookie dough I've been saving for a special occasion."

In the midst of a group cheer, Erik leans toward Aleria to murmur, "Wait until you taste *this*."

PART II

ORIGINS

CHAPTER 12

As soon as she's dropped her things off in her quarters aboard the space vessel, Karena marches the blood-stained blouse directly to Aleria's office. She finds Erik there, talking to his life partner. They stand when she knocks and then enters without waiting for an invitation.

"Sorry," she says, thrusting the shirt forward. "I couldn't wait another minute."

"Of course. I understand." Aleria takes the blouse with great care, fingers avoiding the dark splotches.

"How quickly will you be able to do the DNA analysis?" Karena asks.

"We should know something later today," Aleria says, eyeing the stains. "We have Diastassian, Neksesian, Rajikian, Phaelinian, and of course Sjelian and Earth DNA on file... though I know you already ruled out those last two."

"Run them again, please," Karena says, as the tiniest

spark of hope flickers inside her. What if Janice's equipment was wrong? What if Ludvig was from Earth, after all?

"You have Phaelinian DNA for comparison?" Erik asks Aleria, surprised.

"Yes. When we were evaluating Phaelin, we were able to download their DNA sequence."

"Presumably, we have six of the nine human subspecies' DNA at this point," says Erik. "We know where to get Borjan DNA. With Opik no longer in existence, that only leaves one unknown planet." He pauses, scrunching his face. "Hopefully Ludvig wasn't from that one."

Karena exhales sharply. "I still can't believe he kept all of this from me. Why didn't he tell me the truth before he died?"

Erik squeezes her forearm. "I'm so sorry, Karena."

"Thanks... I just want answers."

Aleria gestures to the blouse. "I'll be in touch when I know something."

Karena nods. With another muttered, "Thanks," she hurries out of the office—but not before Erik spots the glitter of tears in her eyes.

Erik watches her hurry for the evaluation center's exit and decides she probably wants a moment alone. He turns to Aleria and says, "How long do you want to stay on Sjel?"

"I don't know. This will be the first time I've seen my granddaughter, Kayna, in person. Can you believe she is already five years old?"

"I remember when you saw her for the first time. What a beautiful baby."

Aleria nods and reaches for Erik's hand. "That was the most thoughtful present I've ever received. I remember the day... August 28th, 2018."

"You never answered my question," says Erik, kissing her hand.

"I don't know, Erik. Do we have to decide now?"

"No."

"Do you want to return to Earth at some point?" asks Aleria.

Erik ponders what his home planet has become, in the wake of the pandemic. The surveillance, the restricted travel, the nervous energy hanging between friends having private conversations, the unquestioned, unchecked power of the military infiltrating everyday life. "I'll miss Hanna and Olafur, but I have no desire to live on Earth anymore. Maybe... Tria."

"Because Fresler and Karena plan to live there?"

"Yeah, but as long as I'm with you, that's all that matters," says Erik.

"Good answer," she says, bumping his shoulder with hers.

"If we were to live on Sjel... what would I do? Where would I work?"

"You could work in research, with me."

Erik nods, taking a moment to imagine a daily routine with Aleria, working side by side. It's a pretty picture, but it feels a tad incomplete. "I only wish Stephan would stay with us."

Aleria smiles. "He can."

Erik shakes his head. "I'm sure he'll want to return to Earth."

"Well, then let's make sure his time with us, however brief, is memorable."

Erik drapes his arm over her shoulders. "Great point. I can't wait to get to Sjel. I can't wait to meet Emeran and little Kayna."

Aleria nods and closes her eyes, and Erik can imagine the happy picture she's painting: her son and granddaughter wrapped in her arms.

* * *

Stephan's head swivels around at break-neck speeds, taking in every inch of the shuttle's hall. Erik resists the urge to laugh and wonders what exactly Stephan expects to see in the white-washed maze—a speck of color? Maybe even an alien decoration or two? If so, they're heading to the right place.

"He reminds me of you... a little," says Erik, referring to Kralo.

"Why's that?" asks Stephan.

"He is such a good person... to his soul. Like you."

"Aw, thanks," says Stephan, shoving Erik's arm. "I missed you, brother."

"Missed you too."

A few steps behind them, Sarah envies their easy rapport. She and Stephan are both newcomers to the vessel, but he's lightyears ahead of her when it comes to integrating into the community here. Sarah has Kayna, of course, but they only met a few days ago. Erik and Stephan share decades of history.

She sighs, and the sound makes Stephan turn. "Sorry," he says, slowing his pace. "Erik and I always walk too fast."

"Thanks," she says, catching up. "Remind me where we're going? The... Setustofa room?"

"Setustofa," Stephan repeats, his tongue testing the word, drawing it out. "Why do they call it that?"

"Not sure exactly," says Erik. "The word doesn't translate into anything specific. I think it has to do with a person's state of mind." He stops in front of the door and waves his PAD in front of the sensor. "You're going to love this place."

The door whooshes open, and Erik steps aside to let Stephan and Sarah enter ahead of him. Stephan only manages one step inside before freezing in his tracks. He cranes his neck to take in the ceiling with his mouth open. "Wow... it looks like the night sky. How do they make it look so real?"

"Ask Kralo," Erik says. "Maybe he knows." He pauses. "Or Sharon. She was learning a lot about this place the last time we were on board."

Sarah drifts toward the waterfall like a sleepwalker and reaches out to brush her fingers over the pink fronds and enormous purple blossoms of alien plants. The blue-green lights dancing on the water wink at her as she trails a hand through the mini rapids. "Incredible." She turns to beam at Stephan, and for a moment, he's as dazzled by her as he is the room.

Erik spies Kralo by the Slak dispenser. "There's Kralo!" He raises a hand to grab the engineer's attention.

Stephan and Sarah follow Erik to the drink machine, where Kralo waits with a smile.

"This must be Stephan," says Kralo, going in for a handshake.

"Nice to meet you, Kralo," says Stephan, taking the offered hand. "Erik has nothing but nice things to say about you."

"I feel the same way about Erik," Kralo says earnestly. "If it weren't for what he did on Phaelin, I wouldn't be here."

Stephan's eyebrows jump at the statement. "I've heard the story," he says, "but I'd love to hear it again from your point of view."

"Another time," Erik says quickly. He holds out an arm

to usher Sarah forward. "Kralo, this is our other guest, Sarah Solheim. She is the daughter of Kayna's childhood friend."

"Welcome," Kralo says.

"Thank you," Sarah says, shaking his hand.

"Erik tells me you're a medical doctor on Earth," Kralo says to Stephan. "My life partner, Mandal, is also a doctor."

"Yes, I'm an oncologist. I would love to talk with your life partner about Sjelian medicine."

"I will introduce you later. Mandal keeps regular work hours in her clinic."

"Erik tells me you are this ship's pilot," says Stephan. "I'm also a pilot... on Earth."

Kralo nods. "I am the lead engineer, so I guess that makes me the pilot."

"If you're the pilot, then we must be on auto-pilot right now," says Stephan, accepting the glass of Slak Erik holds out with a nod.

Kralo looks thoughtful. "You could say we are on auto-pilot. I don't need to be at the controls of this vessel at all times. But I will be there when we enter the portal tomorrow."

"Erik mentioned the wormholes. Truly incredible."

"We are using Neksesian technology. It is far superior to ours. It once would have taken us nine months to travel from the space station to Sjel. We now can make the trip in five days."

"Five days to travel to another planet!" Sarah exclaims, taking the glass Erik hands her.

"Yes, Neksesian technology is truly groundbreaking," Kralo says, apparently oblivious to the fact that Sarah's awe is also tied to the idea of traveling to another planet.

Stephan takes his first sip of Slak. His eyes pop, and he takes a large gulp. "Amazing," he says.

"Told you." Erik grins.

"Sarah, I understand you're a physicist," Kralo says, leading the group over to an array of couches. "Do you have a specialization?"

Sarah breathes a sigh of relief. Her work is always an easy topic—an anchor that makes her feel less adrift in this strange new place. "What do you know about gravitons, Kralo?" she asks.

The engineer's eyes light with interest. "I have a bit of expertise in the area," he says.

They sit, and Sarah launches into an explanation of her research in terms accessible enough for a neuroscientist and an oncologist to follow along. Stephan sips his Slak, mesmerized by Sarah's passion and knowledge. Erik watches them both, trying not to smile like the Cheshire cat.

* * *

Theran looks around his spacious office. Everything is perfectly in order, down to the angle of each guest chair. His U-shaped desk beckons him into its center, its curves like a friendly embrace. The nearest stars fill the room with lazily shifting patterns of light and shadow through the window at his back. He took this haven for granted in the past. After what he experienced on Earth, he will appreciate his loved ones and the Sjelian way of life more than ever before.

He looks up to watch Kayna walk in behind him, drifting into a chair. Even her smallest movements are lithe and graceful. Sometimes, when he studies her too hard, she seems unreal, like a beautiful spirit of his past orbiting him. He was without her so long that her presence still feels surreal in peaceful moments like this. The thought that he almost lost her a second time on Earth tightens his airway.

Theran reaches down to rub his foot, and Kayna arches a brow. "Is it still hurting you?"

Theran straightens, clearing his throat. "No, it's fine."

"You keep rubbing it."

"Sorry... just thinking about our trip to Earth."

Kayna's face crumples. "They poured acid on your foot," she whispers, tearing up.

Theran leans forward, hands seeking hers atop the cool desk. "It wasn't what they did to me that was painful... it was what they did to you and the others. That hurt more than the acid."

"I feel the same way. It's all my fault."

"No... don't blame yourself. I agreed with you. I didn't want to put Aleria through that again."

Kayna shakes her head. "And yet..."

Theran nods. "She did it anyway. How is she doing?"

"You know... after she used her ability on Diastassi... *and on you*, she was extremely depressed. It was difficult for me."

"What do you mean?"

Kayna tips her head back, studying the ceiling as she says, "Sometimes... my ability to sense emotions is a curse. When you or Aleria are in pain, it's debilitating. And Aleria was in a great deal of pain after Diastassi. I can't explain how intense that feeling was for me, to have my daughter in so much pain. It was hurting me too..." Kayna's voice cracks, but she powers on. "But to answer your question, I don't sense any pain this time. So... I think she is going to be fine. The truth is... I can only sense happiness from her right now."

Theran isn't sure if he should feel as relieved as he does, but now is not the time to ponder his daughter's psyche. "It must be because we are returning to Sjel," he says, believing the words more as he says them. "She will finally see

Emeran and Kayna after all these years. I am looking forward to meeting our great-granddaughter."

Kayna's eyes light up. "Me too... I still can't believe she was named after me. I didn't know that was a Sjelian tradition."

Theran smiles. "It is not."

"When do we meet with the General Council?"

"On our second day on the planet."

"If there is a communication tower on Sjel, do you think they will disclose that information to you?"

Theran releases a deep breath. "I will give them no choice. I must know if there is a signal tower on Sjel and if so, how long they've known."

* * *

"I came as soon as I got your message." Erik enters Aleria's office to find Karena already seated across from his life partner's desk, her crossed legs nervously bouncing. Her eyes are glued to Aleria's back as she fiddles with a little white machine. Erik sits and puts a hand atop Karena's jiggling knee to steady her. "It will be okay," he says.

Aleria sits down at her desk and accesses the DNA results from Ludvig and Winnett's blood tests.

She waves at the holographic screen, flipping a digital page. "Ludvig has three distinct DNA strands."

"*Three?!*" Karena jerks forward. "Janice's findings only indicated one unknown marker."

"Our equipment is much more...advanced," Aleria says, giving Karena a sympathetic smile.

"What are the three strands?" Karena asks, head spinning.

"One is Diastassian," Aleria says. "The other two are...

unknown. Ludvig was not from Earth, Sjel, Phaelin, Rajik, or Nekses."

"Three subspecies in one individual." Karena's mouth is uncomfortably dry, and her voice sounds scratchy as she says, "Sibula told me that you, Aleria, were the first human with three subspecies. Why would she lie?"

"Well, technically, I would have been the first," Aleria says hesitantly. "Our tests indicated that Ludvig was younger than me... albeit older than he probably told you."

"Sibula is a seer," Karena says stubbornly. "Surely she'd know if there was another human running around the universe with three unique DNA strands."

Erik leans back in his chair and rubs his eyes. "I wonder if Ludvig lived on Diastassi."

Karena feels winded, like someone punched her in the stomach. "Is there any other way for us to narrow down the two unknown strands?"

"When we return to Tria," Aleria says, "I'll ask Sibula for a sample of her blood."

"Ludvig didn't look Borjan..." Karena says, frowning as she thinks of Sibula and Utivos's long, pale faces.

"With three DNA strands, it's possible that some traits are more dominant than others," Aleria points out. "We have to rule out the possibility that Ludvig is part Borjan."

Karena nods reluctantly. "What does all of this mean for Winnett?"

Aleria swipes at her screen, and Winnett's results appear. She lets out a long breath before saying, "Your son has five separate human DNA strands: Earth, Sjel, Diastassi, and the two unknowns."

"Oh my God! Five?" Karena gasps as she drops her head into her hands.

"Sibula told you that the more subspecies, the more powerful the ability," Aleria says quietly.

Karena nods. "Her exact words were 'As if human evolution fast-forwarded millions of years.'" She addresses Aleria without looking up. "You're proof of that."

"So then, Winnett...?" Erik can't finish the question.

He's not the only one at a complete loss. Karena scours her memories of her smiley little prince, trying to remember if there have been any hints as to a hidden ability. Nothing... except maybe his propensity for long, searching gazes into people's eyes. But she can't exactly ask two-month-old Winnett why he enjoys staring contests so much.

She returns to questions she might actually get the answers to. "How is it possible that Ludvig died from the morphons? He has three subspecies of human DNA."

"The morphons were Sjelian-made. Only someone with Sjelian DNA would be immune," says Aleria.

Karena huffs, on the verge of tears but refusing to let them loose. "I appreciate your help—so much—but I think I know what I need to do to find out where Ludvig is from."

"What's that?" asks Erik.

Karena sits up and gives her half-brother a grim smile. "I have to confront Sibula."

CHAPTER 13

Sjel — December 20th, 2023

Erik, Aleria, and Stephan are lounging in the Setustofa room when the call to gather in the control room bleeps through their PADs.

"Is something wrong?" Stephan asks, jumping up.

Erik laughs. "If I know Theran and Kralo, they just want to give us a show."

At Stephan's confused look, Aleria says, "We will be entering the Sjelian atmosphere at any moment. My father probably wants you to see our planet from the sky."

"Oh! Then let's hurry!" Stephan leads the way out of the lounge area and then stops with a sheepish look back, completely lost. Five days isn't nearly long enough for an Earthling to learn to navigate the white maze of the vessel.

Erik lets Aleria lead the way, and they find Theran and Kayna leaning over Kralo's seat at the controls. Karena and Kesh hover behind them, Winnett peeking over Karena's shoulder. The door whooshes open again, admitting Fresler, Sharon, and Sarah.

Theran waves them all forward. "Let's get a visual so everyone can see the Sjelian landscape," he tells Kralo.

"Told ya," Erik mutters.

In an instant, the enormous screen turns royal blue. It takes Erik a few blinks to realize he's looking at sky.

"This is incredible," Kesh says.

Karena nods and flips Winnett around so he can see. "This is the planet Sjel. You are part Sjelian," she coos at him, pointing to the seafoam-green ocean zooming toward them onscreen.

Fresler points, too, like an excited spectator at a magic show. "Can you believe it?"

Sharon giggles at him and says, "It's amazing; the water is so clear!"

The white beach flies by in a blink, and they soar over open ocean.

"Did you see that?!" Sarah cries, bouncing on the balls of her feet and pointing over Kayna's head at a long shadow beneath the gentle waves.

Stephan hurries to Sarah's side for a better look. "Yeah, it looks like a... giraffe, but with fins."

"It must be over one hundred feet long," says Sarah. She lets out a soft "ooh" as the creature rises closer to the surface and turns its arched neck. Its head has a soft bump between the eyes that reminds Erik of a brontosaurus. But he doubts the dinosaurs of Earth were the color of orange sherbet.

"A Denia can reach two hundred feet in length," Aleria says. "They can swim at speeds of seventy miles per hour. That one is on the larger side; he's just deep beneath the surface. Visibility here is up to five hundred feet."

"Is the moon always that large?" Erik asks. "It looks so close."

"Yes," says Kayna, clearly relishing the view of the planet she left behind all those years ago.

The moon glows the orange of candlelight, making it look like a setting sun. Kralo keeps close to the water and reins in the vessel at less than five hundred miles per hour, for better sight-seeing opportunities.

"Look over there!" says Sharon.

Fresler follows her pointing finger. "Amazing."

The opposite beach is a white stripe in the distance. Where the water grows shallower, approaching the shore, U-shaped rock formations arch out of the ocean. Purple and green mosses cling to the stone, hanging from the arch like curtains. In their midst, a thin metal column holds up what looks like a covered monorail high above the ocean floor. Kralo maneuvers the vessel through the largest arch, giving the group a better look at the nearby snaking tube. A flash of silver streaks by on the track. It's a train car of some sort, but it travels at speeds that would be deemed irresponsible on Earth.

"They don't seem real," says Sarah, gaping at the stone arches. "How is it possible that they are shaped like that?"

Theran leans closer to Kralo and says, "Take us to the Cithal mountains."

Kralo nods, and the vessel takes a sharp right to fly over dry land. Untamed wildlife rules this region, the plant life high and lush like a rainforest. Every now and then an animal that looks like it came straight out of a storybook appears among the trees. Erik spies a large cat with a bony head plate, like a triceratops. Its blue-striped, sunny yellow fur and green paws make it look like it jumped free of an imaginative child's coloring book.

The Cithal mountain range rises over the jungle ahead, spanning the horizon. Fuzzy green moss coats the dark stone. Kralo flies between two of the smaller clifftops, and the screen displays a paradise below. Every few thousand feet, a blue waterfall cascades over black rock.

"Look how many waterfalls there are," says Fresler, hugging Sharon into his side with one arm.

Erik smiles at Stephan laughing and chatting with Sarah. She points to the screen and leans in to whisper in his ear, her red ponytail mingling with his ginger curls.

Kralo lifts the vessel over the mountains and then dives into the valley where the planet's capital city, Lendar, is nestled. Erik is taken back to his first day aboard the space station, quizzing his room's super-computer about Sjel. The city looks just like the images the AI offered that day —unobtrusive, one with nature. No building rises higher than two stories, and there is plenty of room left for privacy between residences. Not surprising, considering the structures are primarily glass. Pink blossoms act as boundaries running along the tan stone walkways, and little streams weave between the houses, sustaining back-yard gardens.

"The city looks spotless," marvels Fresler.

Sharon chuckles. "A little different than Earth, huh?"

Fresler nods.

Kralo lands the vessel among a dozen others on a landing strip not far from Lendar's downtown area. Theran directs everyone to the shuttle bay.

"Kayna, Aleria, Erik, and I will take the shuttle back to the mountains, where my grandson Emeran lives with his family," Theran says, unable to keep a note of proud antici-pation from his voice. "Reshal will show the rest of you to his apartment here in Lendar, where you will be staying while on Sjel. Then, Reshal, Mandal, and Kralo will give anyone who is interested a tour of the city."

Sharon's hand pops straight up into the air. "Me! I'm interested!"

Laughing at her eagerness, Fresler hugs her close. "I think we'll all take you up on that offer."

"Absolutely," Karena says.

"I will be in touch before our meeting with the General Council tomorrow," Theran continues. "Our delegation will consist of myself, Reshal, Kayna, Aleria, Erik, Fresler, and Karena."

"I'm not going," Fresler announces. "I said it on Tria, and I meant it. What they did to Earth… Sharon lost her whole family to those morphons. I won't meet with the General Council."

"I lost family too," Karena points out, "and I didn't want to meet with the Council, but the situation has changed. We have questions they have to answer."

"You don't need me there," Fresler says stubbornly. "I'm no scientist."

"What we learn about the tower could affect us all," Erik says. "We don't know where the broadcast from Earth is going. We don't know who else is out there." *Or what their intentions are,* he finishes silently.

"You can fill me in later," Fresler says, raising a hand like a crossing guard. "I won't stand in front of those Council members for a second."

"That's fine, Fresler," Theran says. "Of course we won't force you." He looks around the group. "Does anyone else have concerns they'd like to share?" When no one speaks up, he finishes, "I hope all of you enjoy your time on Sjel."

* * *

After a fleeting moment of disappointment at missing out

on the tour of Lendar, Erik finds himself watching the shuttle's display like a riveting film, searching for more animals. The jungle at the base of the mountains thins as they climb, and waterfalls roar down the steep rock, bringing life. Theran slows and hovers over a manicured hill covered in green growth similar to an Earth lawn. The home atop the hill, however, looks like nothing Erik's ever seen. The metal structure wraps twice around the hill, with smaller domed structures that Erik guesses are rooms rising from the loops. The largest dome sits right at the top, overlooking the waterfall. A metal arm juts from the lower loop and extends a landing pad like an open, inviting hand.

Emeran's shiny head glints in the sun as he waves from the pad, one arm wrapped around a dark-haired woman who must be his life partner, Jenta. A small, willowy blonde girl holds Jenta's hand and waves wildly, jumping up and down as the shuttle lands.

The moment the craft powers down, Aleria makes a mad dash to embrace her son. Emeran is tall, like his grandfather, and he bends his head to rest his cheek on Aleria's crown. Erik loiters nearby, beside Theran and Kayna, not wanting to intrude. When Aleria pulls back and cups her son's face in her hands, eyes glittering, Erik feels a flutter in his chest. His eyes sting with tears, thinking of his own child, Eria. Little Kayna, with her bright blue eyes and golden hair, looks like she could be Eria's cousin. But Aleria's granddaughter is only five, with baby fat still clinging to her cheeks. Eria was seven, all knees and elbows, when Erik lost her.

Kayna and Theran take turns embracing their grandson while Aleria hugs Jenta. She then crouches to greet her granddaughter on her level. "Hi, Kayna... I'm your grandmother."

Little Kayna's enthusiasm has shifted to shyness. She hugs her mother's leg with one arm, twisting side to side as she offers Aleria a tiny smile with one fingernail caught between her teeth. She looks up at her mother for a cue, and Jenta nudges her forward. "Go ahead... give your grand-mother a hug."

Aleria waits with arms open, and Kayna smiles wider. Emeran told them she inherited her grandmother's ability to sense emotions, and even Erik can sense the love emanating from Aleria. So, it's no surprise when the girl flings herself against Aleria's chest with an adorable giggle. A soft gasp slips through Aleria's lips, and she closes her eyes. She has waited years for this embrace.

When her granddaughter wriggles free, Aleria stands up and reaches for Erik's hand. She pulls him toward Emeran and says, "I would like to introduce you to my life partner, Erik."

Erik's stomach flips. His nerves are getting the best of him. His hands haven't been this sweaty since he spoke at the neuroscience conference years ago. "Nice to meet you," he says, trying to secretly wipe his hand on his pants before he lifts it to shake.

Emeran smiles and shakes his hand. "Nice to meet you too, Erik. This is my life partner, Jenta, and my daughter, Kayna."

"I'm so happy to meet you both." Erik shakes Jenta's hand and bends down to shake Kayna's.

Kayna hugs the shaken limb to her chest and asks her father, "Why did he do that with my hand?"

Erik smiles as Emeran responds, "Erik is from Earth. On Earth, it is customary to shake someone's hand the first time you meet."

Kayna brushes aside her flyaway hair with an open palm and tells Erik, "I learned about Earth from my dad."

"You did! That's great. What did you learn?" Erik asks.

"That the planet is like ours but…" She looks up at her dad and chews on her lip. "But lots of people died."

Erik nods, his smile fading a little. "Yes… that's true."

Aleria grabs her granddaughter's hand. "Can you show me your room?"

"Yes!" Little Kayna leads Aleria inside the home while her namesake and Theran get their own hugs from Emeran.

Cool air blows onto the back of Erik's neck as he follows behind Aleria. The floor of the looped hallway is white, like the space station, but the walls are a soft gray marble. Little Kayna leads the way up the spiral to her room off the second loop, where she tugs Aleria inside for a private, grand tour. Emeran and Jenta show Erik, Theran, and the older Kayna on to the domed, central living area, decorated with art and mesh furniture. After the full tour of the spacious quarters, they sit outside on the marble deck with glasses of Slak in their hands. The wind carries the spray of the nearest water-fall to the balcony in a fine mist that makes Erik feel like he's sitting by a swimming pool. When Emeran shows him how to recline his chair, Erik sinks back with a sigh of contentment.

Emeran angles his chair to better see his grandmother, Kayna. "Mom told me that she could sense your presence as soon as they reached an orbit around Diastassi. She knew you were on the surface."

"It's true. But I didn't sense Aleria's presence until they landed on Diastassi. Her ability is much stronger than mine. Both of her abilities are." Kayna sips her Slak. "Do you and... my great-granddaughter have the same abilities?"

"Yes... we both do," Emeran says.

"Has it been difficult for her?"

"At times. She should be starting school this year, but Jenta and I decided to keep her at home and hire a private tutor."

"I first used my ability to inflict pain when I was six... when I had just started school," says Kayna. "After that incident, my mother kept me at home."

"It is so hard to believe that you spent the first eighteen years of your life on Earth," says Emeran. He looks over at Erik. "That is something that you both have in common."

"I spent the first *thirty-two* years of my life on Earth," says Erik, chuckling.

"It must have been a shock to find out that there is human life beyond Earth," Jenta chimes in.

"Oh, it was," Erik says. "I'll never forget that day, when I learned the truth. I woke up on the space station and saw Reshal sitting there, staring at me. Talk about trippy."

The slang makes Jenta crease her brow, but before Erik can explain, Emeran says, "Mom told me about your adventures on Phaelin and Tria. She said you were trapped in that anomaly."

Erik notes Emeran's perfect posture and corrects his own. There is a confidence in the set of Emeran's jaw and the straightforward nature of his speech that Erik isn't sure he could emulate. On Earth, Emeran's demeanor would make for a great politician. "Yes, I was trapped for a few days."

"What was it like?"

Erik exhales sharply, hesitant to think back on those dark days with Telfas. "Imagine sitting in your shuttle, trapped in complete darkness. There are no distant stars, no planets... nothing but empty space. The only thing visible in this lifeless void is a white line... so faint you can barely see it. I felt like I was surrounded by death."

"And yet you didn't travel toward that white line," says Emeran.

"No... we didn't. We traveled in the opposite direction. I was conflicted. It seemed logical to travel in the direction of the light, but..."

Emeran tilts his head. "But you'd received a message, sent by someone who'd had a premonition. The message came when you were eighteen, am I correct?"

"Yes. At the time, I thought it was a figment of my imagination." The hairs on Erik's arms still rise at the memory of the veiled woman in black looming in the background of his mother's funeral service.

"It's amazing that you connected her message with the light in the anomaly. I don't think I would have."

"Well, I saw her again, about six years ago. If it hadn't been for that second sighting, I don't know if I would have made the connection."

"Did she speak to you the second time?" Jenta asks.

"No."

"It's incredible when you think about it," Emeran muses.

"Having the ability to glimpse the future."

"I agree," Erik says. Even just getting a peek into tomorrow's audience with the Sjelian General Council would help ease the uncertainty hanging over their heads. Then again, as the group falls silent and Erik sinks back into his chair, looking out over the beautiful Sjelian mountains, he can't help but feel content in the joy of the present.

He hopes the others are having as nice a time as he is.

* * *

Fresler, Sharon, Karena, Winnett, Kesh, Kralo, Mandal, Sarah, and Stephan follow Reshal up his front walk. Like the rooms on the space station, the residences lining the street have very little personality or distinguishing elements. The rectangular, two-story complexes of black metal and excessive glass are partially shrouded by the same species of red-barked tree. There are no ornaments on the lawns or doors, but Reshal's building has chosen a yellow flower for the walkway, while the complex across the street has blue blooms.

"Does most of the population on Sjel live here in the city?" asks Karena, rubbing Winnett's bald head. He coos happily in a carrier strapped to her chest.

Reshal shakes his head as he strolls through the entrance into the lobby area. "No, very few Sjelians live here. Most live near the mountains."

"Is that where Aleria's son lives?" asks Sharon as they all follow Reshal inside.

"Yes."

"Our families also reside in the mountains," Kralo says, arm around Mandal's shoulders. "We'll be staying with my parents and sister tonight."

"How far are the mountains from here?" asks Fresler.

"About... three thousand miles," Kralo says.

"Three thousand?!" Karena cries.

Reshal gives her a perplexed look. "It's only a twenty-minute shuttle ride."

"Why did you decide to live in the city?" asks Fresler.

"I don't have any family... it's just me, and I like it here. Most people like the beautiful scenery of the mountains or the ocean, but not me."

"Haven't you lived on the space station for the last few years?" asks Kesh.

"I have been assigned to the space station for twenty-five years, yes."

"Then why do you keep a place here on Sjel?" asks Karena.

Reshal leads them up the white, blocky stairs and to the right. The building's interior is as nondescript as the outside, with only practical furnishings and pristine surfaces. There's not a single fingerprint on any of the glass walls. "I need a place to stay when we return to Sjel," he says simply.

"Do you have enough room for all of us?" asks Sarah, looking around at the others.

Reshal nods. "Plenty."

Reshal reaches a door at the end of the hall and scans his hand on a pad. The door slides open onto a five-bedroom penthouse swathed in sophisticated creams and grays.

"Wow... this place is amazing," says Fresler.

The walls that aren't glass look like white marble, veined with soft beiges and grays. There isn't a kitchen, but that leaves more room for the main living area, where a holographic screen takes up most of the wall. Reshal has decorated his abode with statues of all sizes—some abstract and others in the shapes of Sjelian animals. Reshal leads them through the living room to the balcony, where five mesh chairs are spread in a wide semi-circle.

"What a view," says Fresler.

"Yes, I get a perfect view of the capitol," says Reshal, pointing to the largest building in the distance, surrounded by a purplish pond.

"I love it," says Sharon.

"I can see why you like this," says Karena. "This place is beautiful. The plants and flowers... the statues..." Karena points to the left of the capitol building, where a marble woman rises out of the pond with arms fanned out like a ballerina ready to twirl.

They walk back inside so Reshal can show them the bedrooms. They look exactly like the rooms on the space station, but with larger beds and some extra space in the bathroom.

"Are we going to see the capitol building?" asks Kesh.

"Tomorrow. We'll meet everyone there at noon, before the meeting with the General Council. Today, I thought we'd visit the research center, followed by Observation Pointe."

"What is Observation Pointe?" asks Stephan.

"It is where we view the different quadrants of the universe, through the lens of the probes."

"Probes?"

"Every year, we send millions of probes into the universe in the hope of finding intelligent life. That is how we located Rajik, Earth, and Phaelin," Reshal explains. "There is currently something quite interesting to see at the Observation Pointe. One of the probes has just captured an image of a geomagnetic explosion created by an eruption on a star... a star that is made up of hot plasma."

"You mean a sun?" asks Karena, face lighting up. She and Sarah exchange a mesmerized look.

"Yes. The auditorium has a one hundred–square-foot hologram. We will be able to view this new discovery at great magnitude."

"Awesome," says Fresler. Beside him, Stephan nods.

"Well," Karena says, "what are we waiting for?"

* * *

Stephan watches Sarah's hair bounce in its silky tie, its strands flaring five different shades of red in the white-gold Sjelian sun. He has never felt more like a tourist, trailing along behind Kralo, Mandal, and Reshal in dark jeans that stick out like a sore thumb among the Sjelians' loose slacks, but he can't seem to fully focus on the scenery. As they pass the capitol building on their way to the research center, he quickens his pace to walk beside Sarah.

She smiles when he appears next to her. "The waterways are incredible, don't you think?"

He redirects his gaze to the pink, purple, blue, and red streams that flow through channels cut into the white stone of the capitol building's courtyard. Their bends and loops form a shape vaguely resembling a Celtic knot. Plants in deep shades of green and purple are planted in alternating patterns inside the confines of the loop, leaving only a single, wide path up to the building's front door.

"Where's the water source?" Sarah asks their guides.

"There is a reservoir not far from here," says Mandal. "The water is pumped into the city." She bends to scoop the purple water into her cupped palms. "You can drink it."

Sarah follows Mandal's lead and takes a sip from the little pool she lifts in her hands. "Amazing." She stands and traces the four streams with her eyes, up the path to where they converge into a pond the color of fine wine that surrounds the building like a moat.

"Do they dye the water?" asks Sharon, taking her turn at a sip from the purple stream.

Kralo chuckles. "No. It just looks that way. It's the lighting."

Fresler shakes his head and reaches out to feel the magenta spray of one of the fountains flanking the walkway that will carry them over the lake. "Incredible. I've never seen anything like it."

"Where is everyone?" asks Karena, turning in a circle. Two people are taking the main path through the heart of downtown and one man sits on a bench nearby, but there is no hustle and bustle of a typical metropolis. "Is this a workday?"

"Every day is a workday on Sjel," says Kralo. "We don't have any shops or restaurants, as you do on Earth. That is why you won't see many people walking around."

"Every day is a workday?" Stephan shoots Sarah an exaggerated look of displeasure that makes her crack a smile.

Mandal nods. "Most of the people that work here don't come in until after noon, and they leave before six. Every five weeks, there is mandatory rest. You have to take six days off from work."

"Okay, I like that schedule," Stephan admits. "I could do that."

"The research center is up ahead," Reshal calls from the front of the pack. He leads their group a few blocks down the main road, leaving the capitol and its surrounding waterways behind. They round a bend in the path and a massive structure comes into view, its sharp, pointed top stabbing a cloud. It balances delicately over a thundering waterfall that wasn't visible from Reshal's side of town.

"Whoa." Stephan cricks his neck trying to take in the five hundred–story structure. Even from a distance, the spray from the waterfall chills his hands, and he shoves them in his pockets. When they get closer, he can see that the building actually juts over the water. He steps to the edge of the walkway and looks down. The waterfall crests over a second lip of stone before crashing into a river below.

"What a magnificent place to work," says Sarah. She lightly grips Stephan's sleeve as she approaches the edge, giving herself an anchor, and the touch warms Stephan's blood.

"Several structures on Sjel are built by or on top of water," says Mandal. "It is conducive to calm and productivity."

Sarah nods. "I read some studies about that effect on Earth."

"This is where all medical research is performed?" Stephan asks.

"Yes. This is where the first macrophage activator was created," says Mandal through a smile.

"It is also where the morphons were devised," says Kralo, far less cheery.

Fresler and Sharon exchange a cynical look.

"Is there a graviton research team?" Sarah asks.

Reshal smiles at her eagerness. "Anyone working on research on Sjel passes through this building. That would include scientists studying gravitons."

Sarah beams, and her hand drifts into her pocket, fingers working inside like she's rubbing a talisman.

Stephan leans in to whisper, "Did you bring your zip drive?"

"Just in case," she murmurs, blushing a little.

Mandal takes the lead as they enter the structure. "Before I was assigned to the space station," she explains, "I worked in this facility."

Inside, the walls are more white-gray marble. There isn't any furniture in the main lobby, but two statues frame the front desk. The plaques at their feet proclaim them as the creators of the macrophage. Stephan looks up at the female of the pair, slender and fairly young, although it's hard to tell with Sjelians. "Now that you have the macrophage, what other medical interventions do you need?" he asks. "It can cure anything, right?"

"Not quite," Mandal says. "We are working on a project involving *regeneration*."

Stephan chokes on his own spit. "You mean, growing body parts?"

"Yes. We have developed the capability to grow limbs, but not internal organs," says Mandal, serene as a summer sky.

"Incredible," Sarah murmurs.

"Did you have that capability on Nekses?" Karena asks Kesh, rhythmically patting Winnett's back as they walk.

"We did not," he says, looking impressed.

As they approach what looks like an elevator, they pass Sjelians dressed in robes with high collars and twisting embroidery on the hems.

"What's with the robes?" Fresler asks.

"It is a tradition that dates back millions of years," says Kralo. "Researchers and physicians on Sjel wear robes. It is a sign of their status."

"But you're not wearing a robe," says Stephan, gesturing at Mandal's brown slacks and turtleneck.

"I did when I worked here," she says. She slides her PAD over the elevator panel and a door slides open.

The elevator looks more like a small shuttle, with two rows of seats. With a push of a button, it zooms them to the top floor in seconds, making Stephan grip the armrests. Beside him, Karena clutches Winnett tighter with a little gasp.

"That was a rush," says Fresler, wind-disheveled hair trapped in his mouth. Sharon snorts out a laugh.

The door opens into a hallway with a window serving as

the left-hand wall. Side by side, Stephan and Sarah look out over the waterfall.

"I've never had a problem with heights, but this makes my stomach feel uneasy," admits Stephan.

"Yeah," says Sarah, taking a step back. "I know it's safe, but still..."

"If you'll follow me," Mandal says from behind them.

When they turn from the window, Stephan and Sarah see their Sjelian guides waiting patiently with hands folded behind their backs and identical placid expressions. Stephan still isn't used to the Sjelians' resting faces. The vacuous smiles are almost... horror movie material. He shudders, feeling guilty for making such an association about his brother-in-law's dear friends.

Sarah's face, by contrast, is expressive and open. The two of them trail after the group, staying shoulder to shoulder as they listen to Mandal's explanation of each area and project. Again and again, Stephan's eyes dart to the woman beside him. Again and again, he wonders if she feels the same spark he does. He hopes it isn't just him.

* * *

On a bench outside the research center, the tour group forces down a Sjelian food cube each for lunch to fortify them for the two-mile walk to Observation Pointe. The city's streets are perfectly level and smooth, and there's plenty to look at. Karena is spurred on by her eagerness to witness the geomagnetic explosion Reshal mentioned earlier. She walks between Kesh and Fresler, perfectly content to just listen as Sharon asks Reshal questions about the native plant life growing all over town. Every once in a while, she twists her head back to look at Sarah and Stephan, who have brought up the rear all day, clearly enjoying each other's company.

Observation Pointe comes into view long before they reach it. It twists gently toward the clouds, looking like a flower bud just before it blooms, the petals still loosely wrapped around the ovary of the plant. In true Sjelian fashion, a series of waterfalls cascades behind the building, thundering over three separate layers of rock that look too perfect to be natural.

Karena takes Kesh's hand as they approach the flat bridge that will take them across the body of water, fed by the falls, that surrounds the tower. "Beautiful, isn't it?"

Kesh nods, looking wistful. "We didn't have any structures like this on Nekses."

Karena can't help wondering if Ludvig ever got the chance to see something like this. Was his home planet a warm and welcoming place to live? Or was it a harsh, militarized wasteland? Did he leave behind family somewhere... loved ones who are still waiting for him? She'd thought she knew his childhood, understood his past. Now she wonders if she'll ever know the true history of the man she loved... or if she even wants to.

Kesh leans in to ask her softly, "Are you all right?"

"Yes," she says quickly. "Just have a lot on my mind."

Kesh's soft smile holds understanding, and she feels a flash of gratitude. To have such a kind, thoughtful person in her life, after suffering such a great loss... it's a blessing. She vows to try to enjoy his company and the novelty of being on Sjel while she can, instead of letting Ludvig's deception cast a heavy shadow.

Reshal leads the way across the water and through the building's main entrance. The silver walls glint in the recessed lighting, and a sitting area beckons from the corner, but Reshal bypasses it on his way to a large metal platform at the back. In its center, a square, digital screen is raised on a slender pedestal. Once everyone is on the platform, Reshal waves his PAD over the screen, and it takes the group to the second floor. They walk off the metal square into an auditorium, and Karena's jaw drops. The enormous holographic screen at the center of the sloped auditorium displays a view of Sjel from space. The blue-green planet rotates slowly, so realistic Karena feels she could reach out and touch it.

Beside her, Kesh grins with anticipation and scientific curiosity.

Reshal gestures to the seats. "There will be a showing in ten minutes."

Only a handful of people occupy the thousands of available seats, so the group has their pick.

Fresler shakes his head. "This is amazing. Why aren't there more people here?"

"Most Sjelians are at work," Reshal points out. "Let's sit in one of the balconies." He points upward to three levels of balconies, twinkling with recessed lights embedded in their guardrails.

They hurry up the stairs, and the lights dim as they take

their seats in the middle balcony, where they are level with the center of the holographic Sjel.

Fresler leans back in his mesh chair, holding hands with Sharon. He turns to Reshal, seated on his other side, and asks, "How often do you come here?"

"I've only been here twice before."

"If I lived here," says Karena, "I would visit this place every week."

Kesh nods. "Absolutely. Imagine if we'd been able to view the anomaly at this scale! What might we have learned?"

"How many showings do they have each day?" Stephan asks.

"One every hour," Reshal says proudly. "Each day, they feature something different. It could be a view of a star, an asteroid, a black hole eruption—it just depends on what the probes encounter."

"A black hole eruption?" asks Karena.

"Yes, five years ago…" The lights flicker on and off, and a horn noise blares from the holographic screen. The group goes silent, and in an instant, the screen resolves, disintegrating the cool-toned planet and reforming it as a giant ball of fire burning in the middle of the room.

"Amazing," says Karena, settling deeper into her seat to enjoy the show.

CHAPTER 14

December 21st, 2023

The next morning, half the group reunites in front of
the capitol, while Kralo, Mandal, Stephan, Sarah,
Kesh, Winnett, Fresler, and Sharon visit the Sjelian
museum. Theran leads the way through the center of the
looping waterways, across the bridge, and up the short steps
to the capitol's front doors.

"I haven't been here in thirty-nine years," he muses as
the doors slide open to admit him. "Reshal and Akril were
the only ones with me then, and the topic of the meeting
wasn't one I looked forward to."

Kayna, Erik, Aleria, Karena, and Reshal follow Theran
to the waiting room just outside the doors to the General
Council chamber—a white domed room that serves as both
the assembly hall and courtroom. They all take a seat and
wait to be escorted inside. The long rows of comfortable
chairs face the massive doors to the auditorium.

Karena is sharing her favorite sights from the tour

yesterday when Aleria senses a familiar, unpleasant presence. She turns to Erik. "I'll be back in a few minutes."

She lets instinct lead her to someone she has wanted to talk to for months—since the day her ability to inflict pain first manifested. Her feet carry her down the hallway to a row of offices. She stops in front of a door bearing Akril's name and title. She braces herself before entering.

Akril jerks at the sight of Aleria and leaps from her seat. She retreats a step, around the chair, and grips its mesh back, studying Aleria with wary eyes. "What are you doing here?"

"I'm sure you're aware that we are here to meet with the General Council," Aleria says. She can sense Akril's nerves, as well as a sharp, acidic tang of fear.

Akril glares at Aleria, her fury unsettling on her petite, childish features. "Yes, my mother informed me of your arrival. She also shared with me the contents of Theran's report." She points a finger at Aleria. "You have an ability to cause neurological pain telepathically! You were the reason I fell to the ground that day! You were the reason I was in excruciating pain!"

Aleria looks through the glass walls at the other offices, expecting shocked stares, but everyone has their heads down, too busy working to notice. "I am sorry for that."

"Sorry?!" Akril's slender chest bounces with short, quick breaths, and her cheeks flush bright red. "You violated a fundamental tenet by attacking me—a fellow crew member."

"I did, and as I said, I apologize." Aleria keeps her voice steady, even though her heart is racing.

"I plan to file a report. You are a danger to all Sjelians. I'll make sure you are banished from Sjel!"

"Akril, you don't seem to understand. If you read Theran's report, you know that the General Council is already aware that I used my ability on Sjelians. They are aware that I have violated a fundamental tenet. They are also aware that Reshal impregnated three women from Earth and that my father knew about this and did nothing. And yet..." Aleria breathes in deep, relishing the outraged expression on the other woman's face. "They are awarding us with a Commendation of Heroism, the highest honor a Sjelian can receive." She steps closer to Akril, who tightens her grip on her chair, positioning it like a shield. "Do you know why they won't prosecute us?"

Akril flares her nostrils but says nothing.

"They don't want the general population to discover the truth: that they knew about the anomaly and didn't disclose it. That they killed billions of humans for the purpose of relocation." Aleria clucks her tongue and offers a sympathetic frown. "You were complicit in those decisions. So... you go ahead and *file your report.*" She turns to walk out of Akril's office.

To her back, Akril shouts, "You and Emeran shouldn't be allowed to live here on Sjel! You both have Earth and Diastassian DNA. You are not full-blooded Sjelians."

"There was a time," Aleria says slowly, "when I actually cared what you thought. Now that I know who you really are... *your opinion doesn't matter.*"

Aleria can feel Akril's glare on the back of her head as she leaves the office, but she can also sense Akril's immense pride and self-assurance faltering.

When she's alone in the hallway, out of sight of everyone, Aleria sags against the wall. She's been anticipating that confrontation. Dreading it. But now that it's over, she feels... relieved. At peace. She can leave what happened with Akril in the past and move forward.

She checks the time and realizes she needs to hurry back to the others. Straightening her spine and brushing imaginary dirt from her clothing, she rushes to the auditorium. She turns the corner just as her group is approaching the large doors.

"Where were you?" Erik asks when she reaches his side.

"Talking to an old friend."

"Ah."

They move down the rows and take seats directly in front of the raised stage, illuminated by the orange moon glowing through the glass panel in the ceiling. A semi-circular white table with thirteen chairs and thirteen square screens looms over them.

One by one, the thirteen robed General Council members enter the chamber through a backstage door. Aleria feels animosity rolling in waves off a robed figure with icy blonde hair spilling from her hood. The woman pushes back the fabric to make her distaste better known, staring daggers at Aleria and Theran, and Aleria's suspicion is confirmed. It's Akril's mother, Fralin.

Beside her, Erik shifts uneasily. The hoods cast deep shadows over the other Council member's faces, obscuring any discernable features. The anonymity brings conspiracy theories and secret societies to the forefront of his mind. While they were waiting outside, Reshal explained that the white garb is a tradition dating back millions of years, but that doesn't make Erik any more comfortable.

Arwed, the lead Council member, pushes back his hood and nods to Theran, his visage smooth and statuesque, with prominent cheekbones and a distinguished, aquiline nose. "Thank you all for coming here today to meet with us," he says to open the session. "We are honored by your presence."

Theran inclines his head.

"We have read your report and are indebted to you and your crew for destroying the anomaly," continues Arwed. "The anomaly would have eventually reached our planet. By destroying it, you changed Sjel's destiny. In recognition of your acts of bravery, we would like to present you each with a Commendation of Heroism."

Theran stands. "I appreciate the gesture. However, we cannot accept."

Erik almost laughs but turns it into a cough as the stoic Sjelians of the Council gawk at each other, their rarely used cheek and forehead muscles twitching with the effort to emote.

Karena turns to Erik, wide-eyed, and mouths, "What?!"

Erik hadn't expected Theran's reaction either, but he shares the sentiment. If denying the commendation is an option, he'll take it. He knows Karena will too.

Reshal rises beside Theran. "I think I speak for my fellow crew members when I say it is difficult for us to accept anything from this General Council. We do not respect your decision to send morphons to Earth. Karena..." his sweeping hand lands on her shoulder, "...lost both her husband and mother to the morphons. This course of action was unforgivable."

Arwed looks over the group. "Do you share Reshal's sentiment?"

Erik, Aleria, Karena, and Kayna each nod.

Arwed sighs and lifts his nose in the air, wearing a put-upon expression. "I am sorry that you feel that way. We made the decision we thought was in the best interest of those on Earth and Sjel."

Reshal scoffs. "You mean those on Sjel, not on Earth."

"No... I mean Earth as well. Every living creature on

Earth would have perished if we did not intercede. This is not in dispute. There are currently over five hundred million humans still alive on the planet, not to mention flora and fauna."

Karena jumps to her feet. "No thanks to your General Council. If Reshal hadn't altered the morphons, there wouldn't have been a vaccine, and without a vaccine..." She cuts off the sentence with a low growl and crosses her arms.

"If you won't accept our commendation, why are you here?!" thunders Arwed. "Surely, it's not to argue with a decision we made decades ago."

"You're correct," says Theran, hands folded politely in front of his waist. "We are not here to criticize the Council's decision."

Arwed looks slightly mollified. "Then why accept the Council's invitation for an audience?"

"We are seeking answers."

Arwed rubs his jaw, as if all the gaping and shouting has strained it. "To what?"

"The signal tower that breached Earth's surface on July 2nd, 2016," Theran says crisply. "We believe you can tell us of its origins."

Arwed looks left and right at his fellows, his shoulders stiffening. "What makes you think that we are aware of its origins?"

"This Council has a history of... *non-disclosure*," says Reshal.

"The tower began transmitting on the same day that the anomaly destroyed the planet Opik," Karena says loudly. "That cannot be a coincidence."

Arwed's eyes follow Karena's gesticulations with a look of trepidation. "How did you discover the fate of Opik?" he asks, rubbing the pronounced bridge of his nose.

"When we were on the planet Tria, a Borjan woman named Sibula told me that it was destroyed on that date," Karena says. "Do you believe this is a coincidence?"

Arwed whispers something into the ear of the man sitting next to him. The man murmurs something in return, and Arwed nods. "No... it is not a coincidence," he says, studying Karena. "There is an identical tower on Sjel in our northern hemisphere, near the base of Mount Heon."

Erik sucks in a sharp breath, and Aleria squeezes his hand. Theran and Reshal exchange a look of astonishment. "Did this tower also breach the surface on July 2nd, 2016, Earth time?" asks Theran.

"It did," says Arwed, his baritone rumbling in the large, open room.

"Why didn't you tell me this when I briefed you about the appearance of the Earth tower back in 2016?" asks Theran, bristling. "For seven years, you've known—"

"Actually, our researchers learned of the tower's existence twenty-five thousand years ago."

"What?!" yelps Reshal.

"If it was buried beneath the surface, how was it detected?" asks Theran.

"Twenty-five thousand years ago, we discovered how to detect and quantify gravitons," Arwed says, sitting perfectly still. "We learned how to use these gravitons as a form of communication. A graviton signal was detected underground. Investigation revealed the buried tower."

Karena leans forward, ready to memorize every word and wishing Sarah was here to hear this for herself. She knows far more about gravitons than Karena does, despite Karena's Nobel Prize.

"Are you saying that this tower was sending signals *before* it breached the surface?" asks Reshal.

"Yes... we believe it has been since the day it was first placed here on Sjel," says Arwed.

"Placed here by whom?" Erik demands.

"We do not know," Arwed says. "But their technology is far superior to ours."

"Sending signals where?" asks Karena.

"To Earth."

Karena's eyes bulge. "Earth?"

"That is how we located your planet two thousand years ago," Arwed explains. "We sent probes in the direction of the graviton signal."

Karena thinks back to her conversation with Kesh, postulating how the Sjelians could have possibly located three human-occupied planets by sending random probes into the universe. Based on what Arwed is saying, there was nothing random about it... which means she was right. It *would* have been impossible.

"Earth's tower is receiving signals from Sjel's tower?" asks Erik, looking astonished.

"Yes," says Arwed. Around him, the other Council members are dead silent, their ghostly presence adding to the chill in the room.

"And the transmissions from Earth," Karena says. "Are they coming back here?"

"No," says Arwed. "Earth's tower is transmitting to a tower on the planet Phaelin."

"That is how we located Phaelin?" asks Theran.

"Yes. We followed the signal trail."

Theran squints at the moon, pondering. "That must mean that the tower on Sjel is receiving signals from Rajik?"

"Yes, that is how we located Rajik."

"Why did it take so long to locate Earth?" asks Aleria, still anchored to her seat by Erik's hand. "We discovered

Rajik twenty thousand years ago and Earth two thousand years ago."

"Until recently, our knowledge of gravitons was rudimentary at best. We were simply making an educated guess as to the locations of Earth and Rajik. Of the two planets, Rajik turned out to be much closer to Sjel, which narrowed the search perimeter."

Karena looks down the row of her friends and family. "Sibula told me that there were nine planets inhabited by humans." She pauses, expecting Arwed to confirm or deny Sibula's claim, but the Council leader only stares at her, waiting. "We now know of towers on Earth, Sjel, Phaelin, and Rajik. What if there was one on Opik?" She stops again, and still Arwed remains silent. So Karena continues theorizing. "What if... the towers are connected? What if the planets are... *tethered by these signals?*"

"Was there any change in the signal when the Sjelian tower surfaced?" Reshal asks.

Arwed nods. "When the tower on Sjel breached the surface, the signal's strength intensified, and it changed directions. It no longer transmits to Earth."

"Where is it broadcasting now?" asks Erik.

"We don't yet know. Perhaps to whomever built the towers," Arwed says.

"Was there a tower on Nekses?" Karena demands. "Is there one on Diastassi? On Tria?"

"Our researchers are hard at work following the new path of the graviton signals—" Arwed begins.

Karena is too deep down the rabbit hole to stop talking. "What if the Borjans built the towers? Utivos said they have been observing each of the nine planets for billions of years. Could the towers be monitoring devices?"

"We don't know—"

"And what about the planets we haven't found yet?" Ludvig's face flashes across Karena's mind. "How can we locate them if the tether is broken?" Her voice cracks as the hopelessness of it crashes down on her head, and Erik loops an arm around her. She leans her cheeks against his shoulder, finally stopping to take a ragged breath. After a beat, she feels a familiar tug in her gut and looks at Theran. "We need to return to Tria. I'm sure Utivos and Sibula can tell us what we need to know." The words come without thought, pulled free by her intuitive ability.

Theran accepts Karena's statement without argument. Her intuition has not yet led them astray. "I believe we should leave immediately," he tells Arwed.

Arwed holds up a hand, signaling them to wait. He and his fellow Council members rotate their chairs to huddle together, mumbling in private. Arwed is the first to turn back around. "Permission granted."

* * *

Later that day, after everyone has returned to the Sjelian vessel, Erik goes in search of Stephan. Finding his room empty, Erik heads for the Setustofa room. He searches the lounge for one red head but finds two. Stephan sits with Sarah in a quiet corner where the walls are painted to look like a beach. They lean toward each other over the arms of their chairs, laughing at a shared joke. Erik smiles at the sight.

"Hi, Sarah... Stephan," says Erik when he's still a few feet away.

Stephan jolts upright in his seat. Sarah nods at Erik with a smile.

"Sorry to interrupt, but can I have a minute?" Erik asks.

"Sure," says Stephan. "Do I need another round of Slak for this conversation?" He wiggles his cup.

Erik snorts. "I don't know. How many have you had?"

Stephan shrugs. "Who cares—there isn't any alcohol in it, right?"

"True." Erik chuckles, thinking of Aleria's face when he'd unwittingly compared the drink to alcohol all those years ago. "So, I wanted to ask you—"

"I'll leave you two alone," Sarah says, starting to stand.

"Actually," Erik says, "you should be here for this. It concerns you too."

"Oh." Sarah looks pleasantly surprised. "Okay."

"What's up?" Stephan asks.

"The Sjelian General Council has granted us permission to return to the planet Tria."

Stephan's eyebrows draw together. "What? I thought we were staying on Sjel for a while, then going back to Earth."

"We have new information about the signal towers."

Sarah leans forward an inch. "Towers, plural?" Erik catches the excitement sparking in her pupils, though she keeps it out of her voice.

"Yes," Erik confirms. "The Council leader told us there is also a tower on Sjel. Up until 2016, it was sending a signal to the tower on Earth. The Earth tower was signaling the planet Phaelin."

Sarah's eyes are like saucers. "Incredible."

"Yes, but in 2016, when the towers breached the surface, the signal changed. Now we don't know where the transmissions are going."

"So, we need to go to Tria to find that out?" Stephan guesses.

Erik nods. "Do you remember when I told you that there are... *were*... nine planets inhabited by humans? Our new theory is that all nine have the same tower, and that they each send and receive graviton signals. They are all connected somehow. It is possible that the Borjans built them."

"Why?" Sarah asks.

"Possibly to monitor the planets... we don't know. But hopefully Utivos or Sibula can provide some answers."

Sarah blurts, "Can I join you?"

"Of course. I was hoping you would. You know more about the tower on Earth than any of us." Erik turns to his brother-in-law. "I know the original plan was for you to go back to Earth after Sjel, but... since our time here was cut short, will you come along to Tria, instead?"

Slowly, Stephan nods. "Yes, I'll come along."

Erik can't help but notice that Stephan's eyes dart over to Sarah as he says it.

"If there's a tower on Tria," Sarah says excitedly, "maybe I can compare the signals to those I measured on Earth." She smacks her forehead. "I wish I could have brought one of those hand-held devices from 1969. Though I guess that would have meant stealing from the U.S. government..."

"Are you talking about the sensors used by the trackers from Diastassi?" Erik asks.

"Yes, I was just telling Kayna how the devices powered on in proximity to the tower. She said they were used to track her ability, but clearly they also sensed gravitons." Sarah stops to think. "How could they track both Kayna's electromagnetic signal and the graviton signal from the tower? Do you think those... Borjans..." Her tongue tangles around the unfamiliar word. "Do you think they'll be able to tell us?"

Erik smiles, both at her enthusiasm and at how much Stephan seems to enjoy watching Sarah gush about gravitons. "I hope so," he says. "The Borjans have been monitoring the nine planets for billions of years, so I bet they know... *something.*"

Whether they'll be willing to share their secrets is another issue entirely.

CHAPTER 15

Tria — January 11th, 2024

Stephan and Sarah bounce experimentally on the spongy, navy-blue earth. Erik makes a beeline for one of the orange, shrub-like plants and plucks two of the fat, pink fruits dangling within its fronds—a favorite sweet treat Aleria discovered on their last visit. He shares a morsel with everyone as they climb the short hill separating them from the Neksesian town. At the summit, Sarah and Stephan "ooh" and "aah" over the green ocean and glittering black sand.

Erik pats his friend on the back and says, "I told you."

"You didn't do it justice," says Stephan.

"The sky is incredible," says Sarah.

"And the air..." Stephan takes in a deep breath. "After three weeks cooped up on that space vessel, it's so... fresh."

The two of them start down the hill after Theran, chatting away. Erik watches them go. This is how it's been for the past three weeks. When Stephan hasn't been shadowing Mandal in the medical clinic and Sarah hasn't been learning from Kralo in engineering, the two of them have been glued at the hip.

"They sure do spend a lot of time together," Erik says, strolling between Karena and Aleria.

"It's sweet," says Karena. She eyes him more closely and pokes his ribs. "Are you jealous he's spending so much time with her?"

"Of course not. It's just that... the entire time I've known him, he's only been out on a handful of dates. It's odd, I guess."

Karena snorts.

Erik returns her poke. "Fine, maybe I was envisioning the two of us hanging out, making up for the time I was away... but I'm happy for him, I swear."

Karena's face softens. "I know you are."

"Never mind me," Erik says. "How are *you* feeling, knowing we might be about to get more answers about the other planets in the tether?"

Karena surveys the scenery, her expression tightening. "Hopeful. But also... not confident. The Borjans have withheld information from us before. And who's to say they even built the towers?"

Erik throws his hands in the air. "They have been monitoring all nine planets for billions of years, so they must know *something*."

"I certainly hope so," says Aleria from his other side.

"There's only one way to find out," Erik says, crooking his arms to help Karena and Aleria down the slope toward the domed huts that house the refugees taken in by the Borjans.

As they pass through the Neksesian village, Kesh taps Karena's arm. "I want to visit my parents, if that's okay."

"Of course."

"Come find me when you've finished your meeting with the Borjans. I hope what you learn is... useful."

Karena gives him a quick embrace.

Kesh adjusts course toward his parents' bamboo home in the distance, waving goodbye to the others.

Fresler holds hands with Sharon as he watches him go. The blue spongy turf puts an extra spring in his step. "This never gets old. I love this ground cover."

"I love this planet," says Sharon.

"As much as I would love to be back on Earth with my parents... you're much more important, and I love this place too."

Sharon smiles wide and hops to kiss Fresler on the cheek.

The group makes their way through the village to the stately, metallic blue capitol building.

As they climb the steps, Reshal gestures to the statues that run along the front of the building. "Clearly, this one represents Sjel." He points to a figure in a hooded robe.

Stephan makes his way to a statue of a short, balding man wearing a suit. "This must be Earth."

Sarah chuckles. "Seriously?"

Before Theran can knock on the massive doors, they creak open to reveal Utivos. He is almost as white as the walls of the Sjelian space station. His droopy, elongated features might make him look like a caricature of a wise old wizard if not for his complete lack of hair. The man doesn't even have eyelashes, much less a beard. "We've been expecting you. Please... come in."

They walk through the vaulted room and take seats at the long glass table where they celebrated the destruction of the anomaly.

Stephan and Sarah whisper to each other, craning their

necks to study the ceiling twenty feet above. Sibula enters silently as a wraith, appraising them all with her murky gray eyes. When she pulls out her chair, Stephan jumps.

"That's the woman in black I was telling you about," Erik whispers to Stephan. Now, however, she is not veiled and is garbed in blue. Though her face is wizened, her black hair is still silky, shiny, and free of grays—stark against her ghostly skin.

Stephan nods as he watches her take a seat next to Utivos.

Utivos turns to Theran and Kayna. "It's good to see you again. Wasn't your original plan to stay on Sjel for a few more weeks?"

"It was," says Theran.

"Then what brings you back to us so soon?" Utivos asks.

"We have questions, and we believe you have answers."

Erik holds his breath, grateful Theran is getting right down to business.

Utivos shares an unreadable look with Sibula. "Questions about what?" he asks Theran.

"We've learned of a series of communication towers linking the planets occupied by humans. This woman—" Theran indicates Sarah, who jolts, surprised to be acknowledged, "—studied the tower on Earth. The Sjelian General Council revealed that there is a similar tower on Sjel, and that the signals it was giving off and receiving led them to find Earth, Phaelin, and Rajik. These towers have been producing graviton signals for thousands of years. Is there such a tower on Tria?"

Utivos nods. "There is."

"Is there a tower on each of the nine planets?" asks Reshal.

"Yes."

"All the towers we know of were buried underground and breached the surface on July 2nd, 2016," says Theran, "the same day that Opik was destroyed by the anomaly. They are no longer sending signals to each other. They are now directed to a common location." He leans in, resting his forearms on the table as he stares down Utivos. "Is it this planet?"

"No."

The word rings through the room, and Erik's shoulders droop. He was convinced that the signals were directed at Tria. Theran looks almost as shocked.

"Then where? Are the transmissions going to Borjan?" asks Erik.

"No, not Borjan," says Utivos, his long earlobes swaying as he shakes his head. "The signal is directed to the people that created the towers."

"That wasn't your people?" asks Erik. "The towers aren't how the Borjans monitor the nine planets?"

Utivos scoffs. "No, we don't need the towers for monitoring. We didn't build them."

"Then who did... and why?" demands Karena.

"I'm sorry. I can't answer that question."

"You mean you *won't* answer," says Reshal.

Utivos doesn't deny it. "You must speak to Borjan's leader, Manerk."

"We have to go to Borjan?!" Erik exclaims, feeling like he's being sent on a wild goose chase.

"Yes."

"How can we possibly visit Borjan?" Kralo asks. "Isn't it in the same dimension as Diastassi? That portal was destroyed, along with the anomaly."

"That portal was not the only way to pass between dimensions," Utivos says, a hint of condescension in his voice. "Our people created a portal millions of years ago. Sibula will travel with you as your guide."

"How can we be certain that Manerk will allow us to land on the surface of Borjan?" asks Theran, no doubt thinking of the conflict-filled trips to Phaelin and Diastassi.

"Manerk wants to meet the hybrids..." says Utivos, milky blue eyes passing over Aleria, Erik, Fresler, and Karena before settling on the baby in her lap. *"Especially Winnett."*

Erik's jaw tightens. He watches Karena shift into Mama Bear mode and hug her son to her chest.

"Why Winnett?" she asks, voice hard as steel.

Utivos turns to Sibula, ignoring the tension in the room. "You will help them locate the portal."

Sibula nods. "We will leave tomorrow."

"Tomorrow," repeats Theran.

Utivos dismisses them without much ceremony, but Theran looks pleased with how the conversation went. Erik, however, mutters in Fresler's ear, "We need to talk."

"Definitely," says Fresler, tapping on Karena's arm and motioning for her to follow.

While the others head down to the black beach to relax, the half-siblings and Aleria wander among the Neksesian huts, looking for a quiet place to debrief.

When they find an unoccupied street corner with a bench tucked away in a patch of overgrown shrubbery, Erik turns to Aleria. "Was Utivos lying? Did the Borjans create the towers to monitor the nine planets?"

"I didn't sense deception," Aleria says, "but he is definitely holding something back."

Fresler scoffs. "What else is new?"

"Do you think Winnett is in danger?" Karena asks, eyes flashing with pent-up anger.

"I don't think so," Aleria says sympathetically, one

mother to another. "I did not get the sense that Utivos means for harm to come to your son."

"Good," Karena says fiercely. "Because... we need to go to Borjan."

Erik recognizes that feverish, bright-eyed look. "Is this your ability talking?"

"Yes..."

Erik exhales sharply. "So, you are going with us?"

"It sounds like I have no choice." Karena's half-smile is uneasy. "Utivos said their leader will only allow us to land if I bring Winnett."

"Is this because of the..." Fresler waves a hand in the baby's direction, "... five DNA strands thing?"

"It must be," Aleria says. "If the Borjans are interested in hybrids, then they would definitely want to see Winnett."

Karena stares into her son's eyes. "I won't let anything happen to you," she murmurs.

"None of us will," Fresler vows.

"We'll keep you safe," Erik adds.

The two men step forward to hug Karena, wrapping her and her child with love.

The familial embrace is interrupted by a throat clearing behind them. They break apart to see Sibula standing nearby, watching them with an odd expression on her long, pale face. "Karena," she says. "May I speak with you?"

"Of course. I had a question for you anyway." Karena turns to her brothers and Aleria. "I'll find you at the beach?"

"Okay," Erik says. The three of them walk away, leaving Karena alone with Sibula... that feverish, intuitive spark alight.

* * *

Stephan marvels at the beautiful green ocean, tinted blueish near the horizon by the setting pink-yellow sun. "This is amazing."

"I could get used to this," agrees Sarah, her arm brushing his as she steps closer to the gently lapping water.

Theran, Reshal, and Kayna sit in the dry sand further from the shoreline, talking about their plans for tomorrow. When Fresler, Aleria, and Erik arrive, they find Sharon searching for purple shells in the water, her pants rolled up to her knees.

"Where's Karena?" Sharon asks.

"She's talking to Sibula. Where's Kralo?" Erik asks.

Sharon points right, where Kralo and Mandal are strolling along the waterline, hand in hand.

"Are you ready for another adventure?" Erik asks.

Everyone bobs their head except Aleria, who says, "No."

Stephan and Sarah approach, standing shoulder to shoulder and laughing at a shared joke. Erik smiles as he closes the distance.

"Hey, Stephan." Erik waves an arm at the horizon. "What do you think of Tria?"

"It's beautiful." Stephan pauses, looking a little worried. "Do you think Borjan will be like this?"

Erik lets out a relieved breath. "Does that mean you're planning to come with us tomorrow?"

"If I can't go back to Earth, I'm going where you're going." Stephan claps Erik on the shoulder with more gusto than his anxious face suggests.

"What about you?" Erik asks Sarah, pretty certain he already knows the answer.

Sure enough, Sarah looks giddy. "I have been thinking about that tower in Wisconsin for seven and a half years. I am not passing up the chance to solve that mystery, once and for all. Never mind the opportunity to travel into another dimension..." She clasps her hands in front of her chest like she's praying. "I can't wait."

Stephan's gaze wanders over Sarah, and the trepidation in his face dissolves into a moony smile.

* * *

Karena tucks the final fold of Winnett's swaddle under his back and strokes his velvet cheek with a finger. The Trian guest hut's crib looks enormous with him inside. Tiptoeing, she leaves him to snooze, but the hut has no doors to close him safely inside. She'll have to keep her interrogation quiet.

Sibula waits in a chair, and Karena stalks toward her, with no desire for small talk or niceties. "I need a sample of your blood," she whispers, arms crossed.

"That won't be necessary," the Borjan woman replies.

Karena can't help letting out a groan of frustration. "I know you and Utivos like your secrets, but—"

"You don't need my blood," Sibula says, "I am prepared to tell you what you want to know."

That stops Karena in her tracks. "You... are?" She narrows her eyes, trying to intuit if this is a trick. "About what?"

"About Ludvig."

At her late husband's name, Karena's legs give out. She sags into the remaining chair.

"You must have discovered Ludvig is not from Earth." Sibula asks.

"Yes, he has Diastassian DNA and two unknown strands."

"The other strands are Tempian... and Borjan."

Karena rocks back in her seat as though struck. "Borjan," she repeats, "and... Tempian. Is that one of the nine planets?"

Sibula looks down at her sandals. "No."

"How do you know all of this?!" Karena yelps.

Sibula puts a hand to her chest. "He was *my son*."

Karena's lungs constrict. "Your son," she manages to wheeze. "Which makes Winnett..."

"My grandson, yes." Sibula looks toward the door that hides the sleeping infant with a sudden fondness. Then she turns back to Karena, who is gaping like a fish.

After a beat, Karena manages to spit out, "Did you know who Winnett was... who I was... when we first showed up here?"

"Yes, of course."

"Why didn't you *say anything?*" Karena demands.

Sibula's eyes grow teary. "I was ashamed."

Karena sees red. "*Ashamed?!*

"Diastassians and Borjans are forbidden to integrate... to be together, and to have offspring. It is considered blasphemy. My father, who was Diastassian, was living on Borjan as part of a diplomatic mission. He had a secret love affair with my mother. I was the result."

"You're a hybrid."

Sibula nods, eyes downcast, like a child accustomed to harsh scolding. The sight pulls at Karena's mother heart, despite her irritation.

"When did you find out? Did everyone know?"

"I always knew... my mother told me. But it wasn't until I used my ability for the first time that everyone else discovered the truth. Borjans are not known for their ability to see the future."

"How old were you?"

"A young adult. I was living on Borjan with my life partner, Utivos." Sibula smiles at the thought. She gathers
herself before saying in a rush, "I had a vision that hundreds
of Borjans would perish. A vessel carrying men, women,
and children would crash due to a solar flare. I felt like I had
no choice but to warn our leader. Utivos pleaded with me.
He said that if I told them, they would discover the truth
about me, but I felt like I had no choice."

"What happened?" asks Karena.

"I warned our leader. She of course didn't believe me...
until the vessel crashed from the solar flare. Then she knew
that I had an ability unlike anyone on Borjan. That is when
they tested my DNA. When the truth was revealed, I was
banished."

"So... it wasn't because you acted on your vision?"
Karena clarifies, remembering their first conversation two
and a half months ago.

Her droopy earlobes shake along with her head. "I was
banished because I was a product of blasphemy. I felt such
shame. I could no longer live on Borjan. Utivos had a choice,
and... he chose to live with me on Tria." Sibula blots away a
tear with the sleeve of her robe.

"What about your parents?"

"They were imprisoned on Borjan. Isolated. Eventually...
they chose to take their own lives."

Karena sucks in a gasp. "I'm so sorry." She shakes her
head. "This makes no sense. They imprisoned your parents
and banished you just because a Diastassian and a Borjan
had a child? That is... *unbelievable.*"

"It is our way of life. Our sacred beliefs."

"So, your ability comes from being a hybrid?"

"Yes. And Erik's escape from the anomaly was not my

only premonition regarding Earth." Sibula takes in a breath, as if gathering her courage. "I saw your car accident."

Karena grips the arms of her chair. "And you sent Ludvig to save me."

"Yes. Ludvig was born with Diastassian and Tempian features." Sibula gestures at her own face. "I knew he would fit in among Earth's humans."

"Tempian," Karena says, recalling the third DNA strand. "Is Utivos also a hybrid? Is that where the Tempian DNA comes from?"

"No, Utivos is only Borjan. Tempians are... another subspecies of humans that also live on Borjan. There must have been an intermarriage in my family. It is of no consequence."

Karena thinks otherwise. Everything about this conversation has incredible consequence for her and for her child. But she moves on to her next question. "Did you know, when you sent Ludvig to rescue me, that I would be the mother of your grandchild?"

"Yes, and that he would be the key to saving the human race."

"Winnett... is the key to saving the human race?"

"Yes."

Karena's breath catches, and she looks through the bedroom doorway with an instinctive urge to clutch her son's crib. "When you sent Ludvig to Earth, did you know that he would die there?"

"Yes. I knew that he would never return to us. By sending him to Earth, I would lose him forever."

Karena stares at her child. She watches his tiny chest rise and fall, rise and fall. "I don't think I could make that same decision. To sacrifice my son, to save the human race."

"Let's hope you don't have to make the same decision someday."

CHAPTER 16

Borjan — January 18th, 2024

By the time Erik and Aleria answer Theran's call and enter the control room, the others are already gathered. Borjan's atmosphere fills the viewing screen with hues of orange and burgundy. The setting sun gives way to a moon that dominates the horizon, its umber form spotted with deep green craters. Displayed on the smaller screens embedded in the control panel are two Borjan vessels, flanked on each side, escorting them to the surface. The black skyscrapers of the capital city look like stacked children's blocks—square levels with rounded corners sitting atop each other from widest to narrowest. The uniform streets create a grid, with waterways filling the spaces between the lines.

"The moon..." says Fresler. "It looks like you could reach out and touch it."

Sharon bobs her head, speechless.

Erik knows the feeling. No matter how many new planets he visits—five now, in total—the sensation never dulls. The exploration, the magnitude of the universe and the discoveries waiting to be made within it, still blow him away. But as he drinks in this new place, his usual awe is tinged with the restlessness that's grown the last six days, as they hurdled through space, aided by the Borjans' secret cross-dimensional gateway. Whatever this Manerk person has to say could affect them all... but in what way? The unknown breeds unease.

Theran is convinced that uncovering the truth about the signal towers will be game-changing. If it weren't, Utivos would have simply told them what they wanted to know on Tria. Erik is inclined to agree. After all, the last time Utivos withheld crucial information, they found Kayna on Diastassi and Aleria discovered true strength of her ability to inflict pain.

What surprise reveal awaits them here?

Sibula disrupts his thoughts when she points out the tallest building on the left. "That is the capitol building. We will be landing on the rooftop."

"Will we need new translators?" Stephan asks, fiddling with the earpiece he was given when he first set foot on the Sjelian space station a little over a month ago.

"No," Sibula answers before Kralo can open his mouth. "Our technology will automatically adapt to your spoken and written languages of choice."

"Great!" Sarah says. "I'd hate to be left out of the conversation."

They land with ease and disembark in a chaotic flock. Theran and Sibula take the lead, approaching the towering man waiting for them by the rooftop door. He is clothed in a floor-length gown similar to the Neksesians' typical attire, with gold trimming and embroidered symbols on the white cloth, but the wide hood shading the man's face looks more like the Sjelian Council's garb.

The man bows his head to Theran but keeps his hands tucked inside his fat gown sleeves. The skin of his face is the same chalky white as Sibula's, and his nose and jowls droop with excess skin.

"Sibula..." the man drawls.

She returns his bow with one of her own. "Janum."

Without another word, Janum turns and enters the charcoal building, leading them down a dark stairwell into a pristine hallway lined with windows. The gray walls are free of decoration. There is not a fleck of dust on the glass nor a speck of dirt on the beige marble floor.

He leads them into a large auditorium that should seat

thousands, but at the moment is completely empty. Janum gestures to the chairs, which look like black leather recliners. In front of the auditorium floats a holographic image of Borjan, towering over two hundred feet high.

As the group gets settled in the first two rows, Karena has déjà vu back to the observatory on Sjel. Winnett sits on her lap, his head bobbing a bit as his neck struggles to hold its weight. He struggles until she turns him to face him, and then he smiles, gazing unwaveringly into her eyes. She kisses his cheek and bounces him on her knee, supporting his head, now covered in super-fine peach fuzz. Kesh tickles Winnett under the chin, but the baby doesn't pull his gaze from Karena.

She wonders what he's thinking... if a three-month-old is capable of thoughts far beyond *hungry, tired, ouch,* and *Mama.* She suspects that *her* three-month-old already has a rich inner life.

She's lain awake at night since departing Tria, mapping out the possibilities. She, Winnett's mother, has enhanced intuition. Sibula, his grandmother, has prophetic visions. And those are just the abilities in his direct line of inheritance. What if his five DNA strands have come together to produce something completely new? Can he read minds, like Telfas? Or is that strictly a Neksesian trait?

She wants to ask Kesh, but she has yet to tell any of her friends or family members what Sibula told her... about Ludvig being Sibula's son, or about Winnett being the key to humanity's salvation. It's just... too much. She wouldn't know where to begin.

But on the off chance her son can read her mind, she stares into his eyes and thinks, *I love you so much.*

"What is the purpose of this place?" Theran asks Sibula,

who stands in the aisle waiting for Manerk to enter the auditorium.

"Our government leaders hold presentations here for the general public," Sibula says, eyes on the door.

"Are we meeting anyone besides Manerk?" asks Kayna.

"No." She blinks at the group, comfortably seated. "Can you please stand? It is a sign of respect."

Theran nods and gestures for the group to stand.

Fresler reaches for Sharon's hand.

"Are you nervous?" asks Sharon.

"Yeah... a little," Fresler admits. Though he and Sharon are rarely in the thick of the action on the space vessel, it would be impossible not to have sensed the rising tension over the past few days.

The door at the back whooshes open, and everyone turns their heads. A robed woman makes her way down the aisle at a dignified, unhurried pace. White-gold hair spills from her hood, but her face is concealed until she draws level with the group. She tips up her chin, and the hood falls back an inch to reveal a ghostly face that looks fairly young... at least compared to Sibula and Utivos.

"Sibula," the woman says in a breathy voice.

Sibula nods and says, "Manerk."

Erik whispers to Aleria, "I thought their leader would be a man."

Aleria elbows his ribs. "Really?"

He shrugs. "Maybe it's the name."

Sibula sits next to Theran, and the others follow her lead, returning to their seats.

Manerk remains standing, head cocked as her eyes find Karena holding Winnett. She smiles, flashing horsey teeth, and glides down the row. She looms over Karena, spindly fingers sliding out from her gown sleeve and reaching for the baby's cheek. "Winnett..."

Karena jerks back reflexively, but Winnett turns his head as if drawn to the Borjan woman.

"Truly amazing," Manerk croons, locked in a staring contest with the three-month-old.

Karena clutches her infant closer to her chest.

Manerk straightens and steps back. She returns to the aisle and walks down to the floor of the auditorium, standing between the group and the large holographic screen. "Utivos informed me that you are seeking answers about the origin of the communication towers." She raises an arm and enters a command in the bottom corner of the holographic screen, which lights up green at her touch. In an instant, the image of the planet Borjan resolves into nine separate planets. "The communication towers were placed on each of these nine planets."

Erik's eyes jump from globe to globe. Earth's continents and oceans are easily recognizable, as is Sjel's now-somewhat-familiar lush landscape. He spots Tria's navy blue ground cover, green oceans, and black sand. Phaelin is dark gray and foreboding. Nekses is displayed as it looked just before the anomaly destroyed it: dusty, rusty red.

There are four planets Erik can't identify until their names appear beneath them, written in unfamiliar characters that resolve, before his eyes, into letters of the English alphabet.

Opik. Rajik. Polemos. Des.

"Why aren't Borjan and Diastassi included here?" asks Theran, over the group's confused murmurs.

"There are no towers on this planet or on Diastassi," Manerk says.

"The nine tethered planets are all in our dimension?" asks Karena.

"That is correct." Manerk waves her hand. A white line shoots between the nine planets, connecting the dots. "Before the anomaly destroyed Opik," she says, "each of these planets was both sending and receiving a message. The signal traveled from Opik to Tria, then to Polemos, to Des, to Rajik, to Sjel, to Earth, to Phaelin, to Nekses, and finally, back to Opik. When Opik was destroyed, the tether was broken. That is when the towers surfaced and started sending messages every five days."

"Where do those new transmissions go?" asks Theran.

"To the creators of the communication towers."

Erik groans loudly. More vague answers.

"Why?" asks Aleria, side-eying Erik disapprovingly.

"We believe that the new transmission was intended to inform the creators that one of the nine planets had been destroyed."

"Did anything change when Nekses was destroyed last year?" Karena asks, casting a glance at Kesh. He's paled to a strawberry color, as he often does when his lost planet is discussed in his presence.

Manerk nods to acknowledge the question. "There was no change that we were able to measure."

Sarah speaks up for the first time, confirming, "Our data on Earth remained stable before and after October 10th, 2023."

The Borjan leader is polite enough not to point out the vast difference between Earth and Borjan technology. She merely adds, "This suggests that once the tether was broken in 2016, there was no need to signal an additional planetary loss in 2023. That said, if there is a more detailed message hidden within the transmissions, we have not been able to decipher it."

"These tethered planets are obviously important to whoever built the towers," Theran says. "Did they seed them? Are we all descendants of these... creators?"

"No. To learn more about our shared origins, there is somewhere else you must go."

"Where?" asks Kayna.

Manerk points to the planet labeled "Des," floating in space between Rajik and Polemos. "You will find the answers you seek on Des."

"Why can't you just tell us?" complains Reshal. "Why make us travel to Des?"

Manerk sighs and stuffs her hands back in her sleeves. "You need to learn the truth from the source."

"The source," Erik repeats, staring skeptically at the image of Des.

"I should warn you..." Manerk says. "You won't like the answers."

Reshal stands up, saying, "But—"

Manerk silences him with a raised hand. She pulls a square electronic device from her sleeve, hands it to Sibula, and then walks up the aisle and out of the auditorium without another word.

Reshal rounds on Sibula. "She just left? How are we supposed to find Des?"

Sibula scans her thumb on the electronic device's screen. It whirs to life, giving off a faint light. She flashes a grim smile. "With this."

Sibula follows Manerk's path out of the auditorium, the rest of the group on her heels. Theran rushes to walk beside her. "How long will it take us to reach Des?"

"Five days to return to the interdimensional portal. Then, three days to Des."

Theran absorbs that information and then asks, "Manerk knows who built the towers and why... doesn't she?"

"She does."

"Do *you* know?"

"I do."

From Sibula's other side, Reshal lets out a frustrated sound. "Then why do we have to—"

"As Manerk said, you must learn the whole story from the source."

"But..." Erik steps closer behind them, eavesdropping. "Why come to Borjan at all?"

Sibula stops so suddenly that Theran and Reshal end up a few steps ahead and have to backtrack. "Manerk wanted to meet Winnett. She needed to communicate with him."

"What?" Karena clutches Winnett.

"How could she communicate with him? He's just a baby," says Kayna, face tense with trepidation.

"He is capable of much more than you could ever imagine." Sibula gives Karena a keen look. Karena is the first to look away. "Manerk believes Winnett is the key," Sibula goes on.

"The key to what?" asks Fresler.

"Human survival."

Sarah's eyes go wide. "Survival? Are we in danger?"

Theran studies Sibula's face, which remains as closed-off as ever. "I have a feeling," he says, "that we'll find the answer to that question on Des."

CHAPTER 17

Des — January 26th, 2024

The control panel lets out an aggravated series of beeps, a red message flashing in Sjelian.

"What does that mean?" Erik asks Kralo.

The lead engineer frowns at his controls. "The vessel's sensors detect no life on Des."

Erik throws up his hands. "How are we supposed to get answers if no one lives here?"

"Maybe the answers are there," says Kralo, pointing to the screen, where three silver structures glint beneath the red sun.

"Try the scan again," orders Theran.

Kralo obeys, making the screen in the panel blink. More angry beeps. Another negative result.

On the cameras, a thick, hazy substance obscures visibility. It blows in the heavy wind, like fine sand stirred into a cloud... or odd orange fog. Three moons of varying sizes hang in the russet sky, but the sun that lights them doesn't penetrate the strange ground cover.

Kralo pilots the ship toward the silver buildings—the only suitable targets in sight. The domed structures look like giant trashcan lids lying half-buried in the orange sand clouds. Unsure how stable the ground is... or where it is exactly... Kralo pilots the vessel to the central building and lands as close as he possibly can.

"There's not enough oxygen to support human life," says Kralo, reading his sensor data.

Reshal directs everyone to a cabinet built into the wall and distributes clear plastic oxygen masks. Sibula leads the exodus from the shuttle and marches toward the building's entrance without a backward glance. She inserts the electronic device that Manerk gave her into a square-shaped hole on the door's lock panel and scans her thumb. The panel flashes blue. When she removes the device, the door opens, revealing a circular room equipped with a single round table and a clear, rectangular screen attached to the far wall. When Sibula's feet cross the threshold, lights flicker on and a panel on the table illuminates. Sibula reads the

instructions on her device and enters something into
the panel.

The wall-mounted screen comes to life, offering an
image labeled "The planet Des." The blue orb looks nothing
like the current barren, red planet. As the camera zooms in,
the landscape fills with greenery. White buildings appear,
tall, spiraling, and majestic, like the Sjelian research center.

Erik reaches for Aleria's hand. Sharon leans against
Fresler. Stephan and Sarah gawk at yet another strange new
setting. Kralo and Mandal slowly take seats at the table, as
does Karena, who shushes Winnett when he lets out a soft
cry, bouncing him while Kesh rubs his little back. Kayna
stands beside her life partner, sensing both his uncertainty
at how to proceed and his distaste for the feeling.

Sibula turns to Theran. "I can program this for any
language. What should I use?"

Theran takes stock of the group. "English."

Sibula nods and enters the command.

Immediately, a woman's voice blares out of unseen
speakers. "This is an image of our planet, Des, as it looked
three billion years ago. We Desians were a peaceful race,
made up of ten distinct human subspecies. Seven of these
subspecies died out long before we developed the technology to travel beyond our solar system, but we kept DNA
samples of those we lost."

Erik and Aleria look at each other, and Erik coaxes her
toward the table. The others left standing follow their lead,
settling into chairs to view the film. The seats recline,
making the whole situation feel oddly like a high-dollar
movie theater.

"We eventually learned how to control gravitons," the
voiceover continues, "which led to the discovery of a
communication tower buried below the surface of Des.

With our new ability to track the signals that were emanating from the tower, we located the planet Polemos— another planet capable of supporting human life, with the perfect balance of oxygen and nitrogen. Using the towers' signals, we eventually located seven more planets. The last planet we discovered had a single, small outpost inhabited by an alien race."

The image of Des dissolves to reform as the green ocean and black sands of Tria.

"These aliens were intelligent life forms, far different from us. We attempted to communicate with them, but we were unsuccessful."

As the audience shifts in their seats, the voiceover adopts an ominous tone, like the trailer for a Nineties horror film, re-enforcing the odd sensation of a dark theater room. Erik can almost smell the popcorn.

"Shortly after we attempted to make contact, our vessel was attacked. We defended ourselves. In the process, we destroyed their vessel... and killed all twenty of the aliens living on the planet.

"Later, after fleeing home to Des, we learned that prior to the attack, the aliens had successfully transmitted a message from Tria. As a result, the towers on all nine planets had breached the surface and were directing a signal to the aliens' home planet. We feared that the aliens would send a scouting party to check on their outpost. They would then discover its destruction... and perhaps find evidence to lead them to our planet."

Fresler holds his breath. He feels like he's reached the climax of an epic sci-fi novel. He wants to turn the page, but dread stays his hand. But this is an audio book, and the story continues without his say.

"We were right to have been concerned," the voice

intones. "Fifteen years after the Trian incident, the aliens returned... with an armada."

The screen shifts again, the camera pulling back to show Tria from space. Alien vessels swarm the globe like a pack of locusts—too many crammed together to distinguish the individual shapes of their ships.

"Thousands of war vessels arrived at Tria," the voice continues. "After investigating the messages left behind by the comrades we'd killed, they traveled toward our planet."

Sharon glances over her shoulder, and Fresler follows her gaze out the window, at the desolate wasteland outside.

"In those fifteen years of waiting, we'd examined the outpost on Tria. We'd determined that the aliens do not use a written or spoken language. They communicate telepathically, using images. When they reached Des, we attempted to communicate with them based on what we'd learned, but we were once again... unsuccessful. They unleashed the full fury of their war machine on our people... our planet."

Gasps echo through the room as images flash across the screen. Sleek black vessels sweep over the streets, firing on the silver, domed buildings of a city. Lasers blast apart occupied streets. Men, women, and children are tossed into the air like debris. Corpses are strewn across ruins.

"After all structures and human lives were destroyed, they fired a large laser from their lead vessel," the woman says. "That started a chain reaction on the planet. The resulting plume of smoke and dust has blanketed our planet for millions of years."

"They obliterated the planet," Aleria whispers, her hand moving to cover her mouth.

"Why destroy the structures and humans first?" Erik asks. "Why not just fire that laser?"

The voice continues before anyone can do more than

shrug. "After destroying our planet, the aliens returned to their galaxy. The communication towers were restored below the surface on each of the nine planets. Once again, they sent signals to each other... as they had prior to our encounter with the outpost on Tria."

"What does this have to do with Sjel... or Earth?" Reshal wonders aloud.

As if she heard him, the voice says, "Long before the aliens arrived, Desian leaders decided to seed the eight other planets in the chain with human life. In those fifteen years between our first encounter with the aliens and our annihilation by them, those seeds were finally planted. The planets Earth, Sjel, Rajik, Polemos, Phaelin, Opik, and Nekses each received one of our seven extinct DNA strands. The planet Tria was seeded with all three strands that remained in existence. We felt that this would ensure the survival of the human race, regardless of Des's fate."

All the wind leaves Erik's lungs in a rush. Karena, Fresler, Sharon, Sarah, and Stephan look exactly how he feels, their jaws dangling, their faces bloodless. They've just learned the origins of human life on Earth in a three-minute slideshow. The absurdity almost makes sense, and Erik stifles a hysterical laugh.

All of humankind... seeded by a dying race.

The people of Des.

Des... *Deus*... Erik chokes on another crazy laugh. The Desians were Earth's creators.

"Hopefully, humanity will continue to thrive," the woman croons, ending the message with a blank screen.

* * *

Sibula is the first to break the stunned silence. "Do you have any questions?"

Reshal leans forward, squinting as he speaks. "The planet Tria," he says, "was seeded with three separate subspecies of human DNA."

"Yes," Sibula says. "Borjan, Diastassian, and... Tempian." Her eyes flicker toward Karena.

"Now there are only Borjans on Tria," Erik says. "And you and the Diastassians each have your own planets. What happened?"

"Millions of years ago, we Trians discovered the other eight planets much like the Desians did... by tracking the signals from the towers." Sibula stares dreamily at the screen. "We discovered this place and this message. We knew after listening to it that the aliens would eventually return. It wasn't a matter of if... but when."

"And whether they'd bring another armada," Erik says darkly.

Sibula nods as if to say, *Precisely.* Then she goes on, "We don't know the true purpose of the towers, but we know they are more than just communication devices. Based on what happened here on Des, we feared that the aliens were planning to end the human race."

"So... you relocated to a different dimension?" asks Kayna.

"Yes. Not long after discovering this message, we created an interdimensional portal. Beyond it, we discovered two planets that, having the perfect balance of oxygen and nitrogen, were capable of sustaining human life. Being in another dimension would keep us safe from the aliens, so we departed as soon as we were able."

"If those planets became Diastassi and Borjan, what happened to the Tempians?" Sharon asks.

"They were a small percentage of Tria's population. They chose to live with us on Borjan. Eventually, they integrated with our subspecies."

"The Borjans and Tempians became one subspecies?" Karena says sharply.

"Not exactly," says Sibula. "About ten percent of our population has both Borjan and Tempian DNA. Most are Borjan only."

"Did any of the Diastassians... *integrate* with the Borjans and Tempians?" asks Fresler.

"It is forbidden to integrate with a Diastassian."

"Why?" asks Sharon.

"They are a violent race. We did not want our DNA to be... *tainted* with theirs."

Kayna narrows her eyes. "Tainted?"

"Tempians and Borjans are peaceful. Diastassians are not."

Theran puts a hand on Kayna's arm at the exact moment Erik puts a hand on Aleria's. Both women bristle but remain in their seats.

"Why are there now Borjans on Tria?" asks Theran.

"We needed an outpost in this universe to observe the nine planets. From Tria, we monitor the towers and the development of the human race."

"Why did the Diastassians create their own interdimensional portal, if the residents of Tria had already made one?" Reshal asks.

"When we lived together on Tria, the Borjan subspecies was the most technologically advanced. When the Diastassians relocated to their own planet, they developed war machines." Sibula pauses for several seconds before concluding, "We feared them."

Fresler waves his arms. "Hold on. Did the Diastassians create the anomaly on purpose?"

"No," Sibula says firmly. "It was an accident. A by-product of their experimentation."

Kralo chimes in, "Why didn't you help them? Or stop them?"

"You have to understand... the two planets lived separately in all aspects. We did not share anything, including technological advancements."

"But you had to have been observing them. That's what Borjans do, right? *Observe?*" Erik filters all his frustration into the emphasis. "If they created that anomaly—accidentally—because you wouldn't share your technical knowledge... doesn't that make you partly responsible for the loss of two entire planets?"

Sibula does not flinch. "It was tradition for us to remain apart."

"You relocated the Diastassians across dimensions when you worried the aliens would come back," Stephan says. "Why bother, if they're so violent? If you're afraid of them?"

"Despite our differences and our desire to remain separate, we still share something very important... we are human, and we will protect each other at all costs."

To everyone's surprise, Karena stands. "There's something you all need to know." She looks at Sibula. "They need to know."

Sibula casts her eyes down, as though readying herself for a blow she saw coming long ago. "I agree."

Karena looks back at the group. "Ludvig had Diastassian, Borjan, and Tempian DNA," Karena announces. "He was Sibula's son."

The Borjan woman shrinks into herself as the room erupts in shocked chatter.

"How is that possible?" Fresler finally shouts, above all the other voices. "You just said—"

"I was a product of a forbidden integration. I am a hybrid," Sibula says. "As a result, my grandson—" she indicates Winnett, sleeping peacefully on Karena's chest, "—is perhaps the most powerful hybrid ever born. We will need him in the years to come."

A renewed hush falls over the room.

"The towers have breached the planets' surfaces, as they did in the past," Sibula intones. "They are broadcasting to the aliens, as they did in the past. We believe the aliens will return... *soon*."

"How long do we have?" asks Sarah. "That recording said... fifteen years?" Beside her, Stephan nods, so Sarah keeps going. "But the tower on Earth breached in 2016. They all did."

As he does the math in his head, Erik can't find the strength to sit up straight. "If they follow the same pattern, they'll be back in 2031. That gives us seven years to prepare."

PART III

DISCOVERY

CHAPTER 18

Tria — January 26th, 2028

Sharon takes the seat Karena offers on the back deck, overlooking the green ocean. In the last four years, the Neksesians have traded their bamboo huts for permanent structures along the ocean's shores that remind Karena of condos back on Earth. When she'd told Kesh that, he got a kick out of the word "condo" and told all their neighbors, many of whom adopted the word as an inside joke that never ceases to amuse Karena.

Out on the black sand, Kesh walks hand in hand with two-year-old Mikaela. "He sure is a loving father," Sharon says, gesturing to the two with a smile.

"He is," says Karena, chest swelling with love. "Fresler too."

"Yes, he's wonderful." Sharon beams down at her life partner and their daughter, building a sandcastle together near the water's edge. Tess is also two, a few months older than Mikaela, and the girls are already on their way to being fast friends.

Mikaela looks up toward the deck and waves at her mother. Her bronze-blond hair is braided out of her face, but flyaway baby hairs still tickle her nose, and she rubs it with the back of her hand. She doesn't have Kesh's pink skin tone, but she's peachier than Karena, and she tans far more easily.

Karena waves back. "I love them both so much." She winks at her older child, nestled on the floor by her feet. "You too, of course."

Winnett hardly notices, engrossed in a book. He may have only just turned four, but he already reads at a much higher level—and in multiple languages. He's currently making his way through a Sjelian engineering manual Kralo gave him for his birthday in October. Karena is sure Winnett will be ready to fly a shuttle on his own before long... not that she'd let him.

"Any update from Sjel?" Sharon asks.

"No." Karena sighs, missing Erik, Aleria, and their adorable three-year-old son, Noah. The three of them, plus Theran, Kayna, and Reshal, have made Sjel their primary residence for almost a year now, overseeing the construction of a fleet of new Sjelian defense vessels. That was one of their first courses of action after learning about the looming threat to humanity: take stock of current defense capabilities and determine how many more vessels could be produced before 2031.

As they'd planned, Karena and Kesh settled on Tria. Together with a few of Kesh's Neksesian colleagues, they launched a research lab within the Borjan capitol building, aiming to reconstruct the various technologies that were lost when Nekses perished. Three years ago, Karena and Kesh became life partners. Mikaela followed in 2025. Being a scientist and a mother keeps Karena busy. She wouldn't have it any other way.

At least she gets to stay in one place—unlike Erik, who is constantly in motion. Sjel, Tria, Borjan… and then there was that ill-fated trip to Polemos that no one likes to discuss.

"Is Sarah coming over?" Sharon asks.

"No. Viktor's not feeling well, so she's staying home to keep an eye on him." Sarah and Stephan are Karena's closest neighbors on Tria. Sarah spends her days researching the transmissions coming from the Trian tower. Stephan studies Neksesian medicine while also taking flying lessons from Kralo whenever the Sjelian pilot is available. Their son just turned two. The party was a delightfully chaotic, exhausting affair full of rambunctious toddlers. Thank goodness for the Slak, or the adults might not have made it through.

Thinking of her friends and everything they've accomplished together, Karena relishes the idyllic beach scene. It's a life pulled straight from a storybook. She has her family. Her friends. Work that fulfills her. A planet that is still mysterious and wondrous and new, even after four years here. The only thing muddying the perfection of her world is the Desians' dire warning, still hanging over their heads. But they'll get through it. She believes in what they've created, what they're doing.

Yes, everything is—

"They're coming," Winnett says suddenly.

Sharon shades her eyes with her hand, staring at Kesh, Mikaela, Fresler, and Tess. "No, it looks like they're still playing."

"They're coming!" Winnett shouts, panic-stricken.

Karena gasps and drops to her knees in front of her son. He's gone pale. His forehead is covered in beads of sweat. But it's his eyes that scare her the most. Though they move so fast they're almost vibrating, they're... vacant. Like he's gone blind. Or, she realizes, like he's seeing something that's not there.

"They're coming," he chants, rocking back and forth. "They're coming. They're coming."

Karena's hand hovers by his cheek, but she's afraid to touch him while he's in this... trance. It might disorient or frighten him, like waking a sleepwalker.

"What's wrong with him?" Sharon asks. "What should we do?"

As quickly as he started rocking, Winnett goes completely still. He breathes deeply, eyelids fluttering. His lower lip trembles.

To Karena's astonishment, her stoic son—the child who never cries—bursts into tears.

She sweeps him into her arms. "Shhh, shhh. It's okay."

"It's not okay!" Winnett wails. "I saw it!"

"What did you see?" Karena asks gently.

"I saw..." Winnett wipes at his wet face, frowning in concentration. "An armada." He looks down at his engineering book and corrects himself. "Vessels. Thousands and thousands of them."

Karena looks up into Sharon's wide eyes. "What else did you see, sweetie?" she prompts, wishing Sibula were here. Winnett's grandmother would know how to handle the aftermath of a vision.

"They had weapons," Winnett says, breathless. "We had vessels too, and weapons. But not enough. We couldn't win. There were too many of them." His tears spill over again. "We were destroyed."

Karena lets her son sob into her shirt as Sharon stands and waves to Kesh and Fresler, jumping to grab their attention. On the beach, the men exchange a worried look, scoop up their daughters, and hurry over.

"Is he ill?" Kesh asks the moment his shoes hit the deck.

Karena shakes her head. "I think he just had... a *vision*."

Kesh startles. "A vision? Of the future?"

Winnett nods fast. "I saw them. They're coming. We're not ready."

Fresler puts Tess down. "Go inside and play with Mikaela."

"Okay!" the toddler chirps. She grabs her bestie's hand, and they charge indoors.

The moment they're gone, Fresler crouches to get on Winnett's level. "What did you see?"

The four-year-old repeats what he told his mother and Sharon. "We were destroyed," he finishes.

"Okay, so we need more defense vessels," Fresler says. "We have to call Erik."

Winnett squinches his eyes shut. "Not vessels," he mumbles. "We need to—"

"The Sjelian General Council needs to hear about this," Kesh agrees.

Winnett tugs at Karena's arm. "I have to go to the tower."

"We only have three more years," Sharon frets.

"Maybe three and a half?" Fresler says. "Opik was destroyed in *July* of 2016..."

"We have to act fast," Karena says firmly. "We have no way of knowing if these aliens follow the same calendar as we do." She stands, grunting as she hoists Winnett and longing for the days when he was small enough to fit in the crook of one elbow.

Winnett speaks louder, gripping Karena's shirt tight. "I need to see the tower."

Karena nods. "We can ask Sarah if we can visit tomorrow. Right now, Mommy has to call Uncle Erik."

"Tomorrow," Winnett says, satisfied. He drops his head onto her shoulder.

Intuition tingling, Karena takes her son inside to make the call she hoped she'd never have to make, about a day she's been wishing would never come.

CHAPTER 19

Tria - October 11th, 2028

"Happy birthday, Winnett!" Sarah crows when her youngest colleague walks through the flap of the black tent that serves as their temporary research office. Karena's right behind him.

"Thanks," the five-year-old says, zipping up his coat. It's always colder out here by the tower than by the beach. The seasons on Tria aren't as regular as those on Earth, but the decrease in temperature by the tower is a constant. Sarah has been tracking that data point with interest, since it wasn't present in the Wisconsin case.

"Where should we begin today?" Sarah asks Winnett.

To an outside observer, it might seem like she's humoring an inquisitive child, but it's a serious question. In the nine months or so that Winnett has been visiting the excavation site, he's become one of the team's most valuable researchers. He's more knowledgeable than some of Sarah's most savvy graduate students back on Earth. He has an eidetic memory, able to read texts once and understand them completely. They've accomplished as much since Winnett came on board as they did in the four years prior.

To be honest, some days, Sarah feels like he's running the site and she's his assistant.

"Let's take a look at the chasm," Winnett says after a moment's deliberation. He accepts Karena's kiss on the cheek and waves her out, already heading for the tent's opposite exit.

Outside, the communication tower spirals into the sky, just like the tower Sarah studied on Earth. Unlike that tower, this one has a massive oval base deep in the dark Trian soil. The wind off the ocean cools the air, and the crash of the waves striking the cliff that protects them from the tide muffles the sound of their footsteps.

They stop side by side, looking down into the chasm, where a few Neksesians are diligently working to excavate samples. Winnett's floppy, perpetually tousled hair blows into his eyes, and he shoves it back impatiently. Its blond hue isn't as icy as his mother's, more strawberry, but he has her nose. Sarah is surprised to realize that he's almost at the height of her shoulder. He's growing like a weed. Despite his height, he still has baby fat in his cheeks.

"I think it's some sort of power source," he declares after several seconds of silence. Most people do a double-take when he speaks. Sarah, however, is used to his adult syntax.

"Why would *this tower* have a power source... but not the one on Earth?" asks Sarah.

Winnett returns to the black tent, and she follows him inside. Computers wink their power lights at him as he enters, but he ignores them, walking instead between the two twenty-foot tables covered with materials unearthed from around the tower.

He stops in front of a sample of gray powder, reminiscent of the mossy material she'd found clinging to cave walls near the Earth tower.

"You found iron oxide, gold, and copper near the tower on Earth," Winnett says thoughtfully.

"Yes, and graphene." Sarah points to the powder. "But... we didn't extract *that* on Earth." She nods at a hefty black rock that looks like charcoal. "Have you determined its chemical structure?"

Winnett nods. "I performed an x-ray crystallography. The bonds in the material are formed by shared electrons in a mix of... *particular* orbital shells. The bonds leave the electrons, which makes it easier for their spins to align. This is what gives it... *ferromagnetism.*"

"Ferromagnetism?! Impossible."

Winnett tilts his head at her, looking stung. "Clearly, it's not."

"Sorry," Sarah says quickly. "I didn't mean to question your research."

"Thanks." Winnett looks back at the rock. "Unlike the graphene..." he gestures to the powdery substance, "... which is not ferromagnetic, this is, and it acts like a permanent magnet at temperatures of 125 degrees Celsius. It is a stable form of pure carbon."

Sarah feels the familiar thrill of a theory becoming likely fact. "Is that this tower's true purpose? To make this... what do you call it?"

"Ferromagnetic pure carbon," Winnett says matter-of-factly. "FP Carbon."

Sarah bobs her head. "I like it. So, do we think this tower's purpose is to create FP Carbon?"

"I need to do more research," Winnett allows, "but... it's possible. Tria, Earth, and the other tethered planets all have one thing in common: the atmosphere is composed of twenty-one percent oxygen, seventy-eight percent nitrogen, and trace amounts of argon and carbon dioxide. If this planet's level of oxygen dips below nineteen percent, we all die. It has to be in perfect balance. The perfect balance exists on all nine planets."

"And it takes that perfect balance to create these substances," Sarah says, gesturing at the samples on the table.

"Precisely." Winnett scratches his head, shaking his mane of hair. "So... yes, it is possible that the purpose of this tower... of all the towers... is to create this FP Carbon."

"Do you think the aliens can't create FP Carbon on their own planet?" asks Sarah.

"I don't know."

"I wonder what they use it for..." Sarah muses next.

Winnett gives her a sharp look. He's an incredibly literal child, not tending toward flights of imagination. He likes to stick to what can and cannot be proven. "We need to first prove that this tower's purpose is to produce FP Carbon."

Sarah puts a hand over her mouth to hide her twitching lips. When he gets like this, Winnett reminds her of a crotchety old professor she once knew at U.C. Berkeley. "Of course. You're right."

"I need to visit the other towers," Winnett says.

"You know your mom doesn't want you leaving the planet," Sarah replies gently.

"What about the trip to Earth in December?" he argues. "I can see the tower in Wisconsin then."

"That trip is for family visits," Sarah says, sentimental euphoria blossoming at the thought of seeing her loved ones on Earth again... not to mention meeting Stephan's parents and introducing them to Viktor. "We won't be stopping by the tower."

"That doesn't' make any sense." Winnett says, shaking his head.

Privately, Sarah agrees with him. As eager as she is for the long-overdue family reunions, she has done her share of arguing for the Earth trip to *also* include research and recruitment. Erik, Karena, and Fresler are on the same page.

But Reshal has been monitoring Earth's rebuilt communications systems. He insists that Earth's leadership will not welcome any overtures for their cause. The governments that rose to power after the pandemic have doubled down on hiding all evidence of life on other planets. Reshal firmly believes that a request for an audience with the president of the United States or the leaders of the Eurasian Alliance will only be granted as a ruse to take them into custody. They will all have aliases and falsified ID cards while they're on the planet, just in case.

Sarah sighs. "We have research teams at the towers on Sjel, Des, and Rajik. I can relay any questions you have to them."

"That won't help," Winnett says. "I need to see those towers for myself." He stalks out the other side of the tent. Sarah hurries after him and finds him observing the abandoned structures on this side of the planet, once home to the Borjans, Tempians, and Diastassians when they lived in something like harmony. "I need to visit those towers," he complains.

"Your mom is the boss," Sarah says carefully, not wanting to undermine Karena as she comforts Winnett. "Let's talk about what we want the teams at the other towers to investigate."

"Is this the only planet with a power source separate from the tower?" Winnett asks, a bit sulkily. "Does this FP Carbon exist on the other planets? And the temperature variation you've been tracking. Is that present anywhere other than Tria?"

Sarah blinks. "I didn't realize you'd noticed I was tracking the daily temperatures."

Now Winnett smiles. "I noticed." He looks younger when he smiles. It crinkles his eyes, cutting back on that odd, hypnotic sensation his stare usually gives off, like he's staring into her soul. Then he says, "Perhaps these towers hold the key to our survival, when the aliens return."

So much for Winnett seeming like a normal five-year-old.

"Aster believes that we need to defend ourselves with force," Sarah says, referring to the Neksesian defense leader. Aster is heading up vessel production on Tria, as Theran is on Sjel.

Winnett huffs. "I don't think that's the answer."

"Well..." Sarah hedges, "it certainly can't hurt."

"It could." Winnett scrunches up his face.

Sarah resists the urge to ruffle his hair, knowing he prefers to be treated as a colleague when he's here on site. "You're a pretty amazing young man, you know that?"

Winnett flushes and stands straighter. "Thanks. So, will you please, *please* talk to my mother about letting me travel to one of the other towers?"

Sarah sighs, knowing it's a losing battle. The more evidence they uncover that the prophecies about Winnett are true, the tighter Karena clings to her firstborn. It took Karena more than two weeks to allow Winnett to study the Trian tower without her... and that was *with* Sarah keeping an eye on him.

"I'll ask her," Sarah finally says, "but no guarantees."

* * *

Sjel — October 12th, 2028

Theran grinds his teeth to hold in a groan. He looks down long enough to smooth his features before addressing the thirteen hooded members of the General Council. "We need to inform the public. We need volunteers to help build and pilot these vessels. It's the only way we are going to win."

Arwed looks down his beak-like nose at Theran. "You can't be certain that these... *aliens*... are traveling to our quadrant of the universe. We have no way of tracking their vessels."

"It's true that we can't track their travel, but..." Theran turns to Reshal for help.

Reshal stands and says, "As you know, the last time the towers breached the surface, the aliens arrived with thousands of war vessels and destroyed Des. We cannot let them do the same to Sjel."

Arwed shakes his head. "I grow tired of hearing the same arguments each time you stand before this Council. What happened in the past is not certain to happen in the future. The circumstances were much different. The aliens destroyed Des because the Desians attacked their outpost. We have committed no such act of aggression. According to your own statements, the tether between planets was broken when Opik was destroyed by the anomaly."

"The anomaly was created by the Diastassians," Theran points out.

Beside Arwed, Fralin scoffs. "You told us the anomaly was an accidental by-product of their attempts at interdimensional portal travel."

Reshal throws his hands in the air. "What if we can't explain that to the aliens? What if they believe the anomaly was a planet-destroying weapon? What happened to the Desians shows us we cannot reason with these beings."

"The Desians initiated an attack," Arwed says stubbornly. "We did not."

Unable to stay silent and seated a moment longer, Aleria jumps to her feet. "What about Winnett's premonition?" The thirteen councilmembers shift her direction in unsettling unison. "Winnett believes they are coming, and that our armada is not ready."

Fralin waves off her words. "Not that premonition again."

Erik takes Aleria's hand as he stands to back her up. "With all due respect, honored members of the Council, we have to assume that Winnett is correct and that history will repeat itself. If we don't prepare for this attack, we could all die."

Arwed stares for a long moment before offering a single nod. "We will continue to provide supplies and technology to support the building of the armada."

"Thank you. And the volunteers?" Theran inquires stiffly. That's really why they're here today. An armada is nothing without manpower to pilot each vessel.

"On that point, we cannot help. We will not inform the general public of an impending attack." Arwed's hooded fellows murmur their agreement, faces entirely shaded above the lips. "An attack... that may or may not ever happen. It would cause a panic. Our people are not capable of killing other life forms. You know that, Theran."

"I do, sir," says Theran with a weary sigh. "If we cannot enlist the help of our citizens, then please consider an evacuation of the planet. The Borjans have already agreed to accept all human refugees from Sjel."

Arwed looks left, then right. The fellow councilmembers nod in unison. "There is no need for that."

Reshal steps forward. "How can you—"

"We have completed the graviton shield," Arwed says. "It is *impenetrable*."

Erik looks at Aleria, mouthing, *Graviton shield?!*

She shakes her head at him. This is the first she's hearing of such a thing. But she senses no surprise in Reshal and Theran. Just outrage.

"If it is not," Reshal spits at the Council, his pointing finger shaking with rage, "you will be responsible for countless deaths."

Arwed cocks his head, as if intrigued by Reshal's display of emotion, and rises to his feet. "Our decision is final."

* * *

That evening, the mist from the waterfall lands like a cool kiss on Erik's cheeks and forehead as he reclines on Emeran's marble balcony. Aleria sits upright beside him, chatting with Jenta but keeping one eye on their rambunctious son, Noah, who's doing laps around the chairs. Every few steps, the almost-four-year-old jumps to try and catch white, fluffy seeds drifting through the air, carried from the surrounding jungle on the strong breeze. His sandy hair blows into his deep-set brown eyes, but it doesn't seem to slow him down.

Kayna lets out a cheer when he finally catches one. Theran, who was watching out of the corner of his eye, chuckles at his grandson, despite his glum mood.

"You knew that the General Council would say no to your request for volunteers," says Emeran, pulling Theran back into the conversation.

"Yes... but I had to try. Winnett's premonition is clear that we are not adequately prepared."

"Do you think additional war vessels will make a difference?" asks Emeran.

"I'm not sure. The message we viewed on Des..." Theran shakes his head while sharing a look with Kayna. "They have a weapon capable of destroying an entire planet."

"The Council said they've improved our defense system." Kayna's eyes roll toward the clouds. "Arwed's exact word was '*impenetrable*.'"

Theran runs a hand over his bald head. "Let's hope it's never tested."

It's been years of this... years of standing before the General Council making variations on the same requests and getting handed scraps in return. It's not that Theran is disappointed in his new armada. He told Erik just yesterday that production is proceeding at a rapid clip, and the vessels are impressive. But after each check-in with the Council, he always looks so downtrodden. Arwed is not taking the threat seriously enough.

Erik glances over. "Did you know they were working on a graviton shield?" he asks.

"I knew the project existed," Theran says. "I did not know the Council had been diverting untold funding and man-hours to complete it in time to deal with this particular crisis. Resources that could have gone to the defense armada." He groans quietly. "They aim to protect Sjel, at the expense of the rest of humanity."

Erik scowls. "What else is new?"

Theran gives him a curious look at the English expression but nods as if he understands the sentiment. "Arwed is short-sighted. Under his leadership, Sjel remains insular. I must find a way to convince him..." He falls silent, staring out over the landscape.

Erik sees an opening. "You know," he begins, "if Sjel is unwilling to provide the aid we need, there are other planets... like Earth..."

"Erik," Theran says, head turning sharply. "We've discussed this."

"We can bypass Earth's leadership and appeal directly to the people," Erik insists. "The new internet—we could post a video explaining the situation and calling for volunteers—"

"Any such message would be removed as soon as it appeared. Communications are tightly regulated."

"Then we'll spread the word underground. When we're on Earth in December, we'll talk to our friends and families. They'll pass along the message. We can use code words..." Erik's enthusiasm falters a bit at Theran's blank face, but he tries not to lose steam as he goes on, "Stephan is proof that Earth's humans can pilot Sjelian and Neksesian vessels, with appropriate training. If enough people volunteer—"

"We cannot afford another Polemos," Theran interrupts.

"It wouldn't be like that," Erik says too quickly, wishing he sounded more certain.

"We must focus on the resources we *know* we have— even when those resources are flawed," Theran says, referring to the General Council. "Promise me you will not do anything rash while on Earth. Don't make me regret granting permission for all of you to make the trip."

With the eyes of Theran, Kayna, Emeran, and Aleria on him, Erik feels like a chastised child as he mutters, "I promise."

An awkward silence follows, ending only when Noah

appears from the other side of the deck and tugs on Erik's hand. "I'm bored. Can you show me how to play Tej?"

"Your mother is better at it," Erik says, nodding toward Aleria.

"Sure, but I want to play with *you*," the child whines sweetly.

Unable to resist that request, Erik nods and straightens his recliner. He leads Noah inside by the hand and settles him on the mesh sofa. "I'm not great at this game, but I can show you how to play." As he fetches the metal cube from his bag, he thinks back on the many hours he spent playing Mario with Eria. When they'd played in St. John, hooting and hollering at each other in good-natured competitive spirit, he hadn't known it would be the last time. He would have cheered louder, hugged her tighter. It's hard to believe she would be eighteen now.

She would have made a great older sister to Noah.

He clears his tight throat as he returns to the couch. "The goal is to find the key that unlocks the vault, which is where you'll find the instructions to build a shuttle, which will take you to your home planet," he explains, turning on the cube. A holographic screen projects itself around the cube, providing buttons and displaying the first geometric problem.

"I know all of that, *Dad*," says Noah with a classic "duh" expression Erik used to give his own parents. "I need to learn how you're supposed to find the clues."

Erik snorts. "Okay..." Erik shows his son the path he is supposed to take to find the invisible boxes that hold the clues. You have to solve the geometric problems you find along the path in order to locate the next invisible box. Tej is a learning game for Sjelian children that's meant for twelve years and up, but Noah has always displayed the intelli-

gence of a much older child thanks to his hybrid genetics—
three subspecies in total.

Erik smiles as he watches Noah solve his first mathematical problem in under two minutes. "Can you sense how I am feeling right now?" he asks. Noah has his mother's ability.

Noah keeps staring at the holographic screen, working the buttons and twisting the geometric shapes with swipes of his fingers. He shrugs and says, "I guess..."

"How am I feeling?"

Noah stops and looks at his dad. "Happy," he says with a smile.

"I am, you know," Erik says, nudging Noah with his arm. "I am so happy when I am around you. I love you more than you could possibly know."

"I know, Dad. You always tell me that." Noah returns his attention to the holographic screen. "Mom's not so happy, though."

Erik has noticed that Aleria's been quietly lately, though she claims all is well. "How is she feeling?"

"Worried," Noah says, without looking up.

"You can sense that, or she told you?"

"I can sense it."

Erik nods, giving his son a one-armed hug. "Thanks for telling me."

CHAPTER 20

"Buckle up, everyone," Stephan says from the pilot's seat as the shuttle approaches Earth's atmosphere. He's joking... mostly. This is his first unsupervised shuttle landing. "No pressure," he murmurs to himself.

From the copilot's seat, Sarah gives her life partner an encouraging smile. "You've got this."

Stephan nods on a stiff neck, focusing on the controls. His pilot training has never failed him before, and he won't let it do so now... even if this vessel is infinitely more complicated than any airplane he flew on Earth. Entrance into the atmosphere is the easy part. There's not even a tremor, just a tiny shimmy. No need for buckles. The hard part comes once he navigates down toward the planet's surface. He must keep the shuttle steady as its speed decreases. When they enter the stratosphere, he allows himself to exhale. Now, he just has to stick the landing.

"Next stop, Washington," he announces, checking that

the shuttle's cloaking mechanism—now upgraded with Neksesian tech—is engaged.

Five-year-old Winnett appears at his shoulder, silent as a ghost. "Are we going to pass over the state of Wisconsin?" he asks, making Stephan jerk in surprise.

Stephan checks his flight path. "Actually, yes."

"We should be stopping at the tower."

"Winnett!" Karena scolds, taking her son by the shoulders. "We've discussed this. You will not be visiting the tower."

"We have a cloaked vessel. We could land in the field right front of the structure, and no one would see us."

"Well... the last time I was there, the farmland was still fairly open..." Sarah says, cringing when Karena turns her frustrated grimace on her. "But we can't be sure it's safe," she adjusts. "We don't know everything that's been happening on Earth since we were last here. A lot could have changed."

Karena pulls Winnett back into the passenger area, ignoring his muttered complaints. They sit beside Erik, Aleria, and Noah. Karena always coaxes Winnett to spend time with Noah, since Noah is the closest in age, and though he's smart as a whip, Winnett's a hard kid to connect with. He's leaps and bounds beyond any kid on Tria, and he'd rather discuss theories of the universe then play a board game. The two get along all right but they never seem to interact for more than five minutes at a time. It makes Karena worry. Is Winnett lonely?

Across from them, Sharon and Fresler are entertaining Tess, Mikaela, and Viktor with a game on a Sjelian tablet device—tapping bubbles of various colors in a specified order. Winnett could clear the highest level at six months.

At the control panel, Sarah turns in her chair to make sure Karena's not giving her the stink eye.

"Nice recovery," Stephan says.

She shakes her head. "I wish we were making the stop. I want to see that thing through Winnett's eyes."

"I know you do, but Reshal is against it."

Sarah sighs. "And Karena doesn't want to let Winnett out of her sight."

Stephan looks back at their own son, on Sharon's lap. "Would you, if it was Viktor in those prophecies?"

"I don't know…" Sarah shifts in her seat, uneasy. "But Winnett is the best scientific mind we have. It's a shame not to let him at least take a look at the tower, while we're here."

"Social visits only," Stephan says, reciting the mandate that Theran gave them when they left the space station this morning. "Speaking of which… ten minutes to Washington Settlement, folks!" he calls out.

Grinning with anticipation, Fresler and Sharon begin gathering their things.

* * *

Washington Settlement, United States — December 24th, 2028 — 9:00 a.m. local time

The settlement looks like a fortress on the outside—concrete and guard posts everywhere—but the fake identification cards Reshal manufactured get Fresler and Sharon inside without incident. Thanks to the restored satellites, the people of Earth are once again transmitting electronic data, which means Reshal has also secured Lars and Gladys's address. The streets make a uniform grid, and Fresler easily follows the numbered street signs to his parents' home.

As they head up the short walk, Fresler looks over at Sharon. "Here goes nothing…"

Sharon picks up their three-year-old daughter and brushes back the girl's wispy blond hair. Her eyes, so like Fresler's, widen as they approach the front door, and she claps as she flashes her mom a smile.

"Tessy seems to think we're in the right place," says Sharon, tickling the girl under her chin. Along with her daddy's eyes, Tess also inherited his ability to sense the presence of her genetic relatives.

Fresler knocks on the door and then shifts from foot to foot while they wait.

When Lars answers, he does a double-take, clutching his chest. "Son!"

Fresler embraces him carefully. He's never thought of his father as delicate, but Lars is in his nineties now, and his body feels brittle and bird-like beneath Fresler's hands. "Hi, Dad. Merry Christmas."

"Gladys!" Lars yells over his shoulder.

Fresler's mother shuffles into the living room a few moments later. She doesn't walk as fast as she once did, but she doesn't need a cane, and Fresler thinks she looks great for her age. "Sweetie!" she shouts. "You're here! And on *Christmas Eve!*"

Fresler steps inside to meet her halfway in an embrace. "Merry Christmas, Mom."

When they break apart, she gives Sharon a one-armed hug. Then she coos over Tess, still propped on her mom's hip. "I have a *granddaughter?*"

"Yes," Fresler says, grinning from ear to ear. "This is Tess, Mom."

Gladys beams while Sharon sets Tess down. When the child's feet are firmly on the floor, Gladys crouches and holds her arms out. She can't bend her knees like she used to, but she gets low enough. "Can I have a hug?"

Tess looks back at Sharon for permission. At a nod from her mom, Tess flies into Gladys's arms, and Sharon winces, extending a hand to catch Gladys should she tumble backward from the force of the toddler's love. But Gladys keeps her balance, and her laugh rings through the room, making Tess giggle too.

Lars walks over. "Can I have one of those?"

Tess latches herself to Lars's leg, and he holds his heart again, eyes welling up as he bends to pat her back.

"How old are you?" asks Gladys.

Tess holds up three fingers.

"Three." Gladys shakes her head.

"Wow, you are such a big girl," says Lars.

Gladys begins to bustle around the room. "I wish we'd known you were coming. We have a spare room, but it isn't ready for guests."

"Whatever you have is fine," Sharon says graciously. "We're just happy to see you."

"How long are you staying with us?" asks Lars.

Fresler responds, "Not long... two days."

"That's it?" asks Gladys.

"Sorry," Fresler says, and means it. "We're in the middle of something really important."

"What is it?" asks Lars.

After a moment's indecision, Fresler says, "It's complicated." As much as he hates to agree with the Sjelian General Council about anything, telling his loved ones that there is an impending threat to humanity won't do much good... yet.

"Complicated." Gladys makes her way over to the sofa, where she sits and pats the empty cushions beside her impatiently. "Sit. Tell us everything."

Fresler and Sharon exchange a quick look, in silent

agreement to keep certain revelations under wraps. "Well," Fresler begins, "we've been living on the planet Tria…"

* * *

Reykjavik, Iceland – December 24th, 2028 — 6:00 p.m. local time

After dropping Karena and her children off at Janice's home in Sweden, Stephan circles back to Reykjavik. The closer they get, the more he understands how Erik must have felt five years ago, when he first showed his face after his first lengthy excursion with the Sjelians. Once he lands the shuttle, he grabs Sarah's hand and tries to calm his nerves.

"Ready?" Sarah asks.

"Not even a little," Stephan admits. He has missed his parents so much… but what if they resent him for staying away so long, when he'd promised only a short visit through the portal? The door to his parents' house has always been open to him. But now that door feels like a barrier to the threshold he hasn't seen in five years, and some irrational bit of his psyche fears the hinges may never swing open that freely again.

"Come on, Stephan!" Erik bellows from outside the shuttle. He, Aleria, and Noah disembarked immediately, apparently feeling none of Stephan's reservations. Then again, Erik has done this before. Maybe it only hurts like this the first time.

"Coming!" He puts the shuttle in protected mode while they're away from it, linking its alarm system to his PAD wristband, and steps out into the fresh, cold air of Iceland in late December.

When they reach the steps up to the porch, Erik hangs

back. "You go first," he says, nudging Stephan forward with a knowing smile.

After a deep breath, Stephan climbs the steps. He raps on the front door and then reaches down to ruffle his son's wavy red hair. Viktor smiles up at Stephan and takes his dad's finger in one little hand, the knuckles like dimples in his baby chub.

The drapes swish to one side, and a giddy scream rings through the window. In moments, Hanna throws open the door and launches herself at her son. He catches her in a hug.

"Stephan..." is all she gets out before the sobs take over.

"Mom..." Then he's crying, too.

Eventually, Hanna steps back. She rubs her eyes and smiles at Sarah, wearing an expression of warm curiosity. Then she spies Viktor, and her mouth pops open. Even as a toddler, his jawline is clearly Stephan's. His face is less rounded than most boys his age, though there's plenty of baby fat in his cheeks. At the site of Viktor, Hanna's sobs renew.

Stephan embraces her again until she regains her composure.

Fresh tears spill as Hanna whispers, "Is this... my *grandson?*"

"Yes... and this is my life partner, Sarah," says Stephan, face stretched in a smile that won't quit.

Hanna hugs Sarah, who says into her shoulder, "It's so nice to meet you, Mrs. Johansson."

"Please, call me Hanna." She narrows her eyes at Stephan. "How old is he?"

"He'll be three next month."

"And you're just now bringing him to meet us?" Clucking her tongue, Hanna bends down to Viktor's level. He shies away at first, but the invitation of her extended arms lures him in... with a little help from Stephan. "What's your name?" she asks.

"Viktor," he says softly.

Hanna pulls him close to her chest and gently strokes his hair. "Hi, Viktor. I'm your grandma."

The boy nods and offers a sheepish grin.

Over Viktor's shoulder, Hanna spies Erik, Aleria, and Noah, waiting respectfully at the bottom of the steps. "Oh!" she yelps. She releases Viktor and makes her way to Noah. "Another grandchild!"

Erik blinks his wet eyes as he introduces Noah.

Once everyone has been welcomed and hugged, Hanna gestures for them all to come in the house.

"Where's Dad?" Stephan asks, looking around the front room. It's strange to see things look the same when so much time has passed—and when so much has happened.

Hanna freezes at the question, her smile vanishing. "Oh, Stephan," she says in a hushed voice. "Your father is... *ill.*" She gestures down the stairwell, to the same office-turned-hospice that she lived in when she had cancer.

Stephan walks down the stairs, dread growing with every step. This part of the households too much sorrow already. The sight of Olafur laid out beneath flannel sheets and hooked up to a ventilator is yet another memory he won't be able to banish. Slowly, he crosses the room to the bed.

Silently, Erik steps up beside Stephan, putting an arm around his shoulder in support.

"It's his heart," says Hanna.

"Dad... it's me." Stephan slides his hand under the covers to take Olafur's hand.

Olafur's eyes spark, but the mask he's wearing prevents him from speaking.

Stephan waves Sarah and Viktor over and introduces them to his father. Sarah leans down to give him a soft embrace, but Viktor clings to her leg, frightened by the tubes and the mask and the rasping, hissing sound of the machine. Aleria, Erik, and Noah stand solemn in the background, hands interlocked in a chain.

"Your father needs a triple bypass, but at his age it is just too risky. So, he decided not to go forward with the surgery." Hanna pulls at Stephan's arm so they can talk in private. She whispers, "The hospice nurse believes he won't make it past this weekend. You came just in time." Her voice wavers. "And on Christmas..."

Stephan looks over at Erik, who gives him a silent nod. Stephan pulls a vial of macrophage activator from his jacket. "I..." He clears his throat and begins again. "I brought this."

At the site of the small vial, Hanna begins to cry. "Is that the same miracle drug that Erik gave me?" says Hanna, hope straightening her spine.

"Yes," Stephan says. "Since I've been gone, I've been working with the lead medical officer on the Sjelian vessel. I brought this with me, thinking that if you had a relapse and your cancer returned, I could give it to you. I never thought I would need it for Dad... he's always been so healthy."

Hanna glances from Stephan to Erik, clutching her hands over her heart. "Do you think it will work?"

"It should," Stephan says, even as his Earth medical training protests that cancer and heart disease can't be cured by the same treatment. "We have to try."

Stephan sets to work removing Olafur's mask and tubes. He helps him sit and tips back his head to let the macrophage trickle down his throat. Olafur sags and stares at the ceiling, glossy-eyed from all the morphine. Stephan lowers him back to the pillows and tucks him in.

* * *

Solna, Sweden — December 24th, 2028 — 7:30 p.m. local time

Janice doesn't bother to mask her amazement, staring openly at Winnett. A five-year-old's been chatting with her about epidemiology for the past fifteen minutes... She's rarely had such an engaged, complex discussion with adult researchers. His breadth of knowledge is astounding... surpassing most of her colleagues.

When Karena reenters the room, after readying Mikaela for bed, and sees the look on her old friend's face, she lets out a tired laugh. "What was it this time?" she asks. "Artificial intelligence? Nuclear fission?"

"Statistical models for future pandemics, based on the way the Sjelian morphons spread through Earth's population," Janice says weakly. She motions toward three-year-old Mikaela, now in a soft purple nightgown, her teeth freshly brushed. "Is she the same?"

Karena ruffles Mikaela's hair fondly. "No... she only has three DNA strands: Sjelian, Earth, and Neksesian. She's just... very intuitive. She has vivid dreams. She's great at guessing games."

Janice shakes her head. "Your children are amazing. You're happy with Kesh, on Tria?"

"I truly am. It's wonderful to see you, but... Tria is our home."

"I am sorry Kesh couldn't come with you this time," Janice says.

"Me too. He sends his regards. But on this trip, we're all

trying to stay out of trouble. He and I agreed that his appearance might... garner unwanted attention."

Janice sighs. "You're right, unfortunately. Your last visit to Earth five years ago is the stuff of legend—the illustrious Karena Wilson reappears for a single day, with a mysterious pink-skinned companion..."

"Illustrious," Karena scoffs, shaking her head.

"Can we tour your laboratories tomorrow?" Winnett pipes up.

"We're closed tomorrow, dear," Janice says kindly. "It's Christmas."

"Sure," Winnett says, not terribly interested in Earth's holidays—even the gift-giving ones. "But you're the director. If anyone can open the building for a private tour, it's you."

"Well..." Janice says, eyes flickering to Karena, asking for permission.

Karena thinks about it for a long moment. It occurs to her that this might be the safest way to satisfy Winnett's never-ending curiosity about Earth's research capabilities. "If we do this," she says slowly, "I don't want to hear another word about visiting the tower in Wisconsin."

Her son's eyes light up. "I promise," he says.

* * *

Reykjavik, Iceland — December 24th, 2028 — 8:00 p.m. local time

Stephan bounces his foot on the living room carpet, checking the clock every few minutes. When he gave the macrophage to his mother, she was feeling relief in no time... but it's been almost two hours since he treated Olafur. Perhaps a failing heart requires different Sjelian medical technology. Sarah takes his hand, which is gripping the couch cushion, and massages out the tension so she can intertwine her fingers with his.

"When will you be leaving us?" Hanna asks them from the easy chair, where she's watching Viktor and Noah play with an old pair of trains that Stephan loved as a boy.

Stephan chews his cheek as he looks to Sarah. "We were planning to leave tomorrow to visit Sarah's father..." he says, sneaking a question into his voice.

"He lives in the states?" Hanna asks.

"Yes, with my aunt," says Sarah. "Well, she's not really my aunt. She's a dear family friend."

"And we were going to stay here two days," Erik says.

Hanna sighs, her lower lip pouting a smidge. "I wish you all could stay longer."

"Me too, Mom," Stephan says.

Sarah opens her mouth to say something, but the stairs to the hospice room creak and make everyone whip their heads around. Olafur wears a triumphant grin as he takes the last step with ease.

Hanna gawks at her husband, spry and smiling, his mask gone. A lively flush colors his hollowed cheeks. Hanna's tears well, then spill out with a sob that's almost a laugh. Stephan embraces his mother and helps her stand as he playfully scolds his father, "What are you doing out of bed?"

"I honestly don't know," says Olafur with a chuckle. He scans the room and does a double-take at Stephan and Sarah on the couch, as if seeing them for the first time. His eyes pop when he notices Erik and Aleria seated at the dining table. "It was that macrophage... wasn't it?"

"Yes, Dad," says Stephan, getting up for a hug of his own. "I wasn't sure it would work with your condition, but..."

"Amazing," says Sarah, patting Viktor's head as he moves in close beside her.

Olafur notices the red-haired boy and his eyes sparkle. "Is that my grandson?"

Hanna watches with tears in her eyes as Olafur crosses the room to the boy. After regaining her composure, she rushes to embrace her husband before he reaches the boy.

"I love you," he says, giving her a gentle squeeze and a peck on the cheek.

They walk together to Viktor. "What is your name?" Olafur asks.

"Viktor."

"How old are you, Viktor?"

"Two."

"He'll be three next month," Stephan adds.

"Wow... such a big boy. You know, you've got my daughter Kristin's nose." He winks, making a tear spill over his lashes. "It's a good nose."

Viktor smiles, though he looks a bit confused.

"And who's this?" Olafur turns his attention to Noah.

Erik pushes his son forward. "Go on, say hi to your grandfather."

"I'm Noah," the boy says. "I'm four years old."

Olafur leans down with a charmed smile and extends a hand that the boy takes. "Well! It's lovely to meet you both!" Olafur exaggerates the handshake, making Noah laugh. He looks back at Stephan. "Are you two... life partners?"

"Yes, we are." Stephan gestures for Sarah to step forward into his waiting arm. "This is Sarah."

Hanna heaves another sigh with her eyes closed. "Stephan and Sarah have to leave tomorrow."

"But we'll be back to pick up Erik, Aleria, and Noah on the 26th," Stephan says quickly, trying to banish the guilt clawing at him. Sarah deserves a family visit, too, after all. "We can spend a few hours then..."

"Well... let's make the most of our time together," says Olafur, standing tall.

Hanna wipes away her lingering tears as she catches Olafur in another hug. She looks around at Stephan and shakes her head. "Your timing..."

* * *

Washington Settlement, United States — December 25th, 2028 — 9:00 a.m. local time

Jackie's home is impeccably tidy, with no dust in sight and no sofa cushion out of place, but it still feels cozy. Soft, handmade blankets are draped over the backs of the chairs and the sofa. The scents of fresh-brewed coffee and a spicy candle fill the living room, along with pine from the Christmas tree in the corner. But it's the sounds of friends and family chatting and laughing from every corner that truly makes it feel like an established home.

Benjamin plays jacks with Tess on the floor. Charles is humming in the kitchen as he pours himself more coffee. Lars and Gladys are enjoying a couple of Jackie's homemade muffins at the kitchen table. Tina picks lightly at her guitar in the chair by the living room window. Jennifer sits with a magazine on her lap, idly flicking through it while her mother dotes over Fresler and Sharon, bringing them blankets and hot mugs.

"I am so happy for you," Jackie says as she settles into a chair near the couch. "You're married with a beautiful daughter."

Sharon rubs Fresler's knee. "Well... not actually married. We're life partners."

"Okay, but it sounds like the same thing to me," says Jackie.

Fresler can't stop gawking at ten-year-old Benjamin. "I can't believe how grown-up you look." He turns to Tina. "He's practically a teenager."

Tina groans. "You have no idea."

The boy rolls his eyes. "Whatever."

"A couple years ago, he demanded that we start calling him Ben instead of Benjamin," Tina informs Sharon and Fresler. "He says it sounds more mature."

According to Jackie, Tina is the one raising Ben, and Fresler can detect the motherly love in the crooked smile she gives him when he says, stubbornly, "It *does* sound more mature."

She chuckles. "You should see his room. I tell him to clean it every day. It's a sty."

Ben shakes his shaggy head. "What are you talking about? It's clean right now... go see."

"That's because you knew Fresler and Sharon would be visiting this morning," says Tina, not bothering to get up.

"Whatever." Ben retreats to the bathroom, letting Tess scoop up all the remaining jacks for herself on the next bounce of the ball.

Fresler nods toward their toddler and whispers in Sharon's ear. "Is she going to be like that in a few years?"

"Probably," Sharon says with a shrug. She turns to Jackie. "How do you like living here?"

Jackie shrugs. "It's nice, I guess."

"There's electricity and running water," says Charles, taking Ben's place on the floor to start a new round with Tess.

"What do you all do, on Tria?" Jackie asks.

Sharon beams, scooting to the edge of her couch cushion. "I'm actually working at an indoor farm and garden! We merged my knowledge of greenhouse growing from Earth with the Neksesians' advanced technology. You'd be amazed at some of the things we can grow."

"And I'm a teacher now," Fresler says.

"Wow, us too!" Jennifer says, motioning between herself and Tina. "I teach first and second grade."

"And I teach high school math," Tina says.

"I teach writing," Fresler says. "I never thought I would teach, but... it's fun."

Sharon smirks at Tina. "I bet Ben is looking forward to having you as his teacher in a few years."

Tina scoffs. "Not exactly. But he did love having Jennifer."

"How sweet," says Sharon.

"You started teaching when you were what... eighteen?" asks Fresler.

"Yup," says Jennifer, flipping a page without looking at it. "That's the legal age when you must be employed in order to live in the settlement."

Fresler blinks, recalling his freshman year of college, which was... aimless, at best.

"The job restrictions did loosen up a little last year," Jennifer continues. "My friend Maddie runs a camp for kids with her husband, Joey. She teaches martial arts, and he teaches swimming, and they have other employees that do hiking and music and stuff. Before, teaching organized recreation wouldn't have been allowed. Maddie and Joey were both working in food services."

"That camp sounds nice," Sharon says, but her smile is lackluster. "What are you doing these days, Jackie?"

"Law enforcement, if you can believe it."

"John would be proud," says Fresler heartily.

The group falls silent for a moment. Tess's bouncing ball is the only sound.

"Is the U.S. government still a dictatorship?" asks Sharon after clearing her throat. Gladys and Lars hadn't wanted to talk much about the government yesterday, preferring to lavish their attention on their granddaughter. But Sharon trusts her friends to tell her what's really going on.

Charles frowns. "They do have three branches again, but the president retained his emergency powers."

"What does that mean?" asks Fresler.

"He has these executive orders that basically bear the same weight as a law," says Charles. "He doesn't need legislative approval, and they cannot be found unconstitutional."

Sharon wrinkles her nose. "What? Executive orders aren't supposed to have the same weight as law."

Charles gives her a knowing look.

"How is it possible that they can't be found unconstitutional?" asks Fresler. "What happened to our constitution?"

"He claims that this is only temporary," says Jackie.

"Good Lord," says Sharon.

"But... starting next month, we are no longer restricted to the two settlements," says Tina, voice brightening. "We can live wherever we want."

Sharon tries to return her enthusiasm, but all she feels is pity and sadness. A sliver of freedom seems like a grand gift to Tina. It's almost as though she's been living in a prison yard for years.

"Yeah, but the problem is that this is where all the jobs are," says Jennifer with a scoff. "If we tried to move out of the settlement, we would have to live without electricity or running water. Who wants to do that?"

Charles raises a hand and blows on his coffee. "I know I wouldn't."

"So, you don't have to carry ID or papers to travel across the country?" asks Fresler, stomach fluttering with hope. "You can live... anywhere?"

Charles nods.

Fresler reaches for Sharon's hand, feeling light enough to float off the couch. "We could live in our cabin in Minnesota."

"You could," says Jackie, "but the government owns it. You'd rent it from them."

Fresler deflates, and Sharon pats his knee. "I would have to get permission to rent my own cabin?" he says in a defeated voice.

"Yes," Jackie says with a sympathetic frown. "They own it now. They own everything. So, you would need to get approval from the government."

"Luckily," Sharon says loudly, before Fresler can get worked up, "we've made a happy home on Tria."

An awkward silence hangs over the room until Fresler admits, "We have."

"We've been thinking about visiting Kentucky... to see the old farm," says Jennifer.

"That sounds like fun," says Sharon.

"The problem is that we would need to buy a car," pouts Jennifer. "One large enough for all of us, and it would have to tow a trailer."

"Why?" asks Fresler.

"The gas stations are not operational," Jackie explains. "We would have to bring our own gas, enough for the whole trip."

"But..." says Sharon, confused. "We saw a gas station not far from here."

Tina strums a chord and says, "Right, *inside* the settle-ment. There are no operational gas stations *outside* of the settlements."

Fresler shakes his head. "I thought things would be better by now. We were gone for five years!" He clenches a fist by his thigh as an outlet for his frustration.

"Well," Jackie says matter-of-factly, "they certainly aren't any worse. We have shelter, food, employment... and of course, we have each other."

"Hear, hear!" Lars calls from the kitchen table. Fresler hadn't realized his parents were listening.

"How long will you be with us this time?" asks Jackie.

Fresler doesn't miss that she doesn't ask, now, if they plan to stay permanently. "We're leaving tomorrow."

Jackie nods with understanding. "I do wish you could stay longer."

"Me too," says Sharon. "But..." She gives Fresler a pained look. He can tell she's itching to warn them about the alien threat.

"We have to get back," he finishes for her. "We'll miss you all."

"We'll miss you too," says Jackie, gaze swiveling between them, clearly sensing the strands of their unspoken conver-sation traveling through the air. "So, you like living on Tria?" she asks, smoothly changing the subject.

"Oh, yes," says Sharon, brightening. "Our daughter is really close to her cousins. It's great for her to have them nearby. I was always close with my cousins. My favorite childhood memories were with them."

Listening to Sharon talk, Fresler has an epiphany: the cabin they shared, *his* cabin... is no longer their family's home. Even if they could live in Minnesota rent-free, their home is on Tria. Maybe it started as a temporary arrangement—calling it "home" only as an empty term—but now it's the honest truth.

And the glow in his life partner's cheeks as she shares what she loves about Tria is enough to ease the sting in Fresler's heart.

* * *

European CDC Headquarters, Solna, Sweden — December 25th, 2028 — 6:00 p.m. local time

"Can we go home?" Mikaela whines, tugging on Karena's arm. "I'm *hungry*."

They've been at the ECDC since 1:00 p.m. Winnett wanted to see every nook and cranny of the building. When Mikaela lost interest, Janice offered her a tablet loaded with some games and set her up in an employee break room. It worked... for half an hour.

"Winnett, sweetie," Karena ventures, leaning into his peripherals and waving. He's been parked in front of a computer terminal in the main research lab for more than two hours. "It's time to go."

"I'm almost done," Winnett says, eyes jumping around as he reads.

"What are you even doing over there?" Karena hobbles toward Winnett, weighed down by the hungry three-year-old now latched onto her right leg.

"I'm memorizing all of the data the United States government has on the communication tower," Winnett says, still enamored by the screen.

"*What?!*" Karena yelps, shaking Mikaela off and rushing to spin Winnett around in his swivel chair. "That's classified! How did you—and what did I tell you about the tower?"

Winnett finally glances at his mother, tilting his head in

polite confusion. "You said not to say another word about *visiting* it. And I won't." He gestures at the computer. "Now, I don't need to."

A snort of laughter from the doorway makes Karena look around. Janice stands in the doorway with keys in hand. "He has you there, Karena."

"Yes, but... hacking into a government database..." Karena runs a frantic hand through her hair. "How did you even do that?"

"It wasn't difficult," Winnett says. "This technology is super basic compared to what we have on Tria."

"I won't tell our scientists you said that," Janice says, eyes twinkling.

Karena moans. "He's already too smart for me, and he's only five. What am I going to do once he's a teenager?"

"You'll do the best you can," Janice says, beckoning them all toward the door.

Reluctantly, Winnett shuts down the computer and hops off his chair. As they walk through the empty corridors toward the main exit, he takes his mother's hand. "Thank you," he says.

Karena can't fight those baby blues. He *didn't* disobey her, after all. "Did you find what you were looking for?" she asks with a resigned smile.

"I did. I'll tell you and Aunt Sarah about it on the shuttle." Winnett turns to Janice. "Do you have any more of those ginger snap cookies?"

"Yes," says Janice, patting her purse, "and you can have some *after* you finish your dinner, young man."

Winnett walks tall, wearing the satisfied smile of someone ready to reap the rewards of their accomplishments.

* * *

Northern Minnesota — December 26th, 2028 — 1:00 p.m. local time

"We'll touch down in five minutes," Stephan says from the pilot's seat. The coordinates Fresler gave him are a green dot on his radar, growing ever closer.

The shuttle lurches a little as he refines his course, and his bloated stomach flips. He and Sarah left Mitchell's restaurant in Salt Lake City this morning with full hearts and fuller bellies. And that was *after* his mom stuffed them with home-cooking in Reykjavik.

It was so wonderful to see everyone... and so hard to leave.

Stephan doesn't think he's alone in feeling a little lost today. He picked up Karena, Winnett, and Mikaela first, noting Karena's red eyes as she said goodbye to her friend Janice. Then, he, Sarah, Erik, and Aleria all cried as they bid farewell to Hanna and Olafur. Their tears upset Viktor and Noah, who soon joined in, clutching legs and consenting to cheek kisses. Finally, Sharon, Fresler, and Tess climbed aboard with solemn faces. Now, everyone sits in subdued silence as they approach their final stop on this planet: Fresler's beloved cabin.

He wants to say goodbye, and no one will deny him the chance.

As the shuttle lands on a snow dune, Fresler leans toward the display screen, where his white-topped cabin is visible on a nearby hill. Fresler hurries into his heavy winter coat and gloves as the door opens, then wraps his scarf on his way down the ramp.

Fresler charges through the snow, clearing a path for the others. The river chatters at him, welcoming him back, but he ignores its call for now. His cabin, his home sweet home, sits vacant and cold. There are no lights on inside. There's no smoke spewing from the chimney. *It looks lonely,* he thinks.

He pauses to reach back and take Sharon's hand. She passes him Tess, and he props her on his hip as he approaches the overhang protecting the front door from snowfall.

Fresler forces the frozen hinges open and is immediately struck by a musty scent that tickles his nose. Cobwebs hang from the ceiling, and dust coats every surface.

Stepping in right behind Fresler, Erik looks around the front living area. "I remember this place."

Fresler smiles. "You were what... five when your parents visited? I can't believe you remember much."

"I remember that fireplace for some reason," Erik says, pointing. The old brick fireplace looks like an open mouth begging for logs to consume.

"That was so long ago," says Fresler.

Tess tugs on Fresler's coat sleeve. "Can I go down to the river?"

Noah bounces by Erik's elbow. "Me too!"

"We can take the kids for a walk," Karena says from the porch. She points to Mikaela, playing in the snow. She pats it cautiously at first, intrigued by its temperature and its texture. They don't have snow on Tria. Satisfied it won't harm her, she shoves her hand in the mound with a squeal of delight. "They all need to run around a little before we head back to the space station."

"Good idea," Sharon agrees. "It's this way." She leads the other moms and the kids down to the river while Stephan, Fresler, and Erik stay in the cabin.

Fresler watches them go, then turns from the window

and says, "You know what's odd... I have so many great memories of this place as a kid and the two years Sharon and I spent here alone, but I keep thinking about the time I spent here during the pandemic." He walks over to the fireplace. "I can see John, Jackie, Jennifer, Larry, and Tina sitting here planning our trip to Littlefork."

"It is amazing that you discovered you were immune," says Stephan, running a finger through the dust on the kitchen counter.

"It's because of Sean," says Fresler reverently. He points through the window at the storage shed. It's leaning left these days. "I'll never forget the two weeks I spent in that shed with Sean."

"That must have been horrible," says Stephan.

"Yeah... watching him die like that." Fresler shakes the memory out of his head.

"Your friend Tina lost both Sean and Larry, right?" Erik puffs a breath out of his nose.

"Yes."

"Everyone lost so much," Erik goes on. *And I wasn't here,* he thinks. He still beats himself up, sometimes, over not making it back in time to prevent the pandemic's first horrific wave. "That boy you found in the mall, Benjamin... his parents had been killed..."

Fresler frowns. "He was so traumatized." He brightens. "But he looks great now. He's ten. He wants to go by Ben. *Ben Claiborne.*"

Erik scrunches his brow. "Ben Claiborne. Wait a second."

"What is it?" Fresler asks.

"How did I not put this together before now?" Erik smacks himself in the forehead. "Stephan, do you remember the patient you referred to our HCP study—the one that survived cancer and multiple sclerosis?"

Stephan nods. "Of course. Timothy Claiborne. Same last name as the kid. Huh."

Erik leans forward. "He told me that his wife was pregnant, and if they had a boy, they would name him Benjamin. That was in 2017, so the baby would have been born early the next year..."

Fresler's mouth drops open. "Ben told me his dad's name was Timothy. You don't think..."

Erik shrugs. "Stranger things have happened to us."

Stephan coughs. "They sure have."

"So, Ben's dad... was your patient who went through that Akureyri portal?" Fresler gapes at Stephan.

"Maybe," Stephan says.

"Timothy Claiborne is the reason I found the cave," Erik says. "Reshal manipulated websites to reach out to me. Without Timothy... none of us would be here."

"And then you saved his son's life," Stephan says, grinning at Fresler.

Erik plops on the sofa, releasing a cloud of dust. "Oh, my God," he says, then sneezes as the dust assaults him.

The three men sit in silence for a moment, thinking about coincidence, tragedy, and silver linings.

Erik gestures to the river. "Let's check on the kids."

He and Stephan head out, but Fresler lingers under the overhang. He crouches and looks under the cabin where he left his foldout chair. It is still there, gathering spider webs. He pulls it out and shakes off the dirt.

Sharon said that we would be back, he thinks to himself, *and she was right.*

CHAPTER 21

Tria – April 10th, 2029

"Where do we stand with the Sjelian General Council?" Aster, the Neksesian defense leader, asks Theran as soon as he steps into the office.

Theran suppresses a groan of exhaustion. He just arrived on Tria a few hours ago, and he doesn't want to think about the Council.

"The Council still doesn't want to inform the citizens of Sjel about the impending attack," Theran says, running a hand over his smooth head in frustration. "They will continue to provide materials and technology, but they will not commit to Sjel providing any additional manpower."

Aster shakes his head, exhaling sharply. "Well, you did predict as much, based on your previous meetings. But that is disappointing."

"They also continue to divert resources to the planet's gravitational shields."

Aster scoffs. "You saw the message on Des. That alien weapon decimated the planet. Not a single living creature survived. Sjel can't rely on a shield. The Council should order an evacuation to Borjan."

"I agree," Theran says, "but they are set against it."

The two of them stare at the wall of screens in the small office. For a few moments, the only sound is the hum of the giant generators powering the war vessel construction effort in the Trian manufacturing plant next door.

Then Aster says, "We are far short of our goal. At this rate, we won't have enough vessels by 2031."

"What do you propose?" asks Theran.

"We return to Polemos."

"No," Theran says immediately. He points to one of the screens. "What about Phaelin?"

Reshal has had probes in orbit around Phaelin for over a year, covertly monitoring communications. Initially, they hadn't expected much activity from what was supposed to be a dying planet. But to everyone's astonishment, they'd discovered Phaelin was not only surviving... but thriving.

Using the Neksesian technology they'd stolen from Gott and Telfas's vessel as a jumping-off point, Phaelin's scientists made their planet habitable again. Phaelin now boasts buildings that are designed to protect their inhabitants from the harsh elements, as well as masks and suits for anyone who must venture outside. Their researchers are working to reverse the considerable environmental damage that resulted from the loss of the planet's oceans. Based on the studies shared over their communication systems, they're not far from a solution.

"We could approach their new leader, Sul," Theran says slowly. "Surely a man who has led his planet's population out of one catastrophe would not want to fall victim to another."

"You of all people must see why attempting to recruit Sul

is a bad idea," Aster counters. He's heard the story of their long-ago escape from Phaelin and now eyes Theran with skepticism. "What would keep him from repeating Skithaell's past actions—capturing our delegation and confiscating our tech? After all, it's stolen tech that's saved their population." Aster nods decisively. "Polemos is the better option."

Theran thinks of an expression Erik taught him: "Better the devil you know." That is how he feels about Phaelin. He knows what to expect from that planet and its inhabitants... whereas all they know of Polemos is that any attempt at contact results in immediate laser fire from their automated defense systems. A "shoot on sight" attitude doesn't lend itself to hope of cooperation.

But he looks at the information displayed on Aster's computer screens and feels his resolve fading away.

Their options are dwindling.

Sjel is aiding their cause... but not enough. Earth isn't sufficiently technologically advanced to help at all, and its citizens don't even know other planets with human life exist. Opik and Nekses are gone. Rajik and Des are barren waste-lands. Aside from Tria, Phaelin and Polemos are all that's left.

On the other side of the interdimensional portal, Borjan has agreed to accept refugees from any of the tethered planets but doesn't want to get involved in the fight. And then there's Diastassi. Even if they weren't vicious, warlike people who'd tried to sterilize both his life partner and his daughter, Theran wouldn't want to go back there.

"Based on the information Reshal's people have gath-ered, Polemos has an armada of over fifty thousand vessels," Aster says, when Theran has been silent too long. "We must convince them to combine our forces. It's the only way we can defend ourselves."

Theran tilts his head. "Do you really think they'll help us, after what happened last time?"

"We must work together," Aster insists. "They must see that we can help them, in return."

"It's risky."

Aster shrugs. "What choice do we have? We need to try." He chews the inside of his lip and stares at Theran for a moment before adding, "I want Winnett to join us for the visit."

Theran shakes his head. "Karena will never agree to that."

Aster cuts his eyes at Theran. "You need to convince her."

* * *

"Absolutely not." Karena's scowl is hard as diamond before the request is halfway out of Theran's mouth. "I am not going to risk my son's life."

Theran bows his head in respect. "I don't blame you. I hope you understand that I had to ask."

"Why is it so important that Winnett join you? Why do you need him, exactly?"

"Aster believes in the prophecy... that Winnett is the key to the survival of humanity."

Karena drums her fingers on her crossed arms. "Does the prophecy include Winnett going to Polemos?"

"I don't know."

Karena growls in the back of her throat. "I hate this. I don't want to believe in it, but..."

"The Borjans believe," Theran says. "The Neksesians believe."

"Do you?" asks Karena, one eyebrow arching to impressive heights.

Theran pauses before saying carefully, "I don't know what to believe."

Karena lets out another growl. "If Aster had a legitimate reason for Winnett to go along... something to do with Winnett's research, perhaps... but this feels like he just wants my son there as, I don't know, a good-luck charm."

Before Theran can respond to that comment, Winnett walks through the front door, looking windswept. He pushes up the sleeves of his Borjan robe, a garment he's taken to wearing since their trip to Earth. It makes him look like a tiny monk.

"Hello," Winnett says to Theran before pouring himself a glass of water.

Theran nods, trying to gauge Karena's expression to determine whether he should head out.

"When are you planning to leave for Polemos?" asks Winnett.

Figuring the boy must have overheard their conversation, Theran responds, "Tomorrow."

Winnett sets down his cup. "I need to join them," he tells his mother.

"No, it's too dangerous," Karena sputters. "You can study one of the abandoned towers instead—"

"This has nothing to do with the towers," Winnett interrupts. "After we visit Polemos, I need to go to Des."

Winnett tilts his head and hypnotizes his mother with his owlish, unblinking stare. "If I don't go with them to Polemos, they won't return," he says evenly.

Karena shakes her head as if to clear it. "What?"

"You have to trust me. I need to go."

Theran stands perfectly still, holding his breath.

Karena looks to the Sjelian commander. "Can you keep him safe?" she demands.

"If I go, we will all return safely," says Winnett, serene as a Sjelian.

"It's not your job to keep everyone safe, Winnett. You're a child. Theran is a military leader." Theran flinches at the word "military", pained by the accuracy of it. "Polemos is violent. You know what they did—"

"You have to trust me." Winnett takes Karena's hands in his own.

Karena swallows hard and eventually says, "I'm going with you."

A smile flickers across Winnett's face. "I'd hoped you would." He walks toward the door. "I'll be back in about an hour."

"Where are you going?" Karena asks.

"I need to talk to Sarah about ensuring the excavation on Des is complete before we arrive." Winnett looks at Theran. "It will take us two weeks to travel to Polemos?"

Theran bobs his head, flabbergasted by how quickly the dynamics of the room changed the moment Winnett stepped inside. It seems Aster was right. They need him, now more than ever.

CHAPTER 22

E rik always enjoys traveling on Neksesian vessels, if only because they provide a little more visual variety than the Sjelian crafts he's accustomed to. As he and Aleria make their way to the command center, they're guided by arrows and signage built into the frosted white walls, and the charcoal floors break up the sea of white. Aster, Theran, Karena, and Winnett await them as they near Polemos.

"We'll arrive tomorrow," Aster says from the pilot's chair. He's at the helm because they're flying with a skeleton crew... just in case. "We are scheduled to meet with their leader, Verad," Aster adds.

"Wait... they are expecting us?!" Erik says, surprised.

"Yes. I just spoke with one of Verad's representatives." Aster sounds a little smug at that. "He is willing to listen to us."

"How do we know it isn't a trap?" Karena asks sharply.

"That is why Aleria is here," Theran says. "She will sense any deception from the Polemosians."

"Since our previous... attempt to communicate with them about the impending attack and need for military support," Aster says delicately, "they have discovered their planet's signal tower. That is why they are now willing to grant us an audience."

"How long ago did they find the tower?" Erik demands. "Why did it take them so long to locate it? We sent them the coordinates."

Theran holds up a hand. "The tower is apparently in an uninhabitable area, and Polemosians don't yet have the technology to measure gravitons. Because of those factors, locating it took some time. Let just be thankful they're talking to us."

* * *

Polemos — April 25th, 2029

When Aster puts the Neksesian vessel in orbit around Polemos, everyone on board holds their breath.

When no shots are fired, they exhale.

Aster pilots the cylindrical shuttle destined for the surface, with the command center gang in tow. They've barely unhitched from the ship, however, before two Polemosian warships flank them. Aster zooms out the camera to take in their hulking silver shapes. To Karena, they look like bulky sting rays.

She grabs Winnett's hand, and he flashes her a smile that says, 'Don't worry, Mom. Everything will be okay.' She wants to trust him... knows from experience that she should... but so many factors are at play. So many things can go wrong.

When the shuttle reaches the atmosphere, blue skies appear. The soft cerulean is eerily similar to Earth. Gray storm clouds gather over a city of skyscrapers. Aster flies them to an enormous airbase on the outskirts. Thousands of fighter vessels, miniatures of their warship escorts, are lined up, ready for takeoff.

The shuttle lands on a circular pad overlooking what Karena can only guess is a training field, outlined by platforms bearing massive satellites. The thunder of hundreds of thousands of feet stomping in single file lines shakes the ground. An army clad in white battle suits turns as a unit to face the shuttle.

Karena's blood chills. She points out the window and asks the others, "Are they trying to make a point?"

"Looks like it," says Erik, looking as uneasy as she feels.

"Translators in, everyone," Theran says, securing his earpiece.

Aster nods. "Stay alert."

Aster leads the way out and is immediately blocked by a towering, bearded Polemosian man dressed in a fitted, padded green military robe decorated with gold and blue medals. After a nod and a grunt to Aster, he escorts the group into the nearest skyscraper, where they are scheduled to meet Verad. Karena nervously eyes the black device hanging from his golden belt. It has to be a weapon, but she can't determine whether it's a gun of some sort or a blunt-force instrument, like a heavy baton.

Once inside the chilly building, the man still doesn't say a word, merely gestures for them to take a seat on cushioned gray benches with no backs that face a raised platform sporting an onyx roundtable. The group complies in similar silence, eyeing the hundreds of soldiers stationed outside the building through the dozens of small windows. Thankfully, these soldiers aren't wearing full battle gear, but the same padded green robes as the bearded escort.

"Are those stun guns?" Karena whispers to Erik, studying the hefty black weapons in greater detail. She can see three blue lights flashing on the ends. Perhaps buttons?

"I don't know," Erik mutters back. "Looks like it, but I'd bet they do more than shock you." He turns to his life partner. "Do you sense anything?"

Aleria's brow furrows as she concentrates. "Mostly... curiosity. They want to know why we're here."

Erik nods. "Okay."

They sit twiddling their thumbs for several minutes, not daring to talk too freely amongst themselves with the bearded soldier standing in a nearby corner. Verad finally graces them with his presence, entering from a back room. He and his two armed bodyguards walk onto the stage. He sits at the empty table, facing his guests. Verad isn't as tall as his escorts, but he's still a hulk of a man. He strokes his chest-length gray beard and appraises them through narrowed eyes that accentuate his crow's feet.

Verad clears his throat. "Which one of you is Aster?"

As he speaks, Polemosian goes in Karena's left ear and English echoes in her right.

Aster stands up and says, "I am."

Verad offers no greeting, only says, "We verified the existence of the tower you spoke of the last time you entered our orbit."

So, you got something *out of the conversation before you shot our ship out of the sky,* Karena thinks bitterly.

"You believe that... *aliens* placed it there," Verad continues, "and that they will return approximately two years from now."

"Yes," says Aster.

"What evidence do you have to support your claim?"

Aster quickly explains about the nine tethered planets,

each with an identical signal tower. He shares how the towers breach the surface of each planet when attacked or otherwise threatened—most recently, in the year 2016 on the Earth calendar, when the planet Opik was destroyed by the anomaly. Finally, he summarizes the message the Desians left behind on their devastated planet.

A heavy silence follows his speech.

Then Verad says, "These aliens pose a threat to all of humanity?"

"They do," Aster says, sounding relieved. "We need to join forces... it's the only way we can defeat them."

Verad nods. "How many vessels do you have?"

"So far, we have built over fifteen thousand war machines."

Verad scoffs. "We have over fifty thousand."

"I know," says Aster, not skipping a beat. "That is why we came to you. Together, we stand a chance of victory."

"What are you proposing?"

"Before Des was attacked, the aliens first visited Tria, the site of their destroyed outpost. Thus, we believe that this time, they will begin their investigation either at Opik's previous location or the former site of my planet, Nekses, which was destroyed by the anomaly in 2023."

The Polemosian leader leans forward in his seat. "What do you believe they're looking for at those sites?"

"A reason for the planets' destruction," Aster says. "Or, more likely, someone to blame."

"Why do these aliens care so much about our planets? What do these towers do? If they're so important, why aren't the aliens here, occupying these planets?"

"We don't have the answer to those questions."

Verad cuts his dark eyes at the group, taking in their varying skin tones and attire. He lingers on Winnett, who definitely looks the most out of place, both because of his age and his Borjan attire. "Assuming that you are correct," he finally says, "and these aliens return, how do you propose we defend ourselves?"

"We monitor both Nekses and Opik's former locations and join forces when the aliens arrive. If they attack, we will destroy their armada."

"How many vessels would you require from us?"

Aster glances at Theran before playing his most desperate card. "All of them."

Verad lets out a bark of laughter. "You'd dare ask us to send our entire fleet on this mission, leaving our planet defenseless? What if you're wrong? What if the aliens come directly to Polemos?"

"They won't arrive here first," Aster says confidently.

"How can you be certain? Do you have the ability to track their vessels?" asks Verad.

At that, Aster falters. "N-no."

Verad raises a salt and pepper eyebrow. "Then how do you know where they plan to be, and when?"

"We believe they will follow the pattern of their first attack."

"A pattern is not evidence," Verad says. "There must be something you aren't telling me."

Instinctively, Karena puts her arm around Winnett's shoulders.

Unfortunately, the sudden movement draws Verad's eye. "The boy..." he says, intrigued. "Why bring a child with you?"

Aster waves an arm toward Winnett. "He had a premonition."

"Premonition?" Verad cocks his head at Winnett. "What does that mean?"

"He can see into the future," says Aster. "He saw the aliens' return."

"Step forward, boy," Verad barks.

Winnett stands and approaches the platform, and Karena can hardly breathe. She grips the hard, uncomfortable bench cushion, digging her nails into the dense fabric.

"What is your name?"

"Winnett," the five-year-old says, voice ringing with confidence.

Verad inclines his head. "You can see the future?"

Winnett nods. "Fragments.... But yes."

"You saw this alien race?"

Winnett nods.

"How many war machines do they have?"

"Thousands... maybe hundreds of thousands."

"Why are they coming?"

Winnett folds his hands behind his back. "To investigate why two of their planets have stopped sending signals."

Verad's brows rise. "Two of... *their planets?*"

"Yes." Winnett seems completely unfazed, carrying on as calmly as if he were chatting with one of his aunts or uncles. "The towers were placed on the nine planets billions of years ago. That means the aliens were here long before we humans built our civilizations. For some reason, these planets are important to the aliens' survival. They feel a sense of... ownership."

"If what you say is correct, then they wouldn't have abandoned them," Verad says stubbornly.

Theran hurries to Winnett's side, and Karena's nails release the cushion. "We don't know why they abandoned them," says Theran. "That's not important at the moment."

"Actually—" Winnett begins, but Theran speaks over him.

"What *is* important is that they will return to find out why the tether was broken. And when they do return, Winnett has foreseen that humanity will not survive their attack."

Verad appraises Theran over a crooked bump on the bridge of his nose, then looks to Aster. "You're proposing we join forces."

Aster slides his hands into the loose sleeves of his gold robe and inclines his pink head in answer.

"You want us to send fifty thousand war vessels to the cause, two years from now."

"Yes."

"I have a better proposal. In two years, you will send your fleet to our planet to help protect Polemos."

Aster rears back, sputtering. "That's ludicrous!"

Verad rolls back his shoulders and harrumphs. "Why should we care whether your people survive, as long as we protect our own?"

On the benches, Aleria stiffens and squeezes Erik's hand. Karena takes note and leans in as Aleria whispers, "Verad is furious. I sense we're in danger."

Verad grits his teeth. "You ask us to abandon our planet and leave our people defenseless! I am no fool. You plan to send your armada to Polemos!"

Aster holds up his hands. "No, you don't understand..."

Karena is on her feet in an instant, sprinting for her son.

"You... Neksesians—" Verad spits out the unfamiliar word as if it tastes bad. "Your planet was destroyed, and you intend to take ours by force." He rises and snaps his fingers. "Seize them!"

Karena grabs Winnett's shoulders and tries to put herself between him and the guards, but they are running into the room from all directions. Theran whirls on his

heel, calling, "Aleria!" just as Aster yells, "You can't
do this!"

A guard twists Aster's arm behind his back, making him
cry out as he's forced to his knees. Guards swarm the
benches. When a black rod is raised at Erik's chest, Aleria
launches her attack, fists clenched.

But before she can shut her eyes and flip the switch in
her brain, electricity pulses through the small of her back.
The blast of blue energy knocks her forward, and she
collapses, twitching, on the ground. Erik dives to her side
and hauls her into his lap, supporting her head. Theran
appears, taking her wrist to check her pulse.

As Erik screams Aleria's name, Karena faces down a
burly guard with his weapon drawn. She pulls Winnett to
her side and raises an arm to shield her face from the electricity sparking at the tip of the weapon. Another guard
grabs her elbow and yanks it down hard enough to make
her scream.

That's when bodies start hitting the floor.

Guards fall where they stand, weapons still sparking
blue. Verad's head strikes his table as he collapses, leaving
him bleeding on his own stage.

In the eerie silence that follows, the group exchanges
shocked looks.

"Aleria..." Karena croaks. "She saved us."

Erik shakes his head, too emotional to speak.

"It wasn't her. She's unconscious," Theran murmurs.

Karena stares at her son with his hood down and his
arms folded across his chest. "It was Winnett. He is the one
that saved us."

The boy looks up at his mother and nods.

She drops down and pulls him into a tight hug, pushing
back his hood to kiss his head.

"Unbelievable," Aster says, getting to his feet.

"Can you carry her?" Winnett asks Erik, nodding toward Aleria.

"Of course."

"Good." Winnett gestures to their shuttle. "We need to get off this planet immediately."

As he gets to his feet and then gently lifts Aleria, Erik scans his surroundings. His mouth pops open in disbelief. Every soldier stationed outside the windows lies crumpled on the ground. That explains why no more have burst through the doors.

But his nephew is right. There are hundreds of thousands of soldiers still waiting for them outside on the training field. They need to get out before anyone notices the bodies.

"Winnett, sweetie," Karena gasps as they quickly retrace the path they took through the skyscraper. "Have you done that before?"

"No."

"Then how did you..."

Winnett shrugs. "It was instinctual."

Karena rubs her sprained elbow. "Thank you," she says faintly.

They reach the exterior doors. Theran motions for them to hide just out of sight. Winnett ignores the order, rushing straight for the exit.

"Winnett!" Theran hisses.

The doors slide open. No alarm sounds. The whole city is quiet.

The soldiers are a mass of indistinguishable white body armor on the ground.

Erik's air leaves him in a barked laugh. "Amazing."

"How...?" murmurs Aster, his eyes bugging out of his

head at Winnett.

The group races to their shuttle, each thinking that this is too good to be true... too easy. But even when their shuttle lifts off and accelerates toward the upper atmosphere, not a single fighter vessel takes off from the airfield. Not a single weapon takes aim.

"Did you incapacitate... every person on the planet?" Karena asks her son, not sure whether she's awestruck, terrified, or both.

"No, not everyone.," Winnett says thoughtfully.

"I still can't believe it and I saw it with my own eyes," Aster says, eyes on the shuttle's controls. A distant blip on one screen makes him pick up speed. "Thank you, Winnett."

Winnett leans deeper into Karena's one-armed embrace, smiling with satisfaction. "I told you we would all make it off the planet safely."

* * *

Neksesian vessel — April 25th, 2029

Aleria slowly opens her eyes and finds herself in a small examination room. The Neksesian medical office looks so similar to the one on the Sjelian vessel, she half expects Mandal to walk through the door. Instead, it's Erik who greets her with a smile.

"How are you feeling?" Theran asks from her other side, startling her.

"A little groggy, but I'll be fine," she says as her heart rate returns to normal.

Erik pulls up a chair to her bed.

Aleria rubs her aching head. "How did we escape?"

"It was Winnett," says Theran.

Erik adds, "He incapacitated everyone in the room."

"What about the soldiers outside the building?" asks Aleria.

"Yes... all of them, too." Erik pauses. "He says he took out everyone in the city."

Aleria sits up and blinks at him, certain she heard wrong. "That's impossible."

Erik shrugs.

Aster knocks on the half-open door. "I see she's awake."

Theran waves him in. "We were just telling Aleria what happened on Polemos."

"I still don't understand it," Aster says, mouth agape at the memory. "There were thousands of soldiers."

"I could never incapacitate so many at once," Aleria says.

"That's not the only unusual thing," Erik tells Aleria. "I watched Winnett when he accessed his ability. He didn't close his eyes or clench his fists the way you do. The expression on his face was no different than it normally is. It was like it took no effort at all."

Aster's amber eyes spark. "The prophecies must be true."

"Where is Winnett now?" Aleria asks.

"With Karena, in their room," Theran says. "She wanted him to rest."

Aleria leans back into her pillows, mind reeling. She's never doubted Winnett's intelligence, but the power of his mind exceeds anything she could have imagined. But... is one child, as powerful as he may be, enough to save humanity?

CHAPTER 23

Tria — July 1st, 2029

Fresler, Sharon, Karena, and Kesh walk along the beach, watching their children play in the surf ahead of them. Tess, now four, and Mikaela, four next month, hold hands as they skip through the water and kick up black sand. Even Winnett enjoys a rare moment of childishness, sneaking up behind the girls to pour a bucket of water over their heads. Their squeals and his laugh of triumph are music to Karena's ears.

To think that, on Polemos, she could have lost him.

You wouldn't have lost him, her rational scientist voice counters. *He's the reason Mikaela still has her mother.*

She pushes that voice to the back of her brain. Winnett is her child. Her responsibility. No... *ability* absolves her of worry or her need to protect him.

"It's nice to see them like this," Sharon says wistfully. "It almost makes it feel like..."

"Like we aren't a year and a half away from the end of humanity?" Fresler says with forced jocularity.

Kesh shoots him a reproving look, still not completely on board with Fresler's Earth sense of humor. Dark comedy still escapes—and shocks—him entirely. "We will prevail," he says firmly.

Sharon glances up at the housing units overlooking the beach. Beyond those structures lie the rest of the city they've built here, practically from scratch. Workplaces. Recreation centers. A school. And of course, Sharon's beloved greenhouse, where she spends most of her days.

"We really made something here," she says aloud. Everyone hears the words she doesn't say.

The home they've built could be obliterated in an instant, like sandcastles in a tidal wave.

Fresler hugs his life partner close. "It's going to be all right," he says.

Before anyone can question this claim, a group of Neksesians approaches the children. As they pass Winnett, they pause and bow to him. He stiffens, shoots an uncertain look over his shoulder at his mother, and then inclines his head at them in return.

"What was that all about?" Fresler asks.

A shiver runs up Karena's spine. "Sarah told me some of the Neksesians at their work site are treating Winnett differently now."

"Differently how?" Sharon asks.

"Less like a colleague," Karena says, "and more like a... celebrity."

"Well," Sharon says uncertainly, "I suppose his new power is more... exciting to them than his super-intelligence."

"Have you two noticed anything different at your lab?" Fresler asks Karena and Kesh. They're deep into a joint project on fusion power, but Kesh has been taking the lead lately, due to Karena's reluctance to leave Winnett's side.

"I have not observed a change, but Winnett is... not my biological child," Kesh says carefully. "And I believe Karena has been... rather preoccupied. With good reason," he adds quickly, when Karena cuts her eyes.

"What about Sibula?" Sharon asks. "Has she had any new... insights?"

Karena and Winnett visit Sibula and Utivos in their grand Borjan mansion just outside the Neksesian settlement for lunch on a weekly basis. Karena is happy to let Winnett get to know his grandmother, but Sibula isn't exactly good at casual chatter. Conversation usually takes an eerie turn into premonitions that leave Karena with goosebumps while Sibula eyes Winnett like he's a stunning piece of art.

"No new visions, if that's what you mean," Karena says. "She still says Winnett is the key to humanity's survival, but... she doesn't say *how* he's the key. If it's his research, or..."

"The other thing," Fresler finishes, when Karena can't finish the thought.

"Well, it's clear what many of the Neksesians believe," Sharon says quietly, glancing at Kesh.

Another trio of Neksesians strolling along the beach spots Winnett in his Borjan robe. They point and duck their heads. They hurry past him, muttering to each other in a lame attempt at casual conversation, as if that will keep him from seeing them. There's no fear or disgust in their faces when the steal glances at him... but rather the kind of awe one might feel at seeing a superhero walking amongst ordinary mortals. They look at their shoes as though they're unworthy, not unwilling, to meet his gaze.

"How does Winnett feel about the extra attention?" Sharon asks.

"I haven't spoken to him about it," Karena says. "Maybe I should..." Even from a distance, she can see the change in her son's posture. Gone is the playful five-year-old, tormenting his little sister. In his place is a young man whose shoulders bear a weight far too heavy for his small frame. Karena looks to the others. "He is still begging to go to Des. I canceled the trip, but... do you think we should reschedule it?"

"It might do him some good to get away," Fresler says thoughtfully. "It might do you both good."

"Des is an abandoned planet," Sharon chimes in. "The only people there are our scientists."

"That seems like a win-win situation to me," Fresler concludes. "He gets to continue his research at a new site. You both get a break from Tria." He squeezes Karena's shoulder. "We'll miss you, though. With Erik and Aleria back on Sjel, and you and Sarah and Winnett leaving... I suppose I miss the days when the gang was together all the time."

"We will be again," Karena says fervently. "One day."

"After all this is over," Sharon says, staring wistfully into the cloudless sky.

Karena kisses Kesh's cheek. "Is that okay with you, for me to take Winnett to Des while you stay here with Mikaela?"

"We'll be happy to watch her while you're at work," Sharon tells Kesh. "It's no trouble."

"Thank you," Kesh says. "I know Winnett will be thrilled at the opportunity."

Karena watches her son watch the ocean, following it to the horizon and the unexplored universe beyond. He's always looked outward, ahead—always with the slightest of private smiles. "He sure will."

* * *

Des — August 15th, 2029

Wind whips at speeds strong enough to push Winnett and Sarah in a zig-zag pattern as they leave the Desian tower and trek the short distance over the desolate orange landscape back to their makeshift research center. Ahead of them, their heavy-duty tent shakes like a leaf, though it's secured with stakes buried ten feet in the unstable soil.

Sarah adjusts her ventilator to better keep out the sandy debris stinging her face. "Hold tight to the railing," she reminds Winnett as they traverse the metal platform that leads away from the excavated base. He gives her a look that says, "I'm not stupid." Sarah chooses not to remind him that she's supervising him at Karena's behest. Winnett may be the lead scientist on their team, but his mother still holds quite a bit of sway—especially in the wake of what happened on Polemos.

What Winnett did... Sarah struggles to fathom how Winnett wields an ability to inflict pain on such a scale, much less how he copes with it. His five DNA strands may make him exponentially more intelligent than most, and obviously exponentially stronger too, but he's a child none-theless. She knows he understands that such power should be used with the utmost responsibility and caution... but does he have the maturity and self-awareness to follow through? That's what keeps her up at night. She trusts him and loves him dearly, but that only increases her worry that he is forced to carry the weight of the universe's wellbeing and his dangerous abilities on his back.

What must it be like to try to parent a child like Winnett, whose mind is so much older than his body? They've been here on Des for a few weeks now, and Karena has finally agreed to stay back at the vessel to focus on her own work uninterrupted, rather than accompanying Winnett to the tower to hover over him like a mother bird. That said, if Winnett gets so much as a scrape or a bruise, Sarah is sure Karena will be here in a flash, her intuition guiding her like a homing beacon.

Winnett, at least, seems at peace here. Each day, he takes his readings. Each day, he compares them to the previous day's measurements. Each day, he stares at the tower and postulates what its true purpose might be... what has the aliens so invested.

Today, he's been singularly focused on the samples of the familiar charcoal-colored powder. When they reach the safety and relative quiet of the research tent, he heads straight back to the chair he pulled up beside the samples this morning.

"I've discovered something," he says after a lengthy silence.

"What is it?"

"We thought this was the same substance being produced on Earth and Tria, but it is not."

"It isn't?!" Sarah exclaims.

"No. It's similar, but with differences at the molecular level."

"The towers are transmitting at the same wavelength. Why would the output be different?"

"I'm not sure. But I do have a new theory about the FP Carbon."

"What's that?"

"I believe that pressure is needed to create it, as well as an electromagnetic wavelength in excess of 10,000 KeV."

"That's not possible. Gamma rays are on the far end of the electromagnetic spectrum, and they have never been measured at that level."

"It is possible... theoretically."

"This tower isn't producing anything like that."

"True... *currently* it's not. But when the towers breached the surface, the signals changed. It is possible that before the breach, it was producing wavelengths in excess of 10,000 KeV."

"Wouldn't that have been extremely dangerous for anyone living near the tower?" Sarah thinks back to the bodies in Wisconsin, their heads pooled by blood that streamed from their orifices.

Winnett shakes his head, making his thick hair fall in his eyes. "Not if it was directed below the surface."

"And the pressure… you believe that came from the towers being buried underground? The weight of the earth pressing down on the structures?"

Winnett smiles. "It's possible."

"Then… why is the Trian tower still producing FP Carbon, while the others have stopped?"

"It must be due to the extra power generator on Tria. The towers on Sjel, Rajik, Des, and Earth don't have such a generator. Although we can't observe them firsthand, I believe it's safe to assume that neither do the structures on Phaelin or Polemos." He pauses, running a finger through the charcoal powder in its petri dish. "The graviton signal is strongest on Tria. I suspect that the generator there was fueling the entire tether. Now that the tether is broken, the graviton signal on Tria has the energy to create an electro-magnetic wavelength. It's those wavelengths that create the FP Carbon."

"Fascinating theory," Sarah says. "It's too bad we don't have more data on the signals that existed prior to 2016."

"Yes." Winnett shakes his head. "The Sjelians' reports are incomplete, as were the Neksesians'. They tracked the transmissions from planet to planet but did not record what the signals were doing to the planets themselves. They looked outward, rather than inward."

"How long do you think it takes to produce FP Carbon?" Sarah asks.

Winnett shrugs. "I'm not sure. We can attempt to calcu-late the age of the residual FP Carbon found on this planet… but those calculations will take time."

Time we don't have, he doesn't add. Sarah hears it anyway.

"I'm not sure that's our most pressing question," Winnett goes on. "We know the towers are billions of years old. We know the aliens have been monitoring our planets for at least that length of time. What we still don't know is, *why?* What does this substance do for them? Is it something they need for survival? Something they cannot produce on their own planet?"

"It must be," Sarah agrees, "for them to go to so much trouble to ensure the towers are safe and operational."

"I don't think the aliens care about humanity at all," Winnett declares. "I think we are incidental. We happen to be able to live on planets that happen to be ideal for the production of this substance."

Sarah finds herself nodding along as he speaks. "In which case…"

"The answer to the coming attack isn't to defend ourselves with force," Winnett says, more urgent now. "We need to understand the purpose of these towers. In order to do that, we need to learn about the signal that existed prior to 2016. I need to visit Borjan."

* * *

Borjan — October 1st, 2029

It took six weeks to get to Borjan: a week to finish up on Des, two weeks to travel back to Tria, two weeks on Tria securing permission and a vessel, then gathering the necessary information to make the most of the trip, and a final week to cross dimensions and complete the journey.

As she did the last time they visited Borjan, Sibula accompanies Karena and Winnett. Having someone familiar with the odd planet and its even odder leader eases a fraction of Karena's anxiety.

Their engineer, a soft-spoken Sjelian trained by Kralo, puts the vessel into an orbiting pattern and then sends them to the surface in a self-piloting shuttle. Once they land, Karena, Sibula, and Winnett are ushered through the Borjan capital, back to the auditorium where they first met Manerk.

The Borjan leader makes a similar entrance, gliding down the aisle like a ghost. Today, Manerk's white-gold hair is plaited and adorned with golden beads. They tinkle when she turns to smile at Winnett.

"Hello, Winnett," she says. "Do you remember me?"

"How could he remember you? He was an infant—" Karena begins.

"I do," he says.

Manerk's droopy mouth barely moves when she smiles, but her eyes crinkle. "Your abilities are so far beyond anything we could have imagined."

He nods.

"You do realize… they won't survive without you."

Karena glances over her shoulder at Sibula. "Yes, we know, the premonition…"

"That is why we're here," Winnett says. "I have questions about the signals."

"The signals emanating from the towers?" asks Manerk.

"Yes," says Winnett. "We found a substance well below the Trian structure that has ferromagnetic properties. The current signal blast would not be able to create this substance."

"You want to learn more about the signals that were produced… *before* they breached the surface?" asks Manerk, that weird little smirk on her face again—as if she has already anticipated how this whole conversation will go and is enjoying being right.

"Yes."

She accesses her holographic computer at the front of

the auditorium. An image of the tower on Tria takes shape, spiraling up to the ceiling. The date on the image is over a billion years ago. "We located the object when we discovered gravitons. We had theorized about them for millions of years but were not able to prove their existence. We eventually developed the technology, and as a result, we tracked the signals."

Winnett tilts his head. "Were there two separate signals?"

"Yes, the gravitons and an electromagnetic signal. The gravitons served more than one purpose."

"To communicate and to create energy," states Winnett, transforming Manerk's smirk into an eye-crinkling smile.

"Yes. The gravitons were used to send a signal and to develop the energy necessary to create an electromagnetic signal."

"Tria is the only planet with a power generator, isn't it?" asks Winnett.

"Only one power source is needed to create a tether," Manerk confirms.

Winnett exhales sharply. "The tether creates the energy needed to power the towers and the electromagnetic signal. Each day, the strength of the tether increases... creating more energy."

Manerk nods. "And the more towers there are, the more energy is created."

Winnett makes what Karena lovingly calls his "faraway face." His mouth goes slack. His eyes are bright but not really looking at anything, as if he's retreated into his own mind to hash out a problem with himself. When he blinks back to reality, he says, "The electromagnetic radiation signals produce the ferromagnetic substance. The greater the energy created by the tether, the more KeV that can be generated by the electromagnetic signal. My theory was correct."

"You have incredible insight," Manerk gushes.

Karena can't contain an eyeroll. In Winnett's presence, Manerk is like a fangirl at a concert.

"Have you determined why this substance is so valuable to the aliens?" Manerk asks.

Winnett shakes his head. "No. I suspect it's something they cannot create on their own planet. Each of the nine planets has the same balance of oxygen and nitrogen and this... *perfect balance* is what is needed to create the substance."

"Their planet must not have the same atmosphere," says Manerk.

"That is my assumption." Winnett stands and walks to the floor of the auditorium for a closer look at the base of the holographic tower. "I did have one more question for you," he says, as an afterthought.

"I will do my best to answer," Manerk says, now adopting a tone of false humility.

Winnett turns to face her directly. "What really happened on Tria?"

At that, Manerk narrows her eyes. "What do you mean?"

"I believe the message left by the Desians, was... *altered*."

"Altered?" Manerk repeats.

Karena cuts her eyes at Sibula, but the older woman looks as confused as she feels. Winnett gave no indication he was going to grill Manerk about a coverup when he requested to visit Borjan.

"The Desians claimed that the aliens attacked them without provocation, and in response they destroyed the Trian outpost and each alien living on that outpost."

Winnett's eyes bore into Manerk's, transfixing her. "Is that the truth?"

Manerk gives herself a little shake. "Your instinct is correct," she says, sounding even more astonished than she did at Winnett's scientific theories. "The aliens did not attack first, as the message indicates. We destroyed their outpost before they attacked us."

"What? It was not the aliens who attacked first?" Sibula yelps.

An incredulous scoff scratches Karena's throat. "Why would the Desians do that?"

"The aliens are not human. We saw them as a threat."

Karena pinches the bridge of her nose. "Why do you keep referring to the Desians as 'we'?"

Winnett answers before Manerk can. "Because Tria was not seeded."

Karena stares at her son. "What? Of course it was."

Now Manerk sighs like a teacher forced to explain to a first grader why the sky is blue for the fourteenth time. "The child is correct. A group of Borjans, Tempians, and Diastassians escaped Des prior to the attack. They returned hundreds of years later to a planet that was no longer habitable. That is when they decided to relocate to Tria... which had not been seeded with one of our extinct DNA strands."

"What, exactly, are you saying?" Karena says, voice low and dangerous now.

"The current inhabitants of the planets Borjan and Diastassi are the direct descendants of the former inhabitants of Des," explains Manerk, talking slowly like she's dealing with someone very dim.

"That is why the Borjans and Diastassians are so much more advanced than the other subspecies," Winnett says. "It is why you have been able to monitor the nine planets for billions of years."

Manerk nods.

Karena glares at her. "Why did they bother to leave that falsified message on Des?"

"Fewer than two thousand Desians fled the planet. Millions stayed behind, despite knowing the aliens would return and possibly destroy Des. Those that stayed seeded the other seven planets. They wanted humanity to survive. They left the message because they wanted humanity to know about their origins."

"Why did millions stay behind if they knew they would eventually die?" asks Winnett.

"They didn't want to live their remaining years aboard a space vessel. They would rather die on their home planet. They assumed those that had fled wouldn't last more than a few years." Manerk pauses dramatically before finishing, *"They were wrong."*

"Did you know about this?" Karena demands of Sibula.

The older woman shakes her head, fixated on Manerk with betrayed, puppy dog eyes. "On Borjan, we are taught the false version of events."

"How do you explain your planet's obvious advancements over the other human subspecies?" Karena asks, skeptical.

"We are told..." Sibula swallows hard. As she composes herself, she stares down Manerk with her mouth in a hard line. "We are taught that we evolved more quickly. That Borjan and Tempian DNA strands are naturally superior."

Karena harrumphs. "What about the Diastassians?"

"We are taught that their warlike tendencies keep them from reaching our level of achievement."

Manerk clears her throat. "That is the truth. It was a

Diastassian commander that fired upon the aliens' Trian outpost. A Diastassian started this conflict billions of years ago. This is why we were so eager to separate our cultures, when the opportunity presented itself."

"How are we supposed to believe anything you're telling us?" Karena asks. "You and your ancestors have lied, again and again and again."

"We have withheld information until it was necessary for you to learn it," Manerk counters.

"It's the same thing!" Karena shouts, stomping her foot. "The survival of the human race is at stake, and you are still not telling us the whole truth!"

Manerk draws herself up to her full height. "There is one point on which we have never prevaricated."

"And what's that?" Karena asks with a heavy sigh.

The Borjan leader turns her focus toward Winnett. "This boy..." she says. "He is the key."

Karena runs her hands over her face. "Everyone keeps saying that. But the key to *what?*"

"To *everything.*"

CHAPTER 24

Tria — October 18th, 2030 — One Year Later

Theran and Reshal meet Aster in his office adjacent to the large manufacturing plant.

Theran strides to the window overlooking the assembled single-manned fighter vessels. "Combining the fleets on Sjel and Tria, we now have almost thirty-five thousand vessels."

"That's not going to be enough," says Aster.

"We don't know how many vessels they have," says Reshal, but his feigned optimism falls flat.

For a moment, the three men are silent, considering their situation. Then, Aster once again brings up the topic that Karena has declared off-limits:

"It won't matter how many vessels we have, as long as Winnett joins us."

"You know that bringing Winnett into battle is a last resort," Reshal says, his daughter's ultimatum replaying in his head. "We are to exhaust all other options."

"But what he did to the Polemosian army—"

"Those were ground forces within a set radius," Theran says. "We have no proof that Winnett's ability can work against pilots and crew operating space vessels across vast distances."

Reshal squints. "We also can't be certain that his ability will have any effect on the aliens. It may only work on human DNA."

"We can't base our strategy around his ability," Theran concludes.

Aster falls into his chair. "But he's our only hope. The prophecy..."

"The prophecy states that he is important, but it doesn't say what role he will play," Reshal says. "His research may yet..." He doesn't finish the thought. Voicing the hope only seems to dry it up faster, like leaving your last swallow of water out in a scorching desert.

In a year of attempting to recover the Desians' data regarding how the aliens communicate, Winnett and his team have come up empty. There is nothing left on Des itself, other than the tower and the building housing the falsified historical record. Meanwhile, the Borjans' extensive archives have proven edifying on many subjects... but not on what these aliens want or how they can be appeased.

It seems that Manerk was not lying when she claimed she did not know why the aliens needed the substance Winnett calls FP Carbon. Any research the ancient Desians conducted on the alien civilization they'd angered must have been destroyed, along with everything else.

"Perhaps we can still defeat the aliens by force alone," Theran says, "without Winnett's help."

Reshal only frowns deeper. A thought that took shape months ago, in the fuzzy moments between lying awake and restless sleep, is now a solid, inescapable idea that looms over him like a dark cloud. Perhaps it's time to voice it. "Before we engage the alien armada, we need to be certain that our laser array will penetrate an alien vessel. If it doesn't, then we can't defeat them… no matter how many fighters we manufacture."

"I agree," says Theran, "but how can we possibly test the effectiveness of the laser array without engaging their fleet?"

"There is a way," Reshal says solemnly. "We need a single fighter to fire its laser at an alien vessel."

"But… that's suicide!" Theran says, appalled.

Reshal scowls at the ugly word. That is not how he sees it. He holds Theran's gaze, willing him to understand. "This person would need to be willing to sacrifice their life for millions of others, yes."

Theran takes a moment to catch his breath, hoping that a steady, rational answer can cool the fire burning in Reshal's eyes. "I am not going to ask anyone under my command to die by suicide. Besides, there is no guarantee that a single fighter could get close enough to test the laser array before being destroyed."

"I agree with Theran," says Aster, but he doesn't sound happy about it. "We need an alternative plan."

"Do you have one?" asks Reshal.

"We abandon this planet and travel to Borjan," says Aster, after a beat. "It is in a different dimension. We'll be safe there."

"Who is… *we*?" Theran asks, eyes narrowing.

"All who have made this planet our home," Aster says.

"You're referring to the general population… not the pilots?" Reshal says sharply. "They're still planning to stay behind and fight?"

"I can't guarantee they will, without a solid plan," Aster says.

"What about Sjel?" asks Theran, barely staving off panic. This whole situation is madness. "If our armada does not have pilots, Sjel is... *all* of the human-occupied planets are... doomed."

"Borjan has declared it will welcome all refugees seeking resettlement," Aster says.

"The General Council has already made their decision," says Reshal with a sarcastic sourness he picked up from Erik that sounds alien in a Sjelian's mouth. "They will not leave Sjel under any circumstances. They believe that their defense system is impenetrable."

"I can't flee to Borjan knowing that everyone on Sjel will die," says Theran, heart sinking at the very thought. "My grandson and great-granddaughter live on Sjel."

"I understand how you feel," says Aster, "but I have talked it over with our leaders, and they all agreed to seek refuge on Borjan."

"Unless we come up with a plan that has a strong chance of winning..." Theran says.

"Yes."

"And your people believe this plan must involve Winnett using his ability."

Aster nods in confirmation.

"Karena will never let us take her son into battle," Reshal says. "She won't risk his life."

"This is about all of our lives," Aster argues. "Perhaps... this is the child's purpose."

Reshal joins Theran by the window, appraising the vessels. "We could use a probe to test our laser array against the alien vessels."

"We can't track the alien vessels." Hopelessness creeps into Theran's voice and chest. "Would we simply deploy probes to the locations where Opik and Nekses once existed and... wait for the aliens to arrive?"

"Yes," Reshal says, warming to his own idea.

"Our probes don't have the capacity to travel through portals on their own," Theran says. "Someone would have to pilot a vessel to both locations and release the probes, as well as monitoring satellites."

"I volunteer," Reshal says.

Theran shakes his head. "It's too dangerous. What if the aliens return while you are in the process of deploying the probes? They will destroy you on sight."

"I'll leave tomorrow, then," says Reshal, quickly doing calculations in his head. "It will take me twenty-two days to travel from Tria to Opikian space. Another thirty days from there to the former site of Nekses. I will complete the mission several weeks before the date Winnett's premonitions have projected for the aliens' return."

Theran stares at his friend and sighs. "We can't be certain that Winnett is correct about the timing. They may arrive earlier."

"It's worth the risk," says Reshal.

"I agree," says Aster.

Theran nods reluctantly. He cannot deny the logic—and he is running out of ways to keep Winnett safe from the fray.

Reshal points to the holographic screen on Aster's desk that depicts the seven planets and the sites where Opik and Nekses once existed. "If they arrive at Opik first, then we have to assume that their second destination will be Nekses. If they follow the tether, then Phaelin would be next."

"But if they arrive at Nekses first," says Aster, "then they will travel to Opik, and then here... to *Tria*."

"Yes. If they follow the tether." Theran doesn't mention the possibility that they won't follow the tether. If the aliens head straight to Sjel or to Earth... there may be nothing they can do.

"Well, then. We will either deploy our fleet here on Tria, or to defend... Phaelin." Aster huffs, and Theran shares the sentiment. No one wants to deal with the Phaelinians less than him... except maybe Erik. "Theran, notify your Sjelian colleagues to have the vessels ready for departure at a moment's notice, destination to be determined."

"I will."

"And... can you at least talk with Karena once more, to try to convince her to let Winnett join us when we engage the aliens?" Aster asks Theran.

The Sjelian sighs. "I will ask her tonight. They depart for Des tomorrow."

Aster's eyes bulge. "What? I didn't know they were planning another trip."

"Winnett has one more idea about communicating with the aliens. He feels this final trip to Des will give him the breakthrough he's seeking."

Aster's breath shortens, his chest rising and falling rapidly. Like so many on Tria, Winnett has become a hero figure to him, and the idea of him leaving so close to the aliens' projected arrival date seems to have him near hysterics. "He must call off the trip!"

"He will not," Theran says, "and denying him a critical avenue of research will not endear him—or Karena—to our cause."

Aster wilts. "Please ensure that they return in time."

Neither of the Sjelians points out that "in time" is relative. With only Winnett's prophecy to guide them, each day that passes could bring them closer to "too late."

* * *

Karena leans against the doorjamb and watches seven-year-old Winnett turn over in his bed. She stands there, drinking him in, until his breathing deepens, lifting the sheet. Wondering what he's dreaming about, she shuts his door, then walks down the hall into Mikaela's bedroom. The five-year-old is sound asleep, one arm thrown up over her head and drool staining her chin. Karena softly brushes it away and kisses Mikaela's warm cheek.

She then heads outside into a balmy night. When she takes a seat next to Kesh on the porch, he asks, "Are they asleep?"

"Mikaela is sleeping like the dead, but Winnett is restless."

"I suppose that's to be expected," Kesh says.

"Yeah. I wish he didn't have so much to worry about," Karena admits. "I wish he could just be a child."

"Me too." Kesh reaches out to take her hand.

Just as their fingers link, they hear a knock at the front door. Karena rushes to answer it before a follow-up knock can wake the kids. Theran is waiting when she opens the door.

"What are you doing here so late?" she asks.

"I'm sorry for the intrusion," the Sjelian says, "but I need to speak with you."

Her gut twists with intuition. "About Winnett."

Theran doesn't bother to beat around the bush. "Yes. May I come inside?"

Karena gestures toward her living room with a suddenly sweaty palm. "What about him?" she asks as he takes the seat she offers.

"Aster believes that we cannot defeat the aliens without Winnett's ability. He is determined to have Winnett on the lead vessel when we engage the aliens."

"No."

Theran nods, looking unsurprised by her immediate rejection. "The situation grows tenuous," he says. "Aster is concerned that many of the Neksesian volunteers will flee to Borjan, rather than fight... if Winnett is not present."

Karena's nails dig into her palms. "Leaving us without enough pilots to fly the vessels we've built."

"Exactly."

She's silent for several minutes, trying to make a rational pros and cons list. But true impartialness is impossible. Winnett's safety always comes out on top of her pros list, overshadowing all else. And yet, now she must battle terrible images of a pitiful vessel force exploding in the Trian night sky, and panic in the streets, and the deaths of hundreds of thousands coming on the wind. Theran doesn't interrupt her thoughts.

Finally, she says, "We don't even know if Winnett's ability will work on such a scale... or on aliens, rather than humans."

"Aster believes it will, and so do his people." Theran inclines his head. "Has Winnett expressed any thoughts on the matter?"

"No," Karena says. "He's completely focused on learning how to communicate with the aliens. He believes we can win this battle without mutual destruction."

"I would very much like for him to be right," Theran says, "but I will not take the chance that he is wrong. I will not leave our planets undefended."

Karena grits her teeth. "And if Aster is wrong... if the prophecy is about something *other* than Winnett's ability... *I could lose my son.*"

Theran changes tactics. "How long are you planning to be on Des?"

"Not long... but it's ultimately up to Winnett."

"The message on Des was clear. The aliens do not communicate with a written or verbal language. It is tele-pathic, based on visions and feelings." Theran leans forward. "Has Winnett uncovered new information? Or... has he demonstrated telepathic abilities?"

"Not that I know of... on either count. But he is certain we will learn something new on Des."

"Then may I make one request of you?"

"You may..." Karena says warily.

"Will you promise to return before the end of the year... before 2031? And if Winnett doesn't find the answers he seeks on Des... will you consider letting him accompany us into battle?"

Karena goes quiet. Theran keeps his face neutral, but he readies his hands on the armrests, like he expects he'll need to flee her wrath.

"I'll think about it," she says.

He exhales. "Thank you." He stands. "Safe travels to Des."

She nods, showing him to the door.

Karena returns to her deck on unsteady legs and collapses in the chair beside Kesh. She's barely done recounting Theran's visit when a second knock sounds at the front door. She looks over at Kesh. "Did Theran forget something?"

He shrugs, so she goes to answer it. To her surprise, this time it's Reshal.

"I apologize for the hour," he says. "I need to speak with Winnett."

Karena crosses her arms, tired of people wanting things from her son. "He's in bed."

"I wouldn't be here if it wasn't important," her father

says quietly.

She groans, knowing it's the truth. "Follow me." She leads him down the hall and opens the door to find Winnett sitting up and staring back at her. "Winnett... Reshal would like to speak to you."

He turns on the light. "Come in."

"Sorry for disturbing you this late," Reshal says as he comes to stand by the bedside table, "but—"

"I can't be certain of the exact date the aliens will return," Winnett interrupts. "I only know that they *will* return to investigate the disappearance of Opik and Nekses."

Reshal blinks and blusters, "How did you...? Never mind." He shifts on the balls of his feet. "If you were to guess which day it would be..."

Winnett sighs. "We've been planning for 2031, but... lately, I've been feeling as though it will be sooner."

"How much sooner?" Reshal asks in a strained voice.

"Maybe in as little as eight weeks. Maybe less."

Reshal sighs. "Thank you, Winnett."

Winnett nods and turns off his light before falling back onto his pillow.

As Karena and Reshal return to the front door, she asks, "What are you planning?"

"I'm leaving tomorrow to deploy probes and satellites at the sites where Opik and Nekses once existed. I need to be gone before the aliens arrive."

"And the uncertainty about their arrival date has you worried."

Reshal avoids Karena's eyes. "How long are you planning to stay on Des?"

Karena tells him the same thing she told Theran. "I don't know."

Reshal looks around the living room, as if expecting

someone to be pressed up against the window, eavesdropping. He puts his hands on her shoulders and quietly says, "Don't return to Tria when you're done on Des... go directly to Borjan. Protect your family."

Her gut flips. "Theran asked me to come back here. He and Aster... they want Winnett..."

Reshal's grip on her tightens. "I'm going to tell Fresler and Erik the same thing. This battle... I don't know if it's one we can win. I want to depart on this mission tomorrow... knowing my offspring and their offspring are safe."

"Erik plans to fight," Karena informs him.

"I know he does," Reshal says ruefully, "but I must try to convince him otherwise."

"I don't know if you can."

Reshal acknowledges that with a sad nod. "But can I convince you to protect your family?"

Karena bites her lip, feeling pulled apart inside by everyone's demands. "I'll do what I feel is right," she finally says, hoping desperately that when the time comes, she'll know what that might be.

CHAPTER 25

Des — October 25th, 2030

Winnett's rummaging sounds like squirrels in the attic, and Karena smiles, transported back to Earth for a moment, even among this cold, Desian technology on this desolate, forsaken planet.

"Can you hand me that?" Winnett asks, voice muffled. His hand appears from the hole he created in the wall beneath the screen that delivered the Desian's final, falsified message. He points to the circular tool on the table next to Karena.

Karena selects the slim, disc-like object and places it into the disembodied, waiting palm.

"Thanks."

"You're welcome."

For several moments, the only sound is Winnett's tinkering. More bits of wire and fat hunks of hardware emerge every few minutes, either tossed from the hole or carefully settled on the ground by Winnett's skinny arms. It looks like chaos to Karena, but she has no doubt Winnett's got a system. The mess reminds her of a story Kayna once told them of her teen years on Earth. Early in 1969—the year she'd fled the planet—Kayna was given access to an expensive computer. Much to her science teacher's dismay, she'd taken the machine apart to learn how it worked. Later, she'd snuck into the high school after hours to rebuild the thing, entirely from memory.

Winnett may not be Kayna's direct descendent, but obviously his multiple DNA strands have given him a similar aptitude. Despite Desian technology's significant differences from the Sjelian, Neksesian, Borjan, and Earth computers he's used to, he's having no trouble dismantling the device that holds the video message they first watched back in 2024. In two days, he's already almost reached the massive computer's central processor.

"I got it!" he shouts, creating an echo inside the wall.

Karena's heartbeat quickens. "What did you find?"

There's a scuffling sound—squirrels in the attic—and then the seven-year-old appears, dusty and triumphant. He holds out his hand, displaying a cube about the size of a die from Earth. Instead of dots to delineate its six sides, it bears six golden symbols. "I believe this is a data storage cube," Winnett says.

"What are those symbols?" Karena asks.

"I'm not sure. Letters, perhaps?" Winnett carefully turns the cube over in his palm, examining it from all sides. "The Borjan archives suggested that the ancient Desians used a unique written alphabet. Perhaps those ancient letters became commonly used symbols in later years, the same way that the letters of the Greek alphabet took on symbolic meaning on Earth."

Karena nods along, though she is unsure what this

discovery has to do with saving humanity from imminent destruction.

"I have digital glossaries from some of the historical Borjan texts on our vessel," Winnett says eagerly.

"And you're hoping to learn...?" Karena prompts.

"How to access this data cube." His perplexed look suggests he expected her to figure that out on her own. "The Desians left this message to tell us of our origins and to warn us, should the aliens ever return. Why would they leave us without any record of their research into the aliens' culture and communication patterns? It must be encoded in this cube."

"I hope you're right," Karena says softly.

As she suits up to follow her son back out to their vessel, she can't shake the feeling—not an enhanced intuition, but an old-fashioned hunch—that they're going to be here a while.

* * *

Opikian Space — November 10th, 2030

Reshal admires the handling of Aster's Neksesian war vessel, crafted with care and artistry despite its formidable purpose. If a Sjelian vessel is a hammerhead, as Erik says, then the Neksesian vessel is a barracuda. Reshal is housed in the tip of the craft's sharp nose, with a double view through the laser-proof windshield and an adjustable display via a computer screen overlaid on the right side of the glass that offers him readouts of incoming data. On the holographic screen projected from his control panel, he can see and speak to Theran and Aster, back on Tria.

"Preparing to deploy satellites and probes," he tells them, pressing the appropriate commands.

The devices smoothly exit the rear of his vessel and propel toward the spot where Opik once existed.

"We see them," Theran says.

"Are the satellites operational?"

"Yes," Theran assures him. "All are transmitting perfectly."

"What about the probes' laser arrays?" Reshal asks next.

In the Trian office, Aster leans toward the monitor on his desk, bumping Theran's shoulder. The rumbling of the manufacturing plant sometimes muffles Reshal's words, so both men stay close, glued to the action. The split screen provides a view of Reshal as well as the former Opik site.

"Preparing to test the laser arrays now," Aster says, a tremble at the end of his words betraying his anxiety.

The three men watch, Reshal from his vessel and Theran and Aster through the satellites' remote video feeds, as each of the probes successfully fires its lasers into open space.

"It works," Aster says, sounding a little surprised. "When the aliens arrive, we will fire on their vessels."

"Let's hope they don't destroy the probes first," says Reshal.

"Let's hope," agrees Theran.

"Are Karena and Winnett back from Des yet?" Reshal asks.

On Reshal's holographic screen, Aster's eyes grow fearful again while Theran's face becomes solemn. "No. Karena reports that they are still... researching."

Reshal is quiet for a moment. "The next time you talk to her, please encourage her to return soon."

"I will."

"Is the first evacuation vessel still planning to depart for Borjan next week?" asks Reshal.

"Yes," says Aster.

"Will your volunteer pilots be among those evacuating?"

Aster shakes his head. "No. They are awaiting news of Winnett's return."

Reshal nods, thinking about his last conversation with his daughter and willing her to take his advice. "Time to input the coordinates to Nekses." He turns his vessel on a dime, inputting the coordinates. As he maneuvers, he marvels at the ease with which a single individual can pilot the craft. The vessel is designed to sleep up to six crew members, but Reshal has no trouble flying it alone.

That was his intention: to place the inherent danger of the mission only upon his shoulders.

"Contact me if there is anything new to report," he tells Theran and Aster, and logs out of the video feed.

Reshal has thirty days of solitude and reflection ahead of him. He has much to ponder.

He hopes he has left a legacy for his children to actually admire, should this mission be his last. He hopes they do not still simply think of him as the man who tricked their mothers in an attempt to undo a heinous mistake he should have stopped much earlier. He hopes that they now have positive tales to tell his grandchildren about him.

* * *

Tria — November 21st, 2030

Stephan shoulders open his front door with a sigh of relief.

"Daddy!" Viktor barrels into his leg.

"Viktor." Stephan leans down to pat his four-year-old son on the back.

"I missed you!"

"I missed you too." Stephan looks up to meet his life partner's eyes, watching him from the kitchen. Sarah smiles at him, but he can see the tension she's held in her shoulders all day. As the battle looms closer, Stephan has been spending more and more time at the training center, helping to ensure that every volunteer pilot is prepared to take off at a moment's notice.

Every other aspect of Trian life is on hold now. The science lab Karena and Kesh ran has gone dark. The school is closed, with half the students already departed on the first evacuation vessel. Those who remain live in limbo, waiting in the refuge of their homes for evacuation... or the aliens' arrival.

"Stephan!" Fresler shouts from the living room. "Come watch Noah play this game. What's it called?"

"Tej," says Noah, who just turned six.

"Right, Tej."

Stephen leads Viktor into the next room, where Fresler sits with Noah on the coach. "He's going to teach me how to do it," says Fresler, slapping his hands on his knees as he eyeballs the metal cube in Noah's palm.

"You'll learn it instantly, like you do with all things Sjelian," Sharon says from the opposite sofa, rolling her eyes good-naturedly. Tess and Mikaela are snuggled under her arms, still exhausted from their joint fifth birthday party yesterday. Technically, Tess turned five two weeks ago, but the two did everything together. They loved the idea of sharing a party.

Stephan sheds his gear and makes his way to the kitchen, where Sarah and Aleria are putting the finishing touches on dinner. "Is Erik on his way?" he asks Aleria.

"He and Kesh will be here soon," Aleria responds.

With the lab closed, Kesh has been recruited as an engineer, putting the finishing touches on the fleet of war vessels. Erik spends his days helping Theran with strategy and people management.

"Smells good," Stephan says to Sarah, giving her a hug and a kiss. "Did you have a good day?"

She hesitates. "Good enough."

Stephan nods. That's about all anyone can expect in this uncertain time. He returns to the living room and makes his customary Dad noise as he settles onto the sofa. His joints thank him.

"Okay," he says to Noah. "Let's see this game."

In the kitchen, Aleria and Sarah make small talk about the work they used to do—Aleria's neuroscience research and Sarah's studies into infrasound and gravitons. Now, Sarah holes up at the Trian tower, hoping to find some use for FP Carbon that might explain the aliens' need for it, while Aleria has been helping to organize the evacuations. Neither woman is usually home in time to prepare a dinner like this one... but family night is sacred.

The tradition started when Erik, Aleria, and Noah first settled on Sjel. Whenever they'd visit Tria, a big family dinner was necessary to catch up on each other's lives. Now that everyone lives on Tria, family night is a weekly affair.

No one wants to say it out loud, but they all know it might not be a tradition for much longer.

"I wish Karena was back," Sarah says.

Aleria glances toward the living room. "Mikaela misses her mother very much."

"She's not the only one." Sarah sighs.

There's a knock at the door. "That should be Erik and Kesh," Aleria says, wiping her hands clean to go answer it.

"I'll set the table." Sarah gathers dishes and silverware as Aleria welcomes her life partner and Kesh to the gathering.

Mikaela's squeals and Noah's cheers warm her heart almost as much as Viktor's greeting to Stephan earlier. These children—her nieces and nephews by love, if not by blood—mean so much to her. So do their parents. She can't imagine what the world will be like if...

No. She won't let her mind go there. Not tonight. She dabs at her eyes with a napkin and heads for the dining table with a smile pasted onto her face.

* * *

Neksesian Space — December 10th, 2030

When Reshal's computer beeps at him that he's reached the Neksesian site, he deploys the probes and satellites as quickly as he can, watching the void of space for a rift in the stars or an alien vessel careening toward him. The moment his task is completed, Reshal calls Theran and Aster to confirm the devices have started transmitting to Tria.

"The satellites are working. We see your vessel," says Theran without the formality of a greeting.

Reshal nods. "Great." He watches the test blasts fire from the probes' laser arrays—bright streaks of light in an abyss.

"Time for you to return to Tria, my friend," Theran says, his relief evident in his voice.

Reshal nods, but he can't bring himself to smile before cutting off the video feed.

He checks his screens, ensuring that the vessel's tracking device is off. He pilots just out of range of the satellites, as if flying toward Tria. Then he spins the vessel around to face the coordinates where Nekses used to be.

Here, he will wait, for as long as it takes.

He won't leave this to chance. Probes and satellites can malfunction or be destroyed. The laser array might not be strong enough to penetrate the alien vessels. No, he will stay and observe, so that he can warn Theran and the others to flee. To abandon the fight.

If he can save their lives, it will be worth the sacrifice.

* * *

Des — December 10th, 2030

The disc tool falls from Winnett's hand with a clang, tumbling from the hole. He clambers out after it, face deathly white.

"What?" Karena asks, already breathless. "What is it?"

"The aliens..." he croaks. *"They're here."*

* * *

Tria — December 10th, 2030

"This should work," says Aster with a budding smile.

Theran doesn't respond. His heart canters as he realizes the holographic screen is no longer tracking Reshal's vessel. He sends a message to his friend. Minutes trickle by. No response.

"Something isn't right," says Theran.

"Maybe he is entering the portal," says Aster.

"No. He is still a few hours away from the entrance." Theran feels the claws of panic digging through his chest and reaching for his heart as he sends message after message to Reshal's vessel. "He's not answering." He jabs his fingers through the holographic keys. "Could the ship have malfunctioned?"

"That ship is in pristine condition. I ran the diagnostics myself before he left," says Aster, mildly offended.

"Well, something's wrong!" Theran shouts, the claws

squeezing his heart now. He sags into his chair, fighting hysterics. "He's up to something, and he's making sure I can't stop him."

"Theran..."

"Is there a way to hack into the—"

"Theran!"

Aster's magenta skin has paled to a dusty rose. His shaking finger points to the larger screen. The alien armada zips through the stars, the ships' sleek black sides blending with the void. Their blue engine fuel leaves dizzying streaks on the black backdrop as the fighters twist in a chaotic formation. The computer estimates over twenty thousand vessels swarming the site where Nekses once existed.

Theran tries to rise, tries to get a closer look at the enemy, but his legs feel like wet noodles, unable to support him. Faint, he closes his eyes and tries to steady his pounding heart with meditation. It's useless. He's locked to the screen. Deep down, he was hoping that it wasn't true... that they wouldn't actually return.

"Winnett's prophecy... they're... early," says Aster.

Theran stands. "We need to fire the laser as soon as they are within range."

Aster nods and scoots his chair in front of the controls on the screen embedded in the desk.

"They should be within range in three seconds," says Theran, his face inches from the readouts displayed on the hologram.

Aster's fingers fly over the controls, entering access codes and taking aim. Blue lasers light the darkness of space, followed by orange bursts of fiery explosions, and a whoop of joy bubbles up from Theran's chest... but it dies on his tongue. The probe readouts cut out, their cameras going dark. The lasers were not theirs. The satellite displays confirm the destruction of the probes.

"It didn't work," says Aster in a tiny voice, turning to Theran in dismay.

Theran swallows hard and stands straighter. "They didn't destroy the satellites... only the probes. We still have visuals to work with."

Aster exhales sharply. "But what are we going to do?"

Theran hails Reshal again but gets no response. Instead, a message from the satellites comes through. A new visual.

No... Reshal's vessel!

Theran's heart skips a beat, the claws of terror latching deeper. "No!" Tears start tracking down Theran's cheeks.

A single tonal note announces the reconnection of Reshal's communication link—audio only. "I need to test the laser," he says.

"Get out of there now!" yells Theran, hot tears stinging his eyes.

"You know I can't do that. We need to know if our plan will work."

"Why would you sacrifice yourself like this?"

"To save you and my three children."

A mini-swarm of black ships breaks off from the group and surrounds Reshal's vessel in a blink. The lead ship's large, cannon-like structure lowers, taking aim from the hull. It's wide mouth fills with sapphire light, and Theran sucks in a gasp... but the cannon holds steady, unfired.

"Why haven't they destroyed my vessel? What are they waiting for?" asks Reshal.

"They may try to communicate with you," Theran says.

But when several tense seconds pass without any such attempt, Reshal says quietly, "It's time." He fires his laser array directly at the mothership. The beam strikes the hull and rebounds uselessly into space. The satellite cameras zoom in at Aster's command. No breach in the enemy's exterior.

"It didn't penetrate," Aster croaks. "Our laser array is... *useless* against their shields."

"*Reshal...*" Theran says quietly, his face wet with tears.

The mothership's cannon blasts a ball of energy twice the size of Reshal's ship, and the vessel blazes white-hot before vaporizing out of existence.

CHAPTER 26

Tria — December 11th, 2030

Theran can't bear to sit in the same seat where he watched Reshal's obliteration. Instead, he paces the office, thankful for the soft brushes of Kayna's fingers along his arm as he passes her chair.

"I just spoke with Karena," he says, pausing in front of Aster's desk and noting the deep purple rings around the defense leader's eyes. "They are aware that the aliens have arrived at Nekses. Winnett... saw it happen. They are about to depart for Des, but..."

"I'm not sure I can convince the Neksesian volunteers to stay behind and fight. You saw the video. Our lasers had no impact on the alien vessel." Aster puts his head in his hands. "This is hopeless."

"Maybe Reshal was right," says Kayna. "Maybe we should all leave this planet and travel to Borjan. We'll be safe there."

"We have a responsibility to stand as a line of defense

between the aliens and the other planets," Theran says stubbornly. "Earth will be destroyed. Sjel as well."

"At least Sjel has its shield defense system," Kayna says with a sigh.

Shield.

Theran closes his eyes as an idea strikes him. Steeling himself with a few meditative breaths, he walks around the desk, scoots between Aster and Kayna, and accesses the video recordings of yesterday's tragedy. He replays the arrival of the armada, quick to restart it before Reshal's vessel is vaporized. He plays the video several times this way, then accesses his PAD.

"Kralo, can you come to my office?"

"On my way," says Kralo.

"What is it?" Kayna asks.

"I have an idea, but I need an engineer's expertise."

"Let me ask Gott to join us," Aster says. Gott responds to the communication in an instant.

When everyone is assembled, Theran begins, "The Sjelians have been working on a graviton shield for thousands of years. It's now operational. It is invisible to the naked eye, unless... *something strikes it.*"

"Something... like a laser array?" asks Aster, voice rising with interest.

"Yes."

With a tap, Theran replays the moment that Reshal fired his laser array at the alien mothership. "Do you see that?" He freezes the video. "It doesn't strike the vessel. It appears to strike a... force field."

Kralo points to the light beam in the holographic image. "Based on the angle of the vessel, the laser would have deflected at a forty-five–degree angle... *not a ninety-degree angle*. You're right. It didn't strike the vessel. It definitely deflected off a shield."

"Kralo, are you familiar with the Sjelian shield project?" Theran asks.

"Yes," the engineer confirms. "I worked in that department before being assigned to the space station."

Theran points to the rebounding laser frozen on the video. "Is it possible for a vessel to use graviton shield technology?"

"In theory," Kralo says, "but the technology is well beyond what we have on Sjel. They would have to have an incredible power source aboard that vessel."

"There is one more thing I wanted you all to see." Theran replays the video. "This is the point where the alien vessel exited the portal."

Everyone leans in ear to ear.

Theran freezes the clip again. "Right there—it looks like there is something reflecting from the vessel not long after it exits."

Aster tilts his head. "Are you saying that the graviton shield was *off* when the vessel traveled through the portal?"

"Yes."

"When Sjelian vessels travel through a portal," says Kralo, "we turn off the gravity generator due to the risk of collapsing the portal. The gravitons can directly impact the integrity of the portal."

Gott clears his throat. "There isn't the same risk with a Neksesian vessel, but if we had an exterior shield, it would have to be turned off while traveling through a portal."

Theran smiles. "The aliens have no choice but to turn off their shields while traveling through a portal."

Aster claps his hands, accidentally jostling Gott. "We could use this to our advantage. We could attack their fleet as they exit a portal." He scoots his chair sideways so that he can turn to face Gott and Kralo. "Can we determine the exact moment when the shields are activated?"

Kralo replays the video. "There. Each vessel produces a glare not long after they exit the portal. That must be the shields coming online."

Gott nods, examining the video's time stamp. "Which means... we have seven seconds from the moment the vessels appear."

"That's enough time," says Theran.

Kayna shakes her head. "The only problem with this plan... is how do we know where they will appear, and when?"

Theran renews his pacing, giving the others more room to breathe. "They arrived at Nekses first. If our satellites next detect them in Opikian space, we can confront them at the Trian portal."

Aster waves his hand across the holographic screen to display a map of the galaxy. A white line appears not far from Tria. "What about the timing?" Aster's finger traces the white line representing the portal.

Kralo rubs out a kink in his neck as he straightens up from the screen. "We don't know what their vessels are capable of. Once we see how long it takes for them to travel from Neksesian space to the former site of Opik, we can project their arrival at the Trian portal."

Theran nods grimly. "We will start planning our attack immediately."

* * *

On the beach, Fresler watches Tess stomp her foot in frustration as Noah runs laps around her in the shallows. He can see her wheels turning, realizing that her petite frame will never keep pace with Noah's lanky legs in a straight sprint. She pauses in the water, crouches, and then pounces on Noah's back when he gets too cocky and passes too close. The two roll in the wet black sand, yelling and laughing.

Smiling wistfully, Fresler turns back to Erik, Aleria, and Sharon. "I wish Reshal were here to play with his... *grand-offspring.*"

The others laugh at the joke, but it's a hollow sound that masks tears.

"Me too," Erik says. "It won't be the same without him."

A moment of silence passes for Erik and Fresler's lost father.

"The evacuation vessels leave tomorrow at noon," says Fresler, taking Sharon's hand. "You're both coming now, aren't you?"

Erik and Aleria share a look that twists Fresler's guts into knots.

"We made a decision," says Erik. "We are going to stay behind and fight."

Fresler's breath leaves him in a whoosh. "Why?" he chokes out. "It's suicide."

"Fresler is right... after what happened to Reshal..." Sharon's blue eyes are huge in her pale face.

"There's a new plan now," Erik says. "Reshal's sacrifice made it possible."

"What if it doesn't work any better than the old plan?" Fresler argues. "What if the aliens don't use the same portal we do? What if they can sense your vessels waiting for them as they exit? What if the new theory about their shields is just... *wrong?*"

Aleria rubs Erik's back and leans into him. "We know

the risks, but we are both trained to pilot the vessels. We have to do this."

"They have enough volunteers," insists Fresler. "They don't need your help. Come with us to Borjan. You have to think of Noah."

"That's what we want to talk to you about," says Aleria.

Fresler's mouth goes dry as Erik steps closer. He struggles to hold Erik's gaze as his brother puts a hand on his shoulder. "We would like you and Sharon to be Noah's guardians if something happens to us."

Powerless to stop the tears, Fresler clears his throat and whispers, "Don't do this. Come with us."

Aleria shakes her head. "We've already decided."

"Why both of you?" asks Sharon, wringing her hands.

"We are both trained," says Erik. "And Aleria has her ability..."

Fresler shakes his head and struggles to draw a proper breath. "Your ability is going to be useless up there!"

Sharon rushes forward, brushing a comforting hand down Fresler's arm on her way to hug Aleria. "It would be our honor to be Noah's guardians."

Aleria relaxes into the embrace and rests her cheek on Sharon's hair with a sigh of relief.

* * *

Aleria and Erik hold hands in Stephan and Sarah's living room, having left Sharon and Fresler on the beach not fifteen minutes earlier.

"Fresler and Sharon agreed," says Erik.

"I'll be there for Noah as well," says Sarah with a melancholy smile.

"Thanks, Sarah," says Aleria.

"Does that mean you've made your decision?" Erik asks Stephan.

Stephan reaches for Sarah's hand. "We've made the decision together. I'm trained. I have to do this."

Sarah's face contorts, as if holding in a sob, but she doesn't let any tears free.

"I am so sorry, Stephan," Erik says around a lump in his throat. "If I hadn't convinced you to come with us, you would still be on Earth with your parents."

Stephan closes his eyes tight. When he opens them, they are moist. "Thanks to you, I have lived more in the last seven years than I ever did on Earth. I met my life partner, had a beautiful son. I have no regrets, Erik."

They reach for each other at the same time, reading each other's minds, and clasp hands in a strong grip, a shared nod passing between them.

"Besides," Stephan says, "I'm doing this for my parents. For Sarah's father and aunt. For everyone we left behind on Earth."

Erik nods again, too choked up to speak.

* * *

December 12th, 2030

Erik drops to one knee beside Noah, and his boy latches around his neck. "I want to stay with you and Mom!"

Erik wipes away a tear and says, "It's not safe here. You need to go with Uncle Fresler and Aunt Sharon. Aunt Sarah and Uncle Kesh will be there too." Erik looks over his son's shoulder with bloodshot eyes to where they all stand on the launch pad. Sharon holds tight to Tess's hand beside Fresler. Sarah has a hand clamped over her mouth to stifle a cry. She holds a wailing Viktor in her other arm, balanced on her hip. Stephan has his arms around them both, weeping silently. Kesh is stoic, but Mikaela clings to him with wide, terrified eyes.

Erik composes himself as best he can before turning back to Noah. He smiles, hoping it's a reassuring one, and drinks in his baby's face. He's getting so big, his baby fat nearly gone. He has his mother's high cheekbones. Erik presses his forehead to Noah's and inhales his scent, trying to memorize it. If this is the last time he sees his son, he hopes that Noah will remember him clearly. Knowing he will be safe doesn't make it any easier to let go, but he pulls away to let Aleria take Noah into her arms.

"I love you, Noah," she says. Her voice is strong, for her son, but Erik sees the pain in the tight set of her mouth, in the way she tucks Noah's head into the crook of her neck, as she did each night she rocked him to sleep as a baby.

Noah bursts into tears and clutches Aleria's shirt in tight fists. Erik guides her toward the evacuation vessel with a hand on her back. She crouches to place Noah's feet on the launch pad, but he's not ready to release.

Fresler thumps Erik's back as they embrace. "Don't take any unnecessary risks."

"You know me," says Erik.

"That's what I'm worried about," Fresler says with a snort that does little to lighten the moment.

Theran and Kayna say their own goodbyes to Noah, coaxing him off Aleria. Kayna gets a second hug and a kiss on the cheek as Sjelians, Borjans, and Neksesians part around them on their way to the boarding ramp. Sharon takes Noah's hand when Kayna releases him. Tess takes his other hand, and they walk aboard between Fresler and Sharon. Noah looks back several times, and Erik makes sure

to keep smiling and waving until he's completely out
of view.

When he lets his hand drop, Aleria leans into the circle
of his arm, gulping down her tears. Nearby, Stephan grips
Sarah and Viktor in one last group hug. He pulls free with a
parting kiss on each of their heads and shoves his hands
into his pockets as he watches every step they take into the
vessel.

Erik walks over to Stephan and claps him on the back.
"We'll see them again, I promise."

"That's not a promise you can keep," Stephan croaks, but
he smiles in solidarity all the same.

Aleria, Erik, Stephan, Theran, and Kayna linger until
the transport vessel lifts off the ground and zips into the
atmosphere, gone in a blink. They watch the spot where it
disappeared, no one wanting to be the first to turn away.

* * *

That evening, Aster stands on scaffolding overlooking the
manufacturing plant floor. Thirty thousand volunteers are
gathered between the silver and blue plasma heaters,
awaiting his directions. The amplifier stuck to his neck
catches the vibrations of his vocal cords and projects them
so even those crammed in the doorways or standing outside
can hear. He points to a holographic screen projected on the
back wall for all to see.

"As you can see, the aliens arrived at the Opik site six
hours ago. Based on the speed with which they traveled
from Neksesian space to the Opikian coordinates, we
believe that they will be entering the portal to Tria in..." He
takes a deep breath. "Approximately thirty-six hours."

Aster waves his hand at the screen and an image of an

orange moon appears, a partial view of a ringed planet visible behind it. "The portal's exit is not far from the Galaxin moon. We will station our vessels near this location." He points to the blue-gray sliver splitting the blackness. "The portal's exit is not large enough for our entire fleet. Therefore, we will align our vessels in two waves. The first will consist of fifteen rows. One thousand vessels per row. The vessels in the second wave will be stationed directly behind the first."

A Neksesian volunteer asks, "How can we be sure they will use that portal?"

Aster responds, "It is the same portal they used when they last arrived... based on the information that Winnett obtained from the archives on Des."

Theran steps forward on the scaffolding and adds, "Remember, they can activate their shields within seven seconds after they exit."

"If a vessel manages to activate its shields, then... we will have no choice but to fly directly into it." Aster practiced these words all morning, but his voice still isn't as strong as he'd like.

A few mutters rise from pockets in the crowd, but Theran speaks up before they spread. "I want to thank each of you for volunteering. You are risking your lives to save humanity." He looks down at his daughter and Erik in the front row. "You are selfless heroes." He tucks his head and bows slightly at the waist in a Sjelian gesture of deep respect. Returned bows send a ripple through the crowd.

Aster rises from his bow first and clears his throat. "We will alert you when it's time. For now... please go home and try to get some rest."

The pilots exit the plant in uniform rows that dissolve into clumps in the empty Trian streets. Erik, Aleria, and

Stephan are among the last to leave, lingering outside the plant's front entrance to wait for Theran and Kayna, who will also pilot a war vessel. *Together, no matter the outcome,* Kayna said when Theran begged her to go to Borjan.

Theran isn't surprised to see his family waiting, but it still brings a melancholy smile. "May we accompany you to your homes?" he asks.

"Of course, but..." Erik shrugs. "I don't know about you all, but I'm not going to be able to sleep a wink."

"Me neither," Stephan says immediately.

Aleria is also twitchy and anxious, in large part thanks to the waves of nervous energy that crackle in the Trian air. "I certainly will not."

"Then let's walk for a bit," Kayna says.

Their wandering feet eventually lead them to the hill that overlooks the Neksesian city—the place where they got their first real glimpse of the planet they've grown to love. Staring out at the view, Erik interlaces his fingers through Aleria's. Stephan throws an arm over Erik's shoulder. Theran and Kayna stand by their daughter's other side. Together, they ponder the battle to come... and everything they're fighting for.

CHAPTER 27

Tria — December 14th, 2030

Thousands of vessels around Erik power up with a synchronized hum that vibrates his bones. The air feels electrified, lifting the hairs on the back of his neck. His stomach sinks. This is it. There is no turning back now. He looks at Aleria, her hair whipped by the launching vessels' slipstreams, and dreads the moment when he must let go of her hand.

Stephan pats Erik's back and says, "Are you ready?"

Erik nods, but his "brave face" feels more like a grimace. "Stay close to us," he says.

Stephan nods. "I will."

Aleria catches Erik in a crushing embrace that she breaks off too soon, murmuring, "I love you."

Erik grabs her hand once more as she tries to branch off to her own vessel. He twirls her into his chest and buries a hand in her hair for a parting kiss. Aleria smiles up at him, tears glittering in her lashes.

"This can't be it," she whispers. "After everything we've been through... this can't be the last time I see you."

"It won't be," says Erik, pressing his forehead to hers.

* * *

Trian Space — December 14th, 2030

Erik scans the holographic monitor on his vessel's laser-proof windshield and directs his exterior camera to Aleria's ship directly above his. Stephan is to his immediate left. The rest of the fleet hovers in formation in all directions, the ship's nose pointed at the silvery mirage of the portal's exit. Erik wipes his sweaty palms on his pants, wishing Aleria and Stephan were far behind him, in the second wave, with Kayna. Erik volunteered to be one of the first in the line of fire, but he should have anticipated they'd insist Aster place them there with him.

His ship's clock counts down the few remaining seconds before the alien fleet is predicted to come flooding through that shimmering rift. He triple-checks that his laser array is aimed directly at the portal's heart and hovers his thumb over the launch button. Seven seconds. That's all they have before the shields go up.

Seven seconds. Just long enough to say "I love you" seven times. One for Aleria, one for Noah, one for Stephan, one for Fresler, one for Karena, one for Kralo, and one for Reshal, wherever he may be.

Erik likes to think Reshal has met Eria by now, somewhere in that other plane of consciousness. He hopes he can make his biological father proud, live up to the hero's legacy he left behind.

Still, seven "I love yous" is not enough. Will seven

seconds save them? It has to—otherwise his life partner and best friend will not survive. Otherwise, Noah will be an orphan.

Static over the communicator startles Erik, and he nearly launches his arsenal.

Erik clutches his chest and shouts, "Holy shit!" Thankfully, he and all his fellow fighters are on ordered radio silence, so that nothing interferes with transmissions from Command.

"Stay alert," Aster's voice blares, transmitting from the Command vessel with Theran and Kralo. "They should be exiting any moment."

Erik wonders if Aleria can sense his emotions from her vessel and just had a mini heart attack, too. Is she too far away? He wishes he could hear her voice.

He tries to restore his focus, thumb back at the ready and eyes glued to the portal instead of Aleria's ship, but his mind keeps drifting off to Noah. His heart seizes at the thought that he may not get to watch his boy grow up, just as he was robbed of watching Eria grow.

He grits his teeth and shoves down the thoughts with a firm, "No. This has to work." For Noah—for all humanity—it has to.

It will. He sends the thought into the universe, praying it has time to blossom.

A shrill siren blares through the cockpit.

"They're here!" Aster screeches through the comms.

Erik blinks at the portal. It's unchanged. Where are they? No alien foes are bearing down on them. He directs his exterior camera to the orange moon. Nothing. Aster must be wrong.

"They are at our stern!" screeches Theran, terror distorting his familiar voice.

Stern? How can they be behind us? Erik switches the view on his holographic monitor. Thousands of blue engine dots blend with the stars, the ships' black exteriors camouflaged by the sky. *Why didn't they arrive through the portal? Where did they come from?* Erik's fingers flitter over the controls but press nothing, at a loss for what to do.

Aleria's face appears on his communication screen. "How is this possible?!" she cries, as clear as if she were sitting next to him.

"They must have known about our plan... but how?"

Stephan joins the conversation, bucking the rules. "Why haven't they attacked us yet?"

Erik makes a garbled, unintelligible sound and throws up his hands. On his monitor, his exterior camera shows the alien vessels approaching the second wave, who are still in the process of turning around in the confusion. Erik grips the manual controls in both hands and follows suit, facing the alien threat and taking new aim.

"Stand down," Aster commands the fleet. "We don't want to be the first to attack. We have to assume their shields are operational."

Aboard the Command vessel, Kralo mutes the communicator. "What should we do?" he asks Theran.

"We can't communicate with them any traditional way. They're telepaths. They have no verbal or written language that we know of."

"We need to try," says Aster, shoving his trembling hands into his gown pockets. He nods to Kralo. "Send a message."

Theran jumps between them, palms out. "Wait, they may think it is—" Kralo has already pressed the button, and the computer chimes. Message received by the alien mothership.

Theran stares at the screen, unable to breathe.

The maw of the mothership's cannon turns sapphire.

"No!" Theran cries, slamming his hands on the control panel. All he can think of is his life partner, out there in the second wave, where he'd hoped to keep her safe. *Kayna*. He lost her once already. And today...

The cannon blast fires, obliterating three fighters in an explosion that rocks the surrounding vessels. The alien fighters open fire, shooting streaks of blue energy at the nearest row of Neksesian ships. In mere seconds, hundreds of human lives are erased.

Aster flips on the communicator and shrieks, "Fire your laser array!"

The fleet fires swarms of lasers, but they bounce off the alien shields like swatted flies, leaving no mark.

In the heart of the chaos, hand sweating on his weapon control stick, Erik fires a third and fourth laser, not bothering to properly aim. There are no longer any friendly vessels obstructing his line of fire, and the aliens take up the whole sky.

Comms come to life with crackles of static as the fighters send up pleas to Command and their fellows.

"I need—"

"They're on my—"

"We have to—"

Each scream is cut short. All around Erik, vessels flare blinding white and disintegrate into powder-fine shrapnel.

Thousands gone in a single minute.

"We need to destroy the mothership!" yells Erik, still linked to Stephan and Aleria.

"How? Our laser arrays are useless!" cries Stephan.

"I won't use the laser. I will fly my vessel directly into the mothership."

"No!" Aleria shrieks.

"Don't!" Stephan shouts at the same time. "Even if you somehow destroy that ship, they have twenty thousand vessels. You can't destroy all of them!"

"Maybe they're linked somehow," Erik says stubbornly. "I have to try."

"Don't! Let's escape through the portal!" yells Stephan.

Erik has a clear shot. The mothership cannon is brewing another ball of energy, but it's barely sparking. He has his seven seconds back ... just a different strategy.

One. *I love you, Aleria.*

"I have to try," he says again.

Two. *I love you, Noah.*

Erik rams the manual controls forward, streaking through space toward the mothership's glowing blue heart —a massive, central engine in its undercarriage.

Three. *I love you, Stephan.*

He tries to look straight ahead, but Aleria's face on the right side of his windshield is a temptation he can't resist. "Don't do this..." she chokes, tears on her cheeks.

Four. *I love you, Fresler.*

Erik rolls the ship to dodge a blue laser.

Five. *I love you, Karena.*

He jukes left to avoid another shot that vaporizes a vessel behind him. It will be a miracle if he isn't destroyed before he reaches his target.

Six. *I love you, Kralo.*

Panting, he straightens out and realigns the nose of his ship.

Seven. *I love you, Dad.*

The cannon sparks silver amid the blue, like dancing lightning, and takes aim at him.

A war cry slips through Erik's clenched teeth as he shuts his eyes, wishing for one more second.

I had to try.

Erik's limbs go numb, his fingers slipping from the controls, but his eyes fly wide open, blinking into space. His neck is immobilized. He can't wiggle his toes. The cannon powers down with a hum that vibrates his bones. His vessel drifts left, unmanned.

This can't be death, Erik thinks, frozen in his chair. *What new trick is this?*

The monitors show both alien and ally vessels leaning and twirling slowly through space, their laser cannons dark.

"I can't move my arms and legs," Aleria says. "I feel paralyzed."

"I can't either," says Stephan. "What did they do to us?"

"Their vessels have stopped firing on us," says Erik. "Maybe they are experiencing the same thing that we are."

Erik fights to free an arm from his side or move forward, but his limbs are bags of bones, as useless as if they were dismembered. His monitor alerts, and his eyes swivel to the screen. Aleria and Stephan's wide-eyed faces shrink while his rearview camera display enlarges to show the portal brightening from gray to shimmering silver. It spews out a small Neksesian vessel.

As it glides carefully through the fray of floating vessels toward the alien mothership, its left wing obscures Erik's windshield. His ship bobs as the vessel passes, tipping him to starboard. It crosses a battlefield that, mere moments ago, was riddled with laser fire, and stops nose to nose with the alien mothership.

"That Neksesian vessel must be responsible for our paralysis," says Erik.

"I'd say since we aren't all vaporized that you're right, but what could do this?" Stephan asks.

"Not *what,*" Aleria says. "*Who.* Winnett is on that vessel."

"You can sense him?" Erik asks.

"Yes."

"But... this happened to us *before* he came through that portal," says Stephan. "There are tens of thousands of us. It's not possible."

Erik relaxes his stiff shoulders, abandoning the fight against the paralysis. "Clearly, it is."

"Why paralyze us? Why not just the aliens?" asks Stephan. "We could destroy them!"

"He wants a truce," says Aleria in that distant, dreamy voice Erik has come to associate with her sifting through the emotions and desires of others. "He wants to talk to their leader."

As if on cue, a shuttle pod shoots out of the Neksesian vessel's belly.

Erik watches the shuttle's route to the mothership. "I hope it works."

* * *

Karena zips her winter coat all the way up to her chin and stifles a wild urge to laugh as she thinks, *My kid is taking me on a field trip.*

She feels rather ridiculous, trudging behind her seven-year-old son down the dim, dank hallway of an alien vessel. The fact that the inside of this ship looks and smells like a cave only adds to the surreal, out-of-body nature of the experience. The black, bumpy walls are covered in a charcoal powder that looks like toxic moss clinging to dark rock.

"FP Carbon," Winnett says with satisfaction, running his fingers through the powder before Karena can tell him not to.

The ceiling must be twelve feet high, which makes

Karena wonder just how big these aliens are. She shivers. Winnett predicted the cold temperatures and the need for the oxygen mask now digging into her cheeks. He got them safely aboard. If there was something to fear from meeting these beings face to face, he would have prepared her... right?

Hell, he seems to know exactly where he's going. He never hesitates before he turns down a new path. She nearly bumps into him as he makes his next right. He tilts his head at a bulky shape on the floor, and then steps over it. Karena gapes. An alien giant is stretched across the corridor, the boots of its black armored suit shoved against one wall, its torso and head crammed against the other. The being is at least eight feet tall, though its scrunched position makes it harder to tell.

It has arms and legs, but the arms look short on its hulking frame. The body suit and helmet hide the being's features and skin... if it even has skin. Karena looks up from the paralyzed body to see Winnett holding out a hand for her. She takes it and hops over the alien's long legs.

Back on Des, after Winnett had his vision of the aliens arriving at the former site of Nekses, she'd expected him to demand swift action. Instead, he'd held the Desian cube gently... reverently... and had gone into a kind of trance. For hours, she hadn't been able to rouse him. He'd sat and stared at nothing, barely breathing, the cube warm in his loose fist.

Just when she'd been about to lose her mind with worry, he'd returned to the present. "It's time for us to go," he'd said, and so they did.

In the days it took them to get here from Des, Karena almost changed course a dozen times. But each time her

mind drifted toward fleeing to Borjan... Winnett was there
to talk her down.

He'd looked her directly in the eye and said, "We can't
leave everyone to die." She'd been powerless to say no. She
wasn't sure if it was his words that had persuaded her... or
something else hidden in his hypnotic stare. Had he used an
ability on her?

She'll have to unpack that later. Right now, they are
about to face down an alien leader.

The hallway brings them to a dark door. Its shiny material stands out, untouched by the charcoal powder that coats
every other surface.

"Is this their command center?" asks Karena when
Winnett stops and stares at the door.

Winnett nods. "Their leader is inside."

"Okay." By now, Karena knows better than to ask how
her son knows what he knows.

"I want to prepare you," he goes on. "They look nothing
like us."

Karena takes a deep breath and nods. "I'm not leaving
your side."

Winnett waves his hand across the width of the door.
The door slides open to show more alien bodies, but none
jump up to attack or greet them. Four are flat on the cold
floor, legs and stumpy arms sprawled out at odd angles. The
other eight are frozen in their seats, which hover four feet
above the floor so that their lanky legs have room to stretch.

The command center is the size of a high school basket-
ball gym, made of the same metallic material as the door in
the same charcoal color as the powder Winnett believes
they prize so dearly. Monitors line the room and blinking
lights illuminate the space.

Winnett leads Karena through the armored bodies to

the largest chair hovering at the center of the room. When they skirt around the chair to face its occupant, Karena's breath catches. The alien leader wears no armor, only a black robe with silver clasps. Its head looks like a boulder. Instead of human skin, its skull looks to be covered in granite, with veins of charcoal and onyx. Its forehead is elongated. Instead of eyes, the being has one thin slit in the rocky skin, filled with a gelatinous substance similar to that of an eyeball, except dark brown and free of a pupil.

The little, foot-long arms sticking out of its robe end in fat stubs instead of hands. Karena wonders what their purpose is. How do these aliens feed themselves or get dressed? And do they eat? She doesn't see anything resembling a mouth, though there is a vertical slit below the eye that she guesses is a nose. No wonder they have no oral or written language. Nothing to write or speak with... except their minds.

Winnett steps forward, and Karena wonders if the alien is already reading his mind... or her mind! She shivers again and resists the urge to run out, dragging Winnett with her.

The leader's eye slit traces Winnett's movement, but nothing else moves an inch. Karena prays Winnett won't relinquish his paralytic hold on the alien as he steps closer and closer with arms crossed inside the fat sleeves of his Borjan robe.

When he's as close as he can get without stepping on the being's feet, Winnett nods to it. With a commotion that sounds like tumbling rock, the alien rises, dwarfing Winnett.

Heart hammering, Karena reaches for her son, ready to snatch him away, but he stops her with a look over his shoulder and a tiny shake of his head. She reluctantly pulls back but keeps her muscles taut and ready to spring at the slightest provocation.

She will protect him from harm, even if it's her final act.

* * *

Winnett keeps his breathing long and steady, compartmentalizing each task his brain must complete in this moment. His ability buzzes in the back of his mind, holding everyone but the leader and his mother in a paralytic state. He checks on that bit, feels the flare of energy still burning strong, and moves it back. He next shoves aside his worry for his mother. It will do him no good.

He focuses instead on the alien leader and sends a telepathic message: *I am not here to harm you.*

Are you responsible for this? The alien's voice fills

Winnett's head, clear but almost musical in its lilt. The alien's head turns slowly as it looks at its paralyzed crew.

Yes. I have an ability that allows me to send signals tele-pathically.

The alien fixes its gaze on Karena. *Does that human also have an ability like yours?*

No, says Winnett firmly, drawing the alien's attention back to himself.

Why did you release me from your control? I can destroy you.

No... you can't.

The alien's boot rises, and Karena gasps. Winnett calls on his ability, directing a spark of energy toward the alien. It jolts and tips off balance, falling to its knees just as Karena grabs the back of Winnett's robe.

"I'm not in danger," Winnett says aloud.

When Karena retreats to a safer distance again, Winnett frees the alien. It rises slower this time, cautious.

Why do you control us? it asks, its voice bouncing around the foreground of Winnett's mind. *Why not kill us? That is what humans do. It is in their nature to kill.*

I have no intention of harming you or anyone else. I came here to broker peace, Winnett responds.

Peace? The being makes a sound that hits Winnett's mind like scornful laughter. *Long ago, humans attacked our outpost without provocation. Now, two planets are gone.*

We are not responsible for the destruction of Opik or Nekses. Those planets were destroyed by an anomaly. Winnett leaves out the fact that technically, the portal and its by-product, the rift, were man-made. *We are not the same as the humans who attacked you before. We have evolved.*

Then why was your fleet planning to attack us the moment we exited the portal?

They were motivated by fear. They saw what you did on Des.

Humans are warlike. They cannot make peace.

I assure you, Winnett replies, making his telepathic voice as firm as possible, *we can.*

The alien ponders in utter silence, stretching Winnett's hope like a rubber band.

It doesn't matter, the alien concludes. *Once you release your hold on us, we will destroy you. We will destroy humanity.*

You didn't come here to destroy humanity. You came for this. Winnett withdraws a leather pouch from his sleeve and dangles it high for the alien to see.

The alien's right arm expands and lengthens like a rubber balloon, and the energy pulsing off its body makes Winnett's hair stand on end, like static electricity. Karena makes a horrified sound at his back but doesn't make another grab for him. The arm is gorilla-like at almost six feet long. The fingers expand last, popping free one by one. Winnett puts the pouch on the alien's palm, and the spidery fingers close around it. The alien unties the drawstring with one finger, tipping the pouch over to spill some of the powder inside. The alien brings the substance close to its eye-slit.

We need this substance... to protect our planet. The alien looks back at Winnett. *It fuels our vessels. It powers our machines. Without it, our species will not survive.*

I know.

You humans have put our survival at risk. We must protect the towers at all costs.

I know that too. But... Winnett draws himself up to his full height and stares into the alien being's eye-slit. *I have made a discovery that will benefit you.*

After a moment of suspense, the alien says, *That is unlikely.*

I can teach you how to create that—Winnett gestures to the substance in its hand—*on your own planet. You won't need the towers.*

That is not possible. Our planet doesn't have the same atmosphere. Only human planets have the correct balance of elements.

There is a way, Winnett says confidently. *Let me show you. Let us end this war.*

* * *

For the next several hours, Karena finds herself standing awkwardly in the background, the only human witness to the silent negotiations between the alien leader and her extraordinary son. The only bit of action to break up the foot-shifting monotony is when the alien directs Winnett to one of the aliens' massive computer consoles. To Karena's partial astonishment, her child begins keying in data with apparent ease. She's come to expect the extraordinary from him, but so far in his short life, today's feats are unparalleled.

She hadn't known he could paralyze two entire space armadas... until he did just that.

She hadn't known he'd mastered the aliens' communication methods... until he began the telepathic conversation in this very room.

She thinks back to Polemos. Then, Winnett said he was unaware he shared Aleria's ability to inflict pain until the moment it became necessary for him to save them all. Perhaps that same rule of necessity was at work today. Was everything they went through to get here preamble to

Winnett discovering his true power in the moment it was needed?

"We're almost finished."

"What did you tell him?" Karena asks.

"How to survive without the towers."

Karena gawks at him. "I don't understand."

"What the aliens did to Des permanently altered the planet's atmosphere," Winnett says. "It made it more like the atmosphere on the aliens' home world."

"Okay..." Karena says slowly. "How does that help?"

"The material the Desian tower has been producing since the attack is different, on a molecular level, than what was being produced at the other towers," Winnett explains. "I discovered a method for producing FP Carbon without the exact atmospheric conditions that our human planets possess."

Karena shakes her head. "This wouldn't have been possible if the aliens had never destroyed Des."

Winnett nods. "True."

"How do you know they won't come back?" says Karena, chewing on her thumbnail as she side-eyes the alien hovering nearby like a wraith. "They were planning to destroy humanity."

"They have what they need. Besides," Winnett says, looking the tiniest bit smug, "they are now aware of what will happen to them if they do return."

Karena pulls her son into an embrace. "You are truly amazing. Your father would be so proud of you."

When she lets him go, Winnett approaches the alien and stares into its eye-slit for one last silent conversation.

* * *

Immobilized inside his ship, Erik has little to do but stare out the windshield. Not the most riveting programming he's ever watched. But when the tiny Neksesian shuttle jets out of the alien ship and returns to its own vessel, he cheers like it's a season finale. Winnett and, presumably, Karena are okay... but what now?

The alien mothership and its fleet power on, and Erik tries reaching for his control stick. Nothing. Not even a twitchy finger.

"Why are we still—" he begins to cry, but the air leaves his lungs when the alien horde turns tail and retreats en masse through the portal. Only when the entire armada has vanished is he released from his paralysis. It falls away like a weighted blanket sliding off onto the ship's floor, starting at his head and shoulders and loosening his muscles systematically to his toes.

His first instinct is to look to Aleria on his screen. "Aleria? Are you feeling that?"

Her voice comes through immediately. "Yes," she says, inspecting her hand.

"Stephan?" Erik asks next.

"I'm okay. I can move again."

"Me too." Erik wiggles his fingers and toes experimentally. He'd expected a pins-and-needles sensation, but everything feels completely normal. "What do you think happened in there?"

"Winnett," Aleria says with certainty. "Our nephew happened."

Theran's voice comes through the comms. The Sjelian leader sounds shaken, but triumphant. "All vessels return to Tria. I repeat, return to the airfield on Tria."

"Is it over?" Stephan asks, when it's clear Theran isn't going to say anything else.

Outside Erik's windshield, Karena and Winnett's vessel pivots and points its nose toward Tria.

"I think..." His smile, reflected to him by the glass, is as hesitant as his voice, but it soon reaches for his eyes. "I think it *is* over."

The Neksesian vessel zips out ahead of the armada, leading the way home.

EPILOGUE

Tria — December 16th, 2030

Beams of light dance on the Trian ocean's surface beneath the magnificent pink glow of the setting sun.

The three siblings stroll down the beach toward Karena's house, where the celebration has already begun. With kids, they don't often get the opportunity to be alone, so moments like this are treasured and treated with a kind of reverence.

"I can't believe I've escaped death four times since Kristin and Eria passed," muses Erik.

"Four times?" asks Fresler.

"Yeah. The first was my attempted suicide. If Stephan hadn't come back for me, I wouldn't be here. Then, during the escape from Phaelin, if Skithaell and Alesta hadn't walked into the viewing room, I would have died on that Neksesian vessel. Actually, I still almost died there. Telfas had to drag me onto that escape pod. And of course, the anomaly. I so badly wanted to travel toward the light, but deep down, I knew that the message from Sibula was meant... *for that moment.*"

"What about the fourth?" asks Karena.

"Two days ago, I was ready to fly my vessel into the mothership. I knew it was suicide, but I didn't know what else to do... to save Aleria and everyone else."

The siblings are quiet for a moment, meditating on all the close calls over the years.

"Maybe... it was all connected," says Karena.

"Connected?" asks Fresler.

"Yeah. Everything is connected. Kristin and Eria's deaths sent Erik looking for the Akureyri portal. And none of this would have happened without the General Council's decision to send morphons to Earth."

"We would have all been better off," grumbles Fresler.

"Would we?" Karena asks thoughtfully. "Reshal impregnated our mothers because of the General Council's decision. If it hadn't been for that, we wouldn't exist."

Erik nods. "And Winnett wouldn't exist."

"He did save humanity," Fresler admits.

"Like I said, it is all interconnected."

Erik chuckles. "Sounds like your intuition."

Karena shakes her head. "No... Winnett. He believes that everything in this universe... including those that have passed... are all linked somehow."

"Who am I to disagree with Winnett?" says Fresler.

"You said it," Erik agrees heartily.

Karena stops to look at her brothers. "Promise me... we will always live together. That our children will grow up together."

Erik wraps his arms around her and says, "I promise."

Fresler joins the group hug. "Me too."

Karena pinches both their cheeks with an ornery grin. "Great. Now, let's join the celebration."

Fresler rubs his face as he and Erik follow Karena up the

beach toward the lights of her Trian home.

Her back deck has never felt more like home. The gang is all back together, settling into a semicircle with cups of Slak in hand. Erik, Aleria, Karena, Kesh, Stephan, Sarah, Fresler, Sharon, Theran, and Kayna all lounge together without a care in the world for the first time... ever?

No pressing crisis looms over their heads. The world as they now know it is as safe as it can ever be.

The kids' laughter and boisterous chatter carries to them over the sand, adding background music to Erik's recounting of the space battle for Fresler, Sharon, Kesh, and Sarah, who just landed back on Tria this afternoon.

Fresler shakes his head. "What was that like? Not having the ability to use your arms or legs?"

"It was terrifying," says Erik, throwing up his palms. "I thought the aliens were causing my paralysis until they stopped firing on us."

"And then Karena and Winnett showed up?" Sharon asks.

"Not a moment too soon," Theran confirms.

"What were the aliens like? What was their ship like?" Sharon asks Karena.

"Their vessel looked and smelled like a cave. I felt like I was outdoors." Karena takes a gulp of Slak to calm her nerves. "The aliens were massive. I think they were over eight feet tall. They don't have skin. It looked like... multicolored stone."

"What colors?" asks Sarah.

"Black, charcoal, brown, and some white. And... they didn't have a mouth."

Erik, who has heard this before, looks amazed all over again at his sister's experience. "Tell them about the stretching arms," he urges.

"Stretching arms?!" Fresler yelps.

Karena curls her lip as the image replays. In her nightmares, the long fingers wrap around Winnett's neck. "They could extend them by a few feet."

"Extend?" Sarah asks.

"Did you ever watch the Fantastic Four?" Karena asks. "Mister Fantastic?"

Sharon shakes her head. "No."

"He was elastic. His arms and legs could stretch. That's what this thing could do."

"It must have been terrifying," Aleria says, as if sensing Karena's lingering fear from across the deck.

"It was," Karena admits, "especially since the alien and Winnett were communicating telepathically. I had no idea what they were talking about until it was over."

Sarah's gaze goes to Winnett, playing with his sister and cousins on the beach. "I can't believe I didn't see the connection between Des's contaminated atmosphere and the FP Carbon before now. Winnett truly is a genius."

"He is," Karena says.

"There's one thing I don't understand," says Fresler.

"Just one?" Sharon jokes.

"Well, there's a lot I don't get about the science of it," Fresler acknowledges. "I'm no Nobel Prize–winning physicist. But if this FP Carbon stuff is so valuable to the aliens, why weren't they here all the time, harvesting it?"

"Winnett said that these aliens have over ten thousand towers across the universe," Karena says. "They all produce FP Carbon. Collection is done on a rolling basis."

Fresler's eyes bulge. "Ten thousand?! That means there are ten thousand planets out there that can sustain human life."

Karena smiles, remembering how floored she'd been

when Winnett first told her. "Yes."

"How many of those other planets do you think already have human life?" Fresler asks.

"I would love to find out," says Erik, exchanging a mischievous grin with Fresler.

"Me too," says Aleria.

"Does Winnett know where these other planets are located?" asks Stephan.

"He does," says Karena, already grinning in anticipation of their flabbergasted reactions.

"All of them?" Sarah exclaims. "How is that possible?"

"Part of communicating telepathically is sharing thoughts," Karena says. "He and this alien leader shared each other's thoughts."

Kayna puts her hand over her mouth. "Oh, my God."

Karena nods. "Before we even boarded their vessel, Winnett had started sharing thoughts with the alien leader. That's how he knew exactly where to find the leader's command center."

"And now he knows how many towers there are and where they are located?" asks Theran.

"Yes. Winnett wants to travel to these planets."

Erik sits straighter. "So do I."

"I would go too, as long as Winnett was there to protect me," says Fresler, winking at Karena.

Sharon nods, saying, "No kidding."

"We can't go yet," says Aleria with a soft sigh.

"Why not?" blusters Erik.

Aleria gestures to the beach. "What? And take children with us?"

"True," says Sharon, looking lovingly toward her daughter.

"Also," Theran says, "I think I need a few months to rest

and relax... without some impending threat."

"I agree," says Kayna, taking his hand.

"But... at some point I would like to," Theran goes on, reclining to look up at the darkening sky. "I only wish Reshal could be there with me. I miss my friend."

Kayna squeezes Theran's hand. "Me too."

Erik raises his glass. "To Reshal."

"To Reshal!" they all repeat, glasses clinking together at the heart of the semi-circle.

Karena downs the rest of her Slak and relishes the warm, fuzzy sensation it produces, amplified when she looks over at Fresler and Erik. She smiles as she recalls the adventures she has shared with her brothers since being reunited.

Dangling over a gorge to disable a capsule that would have destroyed Earth's remaining population.

Running from a crazed polar bear.

Destroying a planet-swallowing anomaly.

Battling fanatical Soldiers of Destiny.

Surviving a showdown with an alien race.

All were terrifying in the moment but are exhilarating and sometimes hilarious after the fact, because they are memories that can be shared again and again. Memories that strengthen a bond that holds together the larger family that fills even her darkest days with love and moments of joy.

Will there be more adventures for the three of them? She sure hopes so.

* * *

If you would like more information about upcoming books by this author, please email ccb@frozen-pandemic.com

Made in the USA
Columbia, SC
03 August 2021